Dear Reader,

This month we are proud to bring you the latest books by two of your favourite authors. You will be delighted with *My Lady Love* by Paula Marshall. We think it's one of her best books ever. You'll also enjoy *Darling Amazon* by Sylvia Andrew, a lively and well-told tale.

In August we have more treasures in store. You'll love *Rakes and Rascals,* two books in a single volume by award-winning author Jasmine Cresswell. *The Abducted Heiress* and *The Blackwood Bride* are two of her finest—an absolute must for Regency lovers. But for now, just sit back and enjoy *Reluctant Bridegrooms.*

Happy reading!

The Editor

Reluctant Bridegrooms

Paula Marshall
Sylvia Andrew

Harlequin Books

TORONTO • NEW YORK • LONDON
AMSTERDAM • PARIS • SYDNEY • HAMBURG
STOCKHOLM • ATHENS • TOKYO • MILAN
MADRID • WARSAW • BUDAPEST • AUCKLAND

ISBN 0-373-31218-0

RELUCTANT BRIDEGROOMS

First North American Publication 1995.

Copyright © 1995 by Harlequin Enterprises B.V.

The publisher acknowledges the copyright holders of the individual works as follows:

MY LADY LOVE
Copyright © 1994 by Paula Marshall

DARLING AMAZON
Copyright © 1992 by Sylvia Andrew

Printed in U.S.A.

CONTENTS

About the Author

British author **Paula Marshall**, married with three
children, has had a varied life. She began her career
in a large library and ended it as a senior academic in
charge of history in a polytechnic. She has travelled
widely, and has appeared on "University Challenge" and
"Mastermind." She has always wanted to write, and likes
her novels to be full of adventure and humour.

Harlequin Regency Romance Books by
Paula Marshall

MY LADY LOVE

Paula Marshall

CHAPTER ONE

"WHAT CAN HAVE possessed you, Shad, to behave as you did? So unlike yourself! Last night's excesses at Watier were the outside of enough. And in front of Cousin Trenchard, too. Shad! Are you listening to me, Shad? You can't still be drunk at four in the afternoon!"

Charles Augustus Shadwell, Viscount Halstead, heir to the third Earl Clermont, always known as Shad since he had been a captain in the cavalry in Wellington's Army—now, in 1818, five years out of it—tried to sit up. He failed. His head, and the room, were still spinning round. His mouth tasted like the bottom of a parrot's cage, and his stomach...!

"Do you have to make so much noise?" he groaned at his younger brother Guy.

"Noise!" said Guy indignantly. "And I thought you never drank, not since the Army anyway. What on earth possessed you?" he repeated. "It's all round the town this morning, and Cousin Trenchard, trust him, has already been to Faa and spun him the yarn."

"What yarn?" ground out Shad, who had sat up on the bed, to discover that he had fallen into a drunken stupor, still clad in last night's clothes. "And why are you ringing such a peal over me? And, for God's sake, Guy, as you love me, don't draw the curtains. I feel bad enough in the dark, but the light—"

"Oh, damn that," roared Guy, and pulled the curtains violently open, to reveal the elder brother whom he had always worshipped, haggard and drawn, his clothes disgustingly soiled, sitting on the edge of the bed, his head in his hands.

Guy's disillusionment was complete. He said so.

Shad tried to remember what he had said or done the night before to cause Guy to behave in such an uncharacteristic fashion—he was usually respectful to his brother. The last thing that he remembered was flinging out of Julia Merton's home in Albermarle Street, yesterday afternoon, head on fire, anger and disgust choking him to such a degree that he was almost outside of himself.

And then he must have got blind drunk, and done something appalling to justify the brouhaha which Guy said that he had created. Only...he could not remember anything. All that had passed since he had banged Julia's drawing-room door behind him had vanished from his memory as though it had never happened.

Guy, his frank young face drawn with grief and disappointment, was still ranting on, "And Faa wants to see you immediately. Good God, Shad, why did you have to do this, just as you and the old man had started to get on reasonably well together? And what about Julia? What will she think when the news reaches her?"

"I don't give a good Goddam what Julia thinks about anything," said Shad inelegantly, rising to his feet and staggering towards the long pier-glass which stood in the corner of his bedroom.

He shuddered at the figure which he saw there. His face was a harsh one, strong and craggy, but it was not normally tinged principally with yellow and purple. His jet-black hair fell in wildly disarranged ringlets, and his deep blue eyes were red-rimmed and bloodshot. A face to frighten women and children.

Well, the more women he frightened the better. He had attracted too many of them over the years, and all of them whores at heart—Julia, God help him, being the latest.

Guy was still reproaching him. "Oh, do give over," he said at last, and reeled to the washstand, plunging his head into the bowl of cold water which stood there—it might help—and with his head under water he could avoid hearing Guy.

He surfaced, water dripping from him, and turned to face his brother.

"At least have the goodness to tell me what it is I did, or am said to have done."

"Oh, you said it, no doubt of that," announced Guy bitterly. "I was there. Who was it who hauled you home, do you think, and stopped Nell Tallboy's cousin from killing you on the spot?"

"Well, thank you for that," ground out Shad, and, face wicked, he launched his full thirteen and a half stone, six-foot-one frame at Guy, and seized him by the throat. "Now, will you tell me what I did? Or do I have to beat it out of you? If I am to be so madly abused, at least let me know what for."

"You mean you really don't know?" gasped Guy, as Shad released him. "Oh, pax, pax," he began hurriedly. "You came into Watier, half-foxed already, barely on your feet, began to gamble like a madman, and then..."

"Oh, God," groaned Shad, collapsing on to the bed. "Enough, Guy. I remember everything. Would that I didn't."

"Well, that's a relief," said Guy sturdily. He walked over to the jug on the washstand, poured water into a glass and handed it to his brother. "Here, drink this. It will make you feel better."

"Nothing will ever make me feel better," muttered Shad, looking up at Guy, and feeling sorry for causing his brother's evident distress. Guy at nineteen was eleven years younger than Shad and had always hero-worshipped him. Perhaps, Shad had often thought, because they were so different, Guy being blond, slim and rather diffident; he took after his dead mother, and Shad after their father.

"Here, let me ring for Carter," said Guy. "If you're going to visit Faa, you'd better spruce yourself up. You look like an unmade bed at the minute."

Shad let Guy order him about. It seemed the least that he could do for the brother who, whatever else, had always loved him and stood up for him.

Later, he waited outside his father's suite of rooms in Clermont House, the Shadwell family's London home. Colquhoun, his father's secretary, had told him, a grieving

look on his old face, "My lord will see you shortly. He is at
his business at the moment."

The business of making Viscount Halstead wait, no
doubt, thought Shad bitterly. Well, closing his eyes, and remembering yesterday, he thought it was no less than he deserved. Nor was he surprised, when Mr. Colquhoun finally
summoned him in, to discover his father, standing stern and
tall before his desk, over which hung Romney's famous
portrait of Shad's dead mother.

"So, you are at last up, Halstead. Is this true, what
Cousin Trenchard tells me?"

"Seeing that I don't know what Cousin Trenchard told
you, sir, it is difficult to say."

"Come, Halstead, don't chop logic with me—this scene
at Watier. Making shameful bets and brawling with the
cousin of the subject of them is hardly the conduct of the
man who is my heir."

Shad's control, insecure since yesterday, broke. He made
no effort to defend himself—he could not—merely replied
bitterly, "I have never ceased to regret, sir, the day that I
became your heir. Oh, I have tried, God knows how hard,
to fill Frederick's place for you, but in your eyes I shall
never be Frederick's equal. He was your...nonpareil."

"Which you, sir, are most definitely not!"

"Yes," said Shad, feeling that he must defend himself a
little, after all. "His untimely death deprived me not only
of a brother whom I had no wish to succeed, but also of a
career in the Army, which I not only loved, but in which I
was beginning to excel. Remember that."

"Come, come, sir," snapped the Earl. "My heir could
not remain in the Army, and, in any case, the wars are over
now. You were needed to learn to run the estate, to take over
from Frederick in every way."

"Which I have tried to do," retorted Shad steadily. "You
can have no grounds for complaint on that score. Green has
told you not only of my application, but of my innovations
at Pinfold. Only I can never be Frederick, and that is the
true ground of the division between us. The only time, sir,
when we were not at odds was when I was away at the wars."

If the Earl thought that there was any truth in this bitter statement, he gave no sign of it. His dislike for his second son was plain on his face.

"You were always a wild boy, Halstead, and became a wild man. Your marriage to Isabella French, against all my wishes—and look what that led to! Your—"

"Spare me," said Shad, his face white beneath the jaundiced shadow of his last night's debauch, "I paid for that, God knows, and in the last five years since Frederick's death I have lived an exemplary life, and done your bidding faithfully. Why should last night's work, which I regret more than you can ever do, cause you to cut me up so severely? One failure after so long..."

"Because, sir, I have been in the country discussing with her uncle, Chesney Beaumont, her mother's brother, an alliance with the very lady, Elinor Tallboys, Countess of Malplaquet, whose name you soiled last night in your drunken folly. We had reached terms. He is to broach your marriage with her today, in her Yorkshire fastness, and I was to speak to you this very morning, when, instead, you lay in your drunken stupor."

Shad, composure gone for once, gaped at him. "Do I hear you aright, sir? You were arranging for me to offer for Nell Tallboys—Nell Tallboys—without so much as a word to me beforehand. You expected me to marry her, at your simple word of command!"

"My mistake," replied his father coldly. "I had thought you almost Frederick, who saw my wishes as his command. I cannot imagine him refusing such a noble prize, so suitable an alliance. You would be...would have been...the richest man in England."

Shad's laugh was almost a shriek, or a curse. "And that's it, sir? That is to be my end? No arguing, agree, or cut line, is it? You knew that I was involved with Julia Merton, intended to marry her...until yesterday, that is," he amended with a shudder.

"Oh, that was never on, sir, never on," shrugged his father. "One more proof that you have not yet rid yourself of your youthful follies. A steady marriage with a steady woman is what you require to settle you, but now...I wonder what the Countess of Malplaquet would think of a proposal from a man who threw her name about in a gaming house? Why did you choose that woman to slight, sir, why?''

What could he say that would not make matters worse than they already were? Only, in his chagrin and, yes, shame, at his conduct yesterday, the more because he had always prided himself on his iron self-control, he muttered stiffly, ''But Nell Tallboys, a plain bluestocking, past her last prayers, with a face to frighten horses, they say, and a virtue so rigid that any man is rendered ice by it, and her very reputation caused me to lose mine last night.''

He stopped at last; his mixed anger and shame had caused him to make matters worse, not better.

''Yes,'' said his father glacially. ''Cousin Trenchard said that you bet an enormous sum—twenty thousand pounds, was it not?—that no woman was virtuous, and that even that paragon would succumb to your wishes without marriage, should you care to try her.''

Oh, God forgive him that he had said any such thing. Was it her cousin Bobus Beaumont's high-minded praise of her which, while he was smarting from his second cruel betrayal by a woman whom he thought had loved him, had caused his drunken self to behave so badly?

''Lightskirts all,'' he remembered roaring. ''Damned mermaids, even the best of them.''

''You may well look ashamed, Halstead.'' His father's voice was so distant, so cold, the dislike which he had always felt for this second son, unworthy successor—as he saw it—to his beloved Frederick, was so plain in his voice that Shad's shuddering, brought on partly by last night's drinking after years of abstinence, increased.

''And now you have the task of trying to mend matters. All may not be lost. Before this news reaches her, I shall use my influence to suppress this latest folly, while you, sir, must go north, to offer for her. An honourable proposal must wipe out what was said. Idle and jealous gossip will explain all.''

Shad stared dumbly at his father. ''Are you light in the head, sir? What can wipe that out? And besides I have no wish to marry Nell Tallboys, would never offer for her, would never have her if she was handed to me on a plate. Nor do I wish to marry again, ever."

"You will do your duty by me, Halstead," was his father's only reply to that. "Or I shall disinherit you. The estate is not entailed, as you well know. I was minded to pass you over and put Guy in your place when poor Frederick died. But my honour would not allow it. If you refuse me now, I shall—"

"You shall, and need do nothing," flashed Shad. "I have worked for five years like the trooper I once was to clear up the mess which Frederick made of running your estates. No, do not shake your head. Green will confirm the truth of what I say. Yes, Father, I tell you that now, what I would not tell you before, and my reward is to be disposed of in marriage, without my consent, and be insulted into the bargain, and what's more..." He stopped on seeing his father's stricken expression—he could not tell him the truth about Frederick; it would break him—and said instead, "You may have your way. I shall leave for my mother's small estate in Scotland, and live there. You cannot take that away from me and you may do as you please with the Clermont lands."

"Glen Ruadh will not finance a luxurious life in London for you," snarled his father.

"Nor do I want it," said Shad wearily. "You do not know me, sir. I shall consider returning to the Army. At least I was happy there. I should never have left it."

"Leave this room, sir, without obliging me over the Countess of Malplaquet, and you may go to the devil for all I care," was his father's only reply to that.

"Willingly, sir, willingly. And since Nell Tallboys enchants you so much, may I recommend that you marry the lady yourself?" ground out his son, and almost reeled from the room. He had thought that five years of hard work and dedication had reconciled his father to the loss of Frederick and his own succession, but the secretly arranged marriage, and his father's response to one night's folly after such devotion, had shown him his own, for nothing had changed.

His only regret was the loss of Guy, who met him at the bottom of the great staircase, and stood back in dismay at the sight of his brother's face, his own white.

"Oh, no, Shad! You are hopelessly at outs with him still, I see."

"So hopelessly that he has disinherited me. He wants me to marry Nell Tallboys, God help me. Has arranged the marriage behind my back, without so much as a by-your-leave. I'm off to Scotland, immediately. For good. I'll keep in touch, Guy. Do what you can for him. He does not live in the world as it is, but as he thinks it is. Frederick's shadow hangs over me still."

"Then I shall tell him the truth about Frederick, Shad, seeing that you will not."

Shad caught his brother by the shoulders. "Indeed, you won't—it would break him. Be a mortal blow."

"And he is not giving you one?" riposted Guy. "Do you still love him, Shad, after thirty years of curses and dislike—still hope that he may care for you a little? To hand you Nell Tallboys!"

"No," said Shad steadily. "I have long surrendered any hope on that score. I should never have left the Army, but I thought... Oh, to the devil with what I thought. It's over at last, and I'm not sorry."

But, as he left the room, and shouted for Vinnie, his late sergeant and now his groom, valet and man of all work, to be ready to accompany him north, on the double, he was. For so long he had hoped to be reconciled with his father, and now all was ashes.

"No," said Elinor Tallboys, Countess of Malplaquet, Viscountess Wroxton, Baroness Sheveborough, all in her own right, mistress of all she surveyed here in Yorkshire, châtelaine of so many properties that even she could not remember them all, wealthy beyond the dreams of man, and woman, too. "No, no, not at all, never. That is my first and last word, Uncle."

"But only consider, my dear," said her uncle, Sir Chesney Beaumont, her mother's brother, closing his eyes against her obstinacy, "only consider."

They were standing in the Turkish parlour at Campions, the Malplaquets' great house on the edge of the Yorkshire moors, a house over three hundred years old, huge, dominating the landscape and the lives of all those who lived near it. The Turkish room was so called because it was filled with rare *objets d'art* from the country, brought home by a former earl of Malplaquet who had been ambassador there. Over the fireplace, carved on a ribbon of stone was the family's motto, "As the beginning, so the end."

Nell Tallboys sometimes thought that she was the only thing in the whole house which could not by any judgement be considered a work of art. She was plainly dressed in a prim grey gown, high-waisted, a small pie frill around its neck being her only concession to any form of decoration. She wore no jewellery, and her hair was tied in a simple knot at the back of her head.

"No," she said, firm again. "I will not consider—nor reconsider, either. I have no wish to marry—let alone consider a proposal from the father of a man whom I have never met and do not wish to meet."

"But you must marry, my dear Elinor—" This was met again with his niece's smiling refusal, laced with a touch of the steel which made her the resolute character she was.

"Must...must...? As good Queen Bess said of a similar suggestion. Not a word to use to me, Uncle, I think." Her smile and her gentle tones took away the sting of her words a little, but her steadfastness, her determination always shone through even her lightest utterances.

He smiled, a little painfully. "No 'must's then, my dear. But you are already twenty-seven years old. You need a husband and the estate and the title need an heir. You do not wish all this—" and he waved a hand to encompass the sumptuous room and the landscape outside "—to go to your cousin Ulric."

"God forbid!" exclaimed Nell, shuddering, thinking of Ulric's debauchery, his wasting-away of his own good estate, and what he would do if he got his hands on the Malplaquet fortune.

"Well, Elinor," said her uncle eagerly. "What constrains you?" And then he added unluckily, "The land needs a master."

"It does?" said Nell, suddenly savagely satiric. "Tell me, Uncle, have you asked Henson how we are faring here since I took over, compared with what we did before I inherited from Grandfather? If his running of Malplaquet's lands is typical of what a master might do, then I am content to remain merely its mistress!"

There was nothing Chesney Beaumont could say to that. He knew only too well that since Nell had inherited at barely twenty-one, and had taken control of the management of her lands, with the help of Henson, whom she had appointed, the Malplaquet estates had multiplied their returns and their efficiency tenfold.

"Nevertheless, I ask you to consider most carefully this offer from Lord Clermont on behalf of his son Charles, Viscount Halstead. A most noble offer, nobly made."

"Nobly made to acquire Malplaquet's lands," said Nell drily. "What I know of Halstead does not attract. One disastrous marriage, after which he killed his wife's lover in a duel, at outs with his father—"

"You are behind the times, Elinor—he is now at ins, is learning to manage his father's affairs."

"Then he does not need to practise on mine," said Nell swiftly. "An arrogant, ill-tempered man such as Halstead is reported to be is the last husband I could wish for. Thank you for attempting to take care of me, Uncle, but the answer is no."

"At least see him," returned her uncle desperately. "Clermont proposes that you meet with Halstead, either here, or elsewhere, wherever you please, to see if you might suit."

"Nowhere is where I please," responded Nell, finality in her voice, "and that must be that. Halstead is the last man I should wish to marry. I would not have him if he brought me a dukedom—nay, if he were a royal prince, on his knees before me," and, as her uncle groaned and shook his head at her implacability, she added, "Come, Uncle, admit it. Even you are acknowledging by what you say that the only

reason why any man would wish to marry me is Malplaquet's fortune. What man of sense could wish for a plain
woman past her last prayers otherwise? Never once, in all
our talks on this subject, have you ever suggested that I
should marry other than to secure the estate and the succession.''

"Now that is unfair, my dear," he said quickly.

"Unfair?" Nell's eyebrows rose. She could see herself
reflected in the beautiful Venetian glass above the hearth. A
plain woman, plainly dressed, too tall, her features too
harsh, too definite, she thought; only the glossy chestnut of
her hair, and her large grey eyes, softened the severity of her
appearance.

That she wronged herself she was not aware. But in a society which preferred pink and white prettiness, Nell's face,
full of strength and character, was not the sort to be in-
shrined in a book of beauty, and, because she had long since
resigned herself to that, she dressed for practical use, not to
attract.

"Come, Uncle," she said gently. "I have long known that
any marriage I make will be one of convenience, but at least
allow me to choose the man I make it with."

"And how will you ever do that, madam, tell me," said
her uncle, at last angry with her obduracy, "when you never
meet a man other than estate servants, old Challenor, your
librarian, even older Payne, your secretary, middle-aged
Henson, and assorted stable hands and flunkeys, led by that
ageing warrior Aisgill, of whom you are so fond?"

He snorted, and then was off again, hallooing himself on,
thought Nell with wry amusement, as though he were out
with the Quorn Hunt and racing for the kill. "You are
grown a hermit, if a female can be such. How can you
choose a man to marry you, unless you consent to go out
into the world, or allow them to visit you here? At least let
Halstead come to Campions. Talk to him. You might deal
well with him. My information is that he is a man of sense,
who was a good soldier, undervalued by the world and his
father.''

"I am content as I am," said Nell, turning away, tears
springing unwanted to her eyes. "And I do not wish for

visitors, male or female. You forget that I have Aunt Conybeare, and all the care of the estate to keep me busy.''

She remembered her one dreadful season in town, nine
years ago, when she was eighteen, and the muttered laughs
and comments which had followed her tall, gauche person.
''Such a great gawk,'' Emily Cowper had drawled in her
spiteful way, ''that, were she not to be Malplaquet's
Countess, the season would be a waste. But, be sure, whatever she looks like, she will have offers aplenty.''

Nell was sure that the comment had been meant to be
overheard—as were others, equally mocking. Nothing, but
nothing, could comfort her after hearing that, and social
disaster seemed to follow social disaster.

She had grown more clumsy by the moment, felt everything about her to be too big, too raw, and, once the season
was over, and half a dozen suitors repelled, their insincerity
so patent that it hurt, she had retired to Yorkshire and happiness in seclusion, and refused to return.

Her grandfather's long illness, and then his death—her
father and mother had died in a boating accident years before—had assisted her wish never to visit London again,
and, once she was her own mistress, Yorkshire had suf-
ficed.

That the years had greatly improved her looks, given her
a poise and command that came from dealing competently
with those around her, she had never found out—nor had
society—for there was none to see, or tell her, and she would
not have believed them if they had.

Her companion, gentle Aunt Conybeare, also hated town,
and the two woman lived comfortably in their isolation.

''You will regret this, Elinor, my dear,'' said her uncle as
he took his leave. ''I do believe it might have been better for
you to have accepted Ulric, rather than live like this.

''And there's no amen to that,'' said Nell lightly, ''and
you know that you don't mean it, Uncle. I shall see Halstead if he arrives here, but I warn you, he won't like what I
have to say.''

And that was that. Only to her horror, this time Aunt
Conybeare hemmed and hesitated, and finally said in her

gentle voice, "I think that your uncle has a point, my dear
Nell, and, if you cannot bring yourself to accept Halstead,
perhaps we ought to try the season again."

"Well, you may," said Nell, harsh, for once, to her aunt.
"But I shan't and that's flat. I shall marry when I'm nearly
thirty, someone old and feeble, just able to give me my heir,
and too fond of comfort to want to interfere with my life."

And then, when she saw her aunt's face crumple a little at
her severity, she went quickly over to her, fell on to her knees
by her chair, and embraced her.

"No, my dear aunt Honey-bear—" which had long been
Nell's pet name for her "—I must not tease you, who have
been so good to me, but you, of all people, know how I feel
about men and women and marriage."

"And I," said her aunt, a little reproving for once, "know
what a good marriage can mean to a woman, and can do for
her. I have never ceased to regret that poor George was taken
from me before his time. No, Nell, do not make faces at me.
I know what you must endure, which I never did, but, believe, as I do, that one day you will meet someone whom you
can love and care for, and who will love and care for you."

Nell grimaced. "Oh, I thank you for that, Aunt, but it is
Cloud-cuckoo-land of which you speak. For I am not you,
and Malplaquet stands in everyone's way, and blinds them
to me, and what I am."

Now what could Aunt Conybeare say to that? And the
look which followed Nell, as she walked away, tall and
graceful, was a sad one, for where would Nell find a man to
whom Malplaquet meant nothing, and Nell everything?

CHAPTER TWO

SHAD DROVE HIMSELF and Vinnie hard on the way to Scotland. The weather was poor, but that meant nothing to him. He had begun to see Glen Ruadh as sanctuary, and could hardly wait to be there. Behind him lay his old life and his old self, which he was beginning to dislike.

The nights were the worst, the worst since Isabella, and he had Julia Merton to thank for them.

How could he have been so blind to fall again into the same trap, and this time with, as he had wrongly thought, his eyes open, and himself armoured against betraying women?

Julia had been so lovely and so clever, quite different from Isabella and her dusky charms. Oh, he had thought that, at last, he had found the one woman. From the moment he had met her he had been in a dream of love. He could see now that he had been as infatuated as a green boy.

For she had sought him out, and day by day had bound him with her magics, and he had worshipped the unattainable and hoped to attain her by marriage. He had laughed at those who had suggested that Julia Merton, still unmarried at twenty-four, might be so for reasons not altogether respectable—not that there were any blots on her reputation, simply the lack of response to the many who had offered for her.

"I was waiting for the right man," she had whispered once, in a scented ballroom when he had gently posed that very question. And then she had looked at him, wide-eyed. "And—do you know?—I think I've found him."

Oh, she had, she had! Her modesty, her gentle wit, the way in which she drew back from him if she thought him over bold. And then, when he had proposed, on his knees, as though the ten years since Isabella had never happened, she had, ever modest, drawn back, said, "All must be proper. I know you are of age, but speak to your father, and then, Halstead, then—" for she refused to call him Shad; that was for his old rowdy, Army life "—I will accept you."

Unknowing of his father's other plans for him, he had thought that the asking would be easy, and on that happy morning he had promised her that he would see his father on the next day, when he arrived from the country—where he now knew that he had been conferring with Chesney Beaumont about Nell Tallboys.

She had told him that she would be resting in the afternoon, but he had been to Bond Street, and seen a ring there, an exquisite thing, as delicate as she was, diamonds and sapphires to enhance her blonde loveliness, and he had rushed to Albermarle Street, his head on fire, to give it to her—surely she would see him.

He burned, he absolutely burned, when he thought of how her maid had tried to put him off, of how he had said so complacently, "Oh, tell her I am here. She will rise for me, I am sure of it," and he had pushed his way so confidently into the little private sitting-room where she usually received him.

He remembered the maid, pulling at him, babbling, "No, my lord, wait in the French drawing-room, rather," but he had hardly heard her, heard anything until he had thrown the door open, and seen the reason for her dismay.

For Julia, his Julia, lay naked beneath Jack Broughton, that noted lecher, married—but his marriage had never stopped that—and a thousand things, half-heard, half-seen, came together, and when she pushed Jack off, and stared at Shad, face white, whispering, "No," as her world collapsed, too, he saw something else which told him why she had pursued him, netted him in her toils.

By her breasts and body she was pregnant, and how she could have hoped to deceive him after marriage, he could not think. Except, of course, once safely married, there would have been nothing he could do without making himself a laughing-stock.

Jack pulled away, and laughed at him, and at the woman both.

"What's this?" he remembered saying in a hoarse voice, and Jack shrugged, even as the woman on the sofa improbably tried to protest innocence.

"Why, Shad, truth will out, I see. She has been my whore these five years, since after I married Nancy. Oh, quiet, Julia," he drawled. "Too late to pretend now. And Shad won't talk, you know. Too full of honour—to say nothing of his pride. He won't tell the world what he so nearly did!"

Shad was not proud of what he did do next. For he seized Broughton and beat him nearly senseless, and then had the privilege of watching Julia wail over his battered form.

"You devil," she spat at him. "Do you think that I could have borne your ugly face, if it weren't that I needed you, or any man, to hide the proof of my love for him?"

"Love?" he said. "What's that?" and walked from the room, but not before throwing the ring at her. "And here's your payment from me," he said. "Sell it to buy baby clothes for your bastard."

And then he had drunk himself stupid and gone to Watier and attacked another woman's good name and ended, possibly forever, the fragile *rapprochement* he had achieved with his father.

So much for that. And it was to exorcise these demons that he drove himself and Vinnie on through the bad weather of that dismal autumn.

At what point he was sure that they were being tracked he did not know. They had stopped overnight at a dirty inn, and after a bad night and a poor breakfast, Vinnie grumbling over his flat ale that it was worse than campaigning, they had set out across the moors, north of Bradford on a poor road which grew worse.

The feeling of being watched grew stronger in him, and Vinnie felt it too. But mile after mile as he drove the carriage north, wishing that he had not brought it, but had travelled on horseback, however hard the journey, nothing untoward happened, so that he began to think that his imagination, fevered with the memory of Julia's betrayal was working overtime, was deceiving him.

They stopped at midday to eat bread, cheese and apples and to drink the bottle of ale which Vinnie had brought with him from the inn, and then water from the spring by the roadside.

He remembered that Nell Tallboys's great house stood near by, and he wondered briefly what she might think if told that her uncle's choice of a husband was passing her by without as much as a how do you do.

Well, judging by reports, she probably wanted him as little as he wanted her. He grimaced, wiped his mouth, and they set off again into the teeth of a wind more suited to November than late September.

And then, just after they had reached the moor's highest point, and the road, now little more than a track along which the carriage lurched, descended before them, all his forebodings came true. His instincts for danger, honed by his Army career, had not played him false.

Two bullets whined at them. One missed him, the other took poor Vinnie, riding by the carriage, in the chest, and dropped him dead from his horse. The French had not been able to kill him, but a group of Yorkshire banditti had done for him.

Shad never did know who or what they were, whether common footpads or poor devils without work, perhaps even old soldiers lost without a war to fight, but whoever they were they knew their business. They came across the moor at him, on horseback, rode over to poor dead Vinnie, and, firing a second shot at him, demanded his valuables on pain of his life.

"You'll have to fight me for them, then," he yelled in feeble defiance, and, another shot catching him across the shoulder, he lost control of the horses, and one of the cutthroats launched himself at him, and struck him such a blow with a bludgeon that he was felled—to lie half in the carriage, and half out of it.

Stunned, but still with some shreds of consciousness, he felt rather than saw them drag his bags and begin to plunder them. They were particularly excited by his fine pistols, and the Baker rifle which he had bought from a friend in the Rifle Brigade who had later died at Waterloo.

Then they pulled him from the carriage, he struggling, weakly and futilely, consciousness coming and going. Once they had him stretched on ground, blood from his gashed shoulder staining his fine coat, they stripped him of his clothing and his possessions, so that he lay naked and shivering on the hard earth.

The leader, a grimy ginger-headed bravo, a man as big as himself, discarded his own filthy rags, put on Shad's, including his top hat, and then, half in malice, half in jest, told his fellows to dress Shad in his discarded clothing.

He struggled with them, was struck again, hard, for his pains, and knew no more until they mounted their own horses, with one of them driving his carriage, with dead Vinnie propped up by his own half-conscious self, bumping and rattling across the moor towards a quarry, earlier glimpsed in the distance.

Shad's last thoughts as they pushed the carriage over the quarry's edge—they had kept his horses as plunder—was that perhaps it was fitting that everything should end here so ignominiously, after he had survived a dozen battles, guerrilla war, and his father's dislike. He'll never know what happened to me—nor will he care, was his last conscious thought.

"And that's the end of my fine gentleman," grinned the man who was now wearing Shad's clothes, watching the carriage break into pieces as it fell towards the water in the quarry's bottom. What he did not know was that Shad, thrown out almost immediately, was caught, a third of the way down, in some bushes, unconscious, but still breathing, and still blindly, instinctively determined somehow to survive.

FOR NELL TALLBOYS that day began like any other. There was little to show that, after it, nothing was ever going to be the same again. She had spent the morning going over her correspondence with old Payne, and she had been compelled to admit that her uncle's criticism of him had been just. He was past his best, and she would need to pension him off soon and find someone younger, which would be a nuisance for she would have to train him—with Henson's help.

She had then gone over accounts with Henson; he had told her of some discontent, not Luddite—that seemed dead, these days—but something similar, over towards Bradford. He hoped that it would not affect Nell's people, but thought not.

The day was fine and sunny, and after luncheon—cold meat and fruit—she had decided on a ride to blow the cobwebs away, and, instead of sending one of the footmen to the stables, she had decided to walk there herself, once she had changed into her riding habit. She liked to come upon the men unawares, see how they behaved when their betters were not about.

Again, she was later to ponder on the might-have-beens, if Nell, Countess of Malplaquet, had not walked into the altercation going on in the stable yard.

The stables themselves were beautiful buildings, large, in the Renaissance style, fine things, with better homes for horses than most men had, she sometimes thought, and the yard was reached by a triumphal arch, with a centaur—half-man, half-horse—galloping across its top.

Beneath, the human centaurs were all gathered, arguing. Aisgill's voice, its broad Yorkshire even broader than usual, was the loudest.

He was railing at Henson, who stood civilised and stolid in his fine black suit, his thin, clever face at odds with the craggy ones around him.

Aisgill stopping to draw breath, Henson began to speak in cold measured tones. Originally a countryman himself, he had adopted the manners and dress of those whom he served.

"Campions cannot," he said, "be the refuge for every wandering derelict plucked from the highway or the moors."

Aisgill began again, "Common humanity—" to be addressed by Nell.

"What is it," she asked, seeing that all the stable lads, the grooms and gardeners, together with some of the house's indoor servants, were clustered around one of the doorways to the stable lads' quarters, "that is worth all this brouhaha?"

Henson and Aisgill began to talk together, and for once Nell spoke with some of the hauteur of the great lady she was.

"One at a time, if you please, and some of you stand back a little. I wish to see what exercises you so." For she had become aware that the cause of the argument was half sitting, half lying on the steps before them.

"To your work, lads," roared Aisgill, suddenly aware of the crowd that had gathered while he disputed with Henson, and then on Nell beckoning him, rather than Henson, to speak, said, "This poor creature was brought in today by Gilbert Outhwaite from Overbeck. He found him wandering on the moor on the way of here. By the looks of him, he had been crawling on his hands and knees," and he indicated the figure on the steps, visible now that all the servants had reluctantly dispersed, leaving their betters to argue.

"Outhwaite knew that you, Lady Elinor—" for Nell was still Lady Elinor to them, as she had been for many years seeing that she had been merely heir presumptive to Malplaquet until her grandfather died, and disliked being called m'lady, or Lady Malplaquet "—were giving charity to such unfortunates, in exchange for casual labour, and thought that we might help this one."

Nell looked at the man on the steps. He was bigger, much bigger than all the stocky moors men who had surrounded him. He had a heavy growth of black stubble on his face, and his hair was a mass of shaggy black ringlets. His clothing was so torn and exiguous that Outhwaite had thrown an old blanket from his cart around his broad shoulders. He was shivering beneath it, his feet were bare and bleeding, and his eyes, suddenly raised to stare at Nell, were a brilliant, feverish blue. They held hers almost challengingly.

"Henson will be after telling me that we cannot take in every vagrant in the Riding," said Aisgill grimly, "but we cannot turn such a poor thing away. He's starving, ate one of the turnips in Aisgill's cart as though he were a wolf, is perhaps simple, for he hardly knows his own name."

"Not true," muttered the man suddenly, his eyes still on Nell. "It's, it's..." He seemed to struggle a moment with himself, then growled something which sounded like "Chad."

"Is that all?" said Nell. "Chad? Ask him what his other name is."

Aisgill spoke to the vagrant, who shook his head, looked puzzled; then, staring again at Nell, his face seemed to lighten.

"That he doesn't know," said Aisgill ruefully. "Only that he's Chad. Nor does he know where he comes from, Outhwaite said, nor even where he is. That is why Mr. Henson here wishes to turn him away. Says he'll only be a belly to feed, won't bring hands to work with him."

"That is so, Lady Elinor," said Henson severely. "Charity is well enough, but Campions cannot support every useless half-wit who roams the countryside. Either the parish supports him, or he finds work on some farm—but who would employ a simpleton?"

Nell looked doubtfully at the man. Beneath his growth of curling black hair she thought she saw a harsh and craggy face, and his body, what she could see of it, seemed a strong one, well made.

"He does not look a simpleton," and then, decisively, "Show me his hands."

The man looked at her again, held out his hands with a smile which showed excellent white teeth, said, "Will they do?" in a tone which was almost provocative, sharp and sure, quite unlike his confusion of a moment before—and then doubt and puzzlement crossed his face again, and he hung his head.

His big hands were torn and bleeding, bruised, the nails broken, the hands of a manual worker, Nell thought, although his speech, what there was of it, hinted that he was more than that. Nell caught his brilliant blue stare again, and something there, something powerful, almost feral, had a strange effect on her. She shivered, and as she did so, he dropped his gaze, and when he looked at her again his face was dull, expressionless.

"He's had a blow on the head recently, or a fall," announced Aisgill suddenly. "There's a half-healed gash on his shoulder. He's been sleeping rough, by the state of him. But he doesn't look a regular idiot to me."

"An irregular one, then," snorted Henson. "He stinks like one. Begging your pardon, Lady Elinor."

"Be quiet, both of you," said Nell sharply, seeing Aisgill bridle and prepare to answer Henson angrily. Both men stared at her; she rarely came the fine lady with them. "We can at least give him a trial, find out what work he can do. Take him in, Aisgill. Feed him, see he's washed, give him some clean clothes. If you think that he might not be well, let Dr. Ramsden look at him, and then, when he's fit again, try him as a stable hand. You were saying you had not enough lads only yesterday."

Henson opened his mouth, saw Nell's expression, said wearily, "Begging your pardon, *my lady,*" and he stressed the title. "If he don't suit, and won't work, as many simpletons won't, then he may go to the parish when he's had his chance."

"He doesn't look a simpleton," said Nell again, but best to make concessions to them both, seeming to favour neither the one nor the other. "But yes. A fair trial with Aisgill first, and if that fails, as you say."

The man of whom they were speaking had fallen into a daze, his eyes on the horizon, apparently unaware of Nell, Aisgill and Henson, and that they were concerned with him.

"Chad," said Nell sharply, "you heard what I said—that you are to be given a trial here?"

He nodded, looked up at Nell, his eyes clearing again. He took her in, standing tall and graceful before him, in her bottle-green habit, elegant boots, and her tiny top hat, a very Diana. Elusive memory, running before him, stirred in Chad. He spoke without thinking, and the words were almost a command.

"Who are you?" he said, blunt.

"Respect due from you," snapped Henson, annoyed, but Nell said,

"No, he means nothing by it. Natural for him to wish to know—especially if his memory has gone. You may call me

Lady Elinor, as the rest of my people do here," she told him gently. "But you must do as Mr. Aisgill here bids you, or be turned away. You understand?"

The man nodded. His puzzled look, so different from the one of a moment ago, had returned. "Do as Mr. Aisgill bids me. I understand," and then, almost as an afterthought, with a slight bow in her direction, "Lady Elinor."

Once more those strange blue eyes were on her, and were doing their work, holding her, trying to tell her something, causing her to be patient with him, affecting her in the oddest fashion. And then he turned to look at Aisgill, for instructions, presumably.

Henson sighed noisily, turned away himself. "Good," said Nell, "then we all understand one another. Now, Aisgill, tell one of the grooms to attend me. I wish to ride on the moor this afternoon," and then as Aisgill nodded, and the man, helped up by one of the hands, for, despite his size, he seemed weak—probably from hunger—was led away, she said, "His voice is educated, Aisgill. I wonder how he came to be a vagrant, wandering the moor half clothed, his memory gone?"

Henson, still standing there, and now suddenly a little ashamed of his harshness before the hands' gentleness with the derelict, said, "Many a man ruined these days, Lady Elinor, with the wars over and business failing. Soldiers ruined, too, their occupation gone."

All three of them watched their new acquisition walk into the men's quarters.

"Well, I don't like us getting a reputation for saving half the riff-raff in Yorkshire, but perhaps one more won't do us harm—if he is willing and able to work, that is, which seems unlikely. Another worthless mouth to feed, no doubt, and throw out after a few weeks."

Later, Henson's words came back, if not to haunt him, but to remind him that even the cleverest of us could make the grossest of misjudgements.

CHAPTER THREE

"I WONDER how the vagabond Aisgill rescued is getting on?" said Nell idly to Aunt Conybeare, who sat stitching at her canvas work before a roaring fire. Early October was colder than usual that autumn.

Nell had been poring over a thick book, not a lady's mindless and agreeable novel, but a report from the Board of Agriculture on hill farming. All her reading seemed to be functional these days, and Lord Byron's latest—and naughty—work, Manfred: a Drama, discreetly hidden from public view by her Quarterly Review on the occasional table by her chair, sat waiting for her to find time to pick it up.

Nell knew it was naughty because Aunt Conybeare, sighing and deploring it as she did so, had eagerly read every word, before telling Nell that, as an unmarried girl, she really ought not to open it.

Nell privately wondered whether an unmarried girl who ran England's biggest and most successful stud could be unaware of anything to do with reproduction, human or otherwise, but discreetly said nothing.

For no good reason, ever since she had seen the vagabond on the steps, and he had raised those amazing eyes to look into hers, the derelict she had taken in had haunted Nell's memory.

Really, this is absurd, she told herself. Whatever had she thought that she had seen there? It had disturbed her so much that she had privately determined to avoid meeting him again, and apart from asking Aisgill once if he was still at Campions, to which Aisgill had said, Yes, and he was putting him to work in the yard, she had not spoken of him again, and had avoided the stables.

Restlessness gripped her, a feeling that life was passing her by—probably the result of Chesney Beaumont's doomings about her unmarried condition. She rose, put down her book, said, "I need air. I think I will go for a walk. No, Aunt," as her aunt raised agonised eyes to her, for the air was keen outside, "I shall take John with me, for protection, if not company, and you may enjoy the fire in peace."

Did her feet take her stablewards consciously or unconsciously? She was interested in the horses, of course. She was a skilful horsewoman, and the Campions stables were nationally famous, particularly the stud, where horses bred by the Malplaquets constantly won the great classic races.

John, the footman, walking behind her, carrying a large green umbrella, although how he was to keep it up in the wind should he need to open it, Nell could not think—she passed through the great arch to stand in the yard.

She was wearing a heavy mannish coat over her light dress, and had put on little black boots against the mud of what appeared to be an early winter.

One of the stable hands stopped currycombing a horse, came up respectfully to take her orders. "Lady Elinor."

"Where is Aisgill?" she said. "I wish to speak with him."

About what? she thought. What odd compulsion has brought me here?

She looked around the busy scene, at the blacksmith in his forge at the end of the row, the lads mending tack, another lad forking feed into a barrow. She could not see Chad anywhere.

"Maister Aisgill's in the riding school, Lady Elinor. Shall I fetch him for you?"

"Thank you, no." Nell was always polite to those who served her. "I'll go there myself," and she set off towards it.

The riding school had been built by the second Earl, a noted horseman, after he had seen the famous one in Vienna on his Grand Tour. Designed to school horses, not only in the elaborate ritual of dressage, but also in their general management, it had fallen into disrepair until Nell, early in her running of the estate, had had it renovated, and had encouraged Aisgill, who needed no encouragement, to bring it into use again.

In the round building, open at the sides, beneath a slightly domed roof, the work of the stable was going on briskly.

Aisgill, suddenly seeing her, came over, his ruddy face welcoming. Dismayed at first by the thought of a woman taking charge, he had found that Nell was his closest ally in restoring Malplaquet's racing pride, and he was now her most fervent supporter.

"Good to see you here, Lady Elinor. We've missed you lately. You wanted me?"

Nell made a vague motion with her hands, her eyes were busy. "Nothing, really. Just to see that all's going well," and then, offered as an afterthought, "What have you been doing with the vagabond you rescued a fortnight gone?"

"What have I done?" he said, with an odd grin. "You might well ask what he's done and doing. He's on Rajah, as you see," and he pointed at the rider and horse completing a neat trotting circle, and coming to rest not far from them.

In the gloom of the arena Nell had not seen him, but she saw him now. He was straight backed, in perfect control of the giant stallion. She saw his head turn, and the blue gaze fell on her again.

"On Rajah! You mean you have let him ride Rajah! And he can control him like that!"

"Oh, he's amazing with the horses, Lady Elinor. He says he can remember nothing, but even on his first day at work when Rajah broke loose he stopped him and quieted him when no one else could."

Aware that the man on the horse was watching them, some delicacy made Aisgill bend his head to speak low to his mistress.

"It's my belief, madam, that he's been in the Army, a trooper, possibly. He rides like a trained cavalryman, and he has the scar of a great wound on his chest. Some poor devil turned away because of the peace, fallen on hard times since. He asked to ride Rajah, and, seeing how he gentled him, I gave him permission, and look at him now. It was a good day when we took him in."

So it was, thought Nell, for Rajah, a great black, the most beautiful horse in the stud, had always possessed a vile, unmanageable temper, and most were frightened to lead him, let alone ride him.

Chad, for so she must think of him now, for he was one of her people, had trotted the horse into the centre of the circle and was teaching him to walk on the spot. Rajah was showing his dislike of the restraint put upon him, but his rider was using his voice, as well as his body, to force his will on him. Nell watched him, fascinated by such power, such control.

"And such patience," she said at last to Aisgill.

"Yes," he replied; he was a little surprised, for Nell, although usually interested in the work of the stable, was seldom so particularly interested. Her whole body had gone quite still, her attention given completely to what she was seeing.

"But it's time he stopped. Rajah is growing impatient."

As though Chad had heard him, he turned the horse towards Nell and Aisgill. He trotted him over, the strength of both horse and rider plainly visible as he controlled the only-half-willing beast. Slipping from his back, to hold Rajah firm where he stood, he touched his forehead to Nell, as he had been taught, said briefly to Aisgill, "He's had enough, sir. Best let him rest."

The words and the actions were servile, those of a good, obedient servant, but despite that there was nothing servile about him, Nell thought.

Now that she could see him plain, it appeared that the vagabond had been tamed and groomed. His crisp black hair had been trimmed, so that it clustered in loose ringlets about his harsh and craggy face, which was now clean-shaven, although a dark shadow shaded his mouth and jaw.

The face was strong, and there was nothing handsome in it, but it was strangely compelling, and not that of a wastrel. His eyes shone bluer than she had remembered them, and they were surveying her, not insolently, but coolly, as though they were simply man and woman together—a strange experience for Nell.

The rest of him, clad in the smart but serviceable green uniform of the stable hand not engaged in dirty work, with his once bleeding and naked feet in bright black boots, was remarkable as well, broad-shouldered, beautifully proportioned, and looking at him Nell felt the strangest stirrings rising in her, stirrings which she had never felt before.

He was so large that he dwarfed her, another pleasant sensation for Nell, who was usually as tall as, if not taller than, many of the men around her.

Allied to all these odd stirrings and throbbings, which grew stronger not weaker the longer she looked at him, Nell was experiencing a strange breathlessness which she had never felt before, and her heart began to beat wildly. She mentally shook her head, reprimanded herself. In God's name, what was coming over her that the sight of a strong stable hand who had been plucked half naked from the moors should cause her to behave like a green girl confronted by her first lover?

For, inexperienced though she was, Nell had no doubt about what was the cause of these strange and involuntary reactions. Desperately she tried to compose herself, for now he was speaking to her in that deep, almost gravel voice, which added to her inward confusion.

"I have to thank you, Lady Elinor, for taking me in. I think I should have died else, my wits were so addled."

Nell inclined her head, fought for control, was surprised how calm and measured her voice was. "If you can tame Rajah," she managed, "it was a good day for Campions, as well as for you."

He smiled, showing his strong white teeth again. Whatever and whoever he was, he had been well fed, and decently educated, and Aisgill's guess that he had been a soldier was probably a good one.

"Oh, no one will tame Rajah," he said confidently. "Only if you show him who's master, he might choose to do your bidding occasionally."

And you too, thought Nell, looking at him. For like Rajah, there was something wild about him, something which, like it or not, called to Nell, who, if not wild, seldom did what was expected of her.

"Aisgill tells me that you might have been a soldier. Have you no memories which might help you to recall who you are, or where you came from?"

His eyes were suddenly shadowed. "No, madam," he said, almost painfully. "But I bear a scar of what I think must be a wartime wound and I have . . . bad dreams."

"Bad dreams?" Nell was aware that she was spending far too much time talking to one poor stable hand, but he intrigued her. "What sort of bad dreams?"

"Of noise, and fighting, and men dying," he said simply. "So yes, I was probably a trooper. I remember riding a horse." He thought a moment. "He was white and splendid . . . and then he fell beneath me . . ."

He paused. "And then?" said Nell encouragingly.

"And then, nothing. The other lads say I wake up shouting, but they cannot tell me what I say."

"You may remember in time, I hope," said Nell, only to hear him reply strangely,

"I may not like what I remember, madam."

She let him go, turned to Aisgill, who had been listening to them, wondering at Lady Nell's interest—but then, she had always been unpredictable.

"Chad," she said slowly. "What name do you use for him on the books?"

"Young Peel said that he should be called Newcome, because that is what he is—new come among us," replied Aisgill with a smile, "and he agreed, so that is how he is styled."

Nell was still watching Chad walk Rajah away, watched him until he left the arena, drawn by she knew not what.

"A corporal or a sergeant, you think," she hazarded. "By the way he speaks, his sureness, he has given orders in the past—and taken them, too. He has had some education—he knew how to speak to me."

"Oh, aye," said Aisgill, who had been a cavalryman when he was a boy, before injury had sent him back to civil life with a permanent limp. "It's passing strange. He cannot remember who he is, nor anything about himself, but he knows how to school a horse, and a dozen other things. He told Seth Hutton off for being careless with a fowling piece. Said that it was no way to treat a weapon!''

"A useful man, then," commented Nell. "And the mare you had in foal—Bluebell—how does she do, these days?" For she thought that it was time that she stopped showing an interest in Chad Newcome, or Aisgill would be wondering what was coming over her—not that she did not make a point of showing an interest in all her people!

CHAD NEWCOME sat on the same steps where Nell Tallboys had first seen him, mending tack. The October day was grey and gloomy, and, to some extent, so were his thoughts.

And yet, in an odd way, he was strangely content. He began to whistle an old song—and where did that come from? he wondered, and how remarkable that he, who could remember nothing about himself, could remember that, and how to school a horse, load and use a gun, and perform a hundred other tasks. Day by day he recovered a little more of what he knew, but, of himself, nothing.

The words of the song ran through his head, and when he came to the phrase, "One is one and all alone," there came the unbidden thought, And shall I always be alone, as I have been in the past?

He frowned, and stopped working, busy hands still. Now, how do I know that? Had he no chick nor child, wife nor father and mother to love and care for him? Had he always been a vagrant wanderer?

No, that could not be true. His good body, and the growing realisation, as his powers slowly returned, that he had been an educated man, told him that once he must have had a settled life, and he knew beyond a doubt that he had had women, and more than one, although how he knew he could not say.

To think of women was to think of Lady Elinor, or Lady Nell, or even "Our Nell," as the men affectionately called her behind her back.

"God send she never marries," he had heard Aisgill say once, "for we should never get a master as good as she is, and I never thought to say that of any woman."

Perhaps it was because his first conscious memory in this new strange life was of her, standing straight and tall before him, that she haunted him a little. He remembered how foolishly pleased he had been that day at the riding school when he had first seen her again, and she had spoken to him kindly about his schooling of Rajah.

It had been difficult not to keep his eyes hard on her the whole time he was with her, and he had frequently looked away because he had not wished to seem insolent, but she drew him in some fashion he could not define.

Or was it, after all, simply that before he had seen her everything had been blurred, a fog through which he had walked unknowing of himself, or his circumstances, uncaring almost, as though he was at one with the few animals which roved the moors?

He shrugged as the song in his head reached the betraying phrase again, and then, as the word "alone" rang out, she was before him, in his mind's eye, and this time he inspected her closely, as he could not inspect the living and breathing woman, the Countess who held all their lives in the hollow of her hand.

She was tall for a woman, but beautifully proportioned, moving with an easy athletic grace. A grace confirmed when he had seen her ride off on horseback, in perfect control of her mount.

And her face! It was neither pretty nor beautiful, but somehow better than either. Beneath the glossy wealth of her chestnut hair, it was as strong and powerful as the face of Diana in an old painting. The high-bridged nose, the full and generous mouth with its humorous set, the grey eyes beneath high-arched black brows, the whole poised on the proud column of a shapely neck.

But best of all was the compassion he had seen there when she had bent that proud head to examine the poor wretch who had been decanted on her very doorstep.

Well, a cat might look at a king, so surely a homeless vagrant, for vagrant he must have been, from his clothes and his condition, might look at a queen—for Nell Tallboys was a queen in Yorkshire.

He rose and stretched. There was a growing pride in him as his faculties returned which Aisgill had noticed, a pride in his ability to control Rajah and to do the menial tasks around the yard well. "He's been a man under orders," Aisgill said to Henson when the agent had enquired how Newcome was faring, "and he's given orders as well. I'd bet my life on his being a sergeant in the Army, and a good one. Wonder why they let him go?"

Henson had shrugged. Newcome might be a bit of a mystery, but not one on which he cared to spend time.

Aisgill came towards Chad now, said briefly, "Lady Elinor needs a groom to escort her on her daily ride this afternoon. You know the lie of the land now, Newcome. Saddle Vulcan, the big gelding, for her, and you may take Rajah, if you think he will behave himself. Without his daily run, he'll be a devil to handle."

So later, smartly dressed, wearing a jockey cap with a green and silver cockade at the side—Malplaquet's colours—he helped his Countess into the saddle, wordless, and then mounted an impatient Rajah, to ride with her across the moors, already clad in their winter colours.

Nell thought that Newcome, riding by her side, looked better than he had done since he had arrived at Campions. The drawn, rather haunted look he had worn in the early days had vanished, and like Aisgill she recognised the pride he was displaying in his work.

And his control over Rajah was greater than ever. That proud beast was suddenly willing to serve an even prouder master. What a strange thought, that one of her stable hands could be proud! She took a covert look at Newcome's harsh profile, and when they reached the usual end of her ride, for she always took the same route—safer so, Aisgill said, if they always knew exactly where she went—a pile of stones known as the Cairn, and they dismounted, she signalled for him to sit by her, on one of the large boulders scattered about the Cairn.

Chad hesitated; he had been prepared to stand by Rajah whom he had tethered to a broken tree, and he knew what the proper place of a groom was, and it was not sitting by his mistress. But orders were orders, and Nell, amused, watched him struggle with his sense of what was fitting, and her command.

She had dressed herself more carefully than usual; indeed, for the last week she had chosen to wear turnouts far more à la mode than she usually did, so that when she was about to leave for her ride Aunt Conybeare had stared at her, and said, "Gracious, Nell, we are fine these days!"

Nell had blushed. She had put on a deep blue riding habit, adorned with silver buttons, and had wound a fine white linen cravat, edged with lace, around her throat and had secured it with a silver and sapphire pin.

Her boots had a polish on them so high that Aunt Conybeare had asked if they had been prepared with champagne; she had heard that the great London dandies did that! And her deep blue top had ribbons of pale blue silk wreathed around it, falling in long streamers down her back. Even her whip was a fine thing, decorated with silver trimmings; it had belonged to the third Earl, a noted fop in his time.

As a final concession to vanity, she had had her maid, Annie Thorpe, brush and brush her chestnut hair, and then Annie had dressed it for her, far more elaborately and carefully than usual, so that the top hat sat proudly on it.

"A pity you're not going to meet your lover—dressed like that," had been Aunt Conybeare's final contribution, and one that had had her going hot all over. Because she had asked Aisgill to assign Newcome to her for the ride, and it was Newcome she was dressing like this for, if she told the truth.

And what would Aunt Conybeare say to that? Or Aisgill, or Henson, or... Well, to the devil with them all!

But she was not thinking of this when Newcome finally sat down, and she said in the most bored, Countess-like voice she could assume, "Tell me, Newcome, have you recovered your memory yet?"

Chad looked at her, and thought that he had never seen anything so superb. Not, of course, that his conscious memory was more than a month old! But Nell Tallboys, who usually walked round the yard looking more like one of the stable lad's girls, shabby clothing pulled on any-old-how, and her hair falling down and blowing in the wind, was truly Lady Malplaquet this afternoon, and he hardly knew how to address her.

Except that his tongue did it for him. "No, Lady Elinor. I still know nothing of myself, and Maister Aisgill—" he pronounced the name as the tykes did; his own speech was accentless "—tells me that Blackwell, your tenant on the Home Farm, found me sleeping by the haystack two nights before Outhwaite brought me to Campions, refused to feed me—apparently I begged for food, although I have no memory of doing so—and moved me on."

"Blackwell is a good tenant but a mean man," said Nell reflectively. "He should have sent you to Campions, but he doesn't approve of Campions charity."

"Well, I approve of it," said Chad sturdily. "Or I should likely be dead on the moor by now."

Nell's laugh at that was not one that any past Countess of Malplaquet would have approved of. "Well, that is true enough," she said appreciatively. "Aisgill tells me that you are a good worker and not only with the horses."

"But I like working with the horses best," said Chad, seeing that Lady Elinor was determined to talk to him. "I have a strange feeling that, while I have often worked with horses, it was not as a groom or a stable lad."

"Which would support Aisgill's belief that you were a trooper. But you don't object to doing the hard work round the yard?"

"It would be a mean soul who would not work for those who had given him his life back, and who were prepared to take him on without knowing of his past."

Seeing Nell look a little puzzled, he added, somewhat stiffly, "A man without a past must be a suspect man, Lady Elinor. Who knows what I have done, or may be fleeing from? It sometimes worries me at night, when I cannot sleep."

Nell looked at Chad's strong face, the face which she hardly dared inspect too closely, it had such an effect on her.

"You do not look like a criminal, Newcome, nor do you behave like one."

Chad shrugged. He did not tell Lady Elinor that in the long night watches his efforts to recall who and what he was often served only to confuse him. Once, when he had been unable to rest at all, and had finally fallen asleep from very exhaustion, he had had a nightmare in which she had figured.

Something about her and himself which had made him cry out so strongly, and throw himself from his bed. His behaviour had been so violent that he had awoken several of the lads and they had been compelled to restrain him because he was not properly awake and he had tried to fight them off. When he had woken up he could not remember what in the dream had distressed him so.

Seeing that he could never have met her before the day on which she had ordered him taken in, and had shown him nothing but kindness, it seemed a strange dream to have.

To take his mind away from unhappy things he did something he knew no good servant should do; he initiated a topic of conversation with his mistress, for the pleasure of seeing her lively face turned towards him, and hearing her beautiful voice.

"These stones, Lady Elinor. Were they put here of a purpose, or did Nature simply pile them up at random?"

Nell looked sharply at him. More and more Newcome was beginning to demonstrate that he had been given a good education.

"The people round here believe that the gods threw them down in play, the old Norse gods, that is. This part of the North was never properly Christianised, they say, until long after the South. There is a book in the library—Challenor showed it to me—which says that people lived in the Cairn long ago, although I find that hard to believe. Think how cold they must have been in winter!"

Unconsciously she had spoken to him as an equal, and he answered her in kind. "If that were true, there must be an entrance."

"And so there is," said Nell. "Look, I will show you." She rose and walked to the side away from the one where they had been sitting, and, pointing to a gap in the stones, said, "Follow me," turned sideways and wriggled through.

With difficulty, Chad followed her, to find himself in a small low chamber, so low that Nell, as well as he, had to bow herself to stand in it.

"They must have been dwarfs!" he exclaimed.

"So Challenor believes," answered Nell, turning to go, but as she did so her foot slipped and she felt Chad catch her, to break her fall.

Nell was suddenly hard against him, could feel the heat from his body, his male strength, and was held there, face to face, her head level with his chin, tall man and tall woman, bowed—then he tried to avoid standing up, so as not to bang their heads, lost his footing as well, and they were on the ground.

It was the first time that he had touched her, other than to hold her foot as she mounted Vulcan, and the sensations Nell experienced were extraordinary. She remembered being in a man's arms, dancing a waltz, being lifted by a boatman, Aisgill picking her up once, when she had been thrown from her horse, and in not one of these encounters had she felt what she now did when Chad Newcome touched and held her.

I am going mad, running a fever, loneliness is making me prey to a disgraceful lust; I should never have brought him in here; whatever would Aunt Conybeare—Aisgill, Uncle Beaumont, Henson—think if they knew how wanton I am grown? ran through Nell's head, before he released her, and they crouched, face to face, in the gloom of the confined space.

Chad was suffering, if suffering was the right word, the same experience as Nell. Loss of memory, he was finding, was leading to some loss of control. He had a mad desire to kiss the woman half kneeling before him. He repressed it, the refrain "And lose your place to be thrown out to starve," running through his mind and stopping him from following his natural inclinations.

Whatever would she think if he assaulted her so? Worst of all, his strongest instinct was to do much more than that to her, it was to bear her to the ground and take his pleasure with her.

Still half crouched, he turned, and pushed his way into the open again, to lean on the biggest stone, fighting for self-control before she came after him.

Once outside, Nell was Countess of Malplaquet again; she said in a voice so false that it frightened her, "I think, Newcome, it's time we went home. I feel strangely tired." She was pleased to see that Newcome appeared his usual stern self, that he merely bowed his head silently, and silently helped her back on to Vulcan before mounting Rajah and waiting for her to lead them home.

Still silent, they rode back to Campions. What neither of them understood was that both of them had reacted in the same way to the other, and each thought that he or she was the only one to experience such savagely strong feelings that rank, decorum, climate, and rules of conduct had meant nothing to them. Had they followed their natural inclinations they would have mated inside the Cairn as though they were at one with the birds and the beasts around them!

CHAPTER FOUR

"NELL," said Aunt Conybeare reprovingly—they were sitting in Nell's private room, overlooking the park, "Your wits are wandering today. This is the second time that I have asked you the same question, and you have not answered me on either occasion. Most unlike you. What can you be thinking of?"

Nell flushed. In her wild and wicked thoughts she had been on the moors again, with Newcome, and then in the Cairn, on her knees before him. How to inform her aunt that she was trying to tell herself that she must have dreamed her reactions to him? An elderly female of twenty-seven, untouched and past her last prayers, could not possibly have felt as she did about a stable hand, a nobody who had arrived at Campions half-naked—and why did she have to think of him in that state? Her whole body flushed hot at the thoughts.

Of course she had imagined the whole thing, including the way in which Newcome had looked at her when they had been crouched in the Cairn together, as though he wanted to eat her, whole. On the ride home, and afterwards, he had been stiffly proper, had helped her down without so much as looking at her, and had led Vulcan and Rajah away, still with his eyes averted. Which, now she came to think about it, told its own story!

Well, she would not look at him, and would try to avoid his company—but, on the other hand, not too much so; unfair to him, to let Aisgill think that he had offended her, when the offence was hers, not his. He had done nothing.

Nell was almost too distracted to read her private correspondence—sorted for her by old Payne, who had looked more decrepit than ever this morning. One badly scrawled

missive was from Cousin Ulric Tallboys, informing her that
he intended to visit her on his way north to the Borders, and
would arrive some time in the next fortnight, he did not
know when. He was staying with the Staffords at Trentham.

"Who probably wanted him as little as I do," said Nell
drily to Aunt Conybeare, "but are too polite to say so. I'll
tell Mrs. Orgreave to make a suite of rooms ready for him—
he is the heir, after all."

Work seemed a way to drive out improper thoughts about
Newcome. She also considered a visit to High Harrogate.
Perhaps more company was what she needed, to meet some
young and sleek gentleman whose smooth and civilised
charms would compare well with Newcome's austere,
straightforward manner.

Newcome again! Nell rose smartly to her feet, said
abruptly, "I'm going to work in the library. Challenor said
that he'd found some old folios, stuffed away in a cupboard, and I ought to look at them."

"Yes, do, dear," said Aunt Conybeare comfortably. "It
might settle you. Your bibliomania is nearly as bad as his,
although the stables seem to have seen more of you lately
than the library."

That did it! Nell almost bolted from the room. Oh, dear,
is it as bad as that, that Aunt Conybeare is noticing something? Humour touched the corner of her mouth at the
thought. Well, some fusty old books, dry as dust, perhaps
containing woodcuts of men and women who looked more
like Mr. and Mrs. Noah in a child's version of the ark which
her grandfather had once given her than the people she saw
around her, might cool her down and drive away these feverish fantasies which were filling her errant mind.

Pushing open the library door, registering old Challenor's pleasure at the sight of her, she said firmly to herself,
I will forgo my usual afternoon ride for a time, come here
instead. Say I don't feel quite the thing—God forgive me for
the lie, I feel too much the thing—and then I needn't go to
the stables at all, and shan't see . . . him.

She did not even want to think of his name, for that seemed to have nearly as strong an effect on her as seeing him.

These splendid resolutions lasted exactly forty-eight hours...

NELL AWOKE EARLY, restless. She could not remember her dreams, only that her sleep had been disturbed and that they were vaguely disgraceful. She remembered crying out once, then sitting up, sweat streaming from her, although the air in the room was cold once she had pushed back the bedding.

Indoors seemed oppressive. She did not ring for Annie, but did what she often did, although Aunt Conybeare as well as Annie disapproved of the habit; she pulled on her clothes rapidly, finishing with her old grey woollen thing, which she wore to work with Challenor, and then a shabby overcoat over that—it had been worn by a young male Tallboys in the last century, and she had rescued it from the bottom of an old press to wear when she visited the stables.

She would, she told herself firmly, go for a walk in the grounds immediately round the house, so she would not need John or Annie to accompany her.

The day was grey and cold, but dry, and the walk exhilarated her. She made a circuit of the house, quite alone; it was so early that the house still slept, all the windows close-curtained, and, at the end, instead of going in again, her wandering feet led her to the stables as though they were leading her home.

Well, Aunt Conybeare, she thought afterwards, wryly, always did say that if I wandered into the stable yard without warning I should end up regretting it, and at last I did.

But did I? Regret it, that is.

As she walked through the arch the place seemed, at first, deserted. And then she turned the corner, into the flat paved area before the stable hands' quarters, a place she rarely visited, but which seemed safe at this hour.

And there, in the morning's half-light, standing in front of the pump, a bucket of water at his feet, and water all about him, was Chad.

He had evidently, despite the cold, taken an impromptu outdoor bath, and his face was hidden by the towel with which he was drying his hair, so that he could neither see nor hear her coming.

But that was not it at all, not at all. What was it, was that he was stark naked, and facing her. Nell was paralysed, except that at the sight of him her body was suddenly prey to the strangest feelings.

The worst was in the pit of her stomach—no, be honest, Nell, lower down altogether—where a most strange ache, exacerbated by throbbing and tickling, suddenly began, and her breasts also had begun to ache, and feel sensitive, and it was exactly as though she, too, were stark naked before him!

For he had lowered the towel to reveal those brilliant and disturbing bright blue eyes, and he was staring at her, as she, dreadfully, was staring at him.

Nell had never seen a naked man before, but she knew at once, without being told, that she had in front of her just about the most superb specimen of the male sex that she could hope to encounter. Almost against her will her eyes drank him in, from the powerful column of his neck, his broad and splendid shoulders, deep chest, covered in fine, curling black hair, a triangle which narrowed into an arrow, and then into another inverted triangular fleece above his...sex...which hung proud and magnificent before her, so that she hurriedly transferred her gaze to his long and splendid legs, muscular thighs, calves and feet, all perfectly proportioned, as though the giant statue of Mars, god of war, in the entrance hall of Campions had come to sudden and inconvenient life.

She also took in the great scar below his shoulder of which Aisgill had spoken, but most shaming of all was that she registered that he had seen her fascinated interest in the figure he presented, and was staring back at her, before he slowly dropped the towel to cover his loins, and began to turn away.

But not before saying in that deep, gravelly voice which so matched his harsh and powerful face, "My apologies, Lady Elinor, I did not know that you were here."

"Not—not at all," she stammered inanely, as though she was addressing a fellow aristocrat, fully dressed in a polite drawing-room. "My fault. I know that I should not have come here without warning."

He half turned back, to speak again, she thought, except that he did not, merely gave her his rare and brilliant white smile, the smile that softened his face, and which, although Nell did not know it, had already won the heart of every female servant at Campions—only Chad had not cared to do anything with or to them, despite its power to seduce.

The paralysis that had gripped Nell left her as suddenly as it had come. She walked briskly away, still dreadfully aware of her own body and its primitive reactions. She had never experienced such a thing before when with any man.

It was a sensation so strong that it frightened her. For she knew, beyond a doubt, that if Chad Newcome had walked over, taken her into his arms and begun to…to…she would have been unable to stop him; nay, more, would have collaborated with him, stable hand though he was, and Countess in her own right though she was!

The primitive call of man to woman which she had always denied had any meaning for her—had denied, indeed, her very sex, and even that a man could ever rouse her—had her in its thrall.

Nell was compelled to face the fact that it had merely been sufficient for her to see him naked, for the pull of him which she had improbably felt on the very first time on which she had seen him, which she had felt again in the Cairn, to be revealed in its purest and most passionate form, to tell her that merely to see him thus was enough to rouse her completely.

Pure! What a word to describe the sensations that coursed through her, and which gripped her still. Nell, unbelieving, shook herself as she walked blindly back through the arch.

It is being on my own so much, and seeing so little of anyone but old Challenor and Aunt Conybeare and the rest, old and middle-aged men, all of them. I really must order my mind a little. It cannot be him, it cannot!

But she could not forget what she had seen, and for the rest of the day, every time her mind strayed, Nell saw before her the form and physique of the perfect athlete that Chad Newcome had revealed to her, accidentally, that morning.

AISGILL WAS WORKING in his little office when Chad came in for his day's orders. He was struggling with his paperwork, the stud book, the accounts of the hands' wages, the expenditure on the stud, everything connected with the stables, and for which he was responsible.

He waved an irritated quill at Newcome, "Wait, man, wait. I'll deal with you in a moment," for the details of his work were refusing to sort themselves out on paper, however clear they were in his head.

He was aware of Newcome, standing there, quiet, and when his pen dropped ink on the paper for the second time, so that he screwed it up and flung it across the room, he saw Chad begin to speak, and then stop, hesitant.

"Yes, man, spit it out, what is it?"

Chad looked at Aisgill, who had been consistently kind to him, if stern, as he was with all the lads; he reminded Chad of someone—who? A vague figure in the mists of lost memory who had given Chad orders which he felt, rather than knew, he wanted to carry out efficiently. He also wanted to be of use.

He decided to speak; after all, Aisgill could always rebuff him.

"Master Aisgill, sir. I have recovered a little more of my memory, not much, but it might be useful to you..." He stopped. Something told him that in his old life, whatever that was, he had given orders, and men had jumped to them, but here he was a menial, and must know his place.

"If you have something to say," barked Aisgill, "then say it. Time is valuable."

Chad threw caution to the winds. "I remember that I know how to keep books, write letters, and, if you wish, I could be your clerk. I know..." he hesitated again, but in for a penny, in for a pound, "...that Henson chases you about the paperwork, and if you used me, he could not."

Aisgill was minded to roar at him, but something in Newcome's humility, a humility which he sensed was not

natural to the man, but which told him that his servant did
not wish to offend, but to help, stopped him. Stupid not to
use a man's talents. More and more it was becoming plain
to him that Newcome was other than a feckless fool who
had ended up walking the roads because of his folly. Bad
luck had probably done for him, as for others. What he actually had been was difficult to gauge.

"I took you in," he said slowly, "at my and Lady Elinor's wish, because we thought that you might be of service. You have proved yourself a hard worker, and, more
than that, your skill with horses and around the stables is
exceptional. If you think that you could be helpful to me in
other ways, then why not? A man would be a fool not to
take up such an offer."

He rose, said with a wry smile, "If you can write without
blots, do so. Do you think you can copy out in fair what I
have writ there in rough."

Chad picked up the quill and sat in Aisgill's chair, looked
at the pile of odd and grimy pieces of paper and scrap on
which Aisgill kept his daily records, said cheerfully, "I think
I have a memory of working with worse than this," and he
let Aisgill instruct him in what was needful, before beginning to transcribe, in a fair copper-plate hand, and swiftly,
what was before him.

"I was not," he said, raising his head, to see Aisgill
watching him intently, "used to doing much figuring, I
think." He frowned; he could not tell Aisgill, for it appeared improbable, that he seemed to remember that other
men had done it for him, and that he had inspected their
work. "But I do have a little grasp of the matter, enough to
keep these simple accounts."

When he had gone, the work done, and some letters
written, still in the same fair hand, with a number of suggestions, diffidently made, which improved their sense,
Aisgill walked over to the table which served as his desk,
picked up the papers, and frowned.

The work before him was meticulous, and he laughed a
little to himself at Henson's probable reaction. There'll be
no grumbling this week, that's for sure, about my careless

indecipheral hand, for he meant to go on using Newcome as his clerk—and then he frowned again. Every new talent which Newcome uncovered only served to demonstrate that he had been a man of more than common affairs.

Which made his arrival here at Campions, a nameless, memoryless vagabond, more than passing strange.

AISGILL WAS NOT the only person Chad Newcome troubled. His mistress hardly knew what to do with herself for thinking about him. She had always prided herself on her downright stability—what the late Dr. Johnson had robustly called bottom. That, she knew, was a quality which denied fiddle-faddle, hemmings and hawings, acknowledged the truth of what was, as another philosopher, Hume, had said, and not what ought to be.

Men—and women—were naked, forked animals, she knew that well enough, and she should not have been so shocked to be reminded of what he, and she, so essentially were.

Be truthful, Nell, she said to herself, severely. You know perfectly well that what is shocking you is not having seen him, but what the sight of him did to you! You can no longer pretend complete indifference to the opposite sex, which you have done since you were nineteen. That is gone forever, along with your innocence. For what happened in the Garden of Eden to Adam and Eve has just happened to you. Be truthful again; you desired him, your stable hand and groom, a nameless nobody, and nothing that you can say or do will alter that one simple and undeniable fact.

And his own cool acceptance of what had happened, there in the yard, no mark of shame about him, at having been so found—what did that tell her about him?

Restlessly, Nell put down the book which she was reading in the library. One of the giant folios which Challenor had found—her predecessors, apart from the fourth Earl, had been careless of their books.

They had been careless of everything, and she had seen it as her duty to put matters in order, and since her succession six years ago order was what she brought to her great possessions.

And inside them her own life had been the most orderly thing of all—but no longer. Outwardly, all was the same, but inwardly—oh, inwardly, was a different matter, and cool Nell Tallboys had gone forever.

CHAPTER FIVE

"WELL," SAID HENSON, "here's a turn-up!" It was a week later, and the Countess of Malplaquet and her advisers, Henson, Aisgill, Challenor and old Payne, her secretary, whom she had privately nicknamed her Privy Council, were having their Friday meeting in her study.

It was a vast room, with windows running from the floor to the ceiling, looking towards the park, which sloped away before them, and then across to the moors, a view so splendid that Nell was thinking of commissioning Turner to come and paint it. One wall was covered with bookshelves containing everything which Nell had thought it necessary to read in order to run Campions and her other properties correctly.

Over the hearth was a portrait of her grandfather, Patricius Tallboys, in all the glory of his youth, painted by Gainsborough, a lovely feathery thing, with the blue of his Garter ribbon glowing like a jewel across his white court dress. Two Canalettos, depicting views of London, were mounted on each side of the hearth above cabinets full of precious porcelain from China, Japan and Germany.

Nell's desk was a work of art, walnut, with inlays showing elaborate flowers, and had a little gilt rail at its back. But its use was practical, not decorative, and she and her cohorts had been doing their weekly examination of the estate's books.

Henson's exclamation had been provoked by the sight of Aisgill's books, which usually evoked either derision or criticism from him. "You've been learning," he accused. "Who taught you?"

The two men had a running battle, half friendly, half not, for Nell's favour. Aisgill, hesitant, decided to tell the truth. Better so.

"Not me," he offered. "Newcome. He offered to be my clerk, and it is his work you are admiring."

Payne picked up the letter written out for him to approve, amend and send out in Aisgill's name. "I need make no alterations or additions to this," he said in his cracked old voice. "I take it that he did not copy it, but wrote it for you."

"Wrong to deny it." Aisgill was brief. "Credit where credit is due. Yes, I told him what to say, and he did the rest."

"A man of parts," commented Henson, the comment grudging. They were all a little surprised by these further revelations of Newcome's abilities, including Nell. She did not let them see how much this news pleased her.

At the end of the meeting Nell made a decision. "Stay behind, Aisgill. I would have a word with you."

Henson looked sharply at them as he left. Nell walked over to the windows, looked out, spoke to Aisgill, uncharacteristically, without turning her head. "I have not taken my daily ride lately. Pray see that Vulcan is saddled for me at two of the clock."

She turned as she finished, to see Aisgill bob his head. "It shall be done," and then, for no conscious reason he could think of, he said, "Will Newcome do as your groom, Lady Elinor?"

"If you can spare him from his clerkly duties, yes," replied Nell lightly, and then, as though idly, "I take it that he has recovered more of his memory—but still has no idea of who he is, or where he came from?"

"That is true, Lady Elinor." Aisgill was hesitant. "It is strange, is it not, how much has come back to him, and yet he does not know himself? I am an ignorant old man, but I sometimes wonder—" And he paused again.

"Yes," said Nell encouragingly. "What do you wonder, Aisgill? You know that I value your opinion." Which was true, she thought. He might not be educated, like Henson and Payne, but he had an earthy and unsentimental shrewdness which was sometimes better than book learning.

"I wonder, which is stupid, I know, whether he does not wish to remember himself. He has such bad dreams, madam."

"You think that he may have done something dreadful, perhaps," said Nell, a little anxious.

"No, not that. I think he may have been unhappy, but is happy now, except when he sleeps."

Nell was glad that she had said and done nothing—such as asking for another escort—to make Aisgill suspicious of Newcome; he seemed to trust him, not only to do his work well, but to protect her. Originally, when he had assigned him to ride with her, he had said, "What better than an old soldier to look after you? If he cannot protect you, no one can."

She was thinking of that, and what had passed in the morning, when she waited that afternoon for Newcome to bring her horse round to the steps before the grand entrance, and when he appeared, leading Rajah, young Peel behind him with Vulcan, there was nothing in the behaviour of either of them to suggest that anything untoward might have happened on their last two meetings.

Nell mounted Vulcan, and they rode off together, Peel watching, in silence, my lady and her respectful groom, riding slightly behind her as though nothing had ever passed between them.

What nonsense! Of course nothing had happened. A couple of mischances, that was all. She had stumbled, and he had saved her, and then they had met...somewhat unfortunately... And not a word of that was true. She had been strongly affected, and, trying to look behind at him without him realising it and failing, she could sense without knowing how that he, too, had been affected, but how, she could not tell.

If Chad had told her the truth, which he had no intention of doing, he wondered how shocked Lady Elinor Tallboys would be. Would she recoil from him, have him thrown back on to the moor from which he had emerged? For what he had felt when she had come upon him, naked, and had felt so strongly that his body had almost betrayed him before her, was a desire for her, that although he did not know it, was no stronger than Nell's for him.

No difference of rank or circumstance had meant anything. Simply, he was a man, and she was a woman, and the accident of their meeting thus, even more than the encounter at the Cairn, had finally told him that what he felt for Elinor Tallboys, Countess of Malplaquet, Viscountess Wroxton, Baroness Sheveborough, all in her own right, was more than simple lust. It was a longing for her as his partner as well as his love!

Which, look at it how you would, was preposterous. For how should he, poor Chad, nobody from nowhere, lucky to have a coat on his back, dare to raise his eyes to that?

No, he must go carefully. Give no hint of his true feelings, be surly, even, and his dour expression made his harsh face so much harsher that Nell, looking at him, felt her heart sink. Was he annoyed with her that she had disturbed his privacy that morning?

Before they left Aisgill, as usual, had seen that they were properly equipped to protect themselves. There were dangerous men about, he had said, and, although he doubted that there might be any on Lady Elinor's land, the moor must not be considered perfectly safe. So each rider had a horse pistol in a holster on their saddle, and Chad had orders to guard his mistress with his life.

Nell always refused to ride with more than one escort, "For who would attack me?" she had said. "And I do not wish to ride out in a procession, and besides I never go far."

But that afternoon, instead of turning for home at the usual point, fairly low on the moor by the Cairn, restlessness overcame her. She swung off her horse, and, turning, said to Newcome, "Tell me, have you ever ridden to the Throne of God?"

To her amusement, the strong face broke up a little as he replied. "No, Lady Elinor. I have not had that privilege."

Nell laughed; she could not prevent herself. With one light sentence he had diffused the tense atmosphere between them.

"Not the real one," she said. "I mean the great pile of rocks there." And she pointed with her whip to the far distance, where a massive cluster of giant rocks and boulders reared, high on the moor. "That is what we Yorkshire tykes call the Throne of God, and, being good Yorkshiremen, we think it natural that God should have made his home on the moors."

It was Chad's turn to laugh even as, standing, he tried to hold the impatient Rajah.

"You surely don't intend to ride there this afternoon, madam," he ventured. "It is hardly wise. The hour is late, and by the looks of it the journey is not a short one."

For whatever reasons, Nell suddenly became skittish, she who was always so full of common sense—and, yes, bottom.

"Are you giving the orders, Newcome? Or is it your Countess's commands that you must, and should, obey? I wish to ride there now, immediately, and you shall accompany me, unless, of course, you prefer to return on your own, and explain to Aisgill why I am not with you!"

Afterwards, she was to curse her light-headed folly, and the behaviour that was so out of character for her. Perhaps it was being with Newcome; perhaps, in some fashion, she wished to tease, to provoke him. She never knew.

Chad was uneasy. While they were standing there, talking, he had been overcome by the oddest feeling. A feeling of being watched, secretly observed. It was a feeling which he knew that he had experienced before, but of the where and when he had no notion. Only that it might be unwise to ignore it.

He tried again. "I cannot," he said, voice grave, "advise your ladyship," and he used her correct title deliberately, "to do any such thing. I have a . . . bad feeling about such a journey."

"Well, I have not," averred Nell gaily, feeling delightfully irresponsible for once in her oh, so serious life. "So spurs to horse, Newcome, and take *my ladyship*—" and she trod on her title comically "—where she commands you to go."

No help for it; against all his instincts and the raised hair on the back of his neck, there was nothing for it but to obey, and they set out again, riding through the withered heather and bracken, dull after the flaming reds, golds, and mauves of autumn.

And now, he thought, the dark was threatening to be on them early, well before they saw Campions again, and the other threat was Aisgill's anger with him if anything happened to the suddenly wilful woman who was now riding alongside him, and if he fell back as a good groom should she reined back so that alongside he was compelled to remain, unless they were to lose even more time.

The feeling of danger grew stronger and stronger as they approached the Throne itself. Nearer to, he saw that several piles of rocks were heaped together, some at quite a distance from the main grouping of stones and boulders which stood in the middle, and which with a little imagination could be seen as a throne of sorts.

Nell, having got her way, was a little ashamed, but not so ashamed that she was above playing games with Chad over riding level with him. But, like Chad, she was beginning to realise that an early dusk would be on them before their return, that they were in a lonely and isolated spot, and she had no business undertaking this mad expedition, just to contradict her groom, and to impress on him who was master—or, rather, mistress!

Master, she thought was better; mistress had unfortunate associations!

They had reached the Throne itself, and were on level ground. She was preparing to dismount, and Chad was dismounting before her—she had difficulty in thinking of him as Newcome—when disaster struck. There was the whine of a bullet coming from the direction of the far group of rocks, and Nell's horse dropped wounded, and probably dying, beneath her.

Fortunately she was thrown clear, to land, stunned and shocked, on the bare earth. Chad, who was still in the act of dismounting, holding Rajah only loosely, was also thrown down, as Rajah, on hearing the shot, flung back his head with a great whinny, and bolted, running at speed across the moor.

Chad rolled away in the direction of the Throne, instinctively protecting himself from a possible further shot, if more than one man was firing at them—he had no doubt that the bullet had been meant for Nell.

Silence had fallen; with both on the ground there was no target for a sniper—if sniper it were—for him to aim at. Chad, memories stirring in him, crawled over to Nell, to find her living and apparently unharmed, only winded by her fall, but shocked, her face grey. On seeing him, apparently unharmed, she gave a little cry and tried to rise.

"No," he said urgently, pushing her down again. "Not yet. Do not make yourself a target." Words, ideas, memories were roaring through his head.

Being shot at from ambush was not a new experience, and he knew how to deal with it. Words of command unthinkingly streamed from him.

"Come," said Nell, a little fiercely, "You cannot believe that the bullet was meant for me. A sportsman's accident, surely."

"At this hour, on the moor, with little on it, from someone who I am sure has been tracking us all afternoon, staying to windward, out of sight," rasped Chad. "Best take no chances. Crawl with me to the Throne, or, even better, wriggle like a snake. Now!"

Nell took one look at his face, hard and set. His tone had been so authoritative, that of a man ordering other men, and expecting to be obeyed.

She shivered. Supposing that the bullet had been meant for her! Prudence dictated that she obey him, and she wriggled away from the screams of her horse on her hands and knees. She reached the shelter of the Throne, turned, to find that Chad had not immediately followed her, had detoured to poor Vulcan, and was pulling her pistol from its holster.

Foolishly, her first thought was that he meant to put Vulcan out of his misery, but no such thing. The pistol once in his possession, he was crawling after her, to push her further beneath the seat of the great Throne, so that she could not be easily seen, or even shot at.

"That's my brave girl," he whispered, as though she were a wench from the village, and not his Countess. "Do as I say, and you may yet be safe."

"And what do you say?" Nell asked of this new man, who seemed to know what to do in a tight corner.

"I say that you will stay here, hidden, and I shall leave you to smoke out who shot at us and why. It may be that I am imagining ghosts, that you were right, a sportsman's accident, that he took himself off when he saw what he had done, but I think not."

"You would leave me?" panted Nell.

"What else to do?" answered Chad, with indisputable logic; a habit of his she and others were to find in the coming months. "If we stay here, we are his sitting targets sooner or later, for we cannot stay hidden forever. I assume that he is better armed than we are. If I track him—and he will not be expecting me to do that—I might...dispose of him...otherwise, he will surely do for us."

He did not add and nobody knows where we are, as you, in your wilfulness, have decreed, but the thought was there, unexpressed, and Nell swallowed at it.

"I'm sorry," she said ruefully. "I broke all Aisgill's rules..."

"No," he said, and then, perhaps not strictly truthfully, for he wanted her to maintain her brave spirit, and not repine at her folly, "If he meant to shoot you, and God knows why, he might have done it at any time, and there are more dangerous places to be than this—at least we have cover. Enough of talking. I must go."

"And if you do not return?" she asked steadily, although her heart was hammering, for his danger as well as her own.

"You are still in no worse case than you are now—for at least if I go there is the chance of my scotching the snake," he replied, "and that is the best I can offer you, for our case, yours and mine, is desperate. Stay here, do not come out, and if I am lost, pray, lady, pray, for only your God can save you."

Nell had to be content with that for he was impatient to be off. She pushed herself farther under the seat, nothing of her to be seen, and he was gone, silently, like the snake of which he had spoken. She remembered what Aisgill had said of him, that he thought that Chad had been a soldier, and almost certainly a good one. She thought by his manner, and what he had said, that he had stalked men like this before, and that after all the outcome might not be too terrible.

Oh, she must hold on to that while she lay hidden beneath God's seat, and time passed with infinite slowness. She prayed a little that he might be safe, and, shocked, realised that she had prayed for him before she had prayed for herself.

Dear God, he must not suffer for my folly. I could not bear that. I might deserve to pay for a moment's lightmindedness, but Chad does not.

And then suddenly, shockingly, there was the sound of two shots, and, after that, silence.

CHAPTER SIX

CHAD REMEMBERED that he had, as Nell suspected, done this before; that was, stalked a sniper who was ambushing him and his men—although when and where this had happened he had no idea, only knowing that he had done it.

Warily, like a serpent, belly to the ground, he worked his way forward as silently as he could, making a wide detour through the bracken to a point slightly below that from which the shot had come, and where there had been no movement, no action, since.

Above him, he suspected, was a man with a rifle, who had carefully stalked himself and Nell, raising Chad's own hackles in the process. He should have listened harder to what his instincts told him, and, if necessary, have thrown her wilful ladyship over Rajah's saddle, and hauled her home, before he had ignored what some kind god was trying to tell him.

And now, with one ball in a horse pistol, he must try to overcome a man armed with a rifle, and probably a pair of loaded pistols as well.

Suddenly, there was the man himself, and his horse, loosely tethered to a dead tree, ready for a quick getaway. He could not have moved since he had loosed his shot at Nell, and yes, he had a rifle, like the ones he had seen in...in... His tortured mind gave up the useless struggle. Suffice it that he knew what he was seeing.

Chad worked his way silently, silently as a guerrilla—what guerrilla? Where—towards his enemy, who was lying prone, his rifle propped on a stone, to hold it steady. He had evidently done this kind of thing before. There was a brace of pistols by him, on the same stone. He was waiting for him and Nell to emerge from their fastness, as sooner or later they must.

He could not shoot the man from where he was, as there was no target to aim at—the prone position protected him—as it was meant to. If he could get nearer ... he wriggled another few yards, and then, his hand closing around one of the small stones which littered the ground, he threw it, to hit the man on the back.

Cursing, the man above him rose, turned, snatching up the pistol to fire at where the stone had come from, probably judging that to raise the rifle and sight would take too long. He was sharp against the skyline, a perfect target, even in the gathering gloom, and Chad, who had leapt to his own feet the moment the stone had left his hand, ran forward, and shot him at point-blank range, in the chest—nothing for it; it was kill, or be killed.

Falling forward, dying, the assassin's finger clenched on the trigger. The second shot, which Nell heard, rang out, and at its sound the dead man's horse broke from the rope which held him, and, like Rajah, bolted across the moor.

Chad waited. His adversary might not be quite dead, might be shamming, might even have accomplices close by, although Chad thought not, but best take no chances.

And then, when nothing stirred, he went over, rolled the man into a position where he could see his shattered chest and grimy face, fringed with a ginger beard.

Something about him and his clothes was almost familiar. Chad shrugged, damned his lost memory, and examined the rifle on the stone with a professional eye.

It was a beauty, a fine thing, delicately engraved, its cost, he would have thought, far beyond what the dead ruffian could have paid for it. Something odd about the rifle, too. He shook his head again to clear it. Trying to remember always troubled him.

Thoughtfully, he put it down, and, no need to be cautious now, he ran back to where he had left Nell, as he had begun to think of her. She would be imagining him dead, and wondering when her turn would come.

Nell, hearing the sound of a man running towards her, cringed a little, and then, when Chad's voice came, "Do not be frightened, Lady Nell, there's no one left to do you harm," she gave a little cry of relief.

"And you are safe?" she called.

"Quite safe. You may come out of hiding now."

Nell, clothes filthy, her whole body one ache from the combined effects of her fall and lying cramped for so long crawled out, tried to stand, needed Chad to steady her.

For a moment they stood, locked together, for her to feel the strength of him, to murmur fervently, "Thank God you are unharmed. My fault, my fault."

Even in this last desperate strait, for they were now abandoned on the moor, their mortal enemy dead, but left to the night and the elements, with none knowing where they were, Chad could not help registering what a vital armful he held.

And then he loosed her from him.

"What happened?" she asked. "I heard two shots. You are not wounded, and he? Where is he?" And she made as if to go look for him.

Nell felt him restrain her. "No," he said. "Best not. He's dead, I fear."

"Dead," she half moaned, and then fiercely, "He meant to kill you, so you shot him."

"No alternative," said this new grave Chad, who had killed to save her, and oh, she honoured him for it. "And a pity, Lady Nell, a great pity."

"Oh, your wish to have spared him honours you."

"No," said Chad, his face hard. "Not that. Dead, we cannot question him, you see, discover why he did it, perhaps who paid him."

"But some Luddite malcontent, surely," said Nell, "who shot at me because he sees me as his enemy."

"Perhaps." Chad was grave. The devious mind which he had recently discovered he possessed was working hard. He thought of the splendid rifle again, and wondered why it troubled him. He also wondered what enemies Lady Elinor might possess. Who, for instance, stood to benefit by her death? He shivered at the thought, and said no more. He did not wish to disturb her.

For they were not yet out of the wood, or, more properly, off the moor!

AISGILL WAS BEGINNING to grow anxious. Lady Elinor and Newcome should have returned long since. He was debating what to do when he saw Henson coming across the yard, struggling against the bitter wind which had sprung up.

"What's this?" Henson said, almost angry. "I was due to meet her ladyship an hour ago, and Mrs. Conybeare tells me that she is not yet back from her ride, and it is almost dark. Where has she gone, and who rode with her?"

He was determined to prove to Aisgill, whom he thought Lady Nell gave far too long a rope, that in the last analysis he, the agent, was master here.

Aisgill regarded him sourly. "You cannot be more worried than I am," he announced. "Yes, she should be back, but Newcome is with her. She should be safe enough."

"Newcome with her!" ejaculated Henson. "You've gone light in the attic, man, to send her out with him. You know nothing of him, and that loss of memory could be all a pretence. Ten to one, he's made off with her."

"That I do not believe," said Aisgill, although he was beginning to have qualms himself about letting the mistress go off in the company of one so dubious, when all was said and done. "I am about to be sending search parties to look for them. Lady Elinor usually rides to the Cairn."

"And if that were where she has gone," said Henson sharply, "she would have been back long since, and I should not be troubling you."

It was while Aisgill was drawing up and instructing search parties, every face worried, for Lady Nell was loved, and Newcome was beginning to be liked, that one of the lads ran up, face alarmed.

"It's Rajah," he blurted. "He's running on the moor, riderless, and none can get near him to bring him in."

"And Vulcan," said Aisgill, desperately, sure now that something was badly wrong.

"No sign of Vulcan, nor either of their riders. Rajah's in a fair old lather, looks to have come a long way."

It took some time to corner Rajah, his weariness letting them catch him rather than any acts of theirs, and while this was going on the first party of lads, carrying lanterns, and with orders to halloo when they reached Lady Nell's usual turning-point, had set off on their mission.

Foam flying about him, Rajah, who bucked and snorted at every hand laid on him, was inspected.

"No sign of hurt," reported Aisgill to the worried Henson, "the pistol still in its holster. No reins broken. All his lines intact. Nothing to explain why he lost his rider, and was parted from Vulcan."

Rajah continued to show his dislike of everyone who was not Chad Newcome before he was finally wrestled into his stall. Both of Nell's senior servants were beginning to be seriously worried, and Aunt Conybeare finally appeared in the yard, shawl about her shoulders, to voice her distress that her darling was missing. Nell was a daughter to her, the daughter she had never borne.

"More search parties," ordered Aisgill, and then, decisively, "and I shall lead one to the Throne of God."

"The Throne of God," snorted Henson, "why there? It's miles away."

"Because Lady Nell loves the place, and think, she might have wanted Newcome to see it. He's never been so far afield to my certain knowledge."

Henson stared at Aisgill. Something odd there. Something both men instinctively felt.

"Lady Nell to take Newcome to see something! Newcome! the vagabond hauled half-naked off the moor. Why should she do that?"

"They deal well together," said Aisgill, almost uncomfortably.

Henson stared again. "What are you saying, man?"

"Nothing," growled Aisgill angrily. "What are you saying? Lady Nell is kind. The man is good with her horses. She might think the Throne of God a good place to show him—and why am I gossiping here with you? The more I think of it, the more likely it seems. The night is drawing on, and if they are unprotected out there in the open . . ." And he ran off, shouting to round up the horses, to order yet another group of Nell's people on to the moor, himself leading it.

Behind him, Henson stared at nothing. "Rainbows," he said finally to himself. "Whimwhams, and dammit, since that man arrived here, nothing has been the same."

THAT MAN SAT with his mistress in the lee of the rocks around the Throne of God. The night was bitterly cold, and a fine rain had succeeded a strong wind. Beside him, Nell, wrapped in the warm green coat from his livery, shivered, and tried to prevent herself from shivering further. Shock as well as the bitter night held her prisoner.

And, to keep her warm, Chad had stripped to his shirt, and must be feeling the cold dreadfully. What was worst of all was that it was her silly irresponsible fault. Without the journey to the Throne, they would have been home and dry hours ago.

She said as much to Chad, who grunted, "Nonsense," at her. "He could as well have tried to shoot you on the journey back from the Cairn, as he did later, when we pressed on."

Nell had suggested that they try to walk towards Campions, but he had said, "Nonsense," to that as well. Since the attempt on her life, and his killing of the would-be assassin, ladyships and stable hands seemed to have flown away; they were man and woman together, struggling for survival.

"There's no shelter on the way should we need it," Chad said, "and it's cloudy tonight, with little moon to help us. God knows where we should end up. Rest here, and we may try to walk at first light. Aisgill will surely be sending search parties after us, and with luck Rajah might have run in, to warn them that something is very wrong."

Nell thought of poor dead Vulcan, whose screams had stopped long ago, and of the other body, lost among the rocks where Chad had left it, beside all the incriminating evidence of guilt and murder.

"Newcome..." she said suddenly—she really must not be thinking of him as Chad.

"Lady Nell?" For Chad had begun to call her by the affectionate name the hands always used of her in her absence.

"You might as well have your coat back," she said, teeth chattering. "It might warm you. I think that nothing is going to warm me."

Chad became quite still, turned towards her where she sat by him, took her small frozen hand in his large one.

"I have been remiss," he said abruptly, memory stirring in him again, for his hand, although he wore less than she, was warmer than hers. "We must do something to warm you . . . or . . ."

Nell knew what the "or" meant. Men and women had died of exposure on the moors in temperatures similar to this. There was, fortunately, no frost, but the wind and rain were working against her instead.

"Come," he said, slipping his coat from her shoulders. "There's no help for it. Forgive me, my lady," he said, all formality, which was ironic enough in the face of what he was about to do.

For he wrapped his coat closely about the two of them, but not before he had drawn Nell into his arms, against his broad chest, to hold her in order to warm her, and then he began to chafe her cold hands, to restore them to life.

Oh, thought Nell dreamily, how comfortable this is, to be sure. She could feel the living warmth of him, the clean male scent of Chad and stables mixed, the latter a smell Nell had known and loved all her life. She could feel the steady beat of his heart, and she turned her head further into his chest, so that its rhythm began to affect her strongly, and as heat passed from him to her another heat began, slowly and stealthily, not outside her, but inside, as though flames were being ignited in her.

What was happening to her? For this new feeling was not only powerful, but was making strange demands of her. For she wanted to burrow further and further into Chad, to put her arms about him, to . . .

Chad knew quite well what was happening to Nell—and to him. He felt her breathing change, took a deep breath, and began to speak, to take both their minds off their errant bodies.

"A strange thing happened out there, Lady Elinor," he said, speaking with exquisite formality to keep his voice steady and his own breathing easy.

"Oh, Chad, what was that?" murmured Nell drowsily, forgetting her resolution to address him as Newcome, the strongest sense of well-being beginning to take her over, repressing a little her desire to seize hold of Chad and stroke him as he was stroking her hands and arms.

"I recovered a little of my memory," he answered . . . and paused for her to say warmly,

"Oh, how splendid. You know who you are?"

He shook his head, as much to clear it as to deny what she had said. The woman in his arms, so warm and soft . . . He started to speak again. "Not that, but I had glimpses of my past, which tell me that Aisgill's guess that I was once a trooper is correct. Flashes only, but I know that I was once in Spain, with the guerrillas there. I must have been cut off from the Army and my officer, because I was giving orders, so Aisgill was right that I was a sergeant."

He stopped again. "Which would explain my clerkly abilities a little, except . . ." How to say that somehow none of these deductions seemed correct to him, there was something missing, but what, he did not know?

And in the meantime, however much he tried to distract himself, Nell's proximity was beginning to affect him so powerfully that it was all that he could do not to begin to make love to her on the spot.

And what he felt for her was not simple lust. The woman he held was not just any woman, she was . . . she was . . . the one woman, the woman the memoryless wanderer had wanted all his life—and never found, until now. And how did he know that? But he did.

It was the Countess Nell, hard-working, proud, compassionate, careful of those who served her, whom he held and wished to pleasure. Countess Nell of the strong, sweet face, whose presence lit up every corner of Campions. Countess Nell who had taken pity on him, and, Oh, god, I want to make love to her, not fiercely, but slowly and gently, to see her fulfilled beneath me, her pleasure more to me than mine, for Countess Nell gives, never takes, and I must give, to her.

And temptation was too much, at last, for he was only a man, and not a saint, and he bent his head, to cup her chin in his hand, and tip her face towards him. To do—what?

Nell, lost in a dream of happiness, hardly aware of where she was, obediently turned her head to help him as she felt his big hand cup her face so gently, and as he tipped it up towards him, before she knew what she was doing, she kissed the palm that cherished her.

For Chad, as for Nell, time stood still. Propinquity, the growing warmth spreading between them, was doing its work. After she had kissed him, he returned her kiss, gently, on the cheek, and then, since she showed no sign of distress at what he was doing, kissed her again, on the other, turning her head slightly, and her response was to make a little noise, almost like a cat purring. For, thought Nell light-headedly, he saved my life at the risk of his, and he surely deserves some reward.

Besides, I like what he is doing!

She was now fully in his arms, body as well as face offered to him, and Chad was desperate. Honour said that he must not take advantage of her, reason said that he would suffer for it if he seduced her, as he now so easily might, but something deep and strong was telling him that what he wanted she wanted too, and that was all that mattered.

His right hand now cupped her breast, stroking it through the cloth, and she purred again, said indistinctly, "Oh, thank you, Chad, thank you," and her right hand stole up around his neck to stroke him in return.

He kissed her again, and this time not on the cheek, for as he bent to do so she turned her own head hungrily towards him, and the kiss found her mouth, and they were suddenly drowning in passion.

From the depths of the memory he no longer possessed, something called, No! so loudly that Chad pulled away for very honour, for it was honour that was calling, and said in a voice husky with desire, "No."

And then still holding her, to keep her warm against him, he said, even more formally than before, "Lady Elinor, it is no uncommon thing, when men and women have been in

danger together that..." And he gulped; how to say this
delicately, without offending, or hurting her?

Nell, cradled in Chad's arms, had never felt so mindlessly happy in her whole life. He was big enough to make
her feel small and delicate—no mean feat—and not since she
had been a little girl could she remember being held so lovingly, been treated with such careful kindness. She was light-
headed enough with shock, excitement, exhaustion, and yes,
true love, not to want him to stop caressing her.

At the back of her mind a little voice was telling her where
this might end, but in her delirium of mingled love and desire she thought, if Rajah can pleasure White Princess, why
should not Chad pleasure me? And she saw no lack of logic
in this disgraceful notion; rather it was as though she, Chad,
Rajah and the Princess were all partners in a dance of nature, where titles, social conformity and duties to God and
King meant nothing.

"Yes?" she said dreamily, aware not only that he had
stopped speaking, but he had ceased making love to her, and
she did not wish him to do that. "You were saying, and then
you stopped. What was that about men and women?"

"That when they have been in danger together they frequently... desire one another afterwards."

"And that, you think," said Nell, wishing all this would
end and that Chad would get down to the true business of
loving again, "is why we are behaving like this now?"

"Yes," Chad said briefly, and, as far as he was concerned, although he was not so sure of Nell, he was lying in
his teeth.

By now, Nell was far gone, already on the edge of sleep,
a sleep induced by his gentle lovemaking on top of her exhaustion and shock.

"You're wrong, you know," she said confidentially and
sleepily, and how good it was to sleep in one's lover's arms,
"I felt like this about you long before tonight,' and, so saying, she finally drifted into a warm slumber, her changed
breathing telling the man who held her not only that he had
warmed his Countess into life, but in return she had frankly
and freely offered him her love.

And what, he thought, still holding her carefully, and giving her one last, chaste kiss on her forehead, would she think when daylight claimed her, and she was the Lady Malplaquet again, and he was Chad, her groom and stable hand? Would she even remember what she had said and he had done?

The moon, long missing, came from behind a cloud, and threw strange shadows on the moor which lay all about them. Chad could not sleep. First his roused body prevented him, and then when desire faded, and it was enough to hold her in his arms and study her sleeping face, the necessity to stay awake, to guard and protect his woman remained.

Even stranger shadows, quite unlike those on the moor, ran through his head. How did he know that he had never felt like this for a woman before, that the other women he had known had always taken, never given? He did not remember their names or their faces, nor how and why they had loved, and why it had not been satisfactory, as it had been tonight—even though nothing had been consummated.

Chad sighed, and Nell stirred in his arms. In her dreams she was in a ballroom, full of people wearing court dress, orders and decorations. She was looking for someone, and then she found him. He had his back to her, was wearing an officer's splendid dress uniform, the uniform of an aide; even from the back she could see the bullion on his broad shoulders.

And then he turned and walked towards her and she saw his face plain, and it was Chad! But as she touched him wonder and delight rising her, his arms enfolding her, the dream faded, and she fell into the deep sleep of oblivion, safe in Chad's arms beneath the Throne of God.

CHAPTER SEVEN

TOWARDS MIDNIGHT as he later discovered, for he did not sleep, but remained awake to protect his lady from any further danger which might befall, Chad heard the noise of Aisgill's party, heading towards them, across the moor.

Nell lay in his arms, face trustfully turned up towards him; once or twice she stirred, and a small smile crossed her dreaming face, his warmth and hers mingling.

All passion, all desire, had leached from him. All he felt was an enormous protectiveness. He had killed for her once, and knew that he would do so again, if necessary. He was at one with Rajah, or the lion who protected his pride, the falcon who stooped to destroy his enemy. What he felt for Nell had been sealed in blood.

The spilling of blood had not been necessary for him to love her—that had come of itself, born from the gratitude for her saving of him from starvation, nurtured by all that he had seen of her since, come to full-blown maturity when he had taken her in his arms to warm her.

But the bond which had been created by what he had done for her was there, a living thing between them, and the instinctive man he was, who needed no memory to guide him, knew that she, being the woman she was, would acknowledge that bond, as she had already acknowledged her love, before she had fallen asleep in his arms.

The noise below told Chad that the everyday world, the world where peeress and lowly servant could not meet as equals, was upon them. He heard the sound of horses and men, voices calling, saw the light of lanterns, knew that rescue was near, and he feared that, despite all, once the bright day was on them again what Nell Tallboys had said would be denied or forgotten—but he could neither deny, nor forget.

They must not be found like this, and he slipped out of the coat which they had shared, wrapped it around her lovingly, and, while she protested in her sleep at losing him, he propped her against one of the pillars of the Throne, and left her—to walk, shouting, towards Aisgill and the men with him.

"Praise be to God," cried Aisgill fervently. "Lady Nell is safe?" And then, "I knew it, I knew it, she took you to the Throne—and what," he demanded fiercely, "happened to your horses, Newcome, that Rajah should come home without you? Where is Vulcan? Never say you let that mild beast get away from you both!"

"A private word with you, Master Aisgill," said Chad, face grim, after he had taken Aisgill's hand, and pointed to the sleeping Nell, half hidden under the Throne's seat, "before you tell the rest." For the search party was now upon them.

"As to Vulcan," he began, leading Aisgill over to the spot where the poor beast lay dead, "it is as you see," and he poured the whole story of the attack and its consequences into Aisgill's disbelieving ear as carefully and lucidly as though he were reporting to his senior officer.

Aisgill's early disbelief did not survive the evidence of the bullet which had killed Vulcan, nor the sight of the body and rifle lying among the rocks parallel with the Throne.

"I was sorry to kill him," said Chad, "for could I have taken him alive we might have learned something of why he attacked Lady Elinor, but I had no choice."

"No," agreed Aisgill. "You did your duty, Newcome, and protected your mistress as a good servant—and a good soldier—should."

Nell had been awakened by the noise of the search party and she walked unsteadily towards them, Chad's jacket still around her shoulders, and for the first time Aisgill saw that Chad was shivering in the night air.

"Come," he said roughly, to one of the lads, "give Newcome a blanket for his shoulders, and you, Lady Elinor," he said reprovingly to her, as though she were the child she had once been, whom he had taught and reprimanded, "may explain to me tomorrow why you should bring Newcome here, so late in the day."

Nell coloured, and put out a hand in Chad's direction. "I was wrong," she said, and then, to Aisgill, "but he saved me..."

Aisgill saw that, despite the sleep she had enjoyed since the ambush, his mistress was exhausted and shocked. He dared to interrupt her. "Enough for now, my lady. In the morning you may both tell the whole tale, although Newcome's bravery is plain to see, and fortunate for us all, the day we took him in."

As they left, beginning the long journey back to Campions, Chad riding one of the horses, Nell's side-saddle transferred from Vulcan to one of the lads' mounts so that she might travel home between Aisgill and himself, he turned once to look at the place of the stones where his Countess had first kissed him in love and gratitude.

NELL SAT UP IN BED the next morning, being petted by everybody. A great fire roared in the bedroom hearth, and Aunt Conybeare was in a chair by her bed, a magnificent four-poster, its crimson curtains looped into a gilt earl's coronet high above it.

Her aunt was worrying over her, exhorting her not to overdo things, then said, almost reprovingly, "You look very well, my dear, for one who has had such an unfortunate experience. Half a night in the open, a man and your horse killed in earshot, a long ride back, and you look blooming, positively blooming. Lately you have looked a trifle... wan... to say the least."

Nell snuggled into her pillows, drank hot chocolate laced with cream, ate new-made white rolls, with delicious homemade jam and butter, and tried not to let the dreadful thoughts she was having show on her face. But oh, dear, from her aunt's comments, they obviously did!

Had she really kissed Chad Newcome last night, before he had kissed her, and virtually invited him to make love to her? Worse, had she actually told him, quite wantonly, that she had been wanting him to make love to her from the moment she had first seen him?

No, surely not. She could not have done *that*. Not she, Nell Tallboys, whose reputation had frightened every suitor away, who could by her cold stare reduce strong men to mumbling inanity when they had tried to court her. Icy Nell Tallboys had lain in the arms of her giant stable hand and had invited him to make love to her, in so many words—no, a very few words, and all of them plain.

But if she had not behaved like a lady, let alone a noblewoman, Chad Newcome had behaved like a gentleman. No, revise that Nell, *better* than most gentlemen. He must have distanced himself from her before Aisgill and the other lads had arrived, to stifle any suggestion of improper behaviour, although how Aisgill thought that she had managed to keep warm she could not imagine.

And what should she say when she next saw him—and what would he say to her? What etiquette governed what she had done? Well, he had saved her life, and she had already heard from Aunt Conybeare, so late had she slept, that Henson, Aisgill, Payne and old Challenor the librarian had met in conclave, talked to Newcome, stared at the body which had been brought in, sent for a constable from Keighley, the nearest village, and had discussed putting up bills to try to find out who Nell's would-be murderer was.

All in all, Aunt Conybeare had told her, interest and excitement between Newcome's astonishing resourcefulness and the mystery of who might want to kill her, seeing that no one, rightly, thought that the shot was meant for Newcome.

"And no more riding on the moors with only one groom, my dear," said Aunt Conybeare tenderly. Nell had only just been able to prevent her spooning bread and milk into her unwilling mouth.

"Oh, no," she had said determinedly when Aunt Conybeare had processed in with a great china bowl of the wretched stuff, "you can take that away," and then mischievously, quoting from *Macbeth*, which she had been told one ought never to do, "'Throw physic to the dogs; I'll none of it.'"

"What in the world has come over you this last week or so, Nell?" sighed her aunt. "You have always been so prim and proper. And now, suddenly, you are a positive hoyden—no, that is not the word. I cannot think of one which fits your goings-on. Why in the world, for example, should you drag poor Newcome to the Throne of God, the last thing a stable lad would be interested in, I dare swear?"

"On the contrary, Aunt," said Nell, looking at her from under her eyelashes, "he seemed so interested in the Cairn when we rode there that I thought that the Throne of God would entertain him even more, and so it did, until that murdering wretch arrived. And, besides, he said that it was a good thing we did go there."

Her mouth was now so disgracefully full of buttered roll and strawberry jam that she had difficulty in getting the next bit out. "He said that we were better off in the shelter of the Throne than on the moor. We were not so good a target for a sniper."

"Aisgill said that you owe your life to his courage," remarked her aunt.

"So I do, and I want to see him, as soon as possible, to thank him," said Nell, mouth free again, "because I didn't thank him properly last night."

"But not in your bedroom, my dear," said her aunt, reprovingly again. Really, what *was* getting into Nell lately?

"Well, the queens of France used to receive their subjects in their bedrooms," said Nell rebelliously, thinking at the same time, What on earth is making me so frivolous and light-minded? Is this what kissing Newcome has done to me?

"But you are not the Queen of France, my dear," said Aunt Conybeare, uncontrovertibly.

"A pity, that," said Nell naughtily, watching her aunt's mouth frame a dismayed circle of surprise. "No, I will see Newcome in my study, with my face so," and she pulled her features into a parody of Nell Tallboys at her coldest.

Her aunt looked helplessly at her. "You will thank him properly or not at all, my girl. But you know he was only doing his duty."

"His duty, Aunt?" Nell was fascinated. "Was it his duty to risk his life for me, and then compound that by giving me his coat? No, Newcome went beyond his duty last night, I think." In more ways than one, Nell, in more ways than one! said the devil which seemed to have taken up residence in her mind.

"Gratitude, no doubt," offered her aunt. "For you did save his for him, when you took him in, after all."

"So I did," said Nell. "That makes us quits, you think? I shall tell him so. No, Newcome, I cannot thank you for what you did for me. It was merely tit for tat, although you risked your life for me when you went after my assassin, and I risked nothing when I gave you shelter."

Except my reputation, said the devil inside her, for I fear that what I so inconveniently feel for him will soon be going to show on my face, or on his!

BUT THERE WAS nothing on either of their faces when she met him in her study after luncheon. She had, for some unknown reason, dressed herself carefully again. Fly away Nell Tallboys seemed to have disappeared for good!

She was wearing green, a deep green high-waisted wool dress, trimmed with saffron lace, and she had wound round her head a turban which Aunt Conybeare had presented to her, and which she had always refused to wear. It was a flaming thing in vermilions, deep oranges, blues and greens, and she pinned an antique jewel set with rubies to its side, to hold it steady.

Even Henson's opaque stare shivered a little when he saw her unaccustomed magnificence. They were all here, all the Privy Council, old Payne looking frailer than ever—and Newcome, of course.

He looked quite splendid, a figure to match her own. As a reward, no doubt, for faithful service, Aisgill had ordered him dressed to perfection in the Malplaquet royal livery, only worn when Malplaquets entertained kings and courts.

His stock was so white, his boots so shiny, his hands so beautiful in their kid gloves, his body so well set off by the splendid green and gold of his bullion-trimmed coat that he

made Nell feel quite weak at the knees—nearly as weak as
she had been in her dream.

He held, of all things, a shako in those hands, with the
most giant Malplaquet cockade pinned to it that she had
ever seen.

And Nell was nervous, as she had never been in her whole
life. Her voice nearly came out in a squeak, until she managed to control it, so that his eyes, previously fixed on the
floor, or his boots, suddenly lifted, and she saw mirth in
them, and yes, an understanding of her predicament—how
to speak normally to him after their intimate moment of the
previous night?

"I have to thank you, Newcome," she said primly. "I was
too overset last night through fright, shock and weariness—" oh, dear, what lies "—to make you properly aware
of my gratitude for your devotion . . ." what a word, devotion, and what a lie to say that he was not aware of her
gratitude, so aware of it had she been that she had virtually
offered herself to him.

And by now Nell was in full flow, one part of her saying
all the proper things, and the other part having the most
improper thoughts at the sight of him, glorious in full fig—
whatever was Aisgill thinking of? Had he no more sense
than to turn Newcome out so completely *à point* that now
it was she who wanted to eat *him*?

"I understand that Aisgill has proposed that you be offered a bonus on your wages for the gallantry which you
displayed in defending me at the risk of your own life."
There, she had said it, without falling on her knees before
him, before them all, and saying, "Take me, Newcome, I'm
yours," like a mad maidservant in a bad French farce, by an
inferior imitator of Marivaux!

She practised it, in French, in her head, while Aisgill,
speaking before Newcome could, said, "He has refused to
accept anything, Lady Elinor. He says that he merely did his
duty and wants neither money nor favour."

"Is this true, Newcome?" asked Nell, willing him to look
at her.

"Yes, Lady Elinor," he replied, looking her full in the
eyes, so that they met there, if nowhere else.

Nell was suddenly frantic. She felt that she was on the edge of a cliff, about to slide over, and nothing and no one there to save her.

Unwittingly, old Payne did. "An illuminated address," he said in his cracked voice, saving her from speaking. "I think I may still be able to limn one, recording the thanks of the House of Malplaquet for saving its jewel." And he bowed to Nell.

"Perhaps a little premature," said Newcome, standing stiff and straight before his superiors. "With respect, I hope that you have considered that whoever planned this might strike again."

For a moment there was silence, then noise, as all spoke together, only Nell and Newcome silent, gazing into one another's eyes.

"Planned this?" said Henson, incredulous. "A malcontent, a Luddite surely, like the man who shot Cartwright."

"Do Luddites own or have access to rifles of such precision and quality that a sharpshooter in the Rifle Brigade might be proud to possess it?"

And how do I know all that? thought Chad. Yes, I was in the Army, but in the cavalry, and suddenly another series of questions shot into his head, which, in the mental stasis produced by his amnesia, he had never thought to ask himself before. When did I leave the Army, and why? I know—how do I know?—that I was happy there.

Aisgill was regarding him steadily. Newcome had told him of his suspicions about the attack the previous evening, but, like the others, he could not bring himself to believe the murder attempt to be by other than a dissident, a Jacobin.

He said so, adding, "The rifle was doubtless stolen," only for him to meet Newcome's hard stare. Chad kept his body still, his voice submissive, but he differed from them and was not afraid to say so.

"The man had been a soldier once, had some grasp of how a guerrilla would strike from ambush. Did you inspect his back? I had not time last night. Lady Elinor's safety was my prime concern."

"His back?" Henson stared at Newcome, puzzled, but Aisgill took the point.

"The marks of the lash, you think, saving your presence, Lady Elinor. The body is still here, awaiting burial. It shall be inspected."

"Not that their presence would prove anything," remarked Henson, annoyed that, once again, Newcome appeared to be instructing his betters.

"No," agreed Aisgill. "But, if there, they would prove he was a soldier, and, perhaps, explain the rifle and his stalking skills. And would add weight to the notion that he was hired."

The room was suddenly so quiet that the ticking of the small French clock over the hearth was loud in it. Nell shivered. She did not like to think herself a target. The face she showed Newcome was now as grave as his.

"My lady should be guarded at all times," he said, "if I may say so. We had a saying in the Army—better safe than sorry."

"I shall arrange it," said Aisgill quickly, before Henson could speak. "The house shall be protected, too. Best, in future, that Lady Elinor does not leave the park to ride."

"And I," said Henson, "with Lady Elinor's permission, shall write to the Bow Street Runners, asking them to send me some of their best men to investigate this whole murky business."

He had hardly finished speaking when Payne, whom Nell had given permission to sit, half rose, uttered a strangled cry, and fell forward on to the carpet.

All of them, paralysed a moment, by surprise, stood staring at him, and it was Newcome, flinging down his shako, who fell on to his knees on the carpet, to take the old man in his arms, revealing a livid and distorted face, the eyes rolled up.

"He has had a fit, he may be dying," he said, and, rising to his feet, the old man in his arms, Chad carried him to the giant oak table in the centre of the room, and swept what was on it to one side to lay Payne down and begin to chafe his wrists and then his poor distorted face.

"The doctor, quickly," commanded Henson, annoyed at Newcome's speed of reaction and the almost unconscious arrogance with which he had taken charge, and begun to give orders.

Of them all, only Aisgill was not surprised. He had seen Newcome behave like this before, when he was not conscious of himself.

Water was fetched, and the doctor and the footmen came to carry him to his room at the doctor's insistence. One thing was plain to them all—if old Payne had not exactly died in harness his useful life was almost certainly over.

"Poor Payne," said Nell, tears in her eyes. "My fault, I should have made him retire."

"No," said Henson, "he would not have been happy to go. He told me so."

"And now my lady has no secretary," said Challenor, suddenly conscious of the weight of his own years. "For Payne has always refused an assistant."

"May Newcome leave us, Lady Elinor?" said Aisgill. "He has duties to perform. Rajah needs gentling after yesterday. Leave off your finery, Newcome, and put him through his paces in the riding school. He needs to be reminded who is master."

"Yes," said Nell, not wishing to lose Chad but, after all, he had his work to do. She watched the door close behind him.

Aisgill turned towards her, Henson and Challenor.

"Now, Lady Elinor, you may think my wits are wandering. But I sent Newcome away so that he would not hear what I am about to say. You need not look far for a secretary. Newcome would do admirably, I dare swear. I should hesitate to lose him, but perhaps you could release him in the afternoons to school Rajah and some of the better horses."

Henson began to argue, only to hear Challenor say, "What an excellent suggestion, if I may say so. The work he has done for you, Aisgill, is exemplary. And he could guard Lady Elinor at the same time. What could be better?"

Nell realised that they were all looking at her, including Henson, who could make no further protests in the light of the other two men's recommendations.

Did she want Newcome as a secretary? Of course she did! Outrageously, proud Nell Tallboys knew that of all things in the world she wanted Chad Newcome to be her secretary, to be by her side... She must be careful in what she did.

Slowly and deliberately she lowered her head, looked at the papers on her desk. "On probation," she said at last, trying to make her voice sound grudging.

"Oh, of course," said Henson, eagerly. "A stop-gap, perhaps."

"Indeed," said Nell. "He might not suit. He seems an outdoors person. Being indoors might be a trial for him."

"True," said Aisgill, watching his lady carefully. Still something odd there, where Newcome was concerned. But even Aisgill could not have imagined the truth of the matter. "But Newcome seems adaptable, and as his memory has recovered, although he has still lost himself, he shows that he has a rare range of skills. Best of all is his application. The Army lost a good man when it turned him out."

"That is that, then," said Henson briskly. He disliked these eulogies of Newcome, a man rescued from ruin, after all. "He cannot have been so remarkable, to end up as he did, wandering the moors, memoryless. Best I keep an eye on him, Lady Elinor."

"A good idea," said Nell, making her face as serious as she could. The person who most meant to keep an eye on Newcome was herself—and what an eye she would keep!

"Speak to him, then, Aisgill. Send him to Henson for his first instructions."

"He'll need some clothes," offered Henson, who disliked the whole idea, but did not care to say so. "He cannot bring the stables in here with him, begging your pardon, Aisgill."

"The tailor can make some for him," said Aisgill, "and in the meantime, if Lady Elinor does not disapprove, he can wear one of her grandfather's old black suits. He has much the same size as Newcome."

"So he was," said Nell, struck. "You are full of invention today, Aisgill."

She could almost feel Henson bridle, added gently, "You can see to that, Henson, I am sure. And my grandfather's old shirts. You could check Newcome's boot and shoe size, as well. Nothing must be wasted at Campions."

After they had gone, Aisgill with instructions to speak to
Newcome when he had finished schooling Rajah, and Henson grudgingly off to check her late grandfather's wardrobe, Nell sat herself down at her desk.

Before he had left the room, Aisgill having gone first,
Henson had fixed Nell with a stern eye, and said, "The
world has turned upside-down since that man came here.
Aisgill has made such a pet of him as I have never seen. Best
watch him carefully, Lady Elinor. After all, we know nothing of him."

"I know that he saved my life from an assassin, and from
the cold after that," said Nell gently.

"And he is a young man," said Henson doggedly. "Not
like having Payne in the room with you."

"Then poor Aunt Conybeare shall sit with me," said Nell
exasperated. "She will not like it, but there it is. Have you
any more instructions for me, Henson?"

"I have only your best interests at heart," replied Henson stiffly.

"Yes, I know that," said Nell, and thought, and you are
right to worry a little, but bonnets over the windmill, Nell,
my girl. You may have your giant stable hand by you at all
times, and your own Privy Council suggested it!

CHAPTER EIGHT

"BEGGING YOUR PARDON, Lady Elinor," said Chad Newcome respectfully, "but I should like to re-organise Payne's records for you. He seems to have fallen into a muddle of recent years—his age doubtless."

Payne was in bed, recovering. He had not died immediately from his fit, but would always be semi-paralysed, and Chad had been her secretary for just under a week.

True to her promise to Henson, Aunt Conybeare sat in a corner of her study, placidly tatting, so that having Newcome with her was not quite the delight Nell had thought it might be.

Besides, he was being most stupidly proper. It was just as though their magic night together, for so Nell thought of it, had never happened.

Perhaps she had imagined it. Except that whenever their fingers touched when he handed letters and papers to her it was almost as though she had been subjected to one of Signor Galvani's shocks. She jumped just like one of his poor frogs was reported to have done. And she was sure that Newcome felt the same. His blue eyes took on a smoky look, exactly as they had done in the Cairn, and that night at the Throne of God.

So it was no use pretending that he was indifferent to her, but what with Henson popping in and out, and Aunt Conybeare sitting there, they might as well be living in a goldfish bowl, and there were times when Nell thought of dragging him off again to see the mere over to Slaitherbeck, and hope that a regiment of Luddites might attack them, so that they could snatch a few more forbidden moments together.

Her study opened into the library—or was it the other way round?—and when he had written the morning's letters he had gone there to do some work for Challenor, that being part of her secretary's duties.

She rose, said loudly, "I wish to check a quotation from Madame de Sévigné," to excuse her leaving the room. "You need not come with me, Aunt. Challenor may play duenna."

Chad was standing at the big map table, with one of the folios Challenor had found lying on it open before him.

Nell had crept in very quietly, to surprise him, and Challenor was nowhere to be seen. But Chad must have had an extra eye, in the back of his head, perhaps, for he said to her, "Yes, what is it, Lady Elinor? May I be of assistance, or do you require Mr. Challenor?"

"No, Newcome," she said severely, "I do not require Challenor, I require you. Pray what are you doing?"

'Mr. Challenor has taught me how to collate books, and I am recording the details of this book for him," he replied, ignoring the challenging note in her voice. "You know I have the oddest feeling that I have seen the book before," and he indicated the map in it.

"Impossible," said Nell, firmly, taking him literally. "Challenor only found it by accident, some three weeks ago."

"Oh, not this book," said Chad, frowning. "Another copy. If I am correct in so thinking, there should be a plate showing Terra Australis near the end," and he turned the pages rapidly, to discover that the last map in the treatise was, indeed, of Terra Australis.

"Yes, you have seen a copy of it before," said Nell slowly. "I wonder where?"

"And so do I," replied Newcome, looking her straight in the eye for the first time since their adventure, and she noticed that his own eyes had gone smoky again. "But you wanted something of me?"

"Yes," said Nell, "I wonder if you would accompany me to the annexe? There is an edition of Madame de Sévigné's *Lettres* there, on a high shelf, and you could hand it down to me, if you would."

The annexe was a smallish, booklined store-room, where works not in good repair were kept, and Nell had purposely chosen one on such a high shelf to have the excuse to take Newcome in with her.

"You would wish to remain here while I collect it?" he enquired.

"Indeed, not," said Nell rapidly; that would not do at all. "I like the annexe—" another lie; Newcome seemed to provoke them "—and I shall certainly accompany you, I may—check what is there," she said wildly, trying to think of a convincing excuse to be alone with him.

So there they were in the annexe, and she made sure that the door was closed behind them before she hissed at him, as he lifted the little library steps over to mount them, to reach her book, "Newcome, pay attention to me and not to Madame de Sévigné. She is not your mistress. Why are you avoiding me?"

Chad put the steps down, and turned to look at her.

"Avoiding you, Lady Elinor? I was not aware that I was avoiding you. We have been constantly together ever since I became your secretary."

"You know perfectly well what I mean. Do not prevaricate, Newcome," said Nell, exasperated.

"Prevaricate, Lady Elinor?"

"And do not repeat every word I say, Newcome. Yes, avoiding me, dodging me. Listen to me, Newcome. I am giving you an order. You are not to avoid me in future. You understand me?"

"Perfectly. I am not to avoid you in future. But I have not been doing so in the present, nor in the past."

"Newcome!" said Nell in an awful voice. "Were it not that I have no evidence to support what I say I should suppose you to have spent a year in a Jesuit's seminary being instructed in the art of Machiavellian dialogue. You do know what I mean, Newcome. You are the most devious creature I have ever met with. Why are you laughing, Newcome?"

For not only were his eyes smokier than ever, but his expression was so full of honest amusement that she wanted to…wanted to… "Quickly, Newcome, speak, or else Aunt Conybeare or Challenor will be upon us."

"My very dear," he said tenderly, taking her by the hand, and bowing his splendid head; he looked so handsome in proper clothing. "You know I must not behave to you as I did that night we spent together. I am your humble secretary—"

"And I am your Countess, Newcome," she said impatiently. "Why do you keep telling me things I know, Newcome?"

"Because, if I speak to you as I wish, it would not only be improper, but it would also be unfair."

"To whom unfair, Newcome? Tell me that, you or me?"

"Both of us. There can be nothing between us, Lady Elinor. You must see that in all conscience. You are a good woman, and to consort with me could only ruin you."

"Suppose I command you to ruin me, Newcome, what then?"

"I don't think you know what you are saying."

"Of course I know what I am saying. I want you to make love to me, Newcome. Is that plain enough for you, Newcome? Would you like me to draw you a diagram, Newcome?"

Her expression as she said this, and the low tones in which they were conversing, had him laughing again, but he said, almost roughly, "Nothing I would like to do better in the whole world, Lady Elinor, than oblige you, but I must not."

How he was able to restrain himself Chad did not know. Her eager face was alight with passion and impudent mockery, a woman enjoying herself in the lists of love for the first time, jousting with him with her tongue, trying to provoke him into action.

By God, if it were action she wanted, she should have it!

He was upon her, all his restraint gone, conquered by her nearness, his own passion for her, she was in his arms, saying breathlessly, before he stopped her mouth with his, "Oh, no, Newcome, you do not need diagrams," and he was kissing her, before common sense ruled, and he released her.

He turned away. "Sévigné, you said," and oh, God, it was torment to know that she was there, but duty and honour, newly returned to his memory, must rule him. He could not throw Countess Nell to the ground to love her, however much she wished him to, and however much he wished to make her his.

Nell tried to hold on to him. The passion which ran through her every time they touched one another had her in its grip, stronger than any duty to her name or to Campions. Ever since her mother and father had died she had lived only for both of them. Her grandfather had seen the steel in her and cultivated it. Careless himself, he knew that Nell was not.

The lonely child she had been had grown into a lonely woman. The education he had given her, intellectually sounder than that of any boy, allied to her natural gifts would have made her senior wrangler had she been a boy. She rode as well as any man, and from seventeen had begun to manage the stud for him, creating it again, making it what it had been in the second Earl's time.

And through it all she had remained proud and cool Nell Tallboys, who at some time in the future would coldly choose a husband, give him a child, but keep her inner self intact. No man should move her, make Countess Nell his toy, his thing, in the end his nothing, as she had seen other women were to their husbands.

Love, what was that? A joke, a myth, something of which poets sang. It had nothing to do with what Nell understood of life. Love was Rajah and the mares he covered, that was all. A name to romanticise lust.

Campions was all she had loved—and all Malplaquet's possessions.

Until she had seen Chad.

Reason had fled, and poetry made sense. The passion previously reserved for Campions was now for him.

Conscience, he had said. Now what was that? Conscience withered and died when she was with him. Was it because he was nameless, and she was the queen who stooped, because to stoop was better than to be equal, that she had come to love him?

No, that was not true, because she gloried in him—all of him. Covertly watched him, walking across the room, driv-

ing his quill across paper, schooling Rajah. And what she
felt for him was of the mind, as well as of the body, no mere
condescension of a great lady, but a woman consorting—his
word—with her equal in the sight of God, if not of man.

Joy ran through her. The humour she had never expressed before, hardly knew she possessed, welled up in her,
to tease him, to play with words, to watch his face light up—
I grow maudlin, she thought, and when he mounted the
steps to find her book, and she heard Challenor approaching, she said loudly, in her best Countess Nell voice, "Oh,
dear, Newcome, I could have found that book a dozen times
were I tall enough. How long you have taken!"

He looked down at her, the book in his hand, said,
"Madam, you are pleased to be wilful. You're sure you really need the book at all?" and her own laughter rang in the
air, as Challenor put his head round the door, said, "There
you both are," and, being innocent himself, saw innocence
in them. "You have visitors, Lady Elinor. Henson has sent
your uncle Beaumont to your study and asked your cousin
Ulric to await you in the Turkish room.

"Visitors!" exclaimed Nell. "We grow strangely frivolous these days. More new faces in Campions in the last few
weeks than are usually seen in a twelvemonth. You may
come down now, Newcome, with or without your book. My
secretary must meet my uncle, I will not say for him to approve of you—he never approves of anyone."

And then she added, with such a look on her as Challenor had never seen, so that he gazed after her in puzzlement, "Do you think that he has come to see me with yet
another proposal from some nobleman who would like to
take Campions from me to waste it away in the turf or the
gaming tables or women?"

Chad would have stayed behind in the library, but she
would have none of it.

"No, you must come with me. Old Payne would have
done, so why not you?"

SIR CHESNEY BEAUMONT, Nell's dead mother's brother,
was a fine-looking man, with a strong urbane face, and was
busy discussing the day's news with Aunt Conybeare. He

had already admired her tatting, and they were well into the affairs of the Princess of Wales, as the Regent's wife was always called.

"My dear," he said to Nell, as she walked in, Newcome behind her, "you look positively blooming. So much better than when I last saw you. You looked a trifle peaky then, not at all yourself. Mrs. Conybeare has told me the sad news about Payne, and that Henson has rightly sent for the Runners to investigate this strange attack on you. Luddites, I am sure. Luddites."

"None of my people think so, uncle," said Nell, adding conciliatorily, "But you may be right."

"And this is your new secretary." Sir Chesney's eyes took in Chad, who thought it best to stand submissive. For some reason, Chesney Beaumont made him feel uneasy, and he could not think why. His very name drew odd resonances from the air.

"Yes," said Nell, walking to kiss him on his florid cheek. "I hope you have not come to tease me about marriage, my dear uncle, for I am more set against it than ever."

Sir Chesney was still exercised by Chad. "I had not thought him to be such a young man," he said doubtfully, "and no, I have not come to talk to you about marriage, least of all with Charles Halstead. Particularly not with Charles Halstead."

He stared at Chad, made waving motions at him. "We could perhaps talk alone, my dear."

"Why?" said Nell coolly. "You would not have sent Payne away. I prefer Newcome to stay. I have no secrets from him," she added, and threw Newcome a killing look, which had Chad coughing, and looking desperately anywhere but at Nell, or Sir Chesney.

"Well, that must be your choice, my dear," he remarked, a trifle miffed. "These matters are delicate."

"From what I have heard of Charles Halstead, delicate is not the word I would have used," said Nell, "but then, fortunately, I have never met him."

"Nor I, my dear," said Sir Chesney, "and now I am glad I never shall, and I am sorry I ever spoke with his father of a match between you. His conduct has been abominable, as you shall hear.''

"Never met him," said Nell, seating herself, with Chad standing at her elbow, a little behind, as befitted a good secretary, ''and yet you recommended him to me in marriage.''

"Oh, I know his father well—Clermont, a sterling fellow. But Halstead—*there* is a horse of a different colour. He, I regret to say, visited Watier in a drunken fit, railed against all women, and when your cousin Bobus was foolish enough to exempt you from his strictures, as an example of strict virtue, you understand, made a dreadful bet that he would, he would..." Sir Chesney ran down, finding it difficult to say exactly what Charles Halstead had roared in his drunken misogyny.

"Would what?" said Nell impatiently, and then, "Oh, you do not like to say. Come, Uncle, Aunt Conybeare had been married, I run a great establishment, and I am sure Newcome will not be shocked by what you have to tell us.''

She was wrong. Newcome, if not exactly shocked, was, for some strange reason, distressed at Sir Chesney's news. And as Sir Chesney elaborated a strange red rage seized him.

"Oh, very well, Nell, if you must. He said that no woman was virtuous and bet that, if he cared to try, he might have you, as he pleased, without benefit of marriage, you understand. What's worse, he bet twenty thousand pounds on it.''

Nell rose, paced to the hearth, stared into the fire, face averted, and said in a muffled voice, "Charles Halstead said that! Before or after you had arranged with his father to offer for me?''

"Oh, before, I assure you. When his father knew what his son had done, he forbade him the house, and withdrew his sponsorship of your marriage to him.''

"Kind of him," said Nell, satiric. "I have never wished more that I were a man. Were I so I would have shot Halstead dead for the insult," and then, a desperate humour in her voice, "but, of course, if I had been a man, you and his father would not have arranged the match with him. What nonsense I am talking." She turned towards Chad, whose rage was now so black and strong that he was shaking with it, had bent over the desk, feeling light-headed with a curious mix of—what was it? Shame, surely not—unless it was for all men who lightly spoke of women thus.

"Newcome," said Nell sharply, "are you ill, that you look so?" and Aunt Conybeare looked up, equally sharply, struck by the note in her niece's voice.

"Nothing," gasped Chad, "a passing malaise. I have had such, once or twice, since I arrived here."

Which was true. He had thought that it was perhaps his lost memory struggling to revive itself, but why Sir Chesney's story should have such an effect on him was a mystery.

Sir Chesney, staring at Nell's concern for her secretary, said indifferently, "I understand from Henson that your cousin Ulric is here. I hope his presence does not mean that you are thinking of marrying him. Most unwise."

Since Chad appeared to be recovering, Nell looked over at Sir Chesney, and said coldly, "I don't think you listened to what I was saying, Uncle. I repeat, I have no intention of marrying anyone, least of all Cousin Ulric. And now I must see him. Disliking him, and his proposal, does not absolve me from practising the common courtesies. Newcome, if you are quite well, you may spend the afternoon in the riding school. Aisgill was asking for you this morning."

She bowed to her uncle, and left him wailing at Aunt Conybeare over Nell's intransigence where marriage was concerned, and glared suspiciously at Newcome when he took his leave. Nell's secretary to work in the riding school—what next?

"REALLY NELL," said Ulric Tallboys petulantly, "it is too bad that I was consigned here alone, while Chesney Beaumont was admitted immediately to you. You should have a word with that butler of yours, and your man, Henson. After all, I am your heir."

"Sir Chesney arrived first," replied Nell briskly. She disliked her cousin, an overweight man, pasty-faced, in his early thirties, and disliked him even more when he continued, still petulant, "Well, I have come here on business, too.

It is high time that you made up your mind to marry me, Nell. That way we keep the Tallboys name in existence, and before you come out with some havey-cavey that you do not love me, let me remind you that you have made it quite plain that you do not wish to marry for love.''

"I don't intend to marry for dislike, either," retorted Nell, goaded into unwisdom. "And the Tallboys name will live on without you, for I intend to have anyone I marry assume it. It will be a condition of my marriage—the lawyers can deal with it when they draw up the settlement.''

"But you should marry me," pursued Ulric blindly. "Safer so. It is all about the North that you were shot at by Luddites, and that you have nothing better to do than make some stable lad your personal secretary. You would be better advised if I were here to look after you.''

His expression was made the sulkier by the thought that if the first Earl had not insisted on the reversion of his title to the female line, because his only child was a daughter, and a sovereign grateful for his victories in the early eighteenth-century wars had not agreed, he, Ulric Tallboys, and not Nell, would now be the proud possessor of Campions and all the lands and title that went with it—a fact of which he never ceased to remind himself almost daily.

"Oh," said Nell dangerously. "And how do you know all that? I never thought that Campions affairs had already become the talk of Staffordshire and Trentham.''

"I heard of your goings-on when I stayed at Habersham Hall with the Gascoynes before I came on here. You are the talk of the Riding, Nell.''

"But then, I always was, wasn't I, Ulric? And I always shall be, because I have no concern in joining Ridings or any other society for that matter.''

"But Nell—''

"Do not 'But Nell,' me," said Nell, feeling more like a reincarnation of good Queen Bess than usual, "or I shall have second thoughts about continuing your allowance.''

"You would not do that?" cried Ulric, aghast. Ever since some eight years ago, after he had squandered his own in-heritance, first Nell's grandfather, and then Nell, had made him, as heir presumptive, a generous allowance, on condition that he did not ever go to London where he had once been involved in a scandal so enormous that Nell's grandfather had almost cut him off forever. Nell had continued to support him on the same terms, and he roved round provincial society, tolerated, if not welcomed, because of his Malplaquet connections.

"And what about this secretary of yours, Nell?"

"What about him?" Nell had never sounded so dangerous, but, unobservant, Ulric galloped on.

"I tell you what, Nell, it is not at all the thing for you to make some yokel your private secretary, particularly when he is a young man—"

"I tell *you* what, Ulric," said Nell savagely, "if I cared to make a one-eyed dwarf, with a hunch back, my private secretary, it is no business of yours. And if you feel so strongly about my doings, why, to save yourself pain, you may leave within the hour. Out of my kind consideration for your own feelings, I would not stop you."

She had never spoken to him so before, had always been courteous and patient, and he stood there with his mouth open. "I say, Nell," he began, only for her to reply, as she strode to the door,

"And I say, Ulric, that if you do not care to remain for luncheon I shall quite understand, and now I must leave you. I have work to do. My days are not spent in fiddle-faddle and gossip."

"Have a heart, Nell," he protested as she swept through the door. "I've only just got here, and dammit, I'm your heir."

"So you keep saying," were Nell's last words, "and a great pity for Campions that it should be so," and she was gone, leaving him gasping, but determined to stay.

After all, he had his own fish to fry at Campions.

LUNCHEON WAS a somewhat constrained meal. Ulric sat there with an aggrieved expression on his face, and Sir Chesney felt strange annoyance with Nell, stronger, perhaps, than her mere refusal to marry deserved. Something odd going on at Campions, but what he could not decide.

As was usual since Nell had taken over, the place ran like clockwork. The food was good, the service perfect, the whole estate was in splendid order, and he looked forward to a visit to the stables and riding school in the afternoon, although he could have done without Ulric's company.

To prevent Nell's sending him away, Ulric stuck like glue to Sir Chesney, whom he disliked as much as Sir Chesney disliked him. He thought that Nell would not be so deuced rude to him before her uncle, and he was right about that, if little else.

The stable and the stud were in splendid fig, too, thought Sir Chesney crossly. It would be nice to have something to complain about, so as to put Nell down a little, but, dammit, with Aisgill there to give his usual friendly meeting, there was little he could say, and like Ulric he was surprised to see the supposedly unmanageable Rajah being given a dressage work-out.

"Who's on Rajah, hey?" he said, to nobody in particular, to hear Ulric grind out,

"I thought Nell said that she never had suitors here, so who the devil's he?"

Chad was up on Rajah, dressed in one of the late Earl's country suits, charcoal-coloured jacket, modest cravat, grey breeches, beautiful boots—his feet, Nell had been pleased to discover, were the same size as her grandfather's—and he was wearing a dated bicorne hat, which made him look particularly dashing.

Swinging Rajah around the circle, keeping him under tight control, for he had been wild ever since the attempt on Nell's life, he was suddenly aware that he had an audience, and that Nell, dressed more smartly than he had ever seen her, had added herself to the group.

Some mischievous devil made him sweep off his bicorne to her as he passed them, and when Rajah, annoyed, reared, he treated the group to a spectacle of a superb piece of horsemanship, which culminated in Rajah performing a splendid caracole—an extravagant sideways leap, which had him apparently standing in the air—much against his lordly will.

"Oh, bravo," cried Nell.

Ulric asked again, "Who the devil's *that*, Nell?" to hear Sir Chesney say, in a hollow voice,

"Good God, it's the secretary! Damme if it ain't."

"You mean that's the yokel?" gasped Ulric, looking from Rajah's rider to Nell, and back again.

Nell's pride in Chad was almost visible, she suddenly realised, and quelled it.

"Yes," she said, in her most bored Countess Nell voice. "I understand he was a trooper once, which I suppose was where he learned to do that."

Sir Chesney looked down his nose. "A trooper who has visited Vienna," he muttered. "Damned difficult trick, that. You've a jewel there, Nell. Wasted as a pen-pusher, if I may say so."

"Well, I need a pen-pusher more than I need a circus turn at Astley's, so a pen-pusher he'll have to stay," said Nell, not wishing to have Sir Chesney begin to make all kinds of suggestions about Chad Newcome's future, and pleased to appear to put him down a little. It would not do for her uncle to begin...suspecting things... And surely, she thought, amused at herself, females must possess a natural talent for intrigue, for no one has taught me to be so devious.

She was thinking this later that afternoon, when she met Chad on the stairs, about to return to his quarters on the top floor, to change out of his riding clothes into his secretary's drab uniform.

"Lady Elinor," he said, staring at her a little. She had already changed for dinner, and was magnificent, simply magnificent. He had heard Aisgill say that the gentry thought Nell plain, but to him she was the most stunning thing he had ever seen.

She was dressed in white and silver satin, high-waisted, with an over-dress of gauze and net floating about her tall person. Around her throat, her wrists and on her fingers, and finally as a crown in her gleaming chestnut hair, were the famous Malplaquet diamonds which she rarely wore. And tonight she wore them like the glorious Diana she was.

They shimmered and sparkled in the light of the chandeliers, fully lit because Sir Chesney and Ulric Tallboys were dining with her.

"You will attend me tonight, Newcome," she said, all arrogance, like her stance, the tilt of her neck, which the diamonds adorned, a monarch to her humble subject.

But Chad, standing straight and tall, was equal to her. If desire roared through him at the sight of her, he quelled it as well as he could. "I think not, Lady Elinor. Unwise perhaps."

"A command, Newcome, you hear me? A command."

"Sir Chesney will not like it, nor, forgive me, will your cousin."

"Servants'-hall talk, Newcome. Henson will be there, and Challenor, too. Old Payne would have sat with us."

"I am not old Payne."

"Very true, and to both our advantages. You will attend me. I will brook no denial."

"You are as wilful as Rajah, my lady, and far less manageable."

"A compliment, Newcome, a compliment. You grow more courtier-like by the instant."

Face to face they stood, and any watcher could not have failed to see the tension which crackled between them.

"Not meant as such, but if you choose—" and she interrupted him, like lightning.

"Oh, I choose, Newcome, to take it as one, and I choose to have you sit at my table, which I would never ask Rajah to do."

As so often, Chad could have taken her, there on the spot, as she was almost defying him to do, for whenever they met the battle of words between them was merely a symbol of the sexual heat which passed between them.

Nell saw his face change, his eyes begin to smoke, and whispered, face wicked, "Confess, Newcome, confess. You wish to call me your lady in every way, Newcome, in every way, and this very moment, too. And if I am your lady you will wear my favour, do my bidding," and she took the scrap of lace which was her pocket handkerchief from where it hung from the fortune in diamonds on her wrist, and leaned forwards to wipe his sweating brow, sweating as much from frustrated desire as from his exertions in the riding school.

He could not deny her further. He took the lace scrap
from her, and put it to his lips, but before he could speak a
door on the landing opened, and Sir Chesney emerged.

Chad stood back, bowed, said submissively, "As you will,
Lady Elinor," and made his way up the stairs, bowing,
equally submissively, to Sir Chesney, who looked after him,
a worried look on his honest old face.

But Nell sweeping an arm into his, as he exclaimed, "My
dear, you look radiant, radiant! Why you will not come to
London and conquer society I shall never understand,"
laughed and replied,

"But Uncle, dear, I have everything I could want, or desire, here in Yorkshire. What could London offer me better
than that?"

And if she was speaking of Chad Newcome, neither Sir
Chesney nor her cousin Ulric could yet have an inkling of
that.

CHAPTER NINE

FOR CHAD AND NELL it was heaven, and it was hell. To be so near, and yet to be now so hedged about by others that they could only enjoy snatched moments, two-edged conversations and the touching of hands, was to suffer the torments of Tantalus in the old Greek Legend.

Not that any yet suspected them. Only as Countess Nell, and still unmarried, she was rarely ever alone. When Chad had only been her stable hand they could go on the moors, mistress and man, but now that he was her secretary they could not even do that. He could school Rajah and her other prime horses occasionally, but that was in public, too, and then she could only yearn at him, in the riding school, on the excuse of seeing her horses being properly trained.

Yes, there was an atmosphere, something in the air, for Nell was now so volatile, after so many years of being sober. Her laugh rang out, her happiness was plain for all to see, but her people were glad merely to see her happy.

The Runner and his assistant arrived. Cully Jackson was a big, raw-boned, red-headed man who questioned them all, made something of Chad's newness, until he heard the full story. Of them all, as he first sniffed about Campions before disappearing into the Riding, he saw what existed between the Countess and her secretary—but said nothing. *That* was not his business.

The year ran towards Christmas, and Newcome was no longer new. The women servants still followed him with their eyes, but he made nothing of them. He burned for Nell; his body, not his memory told him that he had been long continent, and that made the burning worse, but he would not betray the mistress to whom he had never made love.

Sir Chesney left the day after he had arrived; Ulric stayed a little longer, leaving shortly before the Runner was due. The Runner was told of him, the dissolute heir, nodded at the news, but said nothing about that. The dead murderer had borne the marks of the lash on his back as Chad had suspected, but the rifle he carried remained a mystery. "A gentleman's piece," Jackson said to Chad, holding it in his big hands. "You must have seen such in the Army, perhaps?" and he watched his man as Chad shook his head ruefully.

Jackson knew of Chad's lost memory, and tried, Chad was sure, to trip him up, to test him, but left Campions on his journey of enquiry certain that Newcome was not lying about himself.

"And now, Newcome," Nell said teasingly to Chad one morning, shortly after Sir Chesney had left, and Ulric was packing to go, "you know exactly what my worth is, do you not?"

Chad looked up at her. He was writing at his desk, placed near to hers, Aunt Conybeare dozing gently in her corner by the fire. "How so?" he said, abstracted. He was checking accounts for Henson, for though he claimed no special talent for figuring Henson had found him useful with figures, too.

"Why, Charles Halstead set my price," she said gaily, "at twenty thousand pounds, no less. A high price for him, perhaps, but small, is it not, for Campions's owner, and Malplaquet's lady? Would you kill him for his insolence to me, Newcome? He wished to murder my reputation, not my body. I wonder which crime God considered the worse of the two?"

For some reason to hear of Charles Halstead's bet always disturbed Chad. He looked up at his lady, as usual turned out à point these days, her cheeks flushed, and the look in her eyes which was for no one but Chad Newcome.

"I would gladly kill such a cur for you, my lady," he offered, "should you wish it, and should he arrive here to try to win his bet."

"No, I do not wish it, Newcome," she said. "He may stay in exile for me. My uncle said that he has gone to live in

Scotland, and that his father talks of transferring the estate to his younger brother, leaving him only his title.''

Chad cursed beneath his breath. His hand had shaken unaccountably as she spoke and ink splattered over the virgin page.

Greatly daring, there being no one to see her, Aunt Conybeare's snores growing louder, Nell placed her small hand over Chad's large one.

''Does it trouble you so much to hear me traduced, Newcome?''

''Yes,'' growled Chad. ''I'd like to break his damned neck, begging your pardon, my dearest. The sound of his name is enough to distress me.''

He stroked the hand which had been so lovingly offered, and then, as Nell bent her head, Aunt Conybeare growing noisier, and kissed him on the cheek, he lifted the hand to kiss her palm.

Nell felt him shiver, said gently, ''Oh, you burn as fierce as I. Is there nothing we can do, nothing?''

He looked squarely at her. ''Nothing. And there is nothing we should do. I have told you that, my love, my own, and you must believe it.''

Aunt Conybeare's noise stopped, and she gave a great sigh, and said, ''Where are you, Nell? And where am I?''

The lovers pulled away. ''In the study, dear Aunt,'' replied Nell gently. ''Playing chaperon.''

''Oh, yes,'' said her aunt vaguely. ''So I am. Not that you need one,'' and she went back to sleep.

''You heard that?'' said Nell softly to Chad, her face so amused that he leaned forward and kissed her absently on the corner of the mouth, and, pulling away, muttered thickly,

''You almost destroy my resolution with your humour, but mere passion would not answer for us.''

''My passion is not mere,'' she riposted, ''nor, I think, is yours. Tell me, Newcome, if my aunt, wise monkey that she is, the one who places his hands over his eyes, and says, 'I see nothing,' has no suspicion of us, why, then, are we not innocent? And being innocent, may we not do as we please? What the world does not know cannot exist.''

Chad put a hand to his forehead, said hoarsely, "And you accuse *me* of logic-chopping."

"Oh, I learned it from you," said Nell sweetly. "My servant, who will not obey me in the only thing that matters to me in the whole wide world," and she held him with her eyes.

"Lady Elinor—" he began.

"Why, who is that?" she interrupted him.

"The lady whom Mrs. Conybeare chaperons," was his eager answer to her. "My mistress—who can never be my mistress."

"Never, Newcome, never?" She saw his hands rise, to twist together, agonised. The hands which could not hold her. "Is the man who is not afraid of Rajah afraid of me?"

"Shall I be no better than Charles Halstead?" he muttered. "For he betrayed you with his talk, where I shall betray you with your body. Your reputation, your honour, what of them?"

"My spotless reputation did not prevent Charles Halstead from staining it. You see, Newcome, you cannot defeat me in the combat of words. Defeat me in the combat of love instead. I wish to die in your arms. You may kill in that contest. I shall not allow you to win in any other."

Their eyes met, and oh, his smoked, were smouldering into flames. She was winning! She knew it!

There was a knock on the door, and the spell was broken. She called, "Come in," and Chad turned away, was at his desk in a trice, head down, quill driving, and she was at her own, as Henson entered. Nothing there to see, although Nell felt that her recent passion was written in letters of fire in the air.

Henson could only read words on paper. Fire was beyond him. "Ah, Lady Elinor," he intoned. "A dispatch from Jackson. He has traced your murderer," he said, placing a budget of letters on her desk. "I have read what he has to say—do you wish to read yourself, or shall I save you the trouble?"

Nell thought that reading was beyond her. "Tell me," she said.

"Newcome was correct in his suppositions. The man was an ex-soldier, turned off in the peace. He lived at Bradford for a time, turned footpad, had a small gang of men. The rifle was stolen, they say, and some weeks before he shot at you he left his gang and his usual haunts, none knows why. It was supposed by his associates that he was hired."

"Hired!" said Nell. She saw that Chad had stopped writing, was alert. "By whom?"

"Jackson does not know. He will endeavour to find out. Meantime he asks what others beside your cousin stand to gain by your death."

Nell shivered, rose impulsively, walked by Chad, placed a hand on his shoulder as she passed him.

"Ulric! He surely cannot think that Ulric would stoop to that."

She remembered his anger when she had last refused him. "I know he envies me—all this." And she waved a hand at the splendour around her. "But murder, that is quite another thing."

"Desperate men seek desperate remedies," said Henson slowly. "Jackson accuses no one. In the meantime, he says, you should go carefully." He turned to Chad. "You will guard my lady with your life, will you not?"

"Willingly," said Chad, "with my life, seeing that she gave me mine."

He spoke quite levelly, but perhaps Henson could read letters of fire, after all. Something in the quiet intensity of Newcome's speech reached him.

"See that you do," he said roughly. "You will not go out, ever, madam, without Newcome, and a footman, or a groom with you until this snake is scotched."

Nell could not protest. With a sinking heart she faced a future in which few opportunities would be given her to... deal with Chad as she wished.

"I hear you," she said in a hollow voice, staring out of the window at the magnificent view. "But you cannot really believe that it is Ulric who wishes to kill me."

Chad spoke, "With respect, Lady Elinor, you would be foolish to ignore Jackson, and Mr. Henson's advice."

"You hear him," said Henson, face impassive. "We are
of a like mind, and I'm sure that Aisgill and Challenor
would tell you the same. Your advisers are agreed—you
must take no risks, whether it be your cousin, or another,
who threatens you."

The bright day had grown dark, even though the November sun shone cross the moor. Nell shivered, wrapped
her arms round herself, turned to face the two men, Chad
standing now.

"I must obey you," she said, "in all things," and that
message was for Chad, a two-edged one. "Until—" and she
hesitated "—my judgement tells me otherwise. You all advise me—you do not rule. I will not be wilful, but I will be
mistress."

Henson bowed his head. "You are my Countess, madam, and you have never been unreasonable, have always
consented to listen, and to understand." He looked hard at
her. "For that reason your people serve you with love as well
as loyalty. I know you will take heed for yourself, and of
yourself."

Nell looked at the two men. Henson, after his fashion,
loved her, too. He did not merely serve her for his pay. And,
for the first time, she understood Chad's reluctance to take
her without thought.

But I love him, ran through her mind, truly love him, and
I know, because he holds off, that he truly loves me, and
they say love finds a way, and I must clutch that thought to
me—for it is all I have.

THUS, THOUGHT NELL, exasperated, was how it always
went. Snatched moments when, at the crucial point, they
were always interrupted. And now it was worse than ever,
with men guarding her all the time from any possible threat.

Her mind went round and round, a whirligig, she
thought, pondering possibilities. If Rajah wanted Princess,
the whole of Campions arranged for his pleasure, but if
Campions's owner wanted her lover, all of Campions—were
they to know—would conspire to keep her from him.

Why could she not have fallen in love with one of the
sleek young men whom Uncle Beaumont had paraded be-

fore her? They would have handed her over to Charles Halstead without a thought, wretched though he was, but Chad, whom she loved, would be almost whipped from the grounds were it known what she and he felt for one another.

For everyone would assume that it was he who was seducing her, when, ever since the night of the attack, it was *she* who had been pursuing *him*. He thought only of her honour; she thought only of him.

If I were a man, hissed Nell furiously to herself, making angry faces in her mirror, I could have as many lovers as I pleased, and no one would think anything; they would admire me, rather, for my virility. Even well-bred young women would snigger knowingly when I walked in a room, "Look, there is Malplaquet, a devil with the women—won't marry unless he meets one of whom *he* approves and not his advisers. And when he does marry, why, he will *still* go on his merry way."

And I, I can have no merry way. Why was I not a boy, or the Empress Catherine of Russia, who had all the men she pleased in her bed? I only want Chad, none other, and damn them all, I *will* have him.

She rose, walked downstairs, busy brain scheming. The last time that they had been able to meet privately was when she had pursued him into the annexe. Well, she could take him there again, could she not?

But when she reached the library they were all present, the whole Privy council, Newcome with them, wearing the new suit which the tailor had made for him, which fitted him perfectly, showing off the length of his legs, and the strength of his thighs. His cravat was so white that it looked like a fall of snow. His whole appearance did nothing for her equanimity.

Nell stared at them. "What's to do? I had not thought we were to meet today."

They must have agreed that Chad should speak for them all, for he bowed, and said, "The Runner, Jackson, is here, Lady Elinor, and wishes to speak to you. He will not trust what he has to say to the post."

"He is here?" Nell looked around.

"In the ante-room," Henson spoke. "I thought, we all thought, that he ought to speak to you with your council present. It is our duty to guard you, and we must know everything, if we are to do that."

Nell could not argue with them, so inclined her head, said briefly, "Admit him, then."

It was Chad who went to do her bidding, and Jackson followed him in, a rough figure in the splendid room, only Aisgill, sturdy in his country clothes, having any common ground with him.

"My lady..." Jackson made an awkward reverence. "There has been a strange development, of which I must tell you, and your people here. It is about the rifle which Mr. Newcome here thought must have been an Army man's. I have traced it, and an odd turn-up indeed." He paused.

Strangely, of them all, it was Henson who was impatient. "Spit it out, man. Why stand havering?"

"I took it with me, as you know. Returned to London, and showed it to a gunsmith who has his shop in the Strand. I asked him if he had ever seen it before. The piece bore signs of a cunning repair. He recognised it at once, although it was nigh three years since he had last seen it. He would not say who had brought it in until he found its details in his books.

"And there it was, repaired shortly after Waterloo. He identified it by the roses engraved on its steel, and by the coronet he placed upon it for its owner—"

"A coronet?" interrupted Nell. "Not Ulric Tallboys, then?"

"No, indeed," said Jackson, "and here is the puzzle, for Viscount Halstead, old Clermont's heir, bought it off a friend of his, and took it in to be overhauled and repaired, and there is no doubt that it is he who owns the rifle which was used to fire at you, my lady."

There was a babble of voices. "Charles Halstead?" said Nell, incredulously. "You are telling me that *Charles Halstead* owned the rifle? Are you saying that it was he who organised the attempt on me?" She hardly paused before adding, "To prevent the need to pay out twenty thousand pounds when he lost his disgraceful bet? What did he say when you spoke to him of this?''

"He is not to be found, my lady. I went to his father's home. His father refused to see me. I saw only his secretary who said that Lord Halstead was in Scotland. He knows nothing of him, said that Lord Clermont wished to know nothing. I showed him the rifle—although I did not tell him why I needed to know whether it was Halstead's—but the secretary knew nothing of it, merely that it bore Halstead's initials and arms—which I already knew. He added that Lord Halstead had left for Scotland in September. And that is that. A dead end.''

"And we are almost at December,'' said Nell reflectively. "Well, I agree, a strange turn-up. What's to do?'' she added, turning to the men about her. "Can we seriously believe that it was Halstead who hired a man to kill me?''

Jackson spoke again. "If I might advise, I also investigated the affairs of your cousin, Ulric Tallboys, who has the most to gain by your death. It is not commonly known that he is at *point non plus* where money is concerned. He has unpaid bills in every town he frequents. At York, they are for having him consigned to a debtor's prison. There is a lien on the small property he still owns, and his affairs are desperate. His reputation...'' He hesitated, said bluntly, "He has no reputation, whereas Lord Halstead, there's a different matter.''

"In what way?'' It was Chad speaking, his voice hoarse. Whenever Charles Halstead was the subject of discussion, with or without his dreadful bet over Nell, he always felt quite ill.

"This,'' said Jackson, "he has always been at outs with his father, I gathered, but the rest of the world tells a different tale. The servants at Clermont House think the world of him, as do his friends—I made the most discreet enquiries, as you would wish. His reputation as a soldier shows him a nonpareil for courage and ability. The Duke himself commended him, and was sorry when his elder brother died, and he was ordered by his father to leave the Army and take his place. He is reputed to be generous to a fault, unfortunate only with women—''

"He made a disgraceful bet concerning myself," said Nell frostily, "this nonpareil of yours."

"Indeed," bowed Jackson, "and I would not seek to deny that, but I do not think that he is your man, whereas—and I speak with caution, no proof you understand—I think that Mr. Ulric Tallboys should be watched. As for the rifle, I propose we write to Glen Ruadh in Scotland where I understand from the secretary that Lord Halstead has gone, to ask him what he knows of it. It was almost certainly stolen from him."

"So," said Nell, "we are a little forward. Newcome here shall write to Glen Ruadh, and you may arrange for my cousin to be watched. You will continue your enquiries, will you not?"

"Indeed, and I shall remain in touch with you, and you must guard yourself at all times, my lady."

He hesitated. "I must say this. Mr. Tallboys is not nice in his conversation where you are concerned. He hates you, madam, and is foolish enough to let the world know that he does. Which, of course, might mean that he is not our man, but my instincts tell me that he is."

Henson said slowly, after Jackson had gone, "Either way, Lady Elinor, a dreadful thought that he or Lord Halstead should wish to murder you."

Nell shivered. "Do not speak of it. Newcome, write that letter today. At least, with luck, we may clear that puzzle up."

"At once," Chad replied, but she thought that Newcome looked perturbed, and when the others had gone, old Challenor taking himself to his own desk by the library's fire, she signed to Chad to return with her to her study.

"Come, Newcome, what ails you?" she said, for she had developed an extra sense where he was concerned.

"I don't know," said Chad honestly. "There are times when I feel that something of my true past is trying to break through, and just then, in there, while Jackson was speaking, I had the strangest sensation. I felt on the brink of I know not what, I had a sensation of dizziness, a feeling of disaster."

"Disaster," said Nell thoughtfully, "that's an odd word, Newcome."

For the moment her personal feelings were in abeyance. He looked so ill that rather than make love to him she wanted to mother him, feed him gruel, hold his head—there were, of course, different ways of making love to him.

"You wish to be relieved of your duties, to rest a little?" offered Nell tenderly.

Chad looked at her ruefully. "No, indeed. The malaise is merely a passing thing."

"Like Aunt Conybeare struggling to stay awake in here," said Nell, trying to lighten the situation a little. She seemed to have gone from a state of mad desire for Newcome to be in her bed to an equally mad desire for him to be in his own bed—with her as his nurse.

She fantasised him needing to be returned to his room, where she would put on her brown holland apron, feed him soothing drinks, sit on his bed, stroke his brow, stroke his... She blinked.

"I trust you to tell me if you are not well. Campions needs you to be in the finest fettle, Newcome, and so do I." She could hear the note of love in her voice and looked across at Aunt Conybeare, in case that lady had heard it too.

But Aunt Conybeare was sitting there lax, her canvas work forgotten on her knees, dreaming of summer, perhaps, or her coming good dinner.

Impulsively she put her hand on Chad's brow, found it cool; he took the hand, kissed the palm, returned it to her. "You are too kind, my love." For he also had seen that Aunt Conybeare had effectively left them alone again.

"Well or ill, Newcome, I need to see you alone, and soon. You understand me?"

"Too well," said Chad.

"Then we must arrange it," said Nell firmly, ignoring his answer. "Tomorrow, I shall require you to be in the annexe, to solve a matter of grave intellectual import. I am concerned about what Kant actually meant when he spoke of the Moral Imperative. Judging by the answers you have been giving me when I have been trying to seduce you, it would seem that you know a great deal about it.

"Instruct me, I command you, on that topic, Newcome. You are so very moral that perhaps you do not need Kant, whereas I, I need not only Kant, but a whole library of philosophers to make me behave properly. On second thoughts, perhaps I ought to instruct you in Immoral Imperatives! At two-thirty tomorrow, then, on the stroke. Aisgill and Rajah require you this afternoon, and I would not wish to disappoint them."

Chad's expression as he looked at his wilful mistress told its own tale.

"Why are you not making a note of my appointment with you, Newcome? Do so immediately. I want no excuses for your absence. None at all. I need succouring after this afternoon's revelations, and you are large enough to succour anyone. Now, I must go to Henson's office to sign papers, and give silver coins to deserving servants."

She turned at the door, blew him a kiss as Aunt Conybeare slept on. "Tell me, Newcome, what present shall I give to my most deserving servant of all?"

CHAPTER TEN

THE ANNEXE hardly seemed the most romantic of places: no windows, narrow, lined with bookshelves, a glass window in its ceiling the only light, but to Nell and Chad it was a haven, the one place where they might catch a few moments together—if their luck held, that was.

Luck was with them. Challenor was unwell; he had retired to his room, leaving Chad alone there, collating at the map table, for Nell to find him, and Aunt Conybeare was gone to her sitting-room, after her morning's stint in the study overlooking Nell with her secretary.

Nell, aware of Challenor's absence, burning with impatient desire, controlled herself, and as Aunt Conybeare made off said, "A moment—I must consult with Henson, Aunt. I will join you later."

Amorous conspiracy had made such a liar of her that now her voice carried no false overtones, and without the slightest trace of guilt she pushed the library door open to see him standing there, broad back to her.

She did not even need to speak, put up her hand, and he followed her into the annexe where she closed and locked the door behind them and they stood face to face.

But oh, dear, *his* face! He had yet another noble fit of conscience on him, that was plain.

Nell drew a ragged breath, said wearily, "Yes, Newcome, what is it this time? A sudden religious conversation, or another inconvenient attack of honour?"

"Neither," said Chad, face grim. "My wits recover slowly, but they do recover. Two things struck me this morning. First of all, if I accede to your wishes, and my own love and yes, desire for you, the chances of you falling with child are great," and before he could continue she was there before him.

"Oh, Newcome, what of that? Are you fearful that I shall not make an honest man of you, somehow?"

Despite himself his face lightened, even if, as Nell was pleased to see, his eyes began to smoulder. "No, it won't do," he said, blunt with her for once. "Consider—and I must truly have lost my wits as well as my memory not to think of this before—I may have a family, children, somewhere, and, if so, what of them?"

"What indeed?" said Nell, who wondered what her own wits had been doing—struck down by mad desire, she supposed. "You do not seem a married man to me," she offered, "a derelict wandering the moors. Had you deserted them, Newcome? Or have you remembered your family, and this is a kind way of telling me of them?"

Chad closed his eyes, and as so often tried to conjure up his past. Nothing—vague clouds passing over the sun, blackness with lights in it, a dying horse squealing, soldiers shouting, an old man's angry face, despising him, a sensation of falling, sorrow, regret and pain felt—for what?

"Nothing," he said at last, "nothing. The harder I try to remember, the less I can recall. Flashes come when I am not attending to my condition. I do not feel that I was married. On the contrary, my deepest self tells me I was not, but—"

"Oh, what a but that is," said Nell sorrowfully. "Let us think of what you are, and what it tells us. You had an education, a good one. You speak like a gentleman, but you were not in the condition of one when you were found. Aisgill says you were undoubtedly a cavalryman. 'He knows the brand,' he says. A gentleman fallen on hard times, penniless perhaps, enlisted in the Army as a private, one supposes, turned off in the peace with nowhere to go—does all this seem reasonable to you, Newcome?"

Chad nodded. Reasonable but wrong, something beyond reason told him, but he followed Nell's line of logic. "Such hard times that I could find no occupation, began a-wandering, somehow ended up attacked and my memory gone. I do not sound married, and such instincts as I pos-

sess tell me I was not, but oh, my dearest lady, that may be
my wishes, my love speaking, not the truth.''

"What is the truth?'' said Nell softly. ''The present truth
is that you are here at Campions, my secretary who saved
my life, and whom, God forgive me, for reasons which are
no reasons, I love beyond reason. I do not care if you are
married, and have twenty children, Newcome, do you understand me? I do not care. I am Nell Tallboys who lost her
wits, and about whom Charles Halstead was right—when
we love, all women are the same. Light-skirts, every one of
us! He has won his bet—and will never know it. Forget your
conscience, Newcome, as I am forgetting mine. What price
my being a Countess and owning half Yorkshire, and a
quarter of England, if I cannot have the man I love?''

"You love the wrong man,'' said Chad hoarsely. Proximity was fuelling desire; the sight of her, the scent of her,
was working in him. Oh, yes, he might have twenty children, but what of that?

In the here and now there was only Nell, and she was offering herself to him, and if what they snatched together
would be brief, at least he would have that to set against the
dark, which was all that he possessed of himself.

Conscience, honour, reason worked against them both,
but *"Amor vincit omnia"* flashed through his mind; love
conquers all, and against love nothing could stand, nothing.

He moved forward. So did she. Nell saw on his face the
message that she had won. What she offered him he could
not refuse. They were so close together now, in the narrow
room, that no man or woman could be closer, outside of the
act of love itself.

Nell trembled as Chad's hands rose to cup her face, and
then he brought down his face to kiss her. And the kiss was
not like any of his previous ones. It was fierce. It almost
bruised her mouth, which opened beneath his to take him in,
his tongue and hers meeting and touching, as though all the
words which had passed between them had been made flesh,
killing the need for speech.

His tongue was the first hint of him to enter her. She ex-
ulted in the sensation, wound her arms around his neck to

draw him even closer, to feel the long length of him against her, his arms around her, equally demanding, as though they could sink into one another, become an entity which, being both, was neither, but something new.

How long they stood like that Nell did not know. Only, suddenly, his busy hands were at work about her. He was pulling her dress down from her shoulders so that her breasts sprang free, and he was caressing them, first with his hands and then with his mouth, so that her head fell back, and she gave long shuddering gasps, gasps which were in rhythms with the shuddering ecstasy which ran through her body.

The sensations which Nell was experiencing made her knees weak, her head swim, and she gave an inarticulate cry, steadied herself against him, and then her wanton hands did something quite disgraceful, something she had never dreamed of doing.

For she undid his breeches flap and it was his turn to spring, hard, into her hand, which grasped and stroked him, so that he groaned beneath her loving hands, and now his hands peeled her dress up, up.

Nell was on fire, lost to everything but the fact that they were at last on the verge of doing what she had hardly dared dream was possible, and when his hands transferred themselves to her buttocks, to clasp her to him, ready for the final act, she said thickly, "Oh, yes, Chad, yes."

Her voice broke the spell which bound him. He shuddered, put a hand down to take her hand from him, said hoarsely, pulling away a little, "No, Nell, no."

"No?" babbled Nell, who by now had only one idea in her head to impale herself on him...on what her hand held. "What do you mean by no, Newcome? I say yes. Your Countess orders you, Newcome. Yes, immediately. Now."

"No, not like this," was all that he could say, trying to detach himself from her and Nell resisting.

"What do you mean, not like this, Newcome? I thought that this was how one did it. Is there another way? If so, pray show me, at once, Newcome, at once!"

She felt him, rather than heard him, give a half-laugh, half-sob. "Oh, by God, Nell, you tempt me sorely with tongue and body. This way, any way you please, but not here not now, hugger-mugger. I don't want to take you like a drab in an alley. I want to love you, slowly, properly.''

"Oh," she wailed, "I want you now, properly or improperly, my love, or I shall die. Here on the spot I shall die, and how will you explain that, my darling, when Challenor finds me stark and cold, slain by your Moral Imperative, an unwilling sacrifice to virtue?"

"No, never cold," he said, free of her, facing her, trembling with unfulfilled desire, his body reproaching him as much as she. "In life, in death, Nell, never cold. But not now . . . not here . . . It should be a sacrament . . ."

"But where, Newcome, Chad, my own love, where?" Nell was frantic. "No private place for me or you. Oh, here and now is heaven and hell," and she put out her hand to stroke him again, so that he rose on tiptoe, said roughly, chokingly,

"For God's sake, Nell, would you have me pleasured without my knowing you? I can only stand so much . . ."

Nell was on the brink of she knew not what. The excitement she felt was so powerful that it sought release. If he would not pleasure himself within her, then she would give him release without her, for she had brought him to this with her wilfulness, and at least she could give him that.

"I would give you fulfilment," she said, "this way, if not the other."

His grip was suddenly on her wrist, stilling her hand. "No," he said. "No. Without you, nothing."

"For you," she whispered, "for you. For I have done this to you."

"My love, my life, my dearest lady . . ." he was articulate *in extremis* ". . . it is *you* I want. Our pleasure together. Oh, Nell, you must take it, as well as give. Take my unfulfilled flame of love, it is all I have to give you, against what you wish to give me. I will contrive, somehow, that we meet in a place more fitting, that we may make a ceremony of it. Please, Nell, please."

Nell stopped, her head drooping on his chest. They panted together, self-denial more exhausting than fulfillment.

"If that is what you want, then I want it too. Oh, I am greedy, I know, but I want all of you, not just your hands and mouth." She hardly knew what she was saying, and for a moment they stayed there thus, unmoving, content to hold one another. Except, that at the end, Chad turned to face the wall, leaned against it, his whole body shaking, and Nell dropped to her knees, shuddering, her forehead on a low cupboard's top, passion contained, not destroyed.

And then they turned towards one another. He straightened her dress for her, and gently, gently, she restored him, refastened the cravat she had pulled undone in her passion to get at him, rebuttoned him, still without speech between them. They had gone beyond words.

But once outside, in the library, the clock ticked above the fire in the hearth, the busts of the Roman Emperors looked down on them, blind, and the books in their rows behind their lattices as though nothing had happened, as though in their precincts two lovers had not suffered and inwardly bled, torn by their forbidden passion.

Nell walked to the door, turned there before she left, to say but one word. "Soon!"

The word was easily said, the doing difficult. The guard kept on Nell, the duties which bound him, the presence of her aunt, servants, Aisgill, Henson, Challenor, her duties, all contrived to keep them apart. The annexe they avoided.

Christmas, its pleasures and further duties, was upon them. Nell entertained the Riding. Men and women arrived for a great feast. They stared at her. Despite sexual denial, she was radiant, for was *he* not always by her side, to sustain her, if he could not physically love her?

"I never thought Nell Tallboys beautiful before," said one bluff squire to his wife, as Nell moved among them, magnificent in toffee-coloured silk, wearing her rarely seen diamonds, the knowledge of being cherished plain upon her face for the perceptive to see, "but, by God, she's a marvel tonight."

Chad was there, sporting a new silk suit, especially made for him, black, with knee breeches and stockings also of silk, standing in the background with the rest of Nell's council, one or two staring at the size of him.

Memory still lost, he had bad dreams. The night after the scene in the annexe he had shouted so loud in his sleep that he had woken up Sandby, Henson's assistant, who had a room next to Chad's small suite on the top floor, and Sandby had gone in to find him tangled in the bedclothes, sweating and shaken.

He could remember little of what had disturbed him so. Only a feeling of desolation, and of falling, of clawing himself up a steep slope, and then losing himself. Nell had been there, but the sight of her had distressed him so badly that he was suddenly beside himself with pain and shock, after the first joyful sight of her.

He had had such dreams when he had first arrived at Campions, but of late they had disappeared. Perhaps the encounter in the annexe had brought them back. One thing did surprise him, and that was that just before Sandby shook him awake he had seen in his hands, quite plain, the rifle he had taken from the would-be assassin. But the hands that were holding it were wearing white gloves, and he was talking to an officer in full regimentals in terms of cheerful equality, almost of authority, and then the scene vanished into the dark.

Like all dreams, it ran away from him in the day, and little was left of it. He had learned to accept his condition, to accept that perhaps he would never find himself again, and to live with that knowledge. The dogged dedication with which he worked owed a little to his determination to forget himself in his duties, and a great deal to his love for Nell, which he tried, for her sake not to betray to those around him.

But the big event of the Yuletide season for those at Campions was the party that Nell always gave for her staff, the day when the state dining hall was given over to those who created and maintained the estate, and not to those who simply lived off it.

Chad, with the rest of Nell's council, dressed again in his black silk suit, walked in that evening. The hall was decked with boughs of holly, every chandelier was aflame with light, fires blazed in the two hearths, and Nell was even more

stately than she had been on the night she had entertained
the Riding.

She had dressed herself like a bride in white and cream;
she wore not the diamonds but the emeralds which Catherine the Great of Russia had given to the third Earl, when he
had been ambassador in St. Petersburg, after she had taken
him to bed as her lover.

It was a suit of even more splendour than her diamonds,
consisting of a tiara, earrings, necklace, bracelets, rings, and
a belt of gold, set with pearls as well as emeralds, cinched
under her breasts. Her fan matched the suit, huge, decorated with parrots of green and scarlet. Annie had dressed
her hair high beneath the tiara, and if she took Chad's
breath away she had the same effect on everyone else. Even
mild Aunt Conybeare was a little stunned.

The boar's head had been carried in, the plum pudding
served, drink of all kinds handed around, and at a signal
Nell rose, and the company adjourned to the long gallery,
where there was a small collection of musicians, brought
especially from York to play for Nell's people, and a group
of waits who broke into "God rest you merry, gentlemen"
at the sight of Nell.

Chad knew one thing. He had never before been present
on such an occasion—he needed no memory to tell him that.
Old Challenor, her senior council member, led his mistress
out for the first minuet, for court dancing alternated with
the country dances put on for her staff.

"And you," Nell murmured to Chad, after Challenor had
returned her to her place on the small dais set up before the
great window which ran for a third of the length of the wall,
"will take me out for my fourth dance after Henson and
Aisgill. We follow strict precedence here, you see. After you,
the butler!" and her eyes shone with mirth.

Strangely, they had been easy together since their last
powerful encounter in the annexe. It was as though they
knew who they were and how they stood with one another;
that they could be patient, hold off, and work together in a
comfortable amity, even though a cauldron of passion might
lie below the smooth surface of their lives.

"Biding our time," murmured Nell, when he stood up to lead her out. "What good creatures we are, to be sure." The Yule log roared in the hearth, Nell's people clapped their hands each time she took the floor, and many clapped louder when it was Newcome who took her hand. He was liked—and not only by the women, who yearned over his size and rugged charms; the men respected him, too, a pen-pusher who could match them at many of their outdoor pursuits, and beat them in some.

He was Ralph's master, and recently had been discovered to have a punishing blow in the ring. He had stopped one day to watch young Seth training—he was a useful fighter at little bouts in the Riding—had offered him some advice, and then been challenged to put his fists where his mouth was, a challenge he had taken up with some success.

He had arrived in Nell's study with a black eye, but he had managed to put Seth down twice before Seth put him down, and Aunt Conybeare had clucked and fussed over him, to Nell's amusement. She thought that all Campions was falling in love with Chad, not merely its mistress!

They moved through the pattern of the dance, meeting, parting, symbolic of life itself, Nell thought, and thinking so she arrived back at him again, and unselfconsciously, naturally as she met him, there in the centre of the floor, for a fleeting moment all that she felt for him, and he for her, was written plain on their faces.

In the hurly burly of the dance it might have gone completely unnoticed, the spark which betrayed them both. One man, and one man only, saw it.

Aisgill, whom all such occasion as this bored, found his entertainment not in taking part but watching others. He was leaning against one of the pillars of the fireplace, half-cut, but even so the shrewdness and knowledge of man and beast which made him so successful as Nell's lieutenant were still with him. His lazy eye was on the dancers; he saw Nell turn, saw her and Chad meet, and it was as though lightning flashed in front of him to illuminate a landscape he had never seen before.

He had no doubt of what he had seen; his only doubt was how far the lovers had gone. He knew his Countess, and the lightning illuminated something else—the change in her, and what had provoked it.

Nell watched Chad moved away from her, turn, to greet her again, and joyfully, she curtsied before him as the dance ended, and he bowed, to lift her, to take her hand, to escort her to the dais, passing Aisgill on the way, his shrewd, sad old eyes on them both, his mistress and the man he and she had rescued, half-naked, from the moor.

CHAPTER ELEVEN

IT WAS SIX WEEKS since they had broken off their lovemaking in the annexe. Snow covered the moors; Nell thought that her heart was frozen too, and wondered at Chad's. She had not thought it possible that they could be so cool with each other.

They met, worked together, spoke as in a dream. Had she dreamed it, their passion? Had he dreamed it? No, of course they had not, for if they were foolish enough to let their hands touch, ever so slightly, the fever sprang up between them again. Nell felt her body grow lax, saw his eyes begin to smoulder with desire, and then for the rest of the day she needed to control herself.

And how, and when, had he learned to exercise such iron control? For Nell had come to recognise that he did. How fortunate, she thought bitterly, that they were so strong, for none watching them could see what they meant to each other, she was sure of that.

She walked towards the stables in the dim light of early morning. White Princess, her mare, always known as Princess, was in foal, due to bear Rajah's progeny any day. She fantasised herself as Princess, and Chad as Rajah. How simple it was for the members of her stud, and how difficult for her, Nell Tallboys, who had everything, but who had nothing.

Aisgill met her in the yard. "Lady Elinor?"

"I have come to learn of Princess, Aisgill," she said, pulling her coat tighter about her, against the cold. "You said that she was about to foal at any time now." She paused, went on, "You will think me stupid, but I awoke, worrying about her."

"Not stupid, my lady," he answered. "Sometimes I think that where your horses are concerned you have an extra sense. I am worried, too. She has begun to have her foal, but things are going ill. I had hoped that they would go better before I needed to tell you of her."

"I may see her?" asked Nell. She had assisted at births before, insisting that she needed to know all of the work of the stud, not just the pleasant, easy bits.

"Yes," he replied curtly. Nell thought that for some reason Aisgill was short with her, and she wondered why.

He led her to where Princess lay, and there, kneeling by her beautiful mare, now *in extremis,* was Chad, wearing not his fine black suit but the rough clothing he had been given when he first arrived at Campions.

Aisgill saw her eyes on Newcome, sighed. He had thought, after the Christmas dance, when the tenants and the servants had gone, that perhaps he had been wrong, deceived by the drink he had taken; and the impassive masks his mistress and her lover had worn in the days after Christmas reinforced his belief that he had been mistaken. But here, in the gloom, the look which Nell gave to Chad, assisting at the primal moment of birth, told him that after all he had been right.

Nell moved over to Chad, fell on her knees beside him. He had looked up on seeing her enter, and looked away again, fearful that he might betray himself.

Aisgill, behind them, spoke. "I thought that Newcome," he spoke the name roughly, as though Chad were still only one of his hands, not the almost-gentleman he was in the house, "would be of most use here. He helped me when Lady Luck had her foal and things went ill. You owe that foal to him, Lady Elinor. He has good hands for birth, as well as for controlling Rajah."

"Yes," said Nell, almost absently. "What is wrong, Newcome?"

"Her foal is wrongly positioned," said Chad. "Not like Lady Luck's was. Worse, I fear. Her chances are not good."

There were several other stable hands present, all with grave faces. To lose Princess and her foal would be a blow to them all. For no good reason that Nell could think of, it suddenly seemed desperately important that Princess lived. It was almost as though the beautiful beast, lying there helpless, was Nell herself, about to die—or, rather, that Princess symbolised the love she felt for Chad, and could not express.

She rose to her feet, said, "No!" and walked over to the wall, to stand there facing it, leaving them all surprised that she, usually so cool, who had seen all this before and had not flinched, could show such emotion.

Chad could not stop himself. Something of what she was experiencing passed from her to him. He rose, regardless of etiquette, and what Aisgill might think, and he walked over to her, and touched her arm. "Lady Elinor," he said, and the sound of his voice eased Nell's torment a little, "Lady Elinor, we shall do our best to save her, and the foal as well."

Nell turned towards him, showing him a face of such grief that he retreated a little.

"Poor Princess," she said. "There are times when I feel—" and her voice thickened "—that running the stud is more than I can endure."

"It is the way of life, Lady Elinor," he said gravely, fighting the wish to take her in his arms and comfort her. "With or without the stud, mares would be in foal, and occasionally their lives would be at risk because of it."

It was as though they were alone, and the frustration which Nell felt that she could not be Princess, lying there, having *his* foal, even at the risk of her life, was in her voice and manner.

"Where did you learn such wisdom, Newcome? Or have you forgotten that, along with everything else?"

Oh, she was being unfair to him, she knew, and saw that he understood why she spoke as she did, that the rapport between them was now so strong that it went beyond words.

Aisgill spoke sharply. "The mare needs you, Newcome, more than Lady Elinor does."

Both lovers were so engrossed that the full import of what he was saying did not strike them. Chad heard only the command to action, Nell hardly heard him at all.

Until Aisgill added, "This is going to be difficult, Lady Elinor. I think that you should leave us to it. Not a fit place for you."

"My mare," said Nell, proud, "my stud. You would not say that to me if I were the sixth Earl, instead of your Countess. I shall stay."

Aisgill bowed his head. He could not deny her. He knew that she had been present at births before, but in some fashion, and why he did not know, he felt that she should not be present now. But he could not gainsay her, and for the next hour of blood and pain and noise Nell stayed, carrying buckets of water for them, until Princess's foal was pulled into the world, and Princess, though sorely hurt, and beside herself with pain, still lived.

Nell had willed the mare's survival, that Chad and Aisgill should succeed, wanting an omen for herself that she thought to be good, and once all was over her legs turned to water, not with desire, as they had done in the annexe, but for sheer blessed relief.

"And now will you go, madam?" said Aisgill, surlily mutinous for once, Chad washing Princess's blood from his hands and arms in the pail which Nell had carried to him, the foal—which Aisgill had announced was to be called Lightning, in a voice which brooked no argument—staggering about, and Princess trying to rise.

"I will escort Lady Elinor back to the house," announced Chad; he was towelling his face now.

"No," said Aisgill sharply. "Go and eat with the lads. You need to rest. I shall see Lady Elinor back."

"I need no escort in Campions's grounds in sight of both house and stables," said Nell, equally sharply, wondering what had got into Aisgill that he should be so surly. "You need your own breakfast. No, I will brook no denial," and she walked off, head high, Countess Nell at her most icy cold, almost as she had been before Chad's arrival at Campions.

Chad ate his breakfast hungrily, although sorry that he was denied Nell's companionship on the way back to the house. The hands' fare was simple, but good, and he was grateful for the plain food after all the kickshaws at Nell's table. What did that tell him of his old life? he wondered.

Aisgill came late to breakfast, and when Chad rose to return to the house, to dress himself to be Nell's secretary again, said to Chad, still harsh, "A word with you, Newcome, before you leave."

Like Nell, Chad was a little puzzled by Aisgill's manner, the more so when Aisgill led him to the stable yard, away from any overhearing of what he was about to say.

"Do not misunderstand me, Newcome," began Aisgill, his colour high, even for him. "You are a good worker, the best, and I understand from Henson that you have made a good clerk. But remember, the Lady Elinor is your Countess as she is mine, and I do not want to see any hurt come to her, especially from those to whom she has shown kindness. You understand me, Newcome. I should find means to turn you away tomorrow, if I thought that your presence here was a threat to Campions."

The thunderbolt had hit Chad. Aisgill knew! But how? He was certain that he, and she, had done nothing to betray themselves. But Aisgill knew men and animals. Could he scent them, then? And if he could, could not others?

"I would do nothing to bring harm to Lady Elinor, or Campions," he said, "seeing that they have given me life. Without her, I should be cold on the moor."

"Then see that you remember that, man," said Aisgill, showing his teeth. "You are her secretary, who was her stable lad, and before that you were nothing, scum, starving, naked, plucked from the ditch. Keep that well in mind, and you cannot go far wrong."

What could he say? God help me, I love her, and she loves me, and that stands before everything, even my honour, and hers.

Instead, he bowed his head stiffly before her faithful servant who wished only to protect her, while he, what did he wish to do but dishonour her? And Aisgill's words were one more barrier between himself and his love.

NELL, NEWLY DRESSED for the day, elegant in tan, was expecting to find Chad in her study, at his desk. But only Aunt Conybeare was there, placid, her sewing on her knee.

"Where's Newcome?" she said abruptly.

"He came in, went out again." Aunt Conybeare was unruffled. The weeks of sitting in on Nell and Chad and nothing happening had left her used to his presence. The undercurrents between the two escaped her. Gifted at reading novels, Aunt Conybeare could not read life.

Nell sat down at her own desk. There was an envelope on it, her name written there, in Chad's hand.

She opened it, read the short sentence inside.

"Lady Elinor. I must leave Campions. With, or without, your permission," and then his signature, bold, firm, like himself, Chad Newcome, plain, no flourishes.

Nell's heart clenched inside her. She could have screamed, thrown herself about. Of all the things which she could have imagined—never this, never this! To lose him. No, no, it was not to be borne. To be alone again, and this time to know what she was missing. She could never be uninvolved Nell Tallboys again.

Where was he? He must be in the library, if he was not with her, or in Henson's office. She must see him, speak to him. What had brought this on?

He was in the library. He was sitting on the booksteps, a book in his hand. Challenor was nowhere in sight.

Chad saw Nell advancing on him, the letter in her hand, an avenging fury.

She walked to where he sat, waved the letter at him, and, careless of whether Challenor was about or not, said, "What is the meaning of this, Newcome? Tell me at once."

Chad made no effort to leap to his feet, to pay her his due respects, but said, from his sitting position, "I thought the meaning of what I have written quite plain, Lady Elinor."

"Did you, indeed, Newcome? Get down, at once, pay me the respect due to my rank from yours. I am your Countess, Newcome! Remember that!"

Chad rose, stood before her, bowed head, deferential, said, "I am remembering that, Lady Elinor. And *that* is why I have written you my letter."

"Oh!" Nell's desire to scream was almost not to be denied. "Stop it at once, Newcome. You are back in the Jesuit seminary again. Answer a plain question plainly."

He could temporise no longer. The anguish which tore at Nell tore at him.

"It is not right that I should stay. For your honour, I must go. We are . . . remarked upon."

At last something to give Nell pause. To have her staring at him, face white.

"We are . . ." and then the intuitive leap. "Aisgill! I knew it, somehow, this morning. He was odd, strange. But how in the world could he guess at such a thing. For guess it must be."

"Does it matter?" said Chad wearily. "He knows. That is enough."

"He knows nothing, Newcome, for there is nothing to know."

"Now you are enrolled with the Jesuits, Lady Elinor," said Chad. "For there is everything to know. I must go, and soon. To save us . . ." And then since Challenor seemed absent, and for a moment they were safe, "Nell, I would not have written the letter else. I *must* go."

"Go! Where will you go, Newcome, my love, my own? To starve again? To die on the moor this time? You have no home, no haven, not even a name. I will not let you go to . . . nothing."

She but echoed what Aisgill had said earlier.

"What am I," he said, and, since Aisgill had spoken to him that morning he had dredged his mind for memories, something to tell him who he was, but nothing, nothing, "but a piece of scum, found and cared for, betraying those who cared for him, by seeking to dishonour their lady?"

"No dishonour, Newcome, when your lady commands. Was Princess dishonoured by Rajah?"

Chad closed his eyes, that he might not see her face. He would carry the memory of her to his death. His gallant lady.

She took his silence for consent, pressed home her advantage, as she thought. "Besides," she said feverishly, "you are now my secretary. I shall demand three months' notice, you hear me, Newcome? Three months' notice, before you leave. And you are not to try to run away. I shall set the dogs on you, to haul you back.''

The tears were rolling down her face; she was frantic. No thought for those who might find them, her only thought was not to lose him.

"Hush," he said, pulling out his handkerchief, and leaning forward to mop her face with it. "You are brave, my Countess. Remember your ancestor on the field of battle. 'The day is lost, surrender,' his enemies told him, and his answer, 'I scorn to surrender my living body; you may take it only in death.' And saying so he fought on, but not to lose his battle, to win it against all odds, in the end."

"Fine words," she said, thought her tears, "from one who is running away."

"Oh, it is you who carry the banner, not I," he said, his mouth twisted. "I am only your slave, whose duty is to die for you, or sacrifice himself to save your honour."

"But you sacrifice me, too," she wailed, "for what is left for me but a loveless marriage, and an empty life? I have no battle to win, unlike the man whose name I bear. I would be a cottager's daughter and have the man I love rather than be what I am. You must not leave me."

Chad saw that she was distraught, which moved him, and he knew also that what she said and did came from her heart. But he saw Aisgill again, and the contempt in his face for a man who would do what he thought he saw Chad doing.

Again, it was as though she had picked up his very thoughts.

"Am I, are we, to do what Aisgill tells us? Is Aisgill master here—?"

But Chad came back at her, "He thinks of Campions, as well as you."

"Campions!" Nell almost choked on the word. "Do you, does he, love Campions more than you love me? If every great lady who loved where she should not were to be punished as I am, the nobility would be decimated."

"But you are not every great lady. You are Nell Tallboys, brave and true."

"Words, Newcome, words. I cannot compel you, I know.
Whatever you were, you are a strong man. I could not love
a weak one. No," she said, eyes blazing. "If I give you leave
to go, it will not be yet. Give me but a little longer, before my
life closes in on me for good. Only that! I ask only that."

What could he say or do? What was his honour, or hers,
before such suffering?

He hesitated. Nell knew that she had won. "You will stay
a little longer, and we shall be careful. Just to have you near
me will be enough."

But even as he assented, saying, "The usual notice, three
months, and it must be known that I am going," Chad knew
that it would not be enough, for what lay between them was
too strong for that.

CHAPTER TWELVE

FRUSTRATION and desire were one word for Nell—and that word was Chad.

The self-control which had ruled her life for twenty-seven years, which had created the icy Countess Elinor, noted for her stoic uprightness, her austere virtue, the woman who had turned away suitors until suitors had ceased to come, had disappeared when she had met Chad.

The woman who had proclaimed so confidently that love was not for her, that she would marry someone, anyone, when she chose, merely to secure the succession, and, that done, her partner could go hang—she treating him as a man might treat a woman he had married for her money and lands—that woman no longer existed.

She had discovered in herself a well of passion... no, not well, that word was too placid for what she felt for Chad. It was a cataract, or a fire, a raging fire, the flame of which the poets sang, which consumed her.

When she read Lord Byron now, it was not with superior amusement; she knew only too well of what he wrote, and she forgave him for what he was, and what he did, because, knowing what love had done to her, she knew what it had done to him.

How could Chad be so strong? She could almost feel the iron control which he maintained over his emotions, and in the face of the temptation which she knew that she presented to him. For the first time, she truly asked herself what he had been in his lost past. Where and how had he learned to deny himself? And what toll had it taken of him, was taking of him? She knew, because nothing that happened at Campions was unknown to her, that he never touched the women servants who yearned after him, being quite unlike most of the men servants in that respect.

Nell had said to him, and to herself, that she could only love a strong man, and had told true. Otherwise she would have taken Ulric as a husband, and, she now knew, contrary to her earlier beliefs, that she could never have married the weak man whom she thought she could have used to serve Campions.

She had fallen in love with a man whose will and control matched her own—so how had he managed to arrive on the moor and at Campions, abandoned and derelict? And now she must know, somehow, what she thought had never mattered—Chad himself having been all that she had previously wanted—what the man she loved had been before his memory had gone.

Sitting at her desk that afternoon, his resignation formally written out now, lying before her, she made her resolutions. She had three months in which to keep him, to change his mind, to try to bend him to her will.

Chad was at the riding school when Henson came in to her, carrying the account books relating to the estate, and a further budget of letters. Before she opened them in Chad's absence, she showed him the letter of resignation.

Surprisingly, Henson was annoyed and offended. "What maggot's in his brain?" he almost grunted. "Where will he find work to equal what he has achieved here?"

"I thought you disapproved of him," commented Nell mildly.

"I did." Henson was brief. "But the man has compelled me to admit both his competence and his honesty—to say nothing of his courage in saving you. Besides, his devotion to his duty is exemplary. I had not thought him ungrateful to wish to leave what has saved him."

Nell began to close her eyes in pain, said, "I don't think it's ingratitude, Henson."

"Then what the devil is it? Has he recovered his memory?"

"No, it's not that. I . . . taxed him with that. He says—" and Nell invented wildly, and reminded herself to tell Chad of the excuse which she had found for him, for *something* must be said to Henson ''—that he wishes to leave to try to discover who he is.''

''I suppose that makes some sort of sense—so long as he does not end up as a vagabond again,'' replied Henson grudgingly. ''In the meantime, we must try to persuade him to stay. Campions must not lose good servants. To lose first Payne and then Newcome would be too bad.''

Payne still lay in his bedroom in the attic, and would never rise from it again, another old servant dying in harness and cared for by the family.

Nell opened the first letter, read it, handed it to Henson, who had taken a seat at Chad's desk. The letter was from Scotland, and its message was simple. The writer, factor to Charles, Viscount Halstead, had received the letter from Campions asking for information about my lord's rifle, but no answer could be given: the Viscount Halstead was not at Glen Ruadh, and no word had been received of his arriving there. Campions was advised to write to Clermont House in London.

Henson handed the letter back to Nell. ''Another dead end,'' he commented bitterly, ''and where the devil is the man? Saving your presence, Lady Elinor. And isn't it time that Jackson reported back to us?''

''Yes.'' Nell had opened, and was reading, another letter. ''He hopes to be back with us tomorrow. He says he has little to report, but would like to confer with us.''

Henson shrugged his shoulders at that. ''Nothing satisfactory for us today,'' he snorted. ''First Newcome off, then Halstead missing, and now Jackson at *point non plus* by the sound of it.''

''I know,'' said Nell, and then naughtily—cheerfulness would break in, even in her misery, ''I know, Henson, the world is going to the dogs. But it always has done, and it always will.'' And if that doesn't comfort Henson, she thought sadly, why should it comfort me?

''SO THERE IT IS,'' said Cully Jackson to Nell and her council, all in Nell's study the next afternoon. He had arrived, as he had said he would, and his news was that apart from the rifle, which he had asked to keep, he had nothing tangible with which to work.

"I am certain, beyond a doubt, from all I have learned since I last saw you, that Mr. Ulric Tallboys was behind the attempt on you. But I have no proof, no proof at all. One of the dead man's associates awaits hanging in Bradford gaol, and I am to see him there soon. He might, facing his end, tell me a little more of his dead leader—throw light on where Halstead's rifle came from. A slim chance, I fear. And I shall make more enquiries there. I have set up a nice little ring of informers in these parts, who may be of use to me in the future, if not now..."

"And that's all," Henson almost snarled. Of them all he hated the attack on Nell most. A civilised, orderly man, he saw it as a giant crack in his world, as well as an attack on his mistress.

"After that," said Jackson, mildly, ignoring Henson's bile, for he had met such before, "I shall hie me to London again, to try to find a clue to Halstead's whereabouts. He has certainly been in these parts once, but must have left. None here knows of him. Clermont House might have some information on his whereabouts now. And after that, if I fail there, you must save your money. The trail is dead."

"You will stay here tonight," said Nell. "I insist. The housekeeper will find you a room, and the butler will see that you are properly fed."

Jackson bowed. "Before that I should like to speak to Mr. Newcome again, if I may."

They all, Newcome as well, stared at him.

"Oh, I do not suspect Mr. Newcome of any wrongdoing," said Jackson, "but he may know more than he thinks he does. Witnesses often do, and he is our only witness."

Nell rose. "Pray accept my thanks for your efforts so far, and Jackson, I would wish to speak to you alone before you leave. Tomorrow morning, after breakfast, here."

If Nell's council was surprised by this, none indicated that he thought so. Jackson looked across at Chad, said, "I should like to see you in the riding school, Mr. Newcome. I understand that this is the afternoon you work out there. My interest in horses has previously been with the money I have put on their backs, but I have a mind to see a stable in action."

"So you shall." Aisgill was jovial. "You shall see Newcome on Rajah—that is a sight." He felt that he could be generous towards Newcome, seeing that he was doing the decent thing by taking himself and his temptations from Campions.

So, that afternoon, a good lunch inside him, Jackson stood in the riding school watching Chad on Rajah, as Aisgill had promised. Both horse and rider had come on since their early days together. Rajah still hated all men, including Chad, except that with Chad he did strange and wonderful things, and, which, although he did not want to do them, there was an odd magnificence in the doing.

First Jackson watched horse and rider go through a series of tricks which Jackson had seen previously, in simpler forms, at Astley's Circus in London. The caracoles and airs above the ground entranced him, as did the obvious control which Newcome was exercising over the unwilling stallion.

And then the lads put out fences around the arena, and Chad took Rajah over them, snorting, blowing and foaming, hating his rider and the admiring spectators, but compelled to do as he was bid.

And when the show was over two lads warily led Rajah away, and Chad walked to where Jackson was standing. "You wanted to speak to me?"

Jackson was fascinated by Newcome. There was something so ineffably haughty and commanding about him when he was unselfconscious. He had his own theories about what Newcome might have been, and they were not those which obtained at Campions.

"Yes," he said. "As I said earlier, I wanted to ask you some questions about your finding of the rifle."

For some reason Chad did not believe him. His intuition, which he knew—how?—had been powerful in dangerous situations, but not in emotional ones, was working in him. He answered Jackson's innocuous questions calmly; he had no desire to make an enemy of the man. They were now quite alone. It was cold, and the lads had drifted indoors, and Aisgill had gone to his little office.

"And that is all?" asked Jackson. "You have no conscious memory of having seen the man before?"

Chad's expression grew dangerous, his whole body quite still; he said softly, "Are you suggesting that I was in some way connected with the attack on Lady Elinor, that I was a Trojan horse planted here to lead her into danger?"

"No," said Jackson, recognising that the man who had tamed Rajah so easily might not hesitate to tame him. "I have no doubts about your honesty. It was Lady Elinor's decision that you rode to the Throne. She was adamant that you tried to dissuade her to the point of mutiny. But I have the strangest feeling about the rifle every time I hold it, and I have learned not to ignore such feelings—"

"And that is?" prompted Chad, his voice still dangerous.

"That you, Chad Newcome, and the rifle are somehow connected. It is what makes me a good thief taker. Feeling, not reasoning connections."

"I would not argue with you," said Chad, easing a little, the aura of danger about him dispersing. "Because, not from memory but from my own instincts, I know such things may be true."

"And you are leaving Campions, when your notice is up?"

"Yes," said Chad.

"And you will let me know where you are going, when you go. You may do so through Lady Elinor," and then, daring danger, "You are leaving because of Lady Elinor, are you not, Mr. Chad Newcome?"

Jackson was on his knees gasping. Chad Newcome's hands were about his throat. Old campaigner that he was, he had not seen Chad move, only knew that he had done so when he was overwhelmed.

"Say that again, to anyone but myself, and I shall not hesitate to kill you, Mr. Jackson," said Chad, almost conversationally. "It is no business of yours, nor your investigation, why I am leaving. Mention her name to me again and I shall step on you and crush you as I would a beetle."

He released Jackson, who began to laugh, although his throat pained him. "Oh, my fine gentleman," he choked, "I have not properly smoked you out. A trooper, were you? Someone's servant? I think not."

He had the satisfaction of seeing Newcome's face change, lose its colour.

"And what the devil do you mean by that?" Chad grated.

"You may work it out for yourself, sir. In the night watches. It might help you to recover your memory, tell you why you choose to lose it. No, do not attack me again for I know you are not faking. But you might try asking yourself why you do not wish to know yourself, a man of honour, such as you most plainly are."

The Runner strolled off, laughing to himself. He had not needed to bait Newcome to find out that he and Lady Elinor were involved, he had seen that for himself, but he had discovered to his own satisfaction that Newcome was rather more than the poor ex-trooper that Campions thought him to be. What exactly he had been was quite another matter. He took that knowledge with him to his meeting with Lady Elinor.

NELL HAD SPENT her time wondering what to say to Jackson. When he came in with his ill-made, dangerous body and face, the thief taker *par excellence*, she decided that the simple truth might be the safest.

"I have another task for you, Jackson," she said, without preamble, "and it is this. You know that Mr. Newcome has lost his memory, that he is shortly to leave Campions. I am disturbed that he may leave us without being able to sustain himself properly. Consequently, I'm asking you, without his knowledge, to try to discover where he came from, how he arrived, injured and starving, on the moor. It seems to me that you could make your enquiries at the same time that you pursue the mission for which Campions has employed you."

Jackson kept his face straight. He did not fear that Lady Elinor might attack him, as Newcome had done, but it would not be safe to be on the wrong side of such a powerful woman.

"Yes, my lady," he said. "I can do what you wish, and, of course, I shall say nothing to him."

"And I will tell you all I know of his arrival here," began Nell, and proceeded to do so, so lucidly that at the end Jackson said respectfully,

"If I may say so, Lady Elinor, I could do with you as my assistant. Few of the ones I possess are as clear as you in the reports they make to me."

Nell laughed at that. "When I am no longer Countess Nell," she said gaily, "I shall come to Bow Street and ask you for work."

It was not difficult for Jackson to understand why Chad Newcome, and all her people, for that matter, loved her. He determined that if it were possible he would try to find out who was plotting to kill her, and would nail him.

Nell watched him leave the room, dour and honest. She felt as though she was betraying Chad by setting Jackson on his trail, for who knew what he might find?

Jackson turned at the door before he left, and said, "Whatever I discover, of both good and ill about him, you will hear of it from me, will you not?" and his tone was almost a challenge.

"Yes," she said, "yes," and then thought, as he left the room, All's fair in love and war, and only myself and my God know how much I love you, Chad.

CHAPTER THIRTEEN

"NEWCOME!"

Chad was in the library; his time when he was not acting as Nell's secretary was divided between the stables and the library, which Campions did not find strange since their Countess's time was similarly shared.

He was standing at the lectern, working, when Nell came in, his back to the door from her study by which she had entered. The few occasions on which they had been alone together were either in the library proper, or in the annexe. A little earlier Nell had seen Challenor walk by her window, away from the house, knew that Chad would likely be working there, and had immediately seized her opportunity to speak with him unchaperoned.

Chad turned, gave her his smile, which wrenched her heart. Dressed as he was, he was virtually indistinguishable in appearance from the aristocrats and gentry who had once besieged her, except that he was Chad, and none of them had stolen her heart from her bosom.

Nell treasured the smile for it was all that he gave her these days—they had reached the stage where they dared not touch.

"Lady Elinor?"

He was suddenly so grave, so proper, so all that he should be that the devil whispered in Nell's ear. Oh, to destroy his hard-won composure. She spoke, eyes glinting, dark brows lifting, her whole aspect one of such innocent wickedness that the man before her clutched at the shreds of his reason.

"I have not given up, you know, Newcome. I shall never give up!"

"I know," said Chad, his eyes smoking, Nell noted happily. Not so composed, after all, my love, she thought. Let us see if I can shake that nobly intransigent front of yours. "I know, Lady Elinor. You take after your ancestor in that."

"Oh, no," said Nell, still naughty. "It was his body he refused to surrender, whereas the body I refuse to surrender..." and she paused, her eyes hard on his face "...is yours."

Chad could not prevent his smile from broadening at her impudent wit.

"Do not smile, Newcome," commanded Nell severely. "You are not to smile when my heart is breaking."

"If I do not smile, Nell," replied Chad softly, "I shall shriek to the heavens for what they deny me."

"Oh, you feel as I do, then," she said. "How can you be so strong, to deny yourself and me so calmly?"

"As strong as you, Nell," he said, still standing aloof from her. "As strong as you."

"No, I am weak," she returned. "Touch me, Newcome. You will see how weak I am."

Chad put his hands behind his back. They now stood face to face, but apart, neither moving towards the other.

"Infinity," said Nell, pointing at the eighteen inches of parquet floor which separated them.

"An eternity," said Chad. "Two names for the same thing."

"And what name is there for love denied?" asked Nell.

"Honour," Chad returned, as quick as she.

"Honour?" Nell repeated sadly. "I think it a word for men to use."

"Ah, but you play a man's part, Lady Elinor," said Chad. "For you are Countess as a man is an earl. No husband gives you that title. It is yours by birth and by right. So, men's words are your words."

It was as though an arrow pierced Nell's heart, as though a bell had tolled, or a sentence had burned itself in letters of fire before her in the air. She almost staggered and fell. For he had unlocked the door, found the heart of the maze in which they stood, liberated them both from the bonds which bound them.

"Why, so I am," she said. "And their deeds are my deeds, their rights mine. I am blessed among women, for whatever a man can do, so may I do. Oh, Chad," and she laughed joyously. "You have played with words as other men play with dice, and this time your throw is so true that I, your Countess, salute you," and she dipped into a great curtsy before him, as though he were her monarch, chestnut head bent. "And now I must leave you, to think on what you have said—and to act!"

Why, what have I said to affect her so? thought Chad, puzzled, watching her face, glowing as it had not done since they parted, love refused, in the annexe all those miserable weeks ago.

Nell turned at the door, to find that he had not moved, had followed her going with his eyes alone.

"You do not ask me where I am bound, Newcome," she said, her eyes sparkling, her whole mien changed from the stoic one of the recent past.

"To your room, I suppose." For once he was at a loss for words.

"You suppose wrongly, Newcome. I am bound for the long gallery, to where my painted forebears hang, for I think that they have a message for me. You have reminded me of what I am, and what they are, and love may yet conquer all. It is *au revoir* I bid you, Newcome, not goodbye."

EYES STILL SHINING, Nell paced the long gallery, staring up at the family portraits, at the first Earl, godlike in his early eighteenth-century battle dress, banners and plumes, cannon smoking behind him. At the second Earl, Hanoverian George's minister, sardonic in dark blue court dress, the man who had founded the Campions stud, at the third Earl, who had combed Europe for the treasures which filled the house, and had refused office because he disliked his monarch, at the fourth Earl, who had died young, but not before he had created the library which was Challenor's treasure, and at her grandfather, his brother, painted in his old age by Sir Thomas Lawrence.

Their word had been law, they had defied kings, princes, done as they pleased, as the male Tallboyses had always done. She looked at the first Earl again; she had thought him the founder of the House of Tallboys until her grandfather had told her otherwise.

"Oh, no," he had said, one rainy evening, as she sat at his feet, looking at the first Earl. "He simply acquired for us the Malplaquet title. We go further back than that. Not him, my dear. He was already noble. Never forget that we are sprung from nothing, or so the legend says."

Strange that she had forgotten this, and that it should come back to her now.

"What does the legend say?" she had asked him, as he fell silent.

"Why, that one day in the mists of time, long ago, in King John's reign, the unmarried lady of Barthwaite rode from her manor, and, being tired, stopped at a cottage where a tall woodcutter rested on his axe. Ivo of the Woods was all the name he had.

"'You may give me a drink,' she said to him, 'For I have a great thirst.'

"'I would give you more than that, lady,' he said, bold eyes on her, leaving no doubt as to what he meant.

"'Why, so you may,' she said, looking at the size and strength of him, 'and in exchange I will give you myself and Barthwaite, too,' for she knew that here was the only man who could match and master her, and she would have him, for was not she the lady and he the serf?

"'I have no name to give you, lady,' he said.

"'Then I will give you one, woodcutter, and a good French one it shall be, and then you may give it to me when the priest weds us. You shall be Taillebois, the man who cuts wood, and so shall all be to whom we give life.'

"And so it was, and Taillebois—Tallboys—we are to this day, for we are all their descendants, and you, barring Ulric, are the last of the line, my dear."

"And is the story true, Grandfather?" she had asked him.

"I would like it to be so," he said, "if only to show that, noble or simple, we are all the same beneath our clothes. I am at one with the Radicals in that, if in nothing else."

Remembering this, Nell struck her hands together fiercely. She was the last lady of the line, and, through the first Earl's doing, she also stood as the last man, with all of a man's first rights and privileges. She knew what she had to do, and, being practical Nell Tallboys, who organised her life so well, she decided to organise it further—and at once.

"I shall go to York tomorrow," she said aloud, and she almost ran from the gallery, calling on Annie, her aunt Conybeare, and the butler, all of whom she would take with her to her house in York, which stood in the lee of the great cathedral.

"I have a mind to play, to shop, for a week," she lied to a puzzled Aunt Conybeare, "and my council shall rule Campions for me in my absence, for I shall take none of them with me. They may work while I dally, for the house there needs to shelter its owner a little."

EXACTLY WHEN Guy Shadwell first began to worry that he had heard nothing from his brother since he had left for Scotland he could not say.

All Guy's life his elder brother had loved and protected him. His relationship with his other brother Frederick had always been a cold one. But Shad had taught him to swim, to shoot and to ride—not as Shad rode, for Shad was a marvel with horses—and he had always encouraged him to study hard as well, the eleven years between them making Shad more of an uncle than a brother.

And when Shad was away at the wars he had written constantly to Guy. A little reserved in speech, on paper he was a witty and informative correspondent, and Guy had always looked eagerly for the post to bring him Shad's latest letter. He had tried to show them to his father, for Shad's letters to the Earl were stiff, dutiful things, the constraint between them operating on him, but his father had always pushed them away pleading, "No time."

Shad's last words to Guy as he had left for Glen Ruadh had been quite clear. "I shall write to you, Guy—but not immediately."

Time passed, and no letters came. At first, Guy thought nothing of it. He knew that Shad had been mortally hurt by the final breach with his father, but surely, he thought, he must have recovered sufficiently to write to the brother who he knew had always loved him? Unless, of course, he had cut himself off from everything that was related to Clermont, and that included Guy, too, which Guy found difficult to believe.

Shortly before Christmas, growing troubled, Guy wrote to Glen Ruadh, but nothing came back. He wrote again, still nothing, until one day, after his third despairing letter begging Shad to remember that he, Guy, still loved him, on a blustery day in early March, a letter came from Shad's factor at Glen Ruadh.

He wrote that correspondence had arrived so constantly for Lord Halstead that the factor, in my lord's continued absence, had opened it, and was further writing to say that if my lord had set out for Scotland he had certainly never reached there. What was worse was that this first letter had been two months on the way; a second from the factor, written with the last fortnight, was delivered only a few days later and said that my lord had still not arrived and asked for guidance.

Guy stared at the paper before him, face going slowly white. It was now clearly six months since Shad had flung out of Clermont House, announcing that he was off to Glen Ruadh, and no one had seen or heard from him since. Guy had thought him in his Highland fastness, refusing to acknowledge the rest of the world, which was bad enough, but to learn that he had dropped off the edge of the world... Guy had spoken to several of Shad's friends in London, none of whom had heard from him, and were themselves troubled by his disappearance from his old haunts, and lack of any news from him.

Carrying the letter, Guy went to his father's study, put them on the desk before him, and poured out the tale of Shad's disappearance.

"I would have a search made for him, Father," he finished. "But better that such an initiative came from you. Your name is a powerful one."

The Earl, who had stared, face hard, at Guy, while he spoke, looked down at his work again, said coldly, "Most convenient if he has disappeared. You may, after due formalities, be Halstead and my heir. A more satisfactory eventuality than I could have hoped for.''

The obedience which Guy had always shown to his father broke on that.

''No!'' he said violently. ''You shall not speak so. No! You wrong him, Father. You have always wronged him. Shad is good, brave and true, as the whole world knows, aside from yourself. What maggot works in your brain, sir, that you have never given him his due? The Duke himself—''

His father interrupted him. ''Do not bore me, Guy,'' he began.

''Bore you, sir! Bore you! It is time that you knew the truth about Shad—and about Frederick, too. Shad forbade me to tell that truth, but if by bad chance he is dead his death absolves me from my promise to him. It is time you knew what Frederick really was, and what Shad did to save the family honour and to spare you pain.''

He had his father's attention now. The Earl rose, face stern.

''Explain yourself, sir—or I will deal with you as I did with Halstead.''

''Oh, you may cut me off, too,'' said Guy furiously, quite unlike his usual mild and charming self. ''But you *shall* know the truth. Frederick's death was no accident as you and the world thought. Frederick shot himself, committed suicide. He...'' Guy choked on the words, could hardly say them. He ignored his father's suddenly ashen face, began again.

''Frederick loved boys—he always did. He could not live without his... vice. He frequented special houses... Shad knew, he always knew. I didn't know until just before his death when I heard him and Shad talking.

''He was being blackmailed, had been blackmailed for years, was threatened with exposure if he didn't pay large sums of money over. He was bleeding the estate dry to pay the swine off. And when ruin and exposure finally stared him in the face, because their demands became impossible

he . . . shot himself, leaving a letter for you, to tell you what
had happened, and why he did it.

"Shad found the letter, and Frederick, dead in the gun-
room at Pinfold—it was when he was recovering from that
dreadful wound he got in Spain. He knew what it would do
to you, and to the Clermont name, but particularly to you,
who loved him so, if you knew the truth. He fetched me, I
was there that weekend—you were over at Broadlands at the
time—and together we secretly arranged it to look like an
accident. No one ever guessed the truth."

The Earl's face was livid, ghastly. "And how do I know
that this remarkable story is the truth?"

"Oh, the agent knew that Frederick was robbing the estate. He may even have guessed why—but there's more than
that. Shad thought that he had destroyed the letter, but I—
and I don't know why I did it, I was only fourteen at the
time—but perhaps I felt that the truth should not be completely destroyed. I substituted blank paper for it, and Shad
burned that. I have the letter still, and you shall see it. He
never knew what I had done."

The Earl sat down, all his beliefs in ruins about him. He
could not speak. Guy, uncharacteristically voluble, continued. "And that, sir, should tell you how Shad loved you and
protected you and the family name both, for he dealt with
the blackmailers as well—how I never knew—and put
straight the estate which Frederick had nearly ruined. That
should tell you how unworthy you have been to prefer
Frederick to him, and now he is likely dead, taking your
unfounded dislike to the grave with him."

Guy saw that he had broken his father, and, even though
it was for Shad that he had done it, it gave him no pleasure.

"I believe you, sir," said the Earl, at last. "But I would
like to see the letter," and he sank his face into his hands, a
man suddenly grown old before his time. Which son he was
grieving for he could not have said, the one whom he had
wrongly valued, or the one he had never valued—and both
lost.

Finally, he raised his head, said, "You are saying that
Halstead set out for Scotland, but never reached there, and
has not been heard from since he left here?"

"That is so, sir." Guy's throat had closed, his revelations over; he could hardly speak. He had always thought that one day he might tell his father the truth about his two older brothers, but had never thought to do so in such tragic circumstances.

"Then I shall institute enquiries, and also I must...order my thoughts. Come to terms with what you have told me. You say that he did what he did to save me pain?"

"Yes," said Guy sturdily, "and to save Clermont's honour. Think of the scandal if anyone other than Shad had found him." He did not add that Frederick had been careless of that as well as of everything else—he did not need to. "Shad is what I said he was, good, and true, but you were always fixed on Frederick. He understood that, although it grieved him."

The Earl looked sadly at his youngest son, said, "It seems that I have never known any of you. I think that I have never properly valued you either, sir. You showed a shrewdness beyond your years when you saved the letter. When you have given it to me, you will leave me alone with it, and we must both pray that somehow, somewhere, Halstead still lives. My greatest punishment would be never to see him again, to rectify the lost years."

CHAPTER FOURTEEN

NELL HAD ARRIVED back from York late in the evening. She retired to her room without ceremony, without seeing her council; she pleaded tiredness, but sent a message to Henson that they should all meet in her study on the following morning, no exceptions.

She sat in her bed that evening eating buttered rolls and drinking hot chocolate, feeling one moment like the cat that had stolen the cream, and the next moment like the cat turned out into the rain at midnight. What would they say when she threw her bombshell on the carpet before them all in the morning? What would Chad say? Would he kiss her, or kill her? She had no idea how he would react.

She thought she knew how the others would, and she was inwardly bracing herself to face them. She could not sleep for excitement. The lawyer whom she had brought back with her from York was given a room on his own—and told to talk to no one. His cynical old face was even more cynical than usual as he ate his excellent food, and drank his good wine.

Morning broke, the sun was up, and the scents of an early spring were everywhere. Nell dressed with uncommon care in a deep green wool, cut on classic lines, belted high under her waist, and which emphasised the depth of her magnificent bosom, and although the neck was high with a tiny man's cravat the whole effect was voluptuous. She looked a far cry from the icy Nell Tallboys of the past.

She could not eat her breakfast, the food stuck in her throat, and she could hardly wait to reach her study, Aunt Conybeare consigned to the drawing-room; this was not an occasion at which she ought to be present. The lawyer Nell had banished to an ante-room, to be sent for, if required, and Nell had a stack of legal documents on the desk before her. I am armed at all points, she thought. A military metaphor seemed suitable, seeing that she was about to deal with an ex-trooper.

Promptly at ten, the appointed hour, her Privy Council arrived. Almost as though they knew that this was a solemn occasion they were all dressed *à point*. Henson and Challenor were grave in charcoal-grey, Henson was wearing cream riding breeches tucked into shining riding boots; later in the day he was to tour the tenant farms in the Riding around Campions.

Even Aisgill was smart in his country clothing, and Chad was wearing his best black silk suit, and he had, in Nell's honour, although she did not know this, tied his cravat in a waterfall favoured by the late leader of London society, George Brummell.

Standing before his mirror that morning, Chad had had a flash of memory. He had seen himself standing before another mirror with a splendid frame of eagles soaring high above its top. And he was tying his cravat, and talking to someone behind him, whom he could not see, "And this is a waterfall," he had said, and tied the cravat *so*, and then everything disappeared again.

The flashes were disturbing because they were inconsequential, had no beginning, and no end, came from nowhere, and disappeared into nowhere. This one was particularly disturbing because he had felt that his surroundings were luxurious, and how could that be?

All in all, he looked severely magnificent, but then he always did. Severe was a good word to describe him. Well, thought Nell, mischievously, we shall see if severe is a good word for him in another hour. She begged leave to doubt it.

"Lady Elinor," said Henson, almost reproachfully, "this is not our usual day to meet you."

Nell smiled at him. "I agree, but this is not going to be a usual day for anyone."

Henson, she saw, frowned. He did not like surprises, he wanted life to be orderly. Chad, Nell was amused to see, looked wary, as though a sniper were hidden behind the boulle cabinet in the corner. What intuitive message was passing between them that of the four of them he seemed to be the only one to have some inkling that she was about to commit a most outrageous act?

"I have called you in..." she said, quite cool; she was, indeed, astonished at how level her voice was. She could see herself in the Venetian glass over the hearth, and she looked quite calm, the portrait of a lady totally in command of herself, not one about to breach every canon of etiquette which controlled the actions of ladies.

She began again, almost absently, "I have called you all in to tell you that I am about to follow the advice which you have so frequently given me." She paused dramatically; some devil inside her was drawing this out, so that what she was about to say would be all the more devastating to them all when they heard it.

It was Henson who broke when she did not continue. "And that is, Lady Elinor?"

"Oh," said Nell, "there is only one piece of advice on which you have all agreed, ever since I inherited, and I am about to take it. I have decided to marry."

Nell saw Chad's face change. He undoubtedly thought that he had lost her, that she had done the honourable thing, gone to York to arrange a loveless marriage which would remove them both from temptation. She smiled inwardly.

As usual, Henson constituted himself spokesman, forestalling Aisgill. "I think that I speak for us all," he said, "in offering you my felicitations, Lady Elinor. Your decision is welcome, if a little overdue. I take it that we may expect suitors to be arriving here at Campions."

"No, you may not," said Nell, smiling sweetly; she was beginning to enjoy herself, even if Chad wasn't. "I have already decided whom I will marry."

There was uproar. All but Chad began to speak as one, her Countess-ship quite forgotten, she was amused to note. Chad was silent, his face more severe than ever. Oh, how he was suffering, her darling, her poor love; her heart bled for him.

"Not Ulric Tallboys, after all, Lady Elinor," began Aisgill, red in the face. "Not after what Jackson has told us of him. You could not be so unwise."

"No, not Cousin Ulric—" said Nell, to be interrupted, almost rudely, by Henson.

"And not, I hope, to someone whom you met only last week in York, and hardly know, I trust."

"Oh, no," said Nell, "I would not inflict Cousin Ulric on you and Campions. Nor is it someone I met last week in York. That is not my way, either. But it is perfectly true that I went to York to arrange this marriage."

She paused, held them all in turn with her eyes, finally arriving at Chad, almost compelled him to look at her, which he did, so that for a moment it seemed to Nell that there was no one in the room but the pair of them.

"I am," she said, "entitled to arrange my own marriage, for am I not Countess of Malplaquet with exactly the same rights and powers as though I were the Earl? I am, in short, in the same case as a man, and as a man I need no one to arrange a marriage for me and I may propose to my future partner as a man would. I therefore propose a marriage which will please me and benefit Campions.

"I have decided that in view of my...inclination for him, and the talents and devotion to duty which he has shown since he arrived here, I can do no better than to ask Mr. Chad Newcome to marry me, and for you all to support me as I do so. Accordingly, I formally ask you, Mr. Newcome, to take my hand, and Malplaquet, and all that goes with Malplaquet's name with it."

Chad, who had gone quite white, so that Nell's stunned Privy Council could see at once that this was as great a surprise to him as to them, said something inarticulate, strode to the window, and stood with his back to the room and to Nell, staring out at the wild and beautiful view over the moors. It was plain to them all that he was the prey to strong emotion, was struggling to control himself.

The stunned silence gave way to uproar, Henson, Aisgill, Challenor all talking at once. Nell ignored them, and in the moment of silence which followed as the three of them endeavoured to collect themselves and their scattered wits she said steadily, face white, coming from behind her desk, to pass her Privy Council, addressing Chad's straight back, "You reminded me, Mr. Newcome, sir, that I stand in the place of the Earl. I ask you to recognise that fact, turn to face your Countess, and give her your considered answer."

Behind her, her Privy Council muttered as Chad slowly restored his self-control. He now knew why she had reacted as she did that day in the library, when he had so idly said that she stood in the Earl's place, and he could guess why she had gone to York. He refused to turn, for Nell had placed him at a disadvantage by the manner of her proposal, and he was seeking to restore the balance between them.

Henson spoke. "May I advise, madam?"

"No, you may not," said Nell again. "I am Earl and Countess here. I await Mr. Newcome's answer."

Chad stood, unmoving. And Nell, suddenly nervous, for oh, he was strong, stronger even than she might have thought, would give her neither yea nor nay easily, would make her bleed her heart dry, to test how true this proposal was, said, "I may advise *you*, Mr. Newcome, as you have no lawyer, no family to help you. The special license for our marriage, given at York, should you wish to accept my offer, stands on the desk here. The marriage settlement between us, which is the same as I would offer any man, gentle or simple, is also there for you to sign. My grandfather's ring is ready for your finger. As the Earl would give his pledge to the partner he chose, I will give you mine. So do I honour you, Mr. Newcome," and as she had done that last day in the library she sank back in her most elaborate curtsy.

At last, Chad turned, and the man they saw, although neither he, nor they, knew it, was the man he had been before memory deserted them.

His soldiers in Spain would have known his manner, as his fellow officers and the Duke had done. As Jackson had shrewdly noted, when unselfconscious, as he now was, he reverted to the haughty aristocrat birth and military training had made him. Cold, hard and imperious, it was the face of a man who gave orders, and expected them to be obeyed.

"Madam," he said, "though the manner is not one I would have chosen, you do me the greatest honour a woman could do a man. You offer me, a landless nobody, taken naked from the moors, the noblest prize in England. You

are sure that you wish to do this thing? That you understand what you are offering me?''

"None better," answered Nell, quaking internally, for all
her brave front, for here was a Chad she had never seen, nor
her Privy Council either. "I offer you myself, and the
guardianship of Malplaquet, for guardians are what we shall
be. We shall jointly hold it in trust. It owns us. We do not
own it. Those are the terms of the settlement.''

Aisgill spoke, breaking the paralysis which had seized the
three of them at Nell's monstrous proposal. "Madam, I
cannot remain silent in the face of this.''

"But you will, Aisgill, you will," said Nell, not turning
her head. "For I am Earl here, and you would not so have
spoken to my grandfather, without he asked you to. I do not
ask you.''

Aisgill would not be quiet. "The man may have wife and
children, he has no name, he is nobody...''

"As to the first," said Nell, "I think not. As for a name,
I shall give him that. As with the first of the line, so with the
last. Should he so wish, he shall be Tallboys.''

Chad had remained silent. If anything, his hauteur had
grown.

"No," he said. "If I accept, madam, you will take *my*
name. I will not take yours. You may be Countess, and Earl,
I grant you that, but you will still be my wife, and I shall not
be your servant. I shall be your partner—or nothing. And,
should I accept, they—" and he waved a hand with the utmost arrogance at the Privy Council "—they must accept
me, and accept, too, that I had no part in your decision to
do this thing, that you made it freely and without my
knowledge, that I shall be master here, as you will be mistress, but they will still advise.''

Henson had said nothing so far, only now, before Chad
made his final decision, spoke.

"You have still not given a straight answer, man, and
what the world will say if your answer is yes will be a scandal and a year's wonder, and I will advise you now. If
Campions needs a master, and Malplaquet an heir, and you
are her choice, and I would not have chosen you, yet your
answer must be yes.''

Of them all he was the one whom Nell and Chad would have thought the most adamant against such a marriage.

"You may offer me your advice, as I said—" and Chad's face was closed and cold "—I did not say that I would take it."

"So you refuse me," said Nell, white to the lips, head high, bleeding internally; her gamble had failed, after all.

"Oh, no," said Chad, and smiled at her for the first time, his brilliant white smile. "In honour, I could not accept you in less than marriage, in honour, I accept your offer of marriage, and now, in honour, I must offer you. Lady Elinor, will you marry me? I can give you nothing but my signature on a piece of paper, and my love and reverence for you, ever and always."

And he bowed his proud head in answer to her earlier curtsy, while Aisgill hissed, and old Challenor looked bemused, and Henson's face was a sardonic mask.

Nell murmured a whispered, "Yes," suddenly shy, "yes, with all my heart," and curtsied again. He put out his hand to lift her, kissed her hand, and then she pulled from her thumb, where she had placed it before she came into the meeting, her grandfather's ring, the ring which the first Earl had been given by Prince Eugene of Savoy after the battle of Malplaquet.

"I seal our betrothal with this," she said, handing it to him, for him to slip on his finger, and then he pulled from his pocket the lace handkerchief which she had given him at the time of Sir Chesney's visit.

"My lady, I have little to give you, so you would honour me by receiving back the favour which you gave me. I have carried it ever since."

Nell took the handkerchief, after he had kissed it, and she too kissed it, before tying it to her belt.

The ice which had enfolded them both throughout the whole passage broke as Chad finished speaking. The face which he had shown them lost its sternness, Nell's lost her air of cool command, and for a moment the look which passed between them was unguarded, and of the fiercest passion. The Privy Council could have no doubt but that this was a marriage for love.

"And now we must fetch the lawyer who has been patiently waiting in the ante-room, settlement papers shall be signed, the parson brought from Keighley, and the marriage shall be solemnised in Campions chapel tomorrow, with Campions people around us."

"So soon," said Henson.

"No delay." Nell was firm. "Neither he nor I wish to wait, I am sure. And I have no wish for outsiders here."

"Sir Chesney..." began Henson, to fall silent at Nell's raised eyebrows. "No," he said resignedly. "This is enough of a turn-up, without having Sir Chesney's bellowings about it, begging your pardon for my disrespect, Lady Elinor, Mr. Newcome," and his sardonic eye took in Chad. Like the others, he had noticed his changed demeanour during the proposal ceremony, and that Chad had now reverted to the pleasant man he had been since he had first recovered from the confusion which had gripped him on his arrival at Campions.

He was not to know that Chad's own soldiers had always noticed the difference between Chad in a tight corner, the commander on the battlefield, and the courteous man he was in daily life.

Aisgill had the last word when all the legal business was over, and Chad and Nell had retired to the long gallery, where Nell had said that he must be properly introduced to those who had preceded him.

"It might be worse," he said to Henson and Challenor. "He is young, personable, has many talents, has obviously been a soldier, and a gentleman, but who and what he is God knows. We probably never shall." He hesitated. "The thief taker Jackson said a thing I thought was strange at the time when he last left us. He said—and God knows how he knew what even I was not sure of—that passion lay between them—that I was not to worry about the turn events might take, that Lady Elinor and Campions would be safe with Newcome. God grant it may be so. She has leapt into the dark today, and taken Campions with her."

Challenor spoke for the first time. "There was never any stopping Lady Nell. She is a true Tallboys, and the first Earl

would have been proud of her. As for the man, I think him
honest, but as you say, Aisgill, only time will tell.'' He
paused. ''He is a good bookman, and that says much for
him.''

CHAPTER FIFTEEN

NEITHER OF THEM spoke until they reached the long gallery. Once inside, now alone, permitted—nay, encouraged for the first time to be alone, Chad turned to her.

"It is not too late to change your mind—" he began.

Nell interrupted him, her expression dangerous. "You regret your proposal to me, then?"

"No, not that," he said. "Never that. But you, are you sure that you know what awaits you? You rule Campions, but what of the rest of the world? It can be harsh, unfeeling, to those who break the code which binds us."

Chad said "us" without thinking, making himself one of the great ones of the world, part of the cousinry, the network of nobility which owned and ruled England.

Nell was so troubled by his questions that she did not notice this unconscious assumption, and nor did he.

"Oh," she said, lip curling, "they have always disapproved of me. I have simply given them a real reason for their dislike. And you, are you afraid to marry me? Or is your honour troubling you again? It need not; we are to be married, and honourably. I have no fear that you will do other than deal well with me and Campions—which is more than I could have said had I chosen to marry Ulric, or another of his kind."

He took her hand, and kissed it. He could wait now, to love her as he wished to, for when they finally met together in her great bed their union would be blessed, not something illicit, love celebrated hugger-mugger in a corner, but nobly, in the open, Nell's people about her at the wedding ceremony.

"I hope," he said simply, "that I shall prove worthy of what you have given me."

"No fears for me on that score," said Nell, "and now I must show you your inheritance, the painted images of those who have gone before you," and she waved a hand at the Tallboyses who lined the walls, their wives beside them "Bravery and beauty combined," she said with a smile, "until they reach me. For bravery—" and her smile at him was a mischievous one "—I showed today, but as to beauty—I have no illusions about that."

Chad knew that she was not saying this simply for him to deny it indignantly. He took her by the shoulders and turned her towards him, gently held her chin in his big hands, and tipped her head back slightly. "I do not think," he said softly, "that you do yourself justice. Beauty without character is not worth having, and character is beauty, and so you are the most rare of Tallboys ladies, since you possess both."

"Oh, my love," and Nell's smile was dazzling, "you play with words again. Were you a lawyer, after all, and not a soldier? Challenor says that you are a man who should have been a scholar, but I have seldom seen a scholar who looked as though he could go into the ring with the Game Chicken and acquit himself respectably!

Chad laughed at that, and released her so that they paced the gallery together, and before she introduced her recent ancestors to him she told him the story of the lady of Barthwaite and Ivo of the Woods.

He listened to her in silence, and thought of the gulf which she had leapt in order to offer him herself, and thought that in the shock which had followed that offer, against all common sense and urgings of the head, he had followed his heart and now on the morrow, like the lady and her serf, she was to be his.

His bright blue eyes hard on her, the eyes with which he had done such execution, he said, "And you are the lady and I am Ivo?"

"If you like," she answered him. "As the beginning, so the end. I wonder what my grandfather would have said, were he to have known of this day. But he told me once that all men and women are the same under their clothes, so we are not Countess and secretary, but simply Chad and Nell, man and woman.''

"Chad and Nell." His voice was grave. "So be it, then. And you have no regrets?"

"None, and that is an end of that. I know that you and I will serve Campions well, and love one another in the doing, and that is all I need to know. The omens are good, Chad."

Chad nodded his head, and let her tell him of the pictured men and women, long dead, who had sprung from that meeting in the woods. He thought of the dark behind him, and the brightness before him, and paradoxically, now that his future was secure, was settled, he suddenly needed to know his past. He had thought himself reconciled to his loss of memory; indeed, in the days when he had first come to full consciousness of himself and his surroundings, it had been enough for him to know that he existed.

He knew that Henson and the others had made enquiries about him, but everything had led nowhere. He had appeared on the moor as though he had been dropped from heaven, and none had known nor seen him before he had been found lost and wandering.

Short of his memory returning to him, his past was gone, not to be recovered, it seemed, with no clue to lead him to his origins. And then, as Campions claimed him and he became part of it, first in the stables and later as Nell's secretary, that had come to seem enough. The brief flashes of memory annoyed him, and his attempts to remember distressed him so much by their uselessness that he abandoned them altogether.

Except that now he was to marry Nell he had a sudden passionate wish to know himself.

"Perhaps," he said, when her tale was done, and they were to return to the others, "when we have been married for a little, we might try to find where I came from, how I arrived on the moor."

"We must have no secrets between us," said Nell. "When Jackson left us last month I asked him to try to trace your past. He wrote privately to me, two days ago, that all his efforts so far had ended in failure. He had scoured the Rid-

ing, and you had not been seen before you were discovered
begging by the farmer. He also said something I thought
strange—that he connected the rifle with you, and that when
his search in the North was ended he would visit London to
try again to speak to Charles Halstead, to discover whether
he had sold, lost, or even had the rifle stolen from him. His
answer might give us some lead to the assassin, or even, unlikely as it sounds, to the mystery of your origins."

"He told me that, too," Chad said, and frowned. Somehow Charles Halstead's name always had the power to disturb him. "But I cannot think what the rifle has to do with
me, except that I found it by the man who tried to kill you."

"Chad, my love," said Nell quietly, taking his hand, distressed by the unhappiness on his face. "Let us not talk of
this now. I am marrying you, not your past, and what I
know of you, as all Campions knows, and Henson and
Aisgill admit, is good and true.

"The future is all that matters to me. I cannot think your
past disgraceful. Unfortunate, perhaps...and now I fear we
must return to the others. Tonight we dine with the Privy
Council, and after we must retire separately as the conventions must be honoured. We shall not meet again until we
meet in the chapel. I must go to Aunt Conybeare tomorrow
morning, and you will be attended before the wedding by
Challenor. Henson shall give the bride away, and Aisgill, as
is fitting since he first rescued you, shall stand at your side
as your best man."

Her face was full of mischief. "I am only sorry that Rajah cannot be present. He shall have a new set of plumes,
and we shall both visit him after the ceremony so that he
may know that we have not forgotten him!"

Chad bowed solemnly. "It is, as you said to me when we
last parted, *au revoir*, and not goodbye. I trust and pray that
you may never regret today's work, my gracious lady."

"Not I," said Nell. "And now Aunt Conybeare and
Campions must be told that their mistress has found her
master."

AFTER DINNER, a formal occasion, all the participants
splendidly dressed and the best dinner service—the china

from the present given to the third Earl by Catherine the Great of Russia after he had taken her to bed, the silver given him by a Bavarian princess for similar favours, and the great epergne in the centre of the table showing Hercules killing the Hydra, brought home in triumph after a conquest so noble that he never even named the lady—fetched out in honour of Nell Tallboys's marriage to her servant.

Afterwards Nell and Chad, equally formal, bowed and parted to their own quarters, Nell to her splendid suite of rooms, Chad to his small and humble pair in the attic under the roof.

Before he went there, he returned to the study, to pick up his copy of the settlement, to study what he had let himself in for by marrying Nell.

The door to his rooms was ajar, and someone had lit the candles there. He raised his eyebrows, walked in, to discover Henson waiting for him, leaning against a chest of drawers, the book from Chad's nightstand open in his hand. It was a copy of *Les Liaisons Dangereuses* in the original French.

He raised his eyes from it as Chad entered, made no apology for his presence, merely said coolly, "So you read French, too. When did you discover that?"

"Early on," said Chad. "It hardly seemed worth mentioning."

"Difficult to plumb all your talents," drawled Henson, and Chad did not know whether it was praise or criticism which he was being offered. "But the one talent which might benefit you, your personal memory, is still missing."

"Yes," said Chad briefly, "I am not fooling you, though the expression on your face suggests you do not necessarily believe me."

"Oh, I believe you," returned Henson, his face expressionless. "Your choice of reading is interesting—in the circumstances."

Chad chose to ignore any inference which he might draw from Henson's suggestion that a novel which dwelt so constantly on human wickedness and sexual intrigue might have some point, some connection with Chad's own astonishing rise to fortune. He said instead, "To what do I owe your visit?"

Henson closed the book, put it carefully down. He was particularly finely dressed, at all points one with the mighty whom he so faithfully served.

"I came to warn you," he drawled.

"Ah," said Chad, face watchful. "I thought your acquiescence in Lady Elinor's wishes odd, in view of your care for her and her interests. Of you all, I would have expected opposition to such a marriage to come from you."

Henson shrugged his beautifully tailored shoulders. "And what, my fine young man, would the lady have cared for my opposition? Nothing. She was determined to have you. No, I could only lose by gainsaying her. I have watched you since you came into the house as her secretary, and—" He paused.

"And?" said Chad, giving him nothing.

"And—and nothing. From the moment you began to recover yourself you revealed a man of education, a man who has undoubtedly been a soldier. There is also no doubt that at great risk to yourself you saved my Countess's life, and for that I am grateful. Nell Tallboys is a remarkable woman. It is a pleasure to serve her. But, on the other hand, who the devil are you? And have *you*, despite what my Countess believes, angled for this match, used the attraction you undoubtedly possess for her to make yourself master of Campions?"

"Guardian, guardian only," was Chad's answer to that.

"Words," said Henson. "You may or may not be as honest as you seem, but if you are not, beware. My duty is to her, and only to you through her. She is Countess, you but her consort, and if you prove false, why, God help you, for Campions will deal with you, sir, and hardly."

Rage stirred in Chad. The temper which he usually kept in firm control, the temper which he knew must have played its part in his old life—perhaps, unwisely used, he had sometimes thought, might have brought him to destitution and beggary—rose and filled his throat. His hands clenched.

He mastered himself. His true inclination would have been to seize Henson by the throat, force him to his knees, make him retract the unspoken accusation. Reason told him that the man was a good servant, the best, who sought to protect his mistress from harm.

The calmness of his voice did not deceive Henson; the man who could control Rajah, charm Nell, and charm also the men and women about him, was no tame tiger. The hint of wildness behind the self-control was always there. He shivered a little despite himself as Chad spoke, "Rest easy, Mr. Henson, sir. I shall guard Campions, as I would Lady Elinor, with my life. Do you be careful that you are as honest with both as I intend to be."

"Bravely spoken," replied Henson, giving not an inch himself. "Enough—we know where we stand." He walked to the door. "I bid you goodnight, Mr. Newcome. From now on I serve you, not you me. I must tell you that the staff of Campions, indoor and out, have been informed of tomorrow's ceremony. Representatives of all parts of the house and estate will be at the chapel. The rest will attend you later, and you will be expected to show yourself and your lady to them, in due form.

"Tomorrow morning Challenor will escort you to the guest suite, and will help you to dress, with the assistance of old Wilson, the late Earl's valet, brought from his retirement to be of service to the late Earl's successor. From what I have seen of you, you will play your part properly. I bid you goodnight, and I hope that your dreams are more pleasant than I hear they usually are."

He bowed. Chad returned the compliment, saying coolly, "I know, Mr. Henson, that anything you arrange will be both correct and apropos. You need have no fears that I will let my lady and Campions down."

He was gone, and Chad sat down on the bed, his hands sweating, his whole body racked from the necessity to hold himself in. But, in all honesty, he thought wryly, what could he expect? He had told Nell earlier of the commotion which this strange marriage would cause, and he could not fault Henson for seeking to protect his mistress's interests.

He slept at last, for sleep, not surprisingly, was long in coming, but he did not dream until daybreak, and then his dreams were confused, but not painful, until the last one.

He was in a hot and crowded room. He thought that he was
drunk. The men around him were laughing and staring; one
pulled at his arm, saying, "Quiet, Chad, quiet," but he
would not be quiet, he would have his say, and improbably,
as he started from sleep, it was Nell's name that he was crying out, and where and to whom he said it he did not know.

NELL ALSO COULD NOT sleep. First there had been Aunt
Conybeare to tell, to ask her to be Nell's matron of honour, to hold her bouquet when the ring was placed on her
finger. As she had expected, even Aunt Conybeare's usual
placidity was shaken by such momentous news. "But Newcome," she had said, bewildered. "I knew that you liked
him, of course, and he saved you. But to marry him!"

"I love him, Aunt," she had said simply. "And I had
never thought to love anyone." She did not say that she
loved him beyond reason; she did not need to, for even innocent old Aunt Conybeare knew that she would not have
married her servant, of unknown origin, unless her passion
for him was so strong that it transcended common sense,
and the conventions that governed the class to which Nell
belonged.

The servant's hall thought the same. "Wants a man in her
bed, a real man, don't she?" being the most common comment, and said admiringly, not sniggeringly. "Better than
Maister Ulric and them pretty boys what have come up here
from London. One of us now, you might say." For Chad,
although not a seeker after popularity, was popular. From
the moment he had tamed Rajah, he had been accepted, and
there were many who connected that event and the marriage. "Our Nell's a grand lass, and needs a real man to hold
her," being another remark. "Besides, he's almost a gentleman himself, for all he was taken starving off the moor.
You might say that Campions is all he's ever known, seeing
that he remembers nothing before he came here."

The last was the butler's comment, and served as Cam-
pion's opinion of the match. The only thing lacking in him
being, as young Seth said, "Pity he's not really a York-
shireman, but he's a tyke by adoption."

And so, as a fine March day dawned, Campions prepared for the event which many had feared might never happen—the marriage of its Countess, and the settlement of Malplaquet's lands.

And so, once that twentieth day dawned, Catherine proposed his abdication. She hesitated, had written today about
heaven—to surrender with Countess, and the rejection of
Aongabbse it does.

CHAPTER SIXTEEN

NELL HAD AWOKEN that morning with such a feeling of well-
being as she had never experienced before. She stretched
herself, lifting her arms above her head, so that her toes almost touched the bottom of the great bed.

She did not wait for Annie to come, but leapt from it, ran
to the window, pulled back the curtains, and looked out
across the lawns, beyond the giant fountain, where sea-
nymphs and dolphins, the latter spouting water to the
heavens, frolicked in the kind of joy she was feeling, beyond the grove of trees planted by the third Earl, the giant
obelisk commemorating the first Earl's glory, to the moors
above them, rising grand and glorious, until they reached
the Throne of God itself, far, far beyond her sight—but not
her memory.

Oh, she had defeated them all, Chad included! She
thought of his dear face when she had finally cornered him,
how it had changed from the stern severity it normally wore
to the joy and delight he had shown her as they parted in the
long gallery, secure in the knowledge that their love was
outrageous, but that they were about to fulfil it in honourable marriage.

Yes, Nell Tallboys was about to defy them all. Charles
Halstead, when he heard of this, could make further disgraceful bets, tongues would buzz wherever she went—but
what of that? She was the lady of Barthwaite, who had
married whom she pleased, or the first Earl, who had made
his own rules on the battlefield and in life. Tallboyses all,
living up to the house's motto, emblazoned on the ribbon
which ran below the arms: "As the beginning, so the end."

And the arms themselves, the shield which bore three tree
stumps, in honour of Ivo. She hugged herself. I shall peti-

on the College of Heralds. I shall have the shield divided, the trees on one side, Rajah rearing on the other, for Rajah is Chad, the strong man who tamed the strong horse—and is Countess. Unknowingly, she echoed the comments of er staff.

Yes, she was the lady of Campions, and today would marry her choice, the first time both parties to a marriage had proposed to one another, she dared swear.

Annie came in, Aunt Conybeare behind her. Annie was carrying a breakfast tray. Aunt Conybeare carried nothing but a grave face. She said what Chad had. "It is not too late to change your mind, Nell."

"Change my mind!" Nell had jumped into bed again, was stuffing hot rolls into her mouth, drinking coffee this morning. "Why should I do that, when I am marrying my heart's desire?"

Aunt Conybeare sighed. Nell had never looked before as she now did. It was almost, outrageously, as though her lover had already pleasured her, and, had not Aunt Conybeare known for sure that both partners to this mismatch had spent the night chastely apart, she would have thought the opposite. There would be no shy bride in Campions chapel today, that was for sure!

Nell's joy continued, through the bath, its water full of scents, and through the dressing for the ceremony. The parson had arrived shortly after dawn, sent for by Henson, and after she was dressed she went into her drawing-room, so that the bed could be stripped, new linen put on it, herbs strewn between the sheets, a new fire lit in the grate, all to celebrate Campions's proudest day for many years.

Annie had put a little bag under the pillow. "And what is that for?" Nell had said.

Annie blushed. "It is to bless the bed," she said shyly. "Granny Goodman says that the Mother will give you a son, after the night's work, if a virgin places it there, and the bride goes virgin to her man."

"A son!" Nell was enraptured. She, who had scorned men and marriage, could hardly bear to wait for her true love's child. She knew that when Annie and old Granny Goodman spoke of the Mother they meant the Earth

Mother of the old religion which had never really died out in these parts. A century earlier and Granny Goodman might have been in danger of being burned as a witch. Now she prescribed her herbs and simples to the suffering, and blessed marriages, high and low.

The thought of a child changed Nell's mood. She became girlish and trembling, not the madcap who had risen with the dawn. Aunt Conybeare, who had left to eat her own breakfast, returned to find her niece as modest as a bride might be, except that every now and then a fit of such delight passed over her that her face took on the shining aspect of her early morning ecstasy.

Finally, carrying a spray of early spring flowers, brought from the hothouse, Aunt Conybeare, resplendent in deep blue satin, with Nell herself in cream, a pearl circlet in her hair, a small string of pearls around her neck, Chad's handkerchief tucked into the lemon silk sash at her waist, walked downstairs to the great salon where Henson, Chalenor, the butler and the senior servants of the house, including her housekeeper, magnificent in black satin, awaited her.

They bowed as low when she walked in as they would have done had she been marrying Britain's premier Duke, instead of her former stable hand.

Henson, who seemed to have constituted himself as a kind of benevolent grand vizier, despite his private thoughts, said, "Madam, I am to tell you that, if you are prepared, everything is in train. The groom awaits you in the chapel, the priest is at the altar. The ring and the book are ready. If you will take my arm, I shall escort you there."

He bowed low, low, and when he straightened up his eyes were hard on her, and the message was Aunt Conybeare's, "It is not too late," but Nell knew what she wanted, and shy and trembling although she now was, all her bold hardihood quite gone, she was a girl again, the girl Henson remembered from his first day at Campions when he had walked into the Earl's study to see her standing by old Malplaquet's side.

"You know the way, Henson," she said. "And today it is your privilege to give away your Countess and . . . revive

Malplaquet's line, which otherwise would die with me." For she had no faith that Ulric would do anything but waste himself and the estate.

Together, they walked through the great house, past everything which Nell had known all her life, her staff behind her, past lines of her other servants, the occasional, "God bless you, my lady," offered by the bolder spirit.

And there, before her, was the paved forecourt to the chapel, where another group of servants was set, waiting for those behind her to take their places, and there at the altar he stood, Aisgill beside him, magnificent in his livery as master of the horse, a livery worn only on great occasions such as this. Nothing, nothing, was to be omitted from this wedding, all was to be done in proper form, until finally, on Henson's arm, Aunt Conybeare behind her, she walked towards Chad, and they were there together, the wondering parson before them, Challenor now at the pianoforte to play for them.

Joy contained, her face as white as his, bride and groom suddenly nervous, bold spirits though they normally were, faced one another, for life, as it were, he tall, his black curls clustering about his head, wearing a fine suit once worn by Nell's grandfather, possessing neither name nor fortune, only the manifold talents of which Henson had spoken.

Nell, for her part, had been granted a strange beauty, which came from knowing that she was loved, that she had found a mate for whom she could feel respect, as well as passion, who had held off when he could have taken her on the library floor as though she had been a poor girl from the village, but who had preferred to leave her, so that she and he might keep their honour intact.

The service began, and when the priest issued his challenge to any who might gainsay the match there was silence, and then they were man and wife, neither voice faltering, and when Chad pushed on Nell's finger the marriage ring of the Tallboyses the expression on his face and his smouldering blue eyes told Nell all that she wanted to know.

And then they processed out of the chapel. Tables had been spread with food and drink in the long gallery, and the only guests were Nell's people—the marriage was a marriage for Campions and no one else. Bride and groom and the Privy Council ate nothing, but drank a toast proposed by the butler, and enthusiastically seconded by every voice.

Nell thought that the long day would never end; her face ached from smiling. Later, as she had promised, they visited the stables, and Nell's small bouquet was hung over Rajah's stable door.

The day was fine, and hand in hand they walked the length of the gardens to stare together at the moor where Chad had been found, a barely conscious derelict, and now it and Campions were his, as much as they could be anybody's.

But still they were not private. Tenant farmers came in, to see their lady and her chosen husband, until at last evening arrived, and now they were to dine alone for the first time, in the great state dining hall, in the same splendour as the night before, but now as the Countess and her husband.

For a moment, they were alone, and Chad embraced her, kissed her cheek, saying softly, "A pledge for tonight, Mrs. Newcome," and then the door opened, and the servants entered with the food, and facing one another, absurdly, at each end of the table, they ate the fine fare set before them, more to honour the staff who had prepared it than to satisfy their non-existent hunger. The true hunger they felt was for one another.

At the meal's end, the double doors were thrown open by the butler, and Henson entered, the Privy Council at his heels, carrying bottles of wine, for yet another toast.

"It has long been the custom in this part of the world," he announced, his eyes for once merry, "for bride and groom to be publicly put to bed before their servants and dependants. But these, I think, are more civilised times. We shall not demand that of you, my lady Countess. Instead, you shall have Campions to light your way to bed."

He put down his glass, beckoned to them both, said, "Come," and Nell, wondering what she was about to see, walked from the dining-room into the great hall from which the stairs rose for full two storeys of the house.

Before her, to the stairs, was an alleyway of servants, each
carrying a candle. On every step two servants stood, also
holding candles, and along the landing, and all the way to
the state bedroom where Nell and Chad were to sleep, Nell's
lonely days being over, servants lined the way, candles in
their hands, smiling and lighting them, as Henson had said,
to their bed.

Nell felt tears pricking her eyes, and each man or woman
said as she passed, "God bless you both, and Campions,
too," until finally they stood at the great oak doors, which
Henson threw open, bowing—and, at last, they were alone.

Nell sank on to the bed, eyes alight, as though the flames
through which she had passed had found their way home
there.

"You see, my love, you are accepted. Campions wel-
comes you. Let the rest of the world think what it will—here
we are at home."

Chad stood for a moment, looking down at her. The day
seemed unreal. Any moment he expected to open his eyes to
find himself—where? At this point of fulfilled love and triumph his lack of a name and past seemed the doubly cruel;
he felt that he had nothing to offer his mistress, and he said
so.

"No," said Nell, passionately, opening her arms to him.
"You offer me yourself, and what is better than that? Oh, I
am unmaidenly, I should be shrinking. Perhaps—" and she
coloured "—that will come later."

Nell knew that she was not being strictly truthful.
Whether it was the effect of the long day, or the many eyes
upon them which knew exactly what they were going to do
on the great bed, once she and Chad were alone together—
just as though the pair of them were Princess and Rajah,
performing for Campions—she did not know. She only
knew that the maidenly reserve which she had felt for so
long and which had flown away from the moment in which
she had first met Chad had returned some time during the
wedding ceremony and was with her again.

She looked up at him almost fearfully. She felt her legs
weak beneath her, sank on to the bed, and everything about
her alerted the man before her to what had happened.

His viking, his valkyrie had gone; the passionate woman passionately demanding fulfilment from her mate had disappeared. Nell Newcome was what Nell Tallboys had never been with him, the shy virgin, who loved her new husband, but was suddenly aware of what that love meant.

Chad went down on one knee, reined in his own pent-up passion, the desire to take her immediately into his arms and begin to make love to her at last, took her hand, said gently, "Do not be afraid, Nell," and for once she did not spark back at him as she would have done in the past, but looked at him, her great eyes full of a loving demand for his consideration.

"I love you, and I would do nothing to distress you." He hesitated, then added, "Suppose I go to the dressing-room and change there, while you ready yourself for me here?" He saw, in retrospect, that it might have been better if Annie had stayed, to help her to prepare for him, and he had come to her later, but the ceremony which had preceded their entry into the room had preempted that.

Nell looked up at him, grateful for his consideration, his understanding that what had happened today had temporarily quenched the fire within her.

"Yes," she answered him, and then almost with a sob, "Oh, you will think me a fool, after all I have said and done, to behave to you like this, but..." and she shook her head.

"No," he said, "no," and, as he reached the door to the dressing-room, "Oh, Nell, you are as precious to me in your modesty as you were in your pride, and I hope to prove that to you, if not tonight, then another."

He was gone, and Nell was alone with what she had done. Oh, she had no regrets, and the way in which he had reacted to her untoward fit of the vapours, once they were alone together, told her that her choice of him had been no mistake, so considerate was he of her.

She rose, slowly began to take off her beautiful dress, until she stood naked before the roaring fire, which cast its rosy glow on her, so that she was not a marble woman, but a glowing nymph whose image she saw briefly in the long mirror before she took her night-rail from the bed, to hide away what she would so soon share with him.

Nell debated anxiously whether to enter the bed, or sit on
its side, and laughed at herself a little—what matter, either
way? But to enter the bed might look as though she were
trying to hide from him, and Nell Newcome must not be
more fearful than Nell Tallboys had been.

He knocked on the door, another concession to her new-
found shyness, and she called, "Come in," to see him enter, dressed in an overgown which had belonged to her
grandfather, a magnificent brocaded thing, and the familiar sight of it reassured her, and when, after extinguishing
several of the candles which stood about the room, so that
they were bathed in a dim red-gold glow from candle and
firelight combined, he came and sat by her, she said, with
something of her old fire, "Oh, I sometimes think that I fell
in love with you because you so resemble Grandfather, not
in looks and manner, but in body and carriage, the man he
must have been in youth."

Chad took her face in his hands, but gently. "I see that
my fiery lady is back with me again."

Nell blushed beneath his gaze, the touch of his hands
having its usual effect on her. "Not entirely," she said, shyness still with her. "I am stupid with love for you, cannot
really believe in what I, we, have done."

"Believe it," he said, "believe it," and then, "Nell, my
darling, I may have no memory, but I do know this. I am a
man who has not made love to a woman for a long time, and
I will try to be kind to you, but I desire you so passionately
that the body may subdue the mind. I will try not to hurt
you too much, or frighten you by the fierceness of my passion for you, but..." And at the look she gave him, passion and innocence combined, he said thickly, before
bending to kiss her, "Oh, you do understand me, I am sure,
and will forgive me if..."

"Hush," said Nell, beginning to drown in sensation as his
kisses awoke her sleeping senses. "There will be nothing to
forgive, nothing."

"At last," he said, and she echoed the words, but he was
so gentle and so slow with her that his very holding back
excited her, as first his kisses were light, innocent things,
ranging around her face, her neck, before he found her

mouth, and even then the first of them were like a child's, so gentle, until suddenly, giving a harsh sob, he forced her mouth open between his, and they kissed as they had done in the annexe, his tongue meeting hers, and hers welcoming it, so that, as then, fire ran through Nell, and she grasped him by his thick black curls, pulling his head closer to her, to force him even further into her mouth, as though they might consummate themselves there.

By now, his hands were busy about her, unbuttoning her nightgown, to find the treasures of her bosom, his hands on her breasts, stroking, his mouth following, and her hands were a reflection of his, loosening and untying the bed-gown, and even in her passion her wit returned to her, and she muttered as she found his bare chest, the black curls thick on it there, too, "So far, so good, my darling," to hear his choking laugh, as her hands grasped and stroked him there, finding his nipples, like hers, already erect.

"Oh, Nell, you witch, my witch." His voice was hoarse and shaking, his hands now ranging around her naked body, his mouth on her breasts, her own hands wildly stroking him, finding his sex, holding it hot and throbbing in her hand, so that as his hands found her buttocks he stopped, body shaking, to say, "Oh, God, Nell, no, not there. It's difficult enough for me not to take you before you're ready as it is."

Nell hardly knew herself; the need for him, contained over the weeks since they had denied themselves in the an-nexe, the daily necessity to renounce such thoughts of him, had taken their toll. She was more than ready to receive him, on fire all over, her body an aching void to be filled.

"Oh, no, Chad, I cannot wait, either, no need to deny yourself," and, her mouth now on his, he having turned her above him for a moment, he swung her beneath him, strok-ing her inward thighs, until he pulled his mouth away to gasp.

"Be a soldier, my dearest girl, bite the bullet, for a quick hurt is kinder than a slow one," and with one hard thrust he was in her, and they were one.

And being one was so satisfactory that the pain was worth it, even though she cried out at the shock, so that he began to draw back, until she clutched at him, crying, "No, you are mine now, Chad, we are one, not two, and that is all I want."

After that, for both of them, sensation took over; thought and coherent speech flew away. Countess and secretary disappeared, and the great bed consecrated their love as they reached fulfilment together, Chad Newcome pleasuring his Countess so thoroughly that, climax achieved in a great wave of pleasure, Nell was near to fainting from it.

Chad's own pleasure was so strong that his memory, long dormant, almost revived, so that in the aftermath of calling Nell's name he knew that, although he had made love to other women, never before had he felt the satisfaction he had just achieved with this one.

Beneath him, Nell, who had been laughing for sheer joy, now, in the final transports of all, long and slow, was suddenly weeping, her tears—born not of sorrow but of joy run beyond its bounds—slowly falling.

Her sobbings alarmed Chad, who tightened his grip on her, raining tender kisses on her tear-stained cheeks, pausing only to say, "Oh, my love, my darling, what a brute I am, I have hurt you. Forgive me."

"No, no," said Nell, stroking the anguished face he bent over her. "A little pain at first, but, later, what I felt, what you made me feel, was beyond anything."

She kissed him back, and, reassured, he cradled her in his arms as though she were a child, kissing and stroking her gently, until she put a finger on his mouth to stop him, saying mischievously, "I liked it so much, pray tell me, is it possible that we can do it again soon, and often?"

Chad's shout of laughter was spontaneous. "If you look at me like that, and say such things, you will rouse me to such efforts as Hercules might envy! Give me but leave to hold you like this a little, and your pleasure shall be mine. You are as generous in love as you are in life, my own." For she had given herself to him, and to helping him to secure his pleasure, as she had given herself to Campions and its people.

They had both given and taken, they had shared their love in mind and body both, and their mutual pleasure had been so strong because, although Nell and Chad had disappeared when they became one, they still gave and shared, and when they were separate again the knowledge of the one thing remained with them.

Spirit had been involved as well, and, because of that, although their first pleasure was over, he had the impulse to stroke and soothe his partner as he had never done before, so that gradually their sweating, panting selves, for two athletic bodies had celebrated their strength, were slowly brought back to peace and harmony.

"The calm before a new storm," he whispered in her ear. "That was merely the first of many such delights."

"Oh," said Nell, laying her head on his shoulder. "That was even better than I might have hoped. Such joy, such bliss, I wonder anyone is ever out of bed."

"If every man had the pleasure of loving such a beautiful body as yours," was his answer to that, "then I would agree with you."

Shyly, her old fears about her lack of looks reviving again, she said, "Unlike my face, then," only for him to cover her mouth with his big hand.

"You are the most beautiful woman in the world to me, Nell, and, have no fear, few look more strong and true. I have had enough of empty prettiness." And where did *that* come from? he wondered, for the thought to disappear in the glory which his words had evoked on her face.

And later, when they had made love again, this time slowly, so that she had screamed her pleasure at the end, clutching him so fiercely that her nails scored his back, and she lay, half-asleep, a satisfied houri in his arms, she whispered to him, "No regrets, then?" to hear him say,

"For me, Nell, none, but for you? Even in my pleasure I know that gossip will follow you everywhere, the Countess who married her stable hand. Only the thought of what we have shared tonight, and what I hope we share in the future, life and love both, comforts me."

Nell was suddenly all proud fury. She sat up, magnificent in her nakedness, rosy in the fire's ebbing glow. "Gossip!" she said fiercely. "How can you be so foolish? It is not like you. I have done nothing, nothing until I fell in love

with you, and yet gossip has always followed me everywhere. You know as well as I do that Charles Halstead made
his shameless bet about me when I was still virgin, unawak-
ened and untouched. What could be worse than that?''

For no good reason that he could think of, Chad's
breathing became short and painful when Nell repeated this
tale, first heard several months ago. It had affected him
badly then, and did so again.

"Oh, Nell," he said hoarsely, "how can you trouble
yourself about what such a brute as he must be says about
you—?" only to be interrupted by Nell's kiss on his mouth,
and her drawing away to say,

"Oh, come, my love, only a moment ago you were worried about people blowing on my reputation, and now you
tell me not to worry about Halstead's bet. Where is the logic
which you so often show? Of which Henson so often com-
plains?''

"He does?" asked Chad, suddenly sidetracked.

Nell rolled on top of him, kissing him whenever she
reached a comma or full stop in what she was saying, her
whole face and body amused, provocative again. "Oh, yes.
He once said that you must have been a divinity student
gone to the bad, you were so able to rout him with such pit-
iless and carefully reasoned arguments based on such undeniable premises.''

"Now, now," said Chad, imitating her, but giving her two
kisses at each stop, "not only are you funning, my darling,
but of one thing I am sure. I was never a divinity student,
even one gone to the bad.''

"Well, all I can say is that if," remarked Nell, "a divinity student gone to the bad is as good at pleasing a woman
as you are we shall have to arrange special examinations in
which the prize will be failing, not succeeding!''

"For that suggestion, Mrs. Newcome, you shall be properly punished," said her husband, "and the victim shall
choose its manner.''

"When, and if, you fully recover," said Nell thoughtfully, stroking his broad chest, running her fingers again
through the black curls there, "such a *satisfactory* body you
have my darling, a regular work of art—''

"As you saw in the stable yard," interrupted her spouse, equally naughtily.

"Oh, yes," said Nell, not at all ashamed, "I'm sure that from that moment on I was determined to have you in bed with me so that I could do—this," and she tweaked a vital portion of his anatomy. "Why I do believe, Mr. Newcome, you are almost ready to begin to administer punishment! Which of us deserves the praise? You for your virility or me for my powers of temptation—? Oh! Chad!" For he had rolled her beneath him, and the whole delightful business had started again.

"And I was wicked in the stable yard," he said hoarsely, before all speech stopped once more, "for I was so entranced by you and your delighted face—yes, it was delighted, do not deny it—that all my decent modesty flew away, and I was slow to cover myself!"

LATER, MUCH LATER in the night, when, after that final bout, sleep had claimed them both, Chad slowly surfaced for a moment, to find his body lax after loving, Nell in his arms, sleeping quiet against him, body and tongue still at last. He had been dreaming, and dreams of happiness and fulfilment, not the fear and horror which sometimes came to him of a night. How satisfactory it was to make love to a woman who matched him physically. And why, he thought drowsily, did I always believe I liked little, clinging women? Isabella and Julia were both little, and they were similar in their ways, quite unlike Nell, both flutteringly modest and submissive on the outside, but whores inside, whereas Nell—Nell is the opposite, frank and fearless in manner, but at heart a truly modest, good woman.

He sat up suddenly, wide awake, his heart thudding, but instinctively careful, even so, to try not to disturb his sleeping wife. Isabella and Julia! Who were they? He had for a moment remembered them, and then they were gone, into the dark, and, strive as he might, he could not bring them back.

Chad lay down again, Nell turned in his arms, said, half-awake herself, "Chad?" questioningly.

"Nothing, my love. Nothing. Rest easy." For whatever else he had forgotten he knew that he had never felt like this before for any woman, and not simply in the business of sex and bed, but for the whole of living, and that his lost memory had surfaced to tell him so.

Nell's warmth against him, her love freely and frankly expressed, his own sense of having met, at last, his other half, was so strong that the memory could not disturb him, and he slept with Nell in his arms, and both their dreaming was of love crowned, love fulfilled.

CHAPTER SEVENTEEN

EVERYTHING had changed—and nothing had changed. Chad's desk still stood by Nell's, and he worked there daily, but not as her secretary, as her partner. The Privy Council met each week, and Chad, as Nell, was one of them—but the one to whom Nell listened the most. His judgement, as Henson grudgingly admitted, was sound. He proposed some changes, and all were useful, and needed. They involved not only the running of the stud, but the manner in which the estates were administered. He did not put them forward all at once, but was tactful, so that Henson, who had been fearful that, once married, Nell's upstart husband might show himself in colours far removed from those he had worn as stable hand and secretary, was reassured: Campions looked to be in safe hands.

More, Chad suggested to Nell that she lived at Campions too much; that Malplaquet's other lands and homes needed to see more of their mistress, but although she argued with him a little she at last agreed.

"For," he said, after examining the accounts which had come in from Wroxton and Sheveborough, and the Welsh estate. "I think that not all may be well there. Agents left to their own devices may grow careless—and greedy."

Henson was compelled to echo this advice, and was ruefully pleased to see that Nell intended to take it—because Chad had put it forward.

"Grandfather spent most of his time at Campions," she said, a trifle defiantly, one evening, as they sat alone before the fire, the Privy Council, who now dined with them twice-weekly, having left. Aunt Conybeare had taken her leave shortly after the wedding to visit her sister, she said, adding, "You no longer need me now, as chaperon or companion. You have your husband to guard you."

She had never criticised the marriage, was unfailingly polite and kind to Chad, but Nell was not sure what she truly thought.

"You will come back, dear Aunt Honey-bear," she had said.

"Perhaps," said Aunt Conybeare. "When the children arrive, you may need an old woman then."

Chad, who was setting out the backgammon board, looked up at her and smiled. "You have said yourself that your grandfather was not always wise in his rule."

"Sophistry," Nell flung at him playfully, "to turn what one says against the sayer."

He laughed at that, and put out a hand to her. "Come, your turn to win."

"And that," said Nell, "will be a day to run up the union flag, unless you are chivalrous enough to let me win—which I do not want."

"Brave girl," replied her husband affectionately. "For that sentiment you will be suitably rewarded."

Their marriage was, of course, a scandal. The Riding visited, to stare at him, his size and strength, his good manners, and his equally good speech. "A gentleman, down on his luck," was the usual verdict. "But to marry him!"

Chad, and Nell too, bore it patiently. It was inevitable. Sir Chesney did not come immediately; he was away, and the news was late in reaching both him and Ulric. Ulric had left the Riding to visit his mother's family in Ireland, he had said in an ill-scrawled letter, and did not know how long he would be gone.

He would return soon enough, was Nell's wry reaction—when he heard the bad news. Sir Chesney's visit came when they had been married for a fortnight, and were still the wonder of the North, as Nell frequently joked.

Chad was at the stables, working out Rajah, a Rajah who was pleased because they so often took him out on the moors, Nell and Chad riding together, and, if the world disapproved of them, Campions did not.

Nell, working in her room, heard the noise of his arrival, and sighed when the butler told her that Sir Chesney was in the Turkish room.

She put off her brown holland apron, to reveal beneath it the modish dress which she now always wore, her hair carefully coiffed, feet perfectly shod, face soft, the very picture of a satisfied woman, and went to join him; she hardly dared think that he would welcome her, any more than she welcomed him.

He turned as she entered. "Nell! I ask you to tell me that this story is not true. You cannot have married your stable hand!"

She kissed his warm cheek as though this were a normal visit. "Not my stable hand, my secretary," she said calmly.

He dismissed her chopped logic. "Piff-paff, Nell. It's all one, and you know it. How could you do such a thing? What would your grandfather have said? Do you know what the world is saying? Such a marriage cannot stand."

"Come, Uncle," replied Nell, still calm. "The deed is done and I am happy with it. He is a good man, and even Henson approves of him, and you know what Henson is."

"Oh, by God, damn Henson. Who's he to decide who Malplaquet marries? You are wanton, my girl, seduced by a strong body and—"

"Do not say handsome face," responded Nell incorrigibly. "My husband has many attributes, but he is not handsome."

"You have taken leave of your senses and your modesty both," shouted her uncle, now thoroughly roused to anger. "A pity that we are no longer allowed to thrash our womenfolk. A good beating twice a week would soon restore you to your senses."

Before Nell, eyes furious, could respond, a cold voice spoke from the door. Chad had returned, to be told of Sir Chesney's arrival, to hear him shouting even before he opened the door, to be in time to register his displeasure by threatening Nell.

He walked over to his embattled Countess, slipped an arm around her. True, he could never be called conventionally handsome, but even Sir Chesney had to recognise his physical power and the air of effortless authority which had returned to him permanently on the day he married Nell.

"I allow no man to speak to my wife in such a fashion,"
he said, his voice ice and fire, the voice his men had heard
in the Spanish mountains, and on the night before battle.
"Unless you are civil to her both in and out of her presence, you are not welcome in this house, sir."

"Why, you..." Words failed Sir Chesney, faced with the
man himself, standing there so cold and sure. "Who are you
to tell me whether I may or may not visit Campions, see my
niece?"

"My husband, Uncle." Nell was as cool as Chad, and to
Sir Chesney, equally infuriating. "I do not wish to lose you,
Uncle. I have few relatives, God knows, but if you wish to
see me you must respect the fact that I freely chose the man
by my side to be my partner, to run my lands with me, to
father my children, and nothing you can say or do will alter
that. Your choice, Uncle. Go or stay, as you please, but I
will not allow *my* choice or my husband to be traduced."

"You are shameless, madam, shameless," almost gobbled her uncle. "I shall have this piece of trash you have
chosen to elevate from the gutter investigated. Better for you
to have married Ulric than for you to do this."

"I give you leave to go, Uncle." Nell was still calm, but
shaking a little. "You will not, I am sure, wish to remain
here longer, and, much though it pains me to see you go, I
cannot have my husband miscalled. As he protects me, I will
protect him."

"Protects you!" was Sir Chesney's answer to that. "Pillage you more like. Mark my words, my girl. You will rue
the day you married him."

"I am not your girl, Uncle, I never was, and my judgement tells me I have done aright. But right or wrong, done
is done, as we say here, and I joy in the doing. I am sorry
that you have had an unnecessary journey. Should you wish
to eat before you travel home, I will arrange for you to dine
alone, so that we do not disturb you by our presence."

He saw that there was no shaming her, no shaking her.

"God damn it, madam, the food would choke me. What a work you have made of this. What can have possessed you, I ask myself?"

Nell could not resist the opportunity offered. "Why Uncle," she whispered sweetly. "I did but follow the Tallboys motto: 'As the beginning, so the end'. What was good enough for the lady of Barthwaite is good enough for me."

"You were like to have given him a fit," said Chad, a little ruefully, when he had stamped out, "but I could not allow him to speak to you so in your own home."

"Nor I hear you miscalled," sighed Nell. "You were right, of course, when you foresaw trouble. But I cannot allow it to affect me. I am sorry to have made an enemy of him, yet Ulric troubles me even more. I cannot think what he will say or do when he finally hears that I am married—and to whom."

"NOTHING USEFUL," said Guy Shadwell dispiritedly to his father, "and really, after all this time, not surprising. Only an innkeeper in South Nottinghamshire who thought that Shad 'might' have passed through last autumn. He seemed to remember Vinnie—made them all laugh, trust Vinnie—and if Shad's missing, where's Vinnie? He was always watching Shad, guarding him—that was quite a joke, only it ain't one now."

"What I expected," sighed his father. "So it seems that he disappeared somewhere between South Nottinghamshire and Glen Ruadh, which leaves a lot of country to cover after nearly seven months. And the carriage and horses—what happened to them?"

"Attacked by footpads somewhere lonely," hazarded Guy bitterly, "after all he went through in the war, surviving that dreadful wound, to disappear somewhere in England—or Scotland—and be lost without a trace."

"I'll not give up." The Earl rose, his face distraught. "I cannot believe that I shall never be able to see him again, ask his forgiveness for thirty lost years. I cannot refrain from thinking of him. I ask myself why it was I disliked him so much for so long. Perhaps it was because he was always so much his own man, whereas I now think Frederick always consciously sought to please me. The Duke asked after him yesterday, said he was sorry that he was lost to the Army. I nearly told him that Shad—'' the first time that Guy had heard his father use the affectionate nickname ''—was lost to life, but I will not give up hope. The search must go on. See to it, Guy.''

It was Guy who was despondent now; he thought his father's hope was based on a desperate desire to make up to Shad for the cruel indifference he had shown to him all his life. He left, to prepare to visit again the old ex-Runner whom he had employed in the attempt to trace his lost brother.

The Earl sat at his desk after Guy had gone, his head in his hands. Despite his brave words to Guy, who he knew mourned his brother sincerely, he had no real hope that Shad might be found after all this time.

His secretary put his head around the door. ''My lord?''

''Yes.'' The Earl lifted his head—life must go on. ''Yes, what is it?''

''The Runner is back, my lord—says he needs to speak to you urgently.''

''The Runner? What Runner? Guy is dealing with him.''

''Not that one, my lord. The one who came before Christmas about Lord Halstead's rifle. The man you refused to see then—I spoke to him. He insists that he needs to speak to you personally, no one else will do.''

How wrong he had been to refuse to see the Runner. Halstead's rifle might offer some clue to his disappearance. Anything to do with Halstead must be investigated, my lord thought. ''Send him in,'' he said curtly.

Cully Jackson, who had been waiting in the anteroom, carrying the mysterious rifle in its leather case, was not abashed at the prospect of meeting such a great man as Lord Clermont. On the contrary, he stared about him, taking in the splendid room with the trained eye of a man used to summing up his surroundings for his professional purposes.

The study was superb, bookshelves in the bays on each side of a hearth elaborate in white marble, nymphs holding up its mantelshelf. Above the hearth was a giant painting,

which he offered only a cursory inspection—neither the
books nor the painting were of real interest to him; the man
standing behind the desk was. He drew in a long breath, let
it out again. He knew that he had seen this man before, or
someone younger, very like him. One mystery, he was sure,
would have been solved by the time that he left the room.
But he was wary, was Cully; he had to make sure.

"My lord," he began, "I am sorry to trouble you and
your office about this matter again."

The Earl put up his hand. "You are right to do so. I
should have made it my business to see you before. Is that
my son's rifle you carry?"

Jackson lifted the rifle from its leather case, handed it to
my lord. "With respect, you may tell me, sir?"

The man opposite took the rifle, inspected it carefully,
said slowly, "This rifle belonged to my son. His initials are
there, engraved beneath his Viscount's coronet. I remember it." He looked up, his face ravaged. "He showed it to me
once when . . . when we were on good terms. It almost certainly went with him on his journey north last autumn. He
bought it from his best friend who was later killed at Waterloo, and treasured it because of that. He would not lightly
have parted with it. And now he is lost, almost certainly
dead, I fear, and how the rifle came into your possession is
something which you must explain to me."

My lord's face disturbed Jackson. He thought that he
knew why. He had not been on the best of his terms with his
heir, but now that he thought that his son was likely dead . . .
He looked away from naked grief to stare more closely at the
painting over the fireplace.

His stare held. He knew at once that his search was over,
and that my lord's grief was misplaced. But why, and how,
the rifle had come into the possession of the dead thief and
would-be murderer, and my lord's son was—what he was,
Jackson did not know, but was sure that he could find out.

"Forgive me," he said. "The question may seem strange
to you. But is that painting there," and he indicated the
portrait over the hearth, "your son, who is missing?"

The Earl was surprised; it was his turn to stare a little at
Jackson. "Indeed," he said, "that is my son Charles Vis-

count Halstead, done after he came home from the wars, when he had recovered from his wounds. Yes, that is my worthy son," he said painfully, "whom I spent years neglecting for my unworthy son. I am rightly served that I lost him before I found him."

"A cavalryman?" asked Jackson, still staring at the painting.

"Indeed," said the Earl, turning to look at the portrait, which hurt him every time he passed it. "A good one, they tell me. A wonder with horses and at commanding men. Not so fortunate with women."

"Oh, I wouldn't say that, my lord," offered Jackson with a sly grin, referring to the last part of my lord's judgement on his son. "But, I agree, a wonder with horses." He thought of Chad Newcome, the man without a memory, last seen controlling the uncontrollable Rajah in the riding school at Campions.

For the sumptuous painting by Sir Thomas Lawrence, flaming in its glory above the hearth, was of Chad Newcome, but a Chad Newcome whom Campions had never known.

He was standing, straight-backed and tall, face stern, magnificent in full regimentals, black curls blowing in the breeze, his left hand on his sabre, his right hand holding a superb white horse. His breast blazed with decorations, including a giant star. The bright blue eyes gazing down at Jackson he had last seen some weeks ago, and like Chad Newcome's were those of a man of pride, will and astonishing self-control.

The Earl's voice broke into his reverie. "You admire the painting, I see."

Jackson turned, said coolly, London in his speech, "Yes, but I admire the man more."

"You have met my son?" The Earl's voice carried incredulity.

"Yes," returned Jackson, suddenly man to man; Earls and thief takers had no place here. This man was grieving for what he thought was lost—but how would he take the truth? "I beg pardon, my lord, for my effrontery, as you will see it, if I ask you to sit down before I speak to you of

your son and where he may be found, although the finding
may be painful to you, and what it will be to him I canno
even guess."

He held the Earl with the eyes which had frightened
thieves into confession, and consigned murderers to the
gallows, so that the Earl slowly sank into his chair, and be
gan to listen, in mounting shock, to what Jackson had to tel
him.

GUY HAD BEEN SENT FOR, caught as he was about to leave
to initiate further search for Shad.

"And Shad—Halstead—is alone, you say," said Guy,
"and does not know who he is, only that he was Shad,
which, of course, they translated into Chad, and he did not
know enough to correct them? And where, then, is Vinnie,
his faithful shadow and protector?"

"Shad?" said Jackson, for up to now the Earl and his son
had spoken only of Halstead.

"Yes," said Guy, "he was so nicknamed from a boy,
Charles Shadwell, you see—Shad."

"And Vinnie, you said. Who and what was he?"

"Shad's factotum, old sergeant, valet, groom, man of all
work. They'd saved one another's lives in the war. He would
never, living, desert Shad."

"You're sure that he was with him?" asked Jackson—
everything must be double-checked in his line of work.

"Quite sure," replied Guy. "I saw them drive off, and it
was Vinnie who was remembered in the last trace we have of
them."

"All I know," said Jackson, "is that Chad, Lord Halstead, as I believe him, was found alone, starving, half-
naked, mind and memory gone, wandering on the moors.
It's my guess they were set on, robbed, Vinnie killed, Lord
Halstead not quite finished off, horses and possessions, including the rifle, stolen by a gang led by the thief who later
tried to kill Lady Malplaquet."

Even in his relief that Shad still lived, Guy could not help
laughing. "And what a turn-up that is," he exclaimed, "to
be saved and employed by Nell Tallboys, of all people!"

"Oh," said Jackson with a grin, "there's more to it than that. He became her secretary, and, begging your pardon, sir—" he turned to the Earl, who had sat silent, listening '—he and the lady are sweet on one another. So sweet that he gave his notice, and is due to leave any day—doing the honourable thing, you see. We'd best hurry north, the young gentleman and I, to catch him before he disappears again."

Jackson had no knowledge of what had happened at Campions since he left—the proposal and the marriage.

"Sweet on Nell Tallboys!" Guy was incredulous. "Even more of a turn-up. And you're sure he has no knowledge of who he is?"

"Quite sure," said Jackson.

"Poor Shad," said Guy obscurely, thinking of the scene at Watier the night before Shad left, and his oft-repeated statements that the last person he would ever marry would be Nell Tallboys!

The Earl rose. "We owe you our thanks, Mr. Jackson. You have given us hope. And this Chad, you say, who you think is my son, saved Lady Malplaquet from an assassin, worked as a stable hand, and then as her secretary—and that they . . . favoured one another?"

"Indeed, my lord," said Jackson with a grin. "I taxed him with it, and got half killed for my pains. A man of honour, your son, for so I believe Mr. Chad Newcome to be."

"Well, Guy shall go north with you," said the Earl, ringing the bell for his secretary, "to check whether your belief is correct, but what he will do if Charles's memory is still gone he will have to decide when he meets him." He paused and for the first time his stern old face cracked into a smile, albeit a grim one. "I can tell you one thing, Mr. Jackson. If my son does recover his memory to discover that he is . . . sweet on Nell Tallboys, that shock will be a profound one, too!"

CHAPTER EIGHTEEN

NELL FOUND that each day as a new wife brought its own pleasures. She and Chad, who had now been married for a month, an anniversary which they had happily celebrated during the previous night, were due to visit one of Nell's properties situated in north Nottinghamshire, an old hunting lodge-cum-country house known as Penny's Hall. Word had been sent ahead that my lady and her new husband would be expected to arrive on the Friday afternoon, that their baggage would come by coach and cart, and they would ride there, suitably attended by grooms and outriders.

Nell had protested at the state in which she was to travel, but Chad had agreed with Henson and Aisgill that she should not only be protected—the outriders would be armed—but also that the people at Penny's Hall would be flattered by their Countess honouring them so, after all these years without a visit from the family.

"Depend upon it," Nell said ruefully, "the place will be shabby and damp."

"And when did such things trouble you, Nell Newcome?" said Chad, giving her an absent kiss; they were dressing for the journey. Chad was to ride Rajah, Aisgill having given his reluctant consent, but, as Chad had said, the beast deserved some reward for having been so patient in his dressage exercises, and for having also given them four new foals, one of which looked likely to rival his father in beauty, wickedness and power.

"You'll be careful with him," Aisgill had said the previous day.

"As with my life," Chad had replied truthfully.

Aisgill had given him a queer look. "I thought that the lady had run mad when she decided to marry you," he said bluntly, "but now..." And he shrugged his shoulders. 'Now I think she could have done worse. Much worse," he added as an afterthought, watching Chad's face change when Nell came into the yard, dressed as magnificently as she always was these days; flyaway Nell Tallboys had vanished for good. Mrs. Newcome was a fashion-plate.

Breakfast over, and both dressed for the journey, the coach and other baggage gone the previous day, the train they were taking with them assembled on the sweep before the beautiful façade, Vulcan's successor, Pluto, was brought round for Nell, and two lads escorted Rajah, who would still only behave himself for Chad.

Nell felt quite sentimental. It was the first time that she had gone out into the great world as a married woman. They had all decided that the stay at Penny's Hall must be done in style, Nottinghamshire society entertained, Nottingham itself visited for a few days, a boat trip to be taken up the Trent, Colwick Hall and the Musters visited, and all to be done in the intervals of looking at the coal pits there, examining the books and quizzing the obviously lax agent, before deciding whether to keep him.

"Time to go," Chad announced, taking Nell's arm, and they walked out of the front door, through lines of servants assembled to see them off; impossible to do anything these days, thought Nell, amused, without Henson making a pantomime of it, as though determined to show that although Nell Tallboys had married a nobody she was still the greatest lady in the North.

And finally they were on the steps, more of her people assembled, the Privy Council standing in the doorway, the train, all on horseback, patiently awaiting her—at least the men were patient, their mounts less so.

Nell was already up when the first intimation of trouble occurred. A horse and rider, foam flying in all direction from the mad speed of travel, flew through the great arch at the end of the sweep, and came to a stop before them all.

It was Ulric Tallboys. His face was alternately ashen and scarlet, his expression wild in the extreme. He advanced on

Nell and on Chad, who was holding Rajah, a lad controlling the stallion on his other side.

His voice was high, furious, and he had a pistol in his hand, pulled from the holster on his saddle as he dismounted. "So, it's true, then. You've done for me, married this piece of scum," and he waved the pistol dangerously at Chad.

Nell, controlling her fright and unease, tried to stare him down. "What the devil do you think you're doing, Ulric? Put that pistol away, at once. And yes, I've married Mr. Newcome, as I suppose you've just heard. You received my letter?"

"Received your letter?" raved Ulric, waving the pistol at Chad, who had moved towards him. "Keep back, I tell you, or I'll drop you where you stand. Yes, I read your letter, and you've ruined me, you bitch. I only went to Ireland to avoid a debtor's prison. The bailiffs were after me already when it looked as though we were not to marry, and now that you have married this piece of dirt I'm like to be in a debtor's prison all my life, thanks to you. Well, I'm not having it, Nell, be damned to all of you."

He waved the pistol again, and those around Nell, fearful for her, were afraid to do anything that might cause him to shoot her.

"Damn you," he shrieked, "it was only that clod you've married who saved you from death when he killed my man. Be damned to him, what have I to lose now? He shall have his reward." And to Nell's horror he finally stopped waving the pistol, brought it up and fired at Chad, as Chad, careless of what Rajah might do if he loosed him, made for Ulric's throat, fearful that it was Nell for whom the bullet was intended.

This diversionary tactic almost certainly saved his life, since the bullet creased his skull as he lowered his head to charge, instead of taking him in the breast, but it dropped him to the ground, and Ulric, realising that he had failed, and that Nemesis was on him in the shape of Nell's people, suddenly horrified into sense by what he had done, made for Rajah in the hope of mounting him, and escaping on him.

Nell's scream of shock and horror as she saw Chad fall
was lost in Rajah's snortings and whinnyings at the sight of
Chad brought low, and the feel of Ulric's clumsy hands as
he tried to climb into his saddle—he had already broken free
from the lad.

Rajah tossed Ulric from him, and turning, rearing,
trampled him beneath his iron hoofs, transforming him into
bloody rags on the ground, before flinging back his head,
narrowly missing the prostrate Chad, to bolt down the drive,
disappearing through the archway at the end.

Nell had already dismounted from a disturbed Pluto—all
the horses present were distressed by the sudden shot—to
fall on her hands and knees beside Chad, who she feared
had been killed by the man whose maimed body lay a few
yards away from that of his victim. Aisgill dropped down on
Chad's other side, Henson began giving frantic orders. The
sudden nature of the tragedy had shocked them all, but action now followed paralysis.

She was sobbing, wailing, all her normal stoicism gone,
cradling Chad's head, regardless of the blood running down
his face and covering her hands, regardless of Aisgill saying, "Come, Nell," all ladyships forgotten, "you must let
us examine him," for she knew only one thing; Chad might
be dead, and what then did life hold for her, the reason for
it being gone?

GUY AND JACKSON had kept up a good pace on the way
north, for Jackson was fearful that Chad might already have
left. He had no clear idea when exactly Chad was to go from
Campions, only knew that he was working out his notice.

Guy was quite unlike his brother, in looks as well as
manner, but Jackson found him a congenial companion,
although a little *distrait*, his thoughts were with his brother
whom he hoped to meet at journey's end.

And what then? He had asked Jackson his opinion of
Shad's loss of memory, and how likely he was to regain it.
Jackson had shaken his head. He had met such cases before, and they were all different, he said. Some, having re-
trieved it, forgot what had happened in the interval; others
didn't. "And no one knows why, or how," he said. "You

meet some strange things in my line of work, Mr. Guy—I
mean Mr. Shadwell.''

''Mr. Guy,'' said Guy, smiling. He liked the man, there
was a bluff honesty about him, liked him the more because
he seemed to respect Chad—who might be Shad.

And at last they passed into the Riding, where the land
was wild and rough, like its people, Jackson said, and they
were making for Campions, the great house on the edge of
the moors, of which Guy had often heard and never seen,
like the legendary Nell Tallboys, Countess of Malplaquet,
its eccentric owner.

The house was suddenly before them, in the distance,
glowing in the watery sunlight of a late March day, at the
end of a suddenly improved road—the Countess's doing,
Jackson said; she had improved everything to do with her
estate since she had inherited.

The works of past Earls of Malplaquet were everywhere,
follies, stone bridges, triumphal arches leading to nowhere,
until they could see the final great arch through which they
must drive in order to reach the front of the house.

But a quarter of a mile from the arch their driver, nicknamed Pompey—another of Shad's old soldiers, now
working at Clermont House, and brought along to share in
the driving—said suddenly, ''Here's a fine to-do,'' and tried
to pull off the road, as a huge black stallion galloped past
them, narrowly missing the carriage, foaming and bound-
ing, so that it almost seemed that fire might be coming from
his nostrils, finally leaving the road behind them, and running on to the moor.

''Rajah!'' exclaimed Jackson, turning to stare. ''Now
what the devil's up? Drive on, man,'' and so Pompey did,
through the giant arch, and there in front of them on the
sweep before the Corinthian columns and the flight of steps
up to them was a scene like, as Jackson said later, something in a Drury Lane spectacle.

Groups of people were milling about. A dead man was
lying on the ground, broken and bloody, his head at an odd
angle. Another man lay on the ground being attended to, a
woman was being comforted by a middle-aged man in
gamekeeper's clothes, another man in a fine gentleman's

suit was shouting orders, before himself bending down to
the man on the ground, who was wearing, Guy saw, a fine
suit of riding clothes, and beautiful boots.

He had thick black hair in loose ringlets, was big . . . and
Guy gave a hoarse shout. "Stop, Pompey, stop," and, on
Pompey's doing so, hurled himself from the carriage to run
to the group about the prostrate man, ignoring shouts and
attempts to push him away by the man in the fine suit.

"Who the devil are you, sir?" the gentleman demanded,
to have Guy hurl at him,

"Oh, to Hades with you, sir," and then, "It's you, Shad,
at last," to the man on the ground who had begun to stir, as
though Guy's voice had been some sort of signal, recalling
him to his old life.

Nell, Aisgill's arms around her, as though she were a girl
again, began to recover herself. Nell Newcome must be as
brave as Nell Tallboys had been. She was in the act of moving away from Aisgill to question Henson about Chad's
condition, but as he straightened up, shouting for a servant
to go fetch Dr. Ramsden at once, she saw the new actors, as
Jackson would have called them, arrive on the scene.

Astonished, she saw a tall fair young man, shouting
something incomprehensible, hurl himself at poor Chad,
who, assisted again by Henson, had begun to stir, driving
away her first fears that Ulric had killed him immediately.

For Ulric she felt nothing. Later, the horror of his death
would strike her, to visit her occasionally in nightmares,
even though he had brought his death on himself by attempting to kill Chad, but now her only concern was for her
husband, and why the strange young man should throw
himself at Chad, and how it was that he knew the name
which Campions had given him, for Shad, to her ears, had
come out as Chad.

To her infinite relief she saw Chad, blood still running
down his face, try to rise, said hoarsely to Aisgill, "Oh,
thank God, he's not dead," to hear Aisgill answer briskly,

"I told you so, my lady."

And to her astonishment and horror she watched Chad's
gaze pass over her unknowingly, and heard him ask the
young man in a puzzled voice, "Guy, where the devil am I?

And what are you doing here? I thought myself in Spain
when I woke up. Where's Vinnie?''

Nell was suddenly frantic at this non-recognition, the
more so as Chad, ignoring her, attempted to stand, the
young man, Guy—and who was he?—helping him most
lovingly, an expression of acute concern on his face.

And Jackson was there, too, dismounting from the carriage, his sardonic gaze hard on them all, like a sphinx who
knew all the answers, and, if he did, she, Nell Newcome,
wished he would supply them.

Countess Nell at her proudest, she questioned the young
man fiercely, ''Who are you, sir? And how do you know
Chad?'' while Henson, who had uncharacteristically been
struck dumb by this strange turn of events, recovered his
self-possession, and also roared at the stranger.

''Come, sir, who the devil are you?'' and, pointing at
Chad, ''And who the devil's he, since you seem to know
him?''

Behind them, Jackson, the only one of all of them to
realise that Chad had his memory back, watched and
waited.

Chad, now held upright between Aisgill and Guy, stared
at Nell, said thickly, and to Nell's consternation, ''Who are
you, madam, and how did I get here? I thought—'' for as
he recovered consciousness he had been a guerrilla in Spain
again ''—I thought I was in the mountains, but then how
could you be in Spain, Guy? And who are all these people?
What am I doing here?'' and he looked dazedly about him,
wondering who the handsome woman was who stared at
him so poignantly, two great tears running down her face,
as the truth hit her, to bring her almost to her knees again.

Chad had got his memory back, and did not know her!

''Who am I?'' said Guy, loosening his grip on his brother
a little—he had been holding him as though he feared to lose
him again if he were not careful—and at last answering the
questions posed by Henson and the woman, who he had
suddenly realised must be Nell Tallboys, and, if so, report
had lied cruelly about her looks, for what a magnificent
specimen she was, even in her grief. ''Why, I am Guy Shad-

well, Lord Clermont's youngest son, and this—" but he was interrupted by his brother.

"Enough, Guy, enough. It must be for me to...confess who I am."

Even before Guy had begun to speak, the sight of Nell moving towards him, arms outstretched, murmuring his name—for Chad sounded like Shad to him—saying brokenly, "Oh, Chad, never say that you have forgotten me," a look of such love and concern on her poor face, had caused something to move in Shad's head, and he remembered everything—would that he could not!

He knew that Vinnie, poor Vinnie, was seven months dead, knew why he had left London, knew of the attack, knew why he had been found wandering on the moor, knew of his service at Campions, knew why the rifle, and the dead man who had carried it, were familiar to him, knew, to his piercing horror, that he truly loved and had married the woman before him, who would not, could not now love him once she knew who he was—Charles Halstead who had defamed her—but he, and not Guy, must speak the unpalatable truth, even though it destroyed him, for the truth was all Shad had ever possessed, and he had lived by it all his life.

His face a mask of agony, he said, "I have remembered everything. I am—God forgive me, my dearest Nell, for what I said of you, before I knew you—Charles Shadwell, Viscount Halstead. I was set on by footpads, my poor sergeant Vinnie was killed, and I was stripped and left for dead, to be saved by you and become your servant..."

The effort of thought, of speech, was too great for his failing senses. Shad—Chad—welcomed oblivion to give him surcease from pain and shame, and fell gratefully forward into the dark again, unconscious at the feet of the most noble lady, Nell Newcome, Countess of Malplaquet, Viscountess Wroxton, Baroness Sheveborough, all in her own right, whom he had mortally and publicly insulted seven months ago, and who he had loved with a passion beyond reason from the first moment he had seen her, and to whom he was now married.

CHAPTER NINETEEN

"YOU MARRIED HIM?" Guy's voice was almost incredulous.

"Yes," said Nell shyly. She and Guy were in her private drawing-room, Chad's and her possessions all about them. The chessboard was set up, the backgammon board waiting to be set up, Nell's canvas work on an upright stand, books everywhere, the Campions stud book among them, the room left as it was for them to return to—everything bearing witness to their happy and useful life together.

Shad had been carried to the great bed, unconscious, their journey postponed. He was not in any danger, Dr. Ramsden said, but when he had surfaced for a moment and had spoken it was plain that he was greatly confused and shocked. The strain of discovering who he was, and what had happened over the last seven months, coupled with the wound, even though it was not severe—a gash similar to the one which had helped to cause his loss of memory—had been too much for even the strong man that he was to accept easily.

He had been given laudanum to make him sleep soundly. Nell's doctor was a great believer in sleep, and now Guy was talking to Nell, and finding her quite unlike the lady of legend, in speech as well as appearance.

"Well, I'm not surprised that you did marry him," he said slowly, "even if, forgive me, it does seem a trifle odd, for you to marry your secretary, but Shad's such a splendid fellow."

"Yes, he is, isn't he?" said Nell simply.

Guy hesitated, and Nell looked at him affectionately. If he thought Chad—Shad—a splendid fellow, Nell thought that Guy was a chip off the same block.

"You mustn't take any notice of the bet," he said finally. Nell saw that Guy knew that he was on dangerous ground, and spoke to reassure him.

Ever since Chad had told her that he was Viscount Halstead, who had publicly shamed her, her mind had been in a turmoil. Her first thoughts were angry, for Lord Halstead seemed to have nothing to do with Chad Newcome, her husband whom she loved beyond life, so that when she had thought that he was dead she had understood for a moment why some widows threw themselves on funeral pyres, committed suicide.

But to reconcile Chad Newcome and Charles Halstead, that was difficult. Whenever she thought of Halstead, either now, or in the past, she was consumed with a fierce anger. But what had that to do with Chad? He was so unlike what she had assumed Charles Halstead to be from what she had heard of him. But then, wasn't she quite different from the Nell Tallboys of gossip? Her mind went round and round.

"But why?" she said, at last. "Why did he—who you say rarely drank get so blind drunk that he spoke of me as he did? A man who, all the time he was here, was abstemious, respected women, never troubled the female servants—why, I even had to propose to him myself in order…" she paused, said defiantly "…to get him into my bed—whereas he bet that he could have me without marriage. *That* I do not understand."

"Well," said Guy, "it's like this, you see. When I was a little lad, and Shad was barely twenty—he had just joined the Army, not that he wanted to be a soldier at first. He went to Oxford at fifteen, wished to be a scholar there, but Faa…Father…said no, the second son always went into the Army—he met Isabella French, and fell madly in love with her."

He stopped again, and Nell wondered what was coming, he looked so miserable. She said gently, "You needn't tell me, if it makes you unhappy."

"Oh, I have to tell you," said Guy earnestly. "He married her, you see, against Father's wishes, and Father was right—not that he knew what Isabella was. It was just that he never liked Shad for some reason, always wanted to thwart him."

He went on, "Well, at first the marriage seemed to be happy. She was a pretty little dark thing, not a bit like you. All Shad's women, not that there were that many," he hastened to reassure her, "were little. And at first they were very happy. But Shad's duties kept him away a lot, and she...couldn't live without him...it was a kind of sickness, Shad said, and she...well, she gave herself to anyone who would have her when he was away, particularly to Shad's best friend, Harvey Black, who couldn't seem to resist her.

"In the end, Shad found out. He arrived home one day to find her in bed with Harvey, and then it all came out—about him and the other men. What was worse, he fought a duel with Harvey, and then, when Harvey shot at him and missed, Shad deloped, fired into the air—he didn't want to kill him—but Harvey was ashamed of his betrayal of Shad, swore and insisted that the duel be a proper one, Shad must fire at him. They fired again, and Shad wounded him so badly that Harvey died six months later from it. You can imagine what that did to Shad.

"And then, to make it all worse, Isabella was found to be pregnant, and the baby couldn't be Shad's. But he stuck with her, until she died in childbirth. Yes, I know, Nell," he said gently, on seeing her horrified face, and hearing her murmur,

"Poor Chad."

"Yes, I know it's a horrid story, couldn't be worse. After that, he barely looked at women seriously, until last year he met Julia Merton, another little thing, and the whole rotten business began again.

"It turned out that Julia was Jack Broughton's mistress, and was marrying Shad for convenience. It all came out when Shad found her with him—you can imagine what *that* did to him after the business with Isabella, and that was why on the day he found out he drank himself stupid—went to Watier and made that awful bet about you—your cousin Bobus was boasting about your—inaccessibility, and that worked him up. Father was badgering him to marry you,

into the bargain. I know he shouldn't have done it, but you
can see why."

Yes, Nell could see why. She walked to the window,
looked out over the moors, and thought of a young and
chivalrous Shad, his life in ruins—and then for it to happen
again!

"Not Shad's fault," said Guy, "that he picked wrong
'uns—his misfortune. I suppose they picked him because he
was so good and steady at bottom. Everyone envied him Isabella and Julia. It was only afterwards people realised that
they were both lightskirts at heart."

Nell thought of how she had tempted him, and flushed at
the memory—and then of how he had held off. He had been
good and steady with her, too, and that was partly why, in
the end, she had been so wild to marry him.

"He quarrelled with Faa over it," Guy said, "and that
was when he drove north, to be attacked and lose his memory. Was he happy here?" he asked.

"Yes," answered Nell, "very happy. We were both
happy." She thought of their mutual joy, of the badinage
which had passed between them, as well as the passion, of
their shared pleasure in the horses, in their books, and the
running of Campions. "Yes," she repeated, "very happy."

"I'm glad," said Guy fervently. "He's never been really
happy, except perhaps when he was in the Army, doing his
duty—Shad's great on duty—and then he had to give that
up when our elder brother Frederick died. And Father
wasn't even grateful when Shad cleared up the mess Frederick had made of running the estates." And then he added
thoughtfully, "Perhaps he was happy because he no longer
carried the burden of the memories of Isabella, Julia and
Faa's dislike," unknowingly echoing what Jackson had said
to Chad Newcome earlier.

He didn't tell Nell the truth about his eldest brother, but
Nell knew from his manner that he had not loved Frederick
as he plainly loved Shad.

"One good thing about all this—apart from Shad meeting you, that is—is that Faa's wild to make up to Shad for
mistreating him all his life. Wants to be reconciled. I can't

wait to tell him. Shad always loved Faa—God knows why, he was never fair to him.''

Nell walked over to Guy, and kissed him on the cheek. "A present for my new brother,'' she said. "I've never had a brother, and now I've inherited a good one. Welcome to Campions, Guy."

She was amused and touched at his response. "Oh, you're a good 'un, Nell. Not a bit like they said you were. And so handsome, too. Whatever was all the gossip about...?'' He stopped, flushing at what he had almost said.

"That I was plain, you mean?" she said, laughing at him, looking more vital than ever. "Well, I know I'm no beauty."

"Nonsense,'' said Guy sturdily. "You're the finest woman I've ever met, and I really envy Shad. You won't be hard on him when he's himself again, will you?'' he said anxiously. "I know Shad. He'll be worrying himself sick over the bet."

Talking to Guy, listening to him about Shad, and not only the sad story he had told her, but the way in which his face lit up when he spoke of his brother, his unselfish joy that he was alive, when his death would have meant Guy's advancement, touched Nell, told her that her choice of a husband, made blindly, and against all conventional common sense, was a good one.

"No,'' she said. "No. I won't hate him and reproach him. Why, Guy, let me tell you the sad truth about myself. I believe I told my uncle that nothing in the world would induce me to marry Charles Halstead, and then when I met him I couldn't wait to do so, married him in defiance of the whole world!

"You have *no idea* how relieved Henson, my agent, is that Chad is a nobleman in disguise. He had been repressing his misgivings since the wedding-day, and now he's cock-a-hoop. I told him an hour ago that Chad is still Chad, even though he's Shad, but he'll have none of it.''

"Henson's your grand gentleman ordering everyone about?'' asked Guy ingenuously, amusing Nell again.

"Yes, that's Henson. He liked Chad, but not as Malplaquet's master. I can't wait to see him bowing and scraping to Chad—'Yes, my lord, no, my lord.' His universe will be an orderly one again.''

She was suddenly happy Nell Newcome again. Yes, she would tease Chad a little about the disgraceful bet, but be sure to let him know very soon that it was only teasing, that nothing he had said and done in his old life could wipe out what they had come to mean to one another since they had first met.

"And I must write to Faa," said Guy. "Jackson can take the letter back to London with him. And he's cock-a-hoop, too. All his mysteries solved, and he was right about your cousin Ulric, as well."

"Poor Ulric," said Nell. "I can't grieve too much for him. He did try to have me killed, but he was my cousin, and as a little boy he was a bully, yet he was, apart from Uncle Beaumont, practically the only relative I had."

She began to giggle. "Uncle Beaumont! What's he going to say when he learns the truth? Let me tell you about him. What an about-facer that will be!"

"NO," SAID SHAD, bruised and broken though he felt. "I am not staying in bed for a head wound as mild as this is, and, as for damaged nerves and restoring my system, I am not a fourteen-year-old schoolgirl afflicted with the vapours. If you don't send for my clothes I shall take you by the throat, and throttle you until you give way," and he glared at poor Ramsden who said, dodging away as his patient looked thunder at him,

"Now, Mr. Newcome, my lord, pray do not excite yourself, but you really ought to rest a little."

"I don't intend to excite myself," ground out Shad, "merely give myself the satisfaction of half killing you unless you do as I wish," and he threw back the bedclothes and made motions at Ramsden, trying to ignore his swimming head. The one thing that he wanted to do was to see Nell and try to convince her of how much he loved her, and how he regretted what he had said of her in his drunken folly, and this fool was keeping him from seeing her. And he was damned if he wanted to talk to her flat on his back in bed like a . . . mollycoddle.

Ramsden, now with his back to the door, said wearily, "I see that there is no stopping you, my lord. Perhaps it may be wise on my part to allow you to rise. You will soon discover how shaky you are."

All Shad's ill-humour, which was partly caused by his fears about where he really stood with Nell—ludicrous to think that as a nobody he had possessed no such fears, but now as Charles Halstead, her equal, he felt as queasy as a green boy every time he thought of her—leached out of him. Shameful so to speak to a man who was, after all, only doing his duty. All his old charming courtesy, so well known to Campions, returned.

"I'm sorry, sir," he said. "I should not have spoken so. Do but allow me this, I beg."

"Only if you allow me my reservations," said Ramsden stiffly. "I will send for one of the footmen to bring you your clothing, and help you to dress."

And where was Nell? Shad thought, as he allowed the footman to tie his cravat, grateful to allow himself to be nannied for once, he felt so weak and worthless. Was she so disgusted that she had married the brute who had bet on her and maligned her that she no longer wished to see him?

Almost he wished that his memory had not returned, that he was still plain Chad Newcome, and then he thought of Guy's face when he had seen him, and of his duty to his father, and the estate to which he had been born. He could not be Chad Newcome, accountable to no one but Nell who had given him life, love, herself and Campions.

He shuddered at the thought of her, at the possibility of losing her, and her love, and, when Ramsden returned to examine the bandage around his head, said abruptly, beneath his ministrations, "And Lady Elinor, she is well, I trust."

"I hope so," said Ramsden drily. "She spent most of the night at your bedside after she dined with your brother, and I suspect that she is catching up on her sleep—if she is wiser than you are, begging your pardon, my lord, about her health."

She had sat by his bed! Perhaps after all she could forgive him. He jerked a little as the doctor's touch became
painful, called, "Come in," to the knocker at the door.

Henson entered; a cat whose cream had proved satisfactory. "My lord," he said—Nell's prophesy had been correct, the world was no longer turned upside down, and
Henson was happy. "My lord, your brother has suggested
that you be asked if you can remember where you might
have been attacked, and in what circumstances. It might
lead us to where your sergeant's remains may be found. We
have assumed that he was killed when you were attacked, as
you were found on your own, no sign of a companion."

Poor Vinnie. Here he was having the blue devils about
himself, with no thought for what had happened to the
faithful friend with whom he had campaigned both in and
out of war.

"I think I remember," he said slowly. "You must understand that I was barely conscious at the time, and everything is confused. After they killed Vinnie, they stripped me,
and then sat him beside me, and later I remember falling,
and after that climbing. They threw the carriage and the pair
of us into a quarry, you think? Which would account for the
state of my hands when I was found."

"Most like, my lord, most like," said Henson, his manner, previously correctly cool to poor Chad, now almost
unctuous, or as unctuous as such a dry stick could be.
"There are two near Campions land. A search shall be made
at once, my lord. I shall organise it," and he turned to go.

"Henson," asked Shad, "tell me, is Lady Elinor up yet?"

"I heard that she was stirring, my lord, and her maid said
that she had eaten a late breakfast. She slept in the guest
suite, my lord. Dr. Ramsden thought it best that you be left
on your own, my lord." He was gone, and painfully Shad
walked out of the room himself, to find Nell, and learn how
he stood with her.

NELL, SEATED IN HER drawing-room, late up for the first
time in years, was debating whether or not to go and see her
husband, when the door opened, and, to her astonishment,
he walked in.

"Chad!" she said. "Should you be up? I thought you still asleep. Dr. Ramsden refused me entry this morning." His face was white, with great purple smudges under his eyes, and his head bandaged, giving him the appearance of a rakish Arab, she thought.

"Lady Malplaquet," he said, bowing, quite formal, and quite unlike his manner as Chad, so that Nell knew at once that Guy had been correct when he had said how troubled his brother would be.

"Not wise, perhaps, but I am not a great one for lying in a bed, and besides, I needed to see you."

Oh, the poor love, how nervous he was! She longed to go over, hug him, tell him not to worry, but perhaps he deserved to suffer a little for what he had said and done in his drunken folly seven months ago, even if he had got his injury as the result of attacking Ulric when he had thought Ulric might be attacking *her*.

"My lord?" she said, as formal as he, so that suddenly, to her delight, she saw his grim aspect lighten a little.

"Oh, dear, Nell, don't you start. I've already had Henson my-lording me at every second word. You'd think that no one else had ever borne a title."

Nell gave an un-Countesslike giggle. "Did he so? I told Guy that he would."

"Relieved to find me respectable, I suppose," remarked Shad, a little morosely. "Nell, I have so much to say to you, so much to ask you to forgive me for, that I hardly know how to begin. Isabella—"

"No need to speak to me of Isabella, or Julia Merton for that matter," replied Nell briskly. "I've already heard all about them from Guy, and I really do not wish to hear any more, so you may set your mind at ease over that."

Shad hardly knew whether he was grateful to Guy or not; on balance, he thought, probably gratitude was in order. "Now, about the other matter—"

"By other matter," interrupted Nell sweetly, "I suppose, Lord Halstead, you mean your bet. Now, that really does exercise me. I am not sure what you exactly wagered, so I cannot decide whether or not you won or lost. Foolish of you to refuse me in the annexe. You would have been richer by twenty thousand pounds had you done so. On the other hand, if the bet was suitably vague—and only you know that, if, of course, you can recall what you actually said. I believe you were dead drunk at the time, most unlike you, but there it is—then perhaps our marriage may be sufficient for you to win it. You see what a quandary I am in. I don't know whether to congratulate you or commiserate with you.''

At the end of this remarkable speech she had the pleasure of seeing her husband look suitably agonised, so added to further disconcert him, ''I understand that we are a sorry pair. I heard that you had said that of all people you would never marry me, while I told my dear uncle Beaumont exactly the same thing in the same somewhat indelicate terms about you. And here we are, tightly joined to the very partner for whom we had previously expressed extreme aversion. Sheridan, were he still alive, would have found it a suitable subject for comedy, I'm sure.''

''Nell, Nell, it is not a joke,'' protested Shad. ''Here am I trying to tell you how sorry I am for what I said...'' He stopped. His head was thundering away, and his heart was doing the same thing. Had he lost her or not? Difficult to tell when she was roasting him so preposterously—but, after all, he deserved it, did he not?

''Well, I don't propose to cry over it,'' said Nell robustly, ''and it's hardly grounds for divorce, so we seem to be destined to remain firmly attached to one another, legally, if in no other way. I wonder if the terms of the settlement allow me to pay your bet? If you've lost it, that is. And will that noble conscience of yours allow you to accept my assistance?''

''I'm hardly stumped for twenty thousand,'' Shad said, ''little though I shall like paying out such a sum as the consequence of my own folly—why are we going on in this havey-cavey manner, Nell? I came down to apologise to you, and you have done nothing but talk nonsense since I arrived. My head won't stand it,'' he said plaintively.

''Well, let me relieve your deserved misery a little,'' said Nell, deciding not to push the joke too far. ''Guy tells me that the bet was never properly registered. You were too foxed to sign anything, or whatever gentlemen do on such occasions, and consequently the terms of it are immaterial, and there is no chance of your winning or losing anything, and I shall not need to perjure myself by declaring that we... anticipated our wedding vows—you see how delicate becoming a married woman has made me. Goodness knows, by the time we have our first child I shall be so proper that a College of Vestal Virgins would envy me. Why are you laughing, Chad? What are you doing?"

For, thundering head and all, Shad had given a little groan, leaned forward and pulled her from her chair where she had been sitting, looking up at him with the most provoking smile on her face as she teased him beyond endurance.

"I won't have it, Nell," he muttered distractedly. "I don't care how badly I behaved, or what you think of me—I love you, dammit, to distraction, and if you continue as you are doing you will be pleasured on the carpet immediately, thereby either finishing me off for good, or allowing Henson to come in and find us at work, and how he would deal with that I should like to find out, but am unlikely to do so."

And then he had her in his arms and was kissing her willful mocking face, until they both sank on to the sofa, where for a moment it looked as though they might end up celebrating the fact that they were husband and wife despite the possibility of being interrupted, or doing Shad's head a permanent harm.

Sanity suddenly reigned. They pulled apart, Nell rosy, Shad greyer than ever, but happier than he had thought was possible since he had finally remembered who he was on the previous afternoon.

"So, I am forgiven, Lady Malplaquet, for the wicked things I said before I knew you?"

"And I am forgiven, Lord Halstead," she answered, suddenly serious, "for the wicked things I said and thought about you?"

His answer was a kiss, and another saucy look from Nell when lovemaking paused for a moment. "Well, one thing that's certain," she said wickedly, "is that whatever anyone else thinks of our marriage we are sure to please your father and my uncle, and that must be something to cheer about, seeing that neither of them has ever been pleased with us before!"

Shad's shout of laughter at that nearly took his poor head off.

"Oh, Nell," he groaned, "you really must stop, or you will have me back on my bed of pain again, and Ramsden will say, 'I told you so,' and I don't think I could endure that. He's displeased with me enough already."

"Happy to think that my wishes come second to your physician's," Nell riposted, and then, when he reached for her again, "No, Shad, for Shad you will be from now on, I will be serious. We have a great deal to arrange as soon as you are recovered, for, whereas Lady Malplaquet marrying penniless and landless Chad was one thing, I am sure that Lord Halstead marrying the lady will provide the lawyers with work for a twelve-month."

Shad had already thought that life as his old self was likely to be a great deal more complicated than that which he had lived since he had arrived at Campions. He thought wistfully of unencumbered Chad, who was rapidly disappearing into the past—the Chad whom Aisgill had thought *night* have been a corporal, or perhaps even a sergeant, in the cavalry, but who, in reality, had been a captain, and later an aide, and a good one. Landless unknown Chad, actually Charles Shadwell, Viscount Halstead, Clermont's heir, with all that that entailed in duties, responsibilities, as well as rank and privilege.

Campions, and Aisgill, would have to come to terms with Shad, but there were already signs that Campions was happy to discover that the mistress had chosen so truly when she had given poor Chad her heart and her inheritance.

"Not yet," he said gently, pulling her into the crook of his arm, where she fitted as though she had been designed for nothing else. "For the moment, alone here, let us be the Countess and her secretary, duties and responsibilities forgotten." And then, belying his own words, he started up. "Rajah, what happened to him?"

Nell pulled him down again. "He trotted in off the moor late last night, exhausted, like his master, but, like him, he will recover, I hope."

"I am already recovering," announced Shad firmly, "and will continue to do so, provided you do not provoke me too much. A suitable deference to your lord and master would

do wonderful things for me. See to it, Mrs. Newcome, see
to it."

"Willingly," murmured Nell, "willingly, provided always you offer a similar duty to the mistress of Campions."

They lay there, comfortable and settled for life, Chad
Newcome—and his Countess.

DARLING AMAZON

Sylvia Andrew

CHAPTER ONE

LORD CARTERET'S bedchamber was ablaze with light. The huge room was overpoweringly warm, but his lordship had insisted that the fire should be kept burning brightly in the handsome fireplace and that not a single candle should be extinguished. "The dark will overtake me soon enough. Let's keep it at bay as long as we can, eh, Julia?" he had said, smiling grimly at his daughter. That had been before he had suffered his second attack, but since then Julia had ordered the candles to be lit as soon as daylight began to fade and to be kept burning till the dawn. She sat at his bedside now, fanning herself with the newspaper which she had been reading to her father before he had dozed off. She could not reasonably comfort herself with the thought that he was improving, yet she could not imagine life without him. Her mother had died when Julia was just a baby, and for as long as she had been old enough to notice her father had been her world. He had played with her, taught her far more than any of her governesses, and ever since her disastrous London Season had been her favourite companion. She swallowed hard as emotion threatened to get the better of her. He would be disappointed if he saw her give way to tears. It was as well she did so, for there was a slight stirring of the bedcovers and her father opened his eyes.

"Julia?" His voice was low and slurred.

"I'm here, Father."

"Thought you would be." There was a silence only broken by the Earl's laboured breathing.

"Do you wish me to get you anything, Father?"

"No, there's nothing. I've been thinking ... Julia ... how old are you?"

She suppressed a small sigh. For the past week her father had been asking the same question again and again. He never seemed to remember that he had asked it so many times before. The subject was clearly haunting him, and she knew what would follow. She replied patiently, "Six and twenty, Father."

"I don't understand... why you have never married, my dear."

"I never found anyone half as interesting as you to talk to, Father," she said, smiling at him. But this answer served no better than all the others she had produced to comfort the sick man. He gave a faint groan of exasperation and murmured,

"What will you do when I am gone, child? You should be married, have a husband to comfort you, children... Those fribbles you met in London had no notion of your quality..." His voice died away, and he shifted restlessly on the pillow. She had to bend her head as he muttered his next words, though she knew what the gist of them would be.

"I should have listened to your aunt. She told me to give you more time... to pick up a few airs and graces. But I didn't want to wait... I thought anyone could see with half an eye what a wonderful girl my Julia was. Clever as they come, ready to listen to a man sensibly... and know what he was talking about. But all they wanted was a pretty face and a liking for empty compliments, damn them...! I should have listened to your aunt. The woman's a fool in every other respect, but she knows the ways of society. I should have waited." The sick man opened his eyes and his frail hand grasped Julia's. "Forgive me, child, for ruining your chances. I didn't realise..." His voice died away again as he lapsed once more into sleep or unconsciousness. Tears took her by surprise and she looked down unseeingly at the newspaper in her hand. This question of her unmarried state was occupying her father's conscious moments to the exclusion of everything else. His feeling that he was to blame denied him the rest that his enfeebled state so badly needed. What could she do? A husband would appear to be the only answer, but that was an impossibility. Since she had failed to attract an offer in the full swing of a London season there

was little likelihood of finding anyone in the depths of the
Surrey countryside, especially as she was confined to the
house and grounds by her father's illness. It was still less
likely that she would find anyone who would satisfy her
father's exacting standards! She sighed as she walked slowly
over to the window and gazed out unseeingly at the dank
grey February afternoon. There had once been such a
man... She smiled wryly as she remembered her brief acquaintance with Hugo Devenish nearly ten years before. It
was not so surprising that a shy seventeen-year-old, used
only to the sober society of her father, should have fallen
headlong in love with him!

AT THE TIME of Julia's London Season, the old Marquess
of Rostherne was still alive. Lord Hugo Devenish, his
younger son, had newly returned from Greece and was enjoying the flattering attentions of most of the polite world.
Why not? Few maidenly hearts could resist the attraction of
his tall, lean figure, his tanned good looks, and the exciting
breath of scandal which still clung to him. His air of de-
tached cynicism as he regarded the fluttering fans and the
coy approaches only made him seem yet more dangerous,
and therefore more desirable, to the young ladies who were
fortunate enough to meet him. All this would not have
endeared him to their careful mamas, of course, but his
family's wealth and breeding, together with his own impec-
cable courtesy, persuaded them to overlook Lord Hugo's
past indiscretion and to regard him with favour—after all,
there had never been anything more than speculative gossip, and he had been very young at the time.

"But, Mama," exclaimed Sophie during one of the interminable sessions with the dressmaker she and Julia were
forced to undergo before they made their debut, "Mama,
what did Lord Hugo *do*?"

Lady Thornton said with unwonted determination,
"Nothing you need to know, Sophie. More than half of it
was just idle gossip, and it would be better if the whole affair was simply forgotten." She refused to say any more,
instead concentrating her energies on preparing her daughter and niece for their presentation to society. Sophie's vi-

vacity, combined with her rioting blonde curls, china-blue
eyes and rose-petal complexion, assured her of immediate
success. But Julia, who at seventeen was already exception-
ally tall, was another matter. Why, oh, why, thought Lady
Thornton in despair, had the girl's father not followed the
advice she had given him months before?

"Can you not leave it one more year, Richard?" she had
asked her brother. "The child is still very young, and she
might have filled out a little by then. She is, you will agree,
painfully gawk...thin."

"No time, no time, Alicia!" had been Lord Carteret's
brusque response. "Julia must be safely harnessed before I
leave for Greece in the autumn."

Lady Thornton had been roused to protest. "Harnessed
indeed! You talk as if she were a horse!"

"You are well aware of how proud I am of my Julia. But
Greece is no place for a young girl, and by the time I return
she will be twenty or more. No, now's the time to find her a
husband—while I am still in England to vet the candidates.
You get her the right dresses and so on—don't spare the
budget—and bring her out with your own Sophie. I dare
swear she'll make a splendid match in no time at all. And
now there's a fellow I have to see while I'm in London, so
I'll take my leave. Look after Julia for me!"

Lady Thornton knew of old that once Lord Carteret had
made up his mind it was impossible to get him to change it.
But she wished she could be as sanguine as he was about
Julia's chances in the marriage market. The qualities that
her brother rated so highly in his daughter were not those
which would recommend her to the frivolous world of
London society. Julia might well have a razor-sharp mind
and an extensive acquaintance with classical Greece. But she
was also undeniably gawky, moved like an untrained colt,
and had no small talk whatsoever. Nor did she have any of
the conventional accomplishments to be expected of a young
lady. So when Lady Thornton had finally agreed to bring
Julia out, it had been with no great expectation of succeeding in Lord Carteret's ambition for his daughter. She had
promised to do her best for her, however, and now she could
safely say that she had selected a wardrobe for her niece

which rivalled that of her own daughter in prettiness and charm.

Unfortunately Lady Thornton had not stopped to consider that the daintily flounced pink muslins, the lace-frilled silks, the ridiculous bonnets and beribboned straw hats which were so outstandingly successful on her diminutive Sophie did not necessarily flatter Julia. Sophie looked enchantingly fragile. On Julia the effect was less pleasing. Indeed, she resembled nothing so much as a maypole—or so Sophie confided to her best friend. The word quickly spread, and soon Julia was known throughout the polite world as "The Maypole". Perhaps people might have been kinder had they realised how very young she really was, and how much she suffered from their wit. But she was too proud to show her distress and too inexperienced to defend herself. She merely withdrew into what appeared to be a haughty silence, which did nothing to endear her to the world she was supposed to be trying to enter.

ON THE OCCASION of Lady Godfrey's ball Julia had escaped her aunt's vigilance and was hiding in the conservatory, overcome with misery and a longing for her father's companionable conversation. She crept back further into her corner as Sophie came through the doors from the ballroom, accompanied by two gentlemen. Peter Mersham, Sophie's most constant admirer, was a familiar figure, but who was her other companion?

Julia craned her neck as far as she dared in an effort to identify him. He was taller than Lord Mersham, but that was not very difficult. She suddenly froze as his dark head seemed to turn in her direction, but breathed again when he continued his conversation without interruption. Though Sophie was actually addressing Peter Mersham, Julia was unsurprised to observe that her cousin's real interest lay with the stranger.

"I protest, Lord Mersham, you are cruel to tease me so!" Sophie was saying with a pretty pout. "I am persuaded Lord Hugo would never tease a lady in such an unkind manner!"

So that's who it is! thought Julia. Hugo Devenish, society's latest darling! And she wondered somewhat wistfully what it must be like to be so courted and flattered wherever one went. Even Sophie, who was well aware of her own secure position as one of the Season's successes, was positively fawning on him!

"Tell me, Lord Hugo," continued Sophie, "would you liken a lady to someone she had never heard of, and then refuse to explain? Who is this Persephone?"

"Ah, but you must not ask me to undermine Peter's stratagem, Miss Sophie. He is after all my friend. Allow me to tell you that the poor fellow hopes to keep you at his side until he chooses to reveal the answer himself. And who can blame him for that? However, I consider the comparison an unhappy one—it would be an unpardonable waste of your beauty to condemn you to six months' darkness every year..."

"Oh, la!" exclaimed Sophie, clutching Hugo Devenish's sleeve in a tiny hand. "Whatever did the lady do? Lord Mersham, you are too cruel. Pray save me, Lord Hugo!"

Julia saw Hugo look at Lord Mersham's downcast countenance. Then, courteously but firmly removing Sophie's hand from his sleeve, he said, "Peter, you should not bore a lady as charmingly pretty as this with classical allusions."

"Classical?" cried Sophie in mock horror. "Like those old statues that everyone is forever prosing on about? Why, the only time I ever saw them I was bored to tears—when I wasn't being put to the blush by them. And one of them was at least ten feet tall! Lord Mersham, I declare I am quite out of humour with you. Do you really find me such an Amazon? Or are you perhaps confusing me with my cousin?"

The expression of cynical amusement grew on Hugo's handsome face as Lord Mersham stammered and stuttered in his eagerness to correct this mistake, but the latter's laborious explanations were interrupted by the entry of Sophie's friend, Maria.

"Lady Thornton is looking for you everywhere, Sophie! And have you seen Julia? She's missing, too."

"How on earth could anyone miss Julia?" exclaimed Sophie, looking roguishly at Lord Hugo. His expression

changed and a slight frown appeared at her words. Lord
Mersham laughed and offered to escort naughty Miss Sophie to her mother, but she refused. With a last smile at the
two gentlemen, she tripped off with Maria.

"I'm demmed if I don't think Miss Sophie the most
charmin' girl in the whole of London," said Lord Mersham fervently.

"She is certainly prettier than most, Peter." Lord Mersham looked askance at the reserve evident in his friend's
voice and Hugo continued, "I found her unkind about her
cousin. The girl is surely not such a quiz."

"Believe me, she is, Hugo! Have you never met her? I'll
allow she has the Marchant fortune behind her, but that
alone ain't enough to justify her top-lofty air! She makes
not the slightest effort to please and, believe me, a...a poker
would be easier to dance with! Look at the way she apes her
cousin in her dress, too. She looks like a...a dashed May
horse! I tell you, Hugo, you'd never believe the two were
cousins. Miss Sophie is such a fetchin' little thing. A...a
pocket Aphrodite!"

Hugo laughed. "Take my tip and give up the classical
comparisons, Peter. She'll like your compliments a great
deal better if you just compare her with spring and have
done. Your Sophie is as ignorant as she is pretty, you
know."

"Oh, Miss Sophie has all the accomplishments to be expected of a lady," said Peter, a little stiffly. "Too much education for women is not desirable. They tend to become
opinionated."

Hugo laughed again, less pleasantly. "If you think Miss
Sophie is not fully as determined to have her own way as the
rest of her sex then you are more of a fool than I thought,
Peter. Don't be misled by the Dresden china appearance, my
friend."

This was too much for Lord Mersham, and he announced rather coldly that since the conversation was taking a deucedly disagreeable turn he was going to join the
others. Hugo bowed ironically and sat down. After a minute or two he said, without turning his head, "You can come

out now. I imagine you would prefer not to stay there the whole evening.''

Shrinking back into her plant pots, Julia gasped, ''How did you know I was here?''

''My dear girl, I saw you when I first came in.''

''It's true that I'm difficult to miss,'' she said bitterly.

''Why the devil should anyone want to?'' was his surprising response. ''Stop cowering in there and dance with me instead.''

''Oh, I couldn't!'' Julia exclaimed in horror. ''You don't know who I am! I'm ... I'm—''

''You're Julia Marchant, Sophie's cousin, unless I'm very much mistaken. I'm Hugo Devenish, by the way.'' When she still did not move he got up and came towards her. ''Come on, I'm not going to eat you.'' The cool, cynical voice was not reassuring. She shrank back further, shaking her head. After a pause he said, ''I'm sorry if our remarks a moment ago offended you.''

''They didn't, not really,'' Julia said sadly. ''I suppose I'm getting used to it. But it's all very different from what I imagined ...''

''What did you think it would be like?'' he asked more gently.

Julia took a tentative step forward. ''London is so big! And it has so much history behind it, and all the exhibitions, and ... and theatres and libraries. I thought it would be full of people who knew things—things I'd like to learn more about. Of course I was looking forward to the balls and so on, but I don't seem to be very good at dancing. I stumble a lot and ... and ...'' She lifted her chin defiantly and said, ''The melancholy truth is, Lord Hugo, that I simply don't have the art of pleasing. And now they all laugh at me and say unkind things about me. You heard Sophie and Lord Mersham.'' She waited for him to say something, but he remained silent. Something in his face however prompted her to add, ''I try not to show I mind, but I do really.''

''Of course you do! Anyone would. But now you must put it behind you and dance with me. I won't let you stumble.''

Julia slowly emerged, staring at this odd man who actually wanted to dance with her. As she straightened up she realised that he was fully three inches taller than she and startlingly handsome.

"Well, well," he murmured slowly, removing a leaf from her shoulder. "What silver-eyed Athene have we here? Have you left your owl in the bushes?" An unmistakable giggle came from Julia. Her grey eyes sparkled as she said demurely,

"I thought you disapproved of classical allusions, Lord Hugo? And I don't think it's very kind in you to compare me with someone who sprang fully armed from her papa's head, do you? That's almost as bad as poor Persephone's six months in Hades."

His face was transformed as he gave a shout of laughter and said, "At least you didn't ask me who the lady was. But tell me, Athene, which of your manifestations do you favour at the moment? Do you carry the owl for wisdom, or the sword for war? Are you going to dance with me, or slay us all with a glance of disdain from those silver eyes of yours?" The music struck up in the next room. "We'll debate it while we dance," he said with a wholly natural grin. "Come!"

He dragged her half protesting into the ballroom and proceeded to dance with her, guiding her so firmly that she never once faltered. Indeed she was so fascinated by the laughter in the hazel eyes looking into hers that it didn't occur to her to be nervous about the onlookers—or even to think of them at all. The supper interval followed and, to her astonishment, he did not return her to her aunt, but instead escaped with her to an alcove where he plied her with delicacies. He invented a ridiculous game called "Classical Allusions", challenging her to recognise the ladies he described, and demanding responses from her. She spent the time in a ripple of laughter which was only stilled when he leant forward and lightly kissed her. Then her eyes grew wide and her lips opened in astonishment. He laughed and kissed her again, this time with more feeling. Then with a slight frown he asked suddenly, "How old are you, Athene?"

"Sev...seventeen, Lord Hugo."

"Is that all? I had thought you were older."

"It's because I'm so tall. People often mistake my age."

He frowned more heavily and said, "It's time I took you back to your aunt, little Athene. I mustn't expose you to more gossip. Come!"

He escorted her back to her aunt, smiled somewhat ruefully at her, and went. For the rest of the evening she sat in a daze, unheeding of the curious glances cast at her. In bed that night she lay awake, humbly astonished at her good fortune and dreaming of future delights in Lord Hugo's arms. Her wide knowledge of the classics and her razor-sharp mind were no help to her as she fell under the spell of a pair of laughing hazel eyes and those two enchanting kisses. He had made her feel beautiful. The fact that he had not danced with her again was easily accounted for—he had not wished to expose her to more gossip. The next night she told herself that his failure to call that day would soon be explained. Perhaps he had important business elsewhere? After all, he could not have known, any more than she, that he was going to meet his fate at Lady Godfrey's ball... This wilful self-deception lasted less than a week, and at the end of it she was faced with the fact that what had been an earth-shaking experience for her had meant nothing to him. Perhaps he had even laughed at her! Full of angry hurt she haunted the park when he went riding in order to ignore him, sought him out at the balls and rout parties they both attended in order to turn her back on him. Soon the whole of London was laughing at The Maypole's persecution of Hugo Devenish. Julia did not care that she was making herself ridiculous. A kind of madness had her in its grip, in which Hugo was the enemy and had to be punished, regardless of personal cost. And soon her prejudices about him received unexpected confirmation.

She had retreated one day to a favourite window-seat in her aunt's drawing-room. Here, hidden from the rest of the world behind the heavy curtains, she could indulge herself in daydreams in which a desperate Hugo was contemptuously rejected. The sound of her own name brought her back to reality. Her aunt was speaking.

"Julia is a great worry to me, Lady Crichel, I will admit. Her behaviour seems to have become even worse since Lord Hugo has been so particular in his attentions to Miss Strangway. I have written to her father, but he is at the moment away. The dear child is so very unhappy."

"Unhappy!" snorted Lady Crichel, a disagreeable dowager and one of society's severest critics. "The gel deserves to be whipped for her behaviour! Has she no sense of propriety? Mind you, it's no more than I expected. Mark my words, I said, did I not? Allow Hugo Devenish back into your drawing-rooms and there will be trouble. Any man who makes off with his own brother's wife doesn't deserve his place in society!"

"Pray do not say such things," said Lady Thornton in distress. "There is not the slightest evidence that those rumours were true. You might well be doing Lord Hugo a grave injustice, Lady Crichel."

"Ha! Evidence! I don't need evidence," said the Dowager with perfect truth. "I ask you, what is the world to think when a handsome young whipper snapper, who has been constantly in his sister-in-law's company, suddenly disappears abroad after a very public scene with his brother, and then..." She paused for effect. "And then less than a month later, mind you, his brother's pretty wife—barely married above a twelvemonth—equally suddenly vanishes, also abroad." She sat back. "You may call me a suspicious old woman if you wish, but I believe I am up to snuff—and a pinch above it, too!"

"It is true that John Devenish has never been the same since his wife left him—for whatever reason."

"He's a poor creature—" Lady Crichel's contempt was evident "—with his drinking and his gambling. His father has had to rescue him more than once. He should never have married the foreigner in the first place—what was her name? Thérèse de Lachasse. Pshaw! Plenty of English girls, with respectable fortunes, too, would have been glad to marry the Marquess of Rostherne's heir. In my day..."

Julia's attention strayed here, since the conversation appeared to be drifting away from the subject of Hugo, but her mind was busy with what she had already heard. It was just

as she had thought—Hugo Devenish was a heartless phi-
landerer. He had probably abandoned that poor girl,
Thérèse, and was now seeking new conquests here in England. What a fool he had made of her at Lady Godfrey's
ball! She stared miserably out of the window. She was desperately homesick. Her experiences in London were gradually destroying everything she valued—her belief in herself
and others, her sense of ordinary propriety, any consciousness of what she owed to her aunt... She was overcome with
remorse. But all her dislike of Hugo Devenish flared up
anew when he called a few days later and asked to see her.
Her aunt, who was in despair at her niece's conduct, insisted that Julia should receive him.

When Lord Hugo came into the library where Julia was
waiting he smiled at her so kindly that she almost responded. But then she drew herself up and said with fierce
dignity, "Sir?"

"Lady Julia, your aunt has allowed me to see you alone
so that I may beg you to stop this ridiculous behaviour. It
reflects credit on neither of us. The truth is—"

"The truth is that you have lost interest in making sport
of me. Is that it?"

"You are wrong, Athene. I gave in to an absurd impulse,
reprehensible, I admit, to surprise all the tabbies who were
treating you so unkindly. But I didn't allow for the fact that
you were so young—and so...and so impressionable. I was
thoughtless, but I swear I was never malicious. Show your
wisdom, Athene. Forgive me and be friends."

"I wish you not to call me by that ridiculous name!" she
exclaimed. "Was this why you went to such lengths to see
me, Lord Hugo? Just to tell me this?"

"When it only concerned myself I bore your childish
pranks—for that is what they are—with patience, aware that
I had brought them on myself. But the gossip arising from
your conduct is disturbing a lady for whom I have some regard. That I cannot allow. Your campaign must stop, Lady
Julia, from this moment."

She stood in silence, a desire to burst into tears at war with
a passionate determination not to show how mortally hurt
she was. Then she went over to the bell, saying as she pulled

the rope, "You may tell Miss Strangway that she will no longer be 'disturbed' by my behaviour. I am returning to my father at the end of the week, and London will see no more of me." She paused for breath. "You called me 'Athene' a moment ago, reminding me of an episode I would rather forget. But I tell you this..." Her voice became fiercely resentful. "Your so-called pity for my situation, your condescension at Lady Godfrey's ball, your heartless desire to look well in your own eyes have caused me to look an even bigger fool than before. I shall never forgive you for that! You can keep your owl of wisdom, Lord Hugo. In the unlikely event that we ever meet again you will remember that I'm your enemy!" Hugo's lips twitched at these melodramatic words, but his amusement vanished when Julia added her parting shot, "And in view of your past history, I consider myself lucky to have escaped your attentions!" The look on his face frightened her as he took a step forward. But then the footman appeared at the door and Julia said coldly, "Lord Hugo is leaving. Pray show him out."

Hugo looked furiously at her for a moment, then turned on his heel and went out. Julia left London after a few days and in the autumn of that year she persuaded her father to take her to Greece. By the time they returned three years later she had managed to dismiss most of her unhappy experiences in London from her mind. But though several young men had shown an interest in her, not one of them had managed to chase away the memory of laughing hazel eyes in a tanned face, and two kisses...

CHAPTER TWO

THE LITTLE CLOCK on the mantelpiece struck five and recalled Julia to the present. Five o'clock. The doctor would soon be here for his evening visit. She went back to her father's bedside and sat down to wait. The minutes ticked by and there was still no sign of Dr. Carfax. He must have been delayed. Idly she started to read through those items in the newspaper which had held no interest for her father—and sat up sharply as a paragraph leapt to her eye.

An announcement concerning the Matrimonial Plans of a certain Sixth Marquess of R. is expected within the month. The Polite World is eager to learn the identity of the Mystery Lady who is to make the Marquess the happiest, or at least the most Fortun-ate, of Men. But the Writer will Keep his Counsel, saying only that she is not to be found in the Ranks of London Society at Present.

Julia could hardly believe her eyes. She had just spent the afternoon thinking of Hugo Devenish, and here was an item in the newspaper about him! That it did concern Hugo she had no doubt. Ever since both his father and his elder brother had died, Hugo had been Lord Rostherne, Sixth Marquess of Rostherne. And it had long been public knowledge that the Devenish fortunes were in dire need of repair. Hugo must be planning to marry one of the latest generation of heiresses—girls whose fathers had made fortunes out of the new manufacturing industries in the Midlands or the North. She wondered how he would feel when he saw this piece of malicious impertinence. For a Devenish to be considering what would clearly be a shocking misalliance, the situation must be desperate indeed ... ! Julia pulled herself up short. Hugo Devenish was in the past, as far as she was concerned. And there he must stay. It had not always been easy to ignore him over the years, for Hugo had spent months in Greece visiting the ancient sites of Greek civilisation, and over the years Lord Carteret had been keenly interested in the notes and drawings Hugo had made there. There had been a regular correspondence. But in all that time Julia had studiously avoided any contact.

The sound of voices on the stairs heralded the arrival of Dr. Carfax. Julia rose eagerly to meet him, her musings on the past forgotten.

The doctor was accompanied by Lady Thornton, who took Julia by the hand and said, "My love, how is your father? Has he·spoken at all? My dear child, you look worn to a shadow. Why did you miss dinner? I insist that you come downstairs with me while Dr. Carfax is here. You must take a small glass of wine and a little of the excellent beef Cook prepared for us. No, I will take no excuses, I insist!"

Dr. Carfax brusquely overrode Julia's objections. "Your aunt is right, Lady Julia. You won't be much use to your father if you are ill yourself. Mrs. Tomkins will take over from me when I have finished here. I will see you later."

As Julia reluctantly closed the door of her father's bedchamber, her aunt looked anxiously into her face. "I have something to tell you, Julia. I hope you will not be too disappointed, but Sophie has decided to return to London tomorrow." That her cousin had grown bored came as no surprise to Julia. She was considering what she could tactfully say when her aunt continued, "It was kind of Sophie to offer her support to us down here, but I am afraid she has found it very hard. Her nerves are not at all strong, as you know, and her fears for your father's health have quite worn her down. Besides, as I told her myself, her husband and children have need of her too, and indeed I think she is missing them."

Even in her present melancholy state Julia could hardly forbear to smile at this masterly presentation of Sophie's case. In fact, Sophie had left London to demonstrate her displeasure at Lord Mersham's refusal to buy her a new carriage. However, she had soon regretted her decision to join her mother at Downings, for the enforced quiet of a household which revolved round her uncle's sick room was not at all to her taste. In the last two days she had become very tiresome, and Julia was prepared to wager that her aunt had actively supported Sophie's decision to forgive her long-suffering husband and return to the bosom of her family.

"Mama, I should have thought it was perfectly reasonable for you to return to London with me," was Sophie's greeting as they came through the door of the salon. She was obviously continuing a discussion which had been interrupted by the arrival of the doctor. "I am sure Julia would manage very well without you. You hardly see her as it is, for she is forever upstairs with my uncle. And what if Mersham is still so stupidly obstinate—how will my nerves stand it? I need you, Mama. You must come!"

"Julia needs my support, Sophie—"

"So do I," said Sophie petulantly, her lower lip beginning to tremble. Julia hastily intervened.

"I think Sophie is right, ma'am. And even though the journey is not long, I am persuaded that Lord Mersham would not approve of her travelling unaccompanied. There is little enough to do here—" She was interrupted.

"There, you see! Julia doesn't need you, Mama, and I do! You can always come back if my uncle should d..." Even Sophie could not finish this last sentence. "If my uncle should get worse," she finished.

Lady Thornton looked irresolutely at the two girls, Julia with a steady smile on her lips and Sophie beginning to frown. "If you're sure, Julia..."

"Of course I am, ma'am. I have been truly grateful for your company these past weeks, but I must not be selfish any longer. Sophie is right. And the children will be glad to see you again." This clinched the argument. Lady Thornton's devotion to Sophie was only rivalled by her devotion to her grandchildren. Sophie hurried off to supervise the packing. Her mother waited until she had gone, then said,

"I would not dream of leaving you like this, Julia, but I will own that I am seriously worried about Sophie and Mersham. The cause of their quarrel was trivial, but they

have had too many such disagreements of late. I fear Mersham does not always allow for the delicacy of Sophie's
nerves. My presence in London might well help to avoid a
disaster. Are you sure you can manage by yourself, my
dear?''

"My dearest aunt, of course you must go with Sophie.
My father's illness was a shock at first, but I am now well
used to the situation. Pray do not worry. Sophie's marriage
must be your chief concern. I will send for you if I need you,
you know that.''

Still looking doubtful, Lady Thornton followed her
daughter, and Julia was left with her own sad thoughts. A
few minutes later one of the maids brought in a tray laid
with an appetising array of meats and a glass of wine. Julia
looked at them with disfavour, but her aunt's concern
touched her and, mindful of Dr. Carfax's warning, she tried
to eat. She had not swallowed more than a mouthful however when she heard the doctor's step on the stairs. She
hurried to him. "How is . . . ?" Her voice faded as she saw
the doctor's face.

"I will not beat about the bush, Lady Julia. Your father
is very ill. With careful nursing and absolute quiet he might
survive a month. I cannot promise more than that. I am
sorry—I know how close you are.''

Julia nodded and swallowed. The doctor looked at her
with concern and suggested he should send for her aunt.

"No, no!" said Julia. "You must not! Indeed I would
prefer you not to say anything that might upset Lady
Thornton. She has to return to London tomorrow and I do
not wish her to be burdened with anxiety about us. Please
do not repeat what you have just said to anyone else." She
sank into a chair and gratefully sipped the wine the doctor
handed her from the tray. When she repeated her determination to keep the true state of her father's health from her
aunt the doctor left, shaking his head and looking grave.

JULIA WAS still staring into space when her cousin returned. Now that she had achieved her own way, Sophie was
disposed to be pleasant. She sat down by Julia confidingly.

"Lord, Ju, I don't know how you stand the country! I would die of boredom, I swear. But then you always were a sobersides. Hugo Devenish called you a little philosopher once, and so you are! I remember I screamed with laughter at the time—you being called little, I mean. He was a great wit in those days. Do you remember him, Ju? It must be nearly ten years since."

Julia replied in a constricted tone that she did indeed remember Lord Rostherne, and asked Sophie if her mother needed any help in arranging her packing. But this effort to divert Sophie failed. She said slyly,

"Do you know you've gone pink, Julia? Of course you were nuts on Hugo, weren't you? What a fool you made of yourself over him, remember? Of course it's all forgotten now. Hugo is hardly seen nowadays." Julia looked her surprise. "Well you can't really blame people for cutting him, can you? After all, it was bad enough when he ran off with his brother's wife, though that was all over before we knew him, and Mersham says it's all nonsense anyway. But there, he's Hugo's friend. In my opinion there must have been something, don't you agree?" Without waiting for Julia's reply, Sophie went on, "It was the scandal about John Devenish and those awful suicides that ruined Hugo. That and the fact that he now has no money, of course. Oh, don't look so puzzled, Ju, you must have heard about it!"

"I . . . knew that the Devenishes had lost a great deal of money. But Father and I were in Greece when the old Marquess died. I suppose people had stopped talking about it by the time we got back. I don't spend much time in London."

"No, you've buried yourself alive down here. So you don't know that John Devenish stole vast sums from the Navy Office?"

Julia was shocked. "But I couldn't have missed hearing about that! The trial—"

"He wasn't tried! To tell the truth, the story was never generally revealed. But everyone knows he did it."

"Trial by 'everyone'—is that it? Poor Hugo! However, I don't want to hear any more, Sophie. When do you plan to leave tomorrow?"

Sophie ignored her, got up, and went over to pat her golden curls complacently before the mirror. "You know, Ju," she continued, "I expect I could have got Hugo Devenish if I'd tried a bit harder. And at one time I'd have liked to be Lady Hugo above anything. I'd have been a Marchioness now, too. But how providential it was that I decided to accept Mersham's offer—I simply couldn't have borne Hugo's disgrace. And now the Devenish estate might soon be up for sale. Whatever will Hugo do then? He's nutty on Donyatt, you know. In fact, he can be quite boring about it." Sophie came back and said in a confidential tone, "I don't suppose you know what they are saying now?"

Julia shook her head. She desperately wanted to end this conversation, but her tired brain refused to help her. Her cousin said with relish, "Well, the latest *on dit* is that Hugo is trying to rescue his estates by making a marriage of expedience. And no one knows who the lady is! Everyone is waiting to see if Hugo is going to marry the daughter of a merchant—or worse! Dear Lord, when you remember how stiff-necked the Devenishes were! Oh, you have the paper, I see! Listen to this, Ju!" Sophie cleared her throat and read out the malicious little paragraph. "Is not that shockingly spiteful?" she asked, her face full of enjoyment. "I wonder who can have written it?"

But Julia could take no more. She looked wearily at her cousin and said, "You were an unpleasant child, Sophie, and I am sorry for my aunt's sake that you do not improve with age. Go back to your husband. You would be wise to make your peace with him before it is too late."

Sophie's face grew scarlet. "At least I have a husband, Cousin! Don't you dare look down your nose at me! I didn't make myself the laughing-stock of London—you're the one who's an old maid, and likely to remain so for all your cleverness and handsome fortune!" She flounced away and went to her room. Julia sighed. Sophie's reply had struck at the very heart of her problem, but it had been an unedifying exchange none the less. And if Sophie's reaction to the paragraph was what Hugo was to expect from his friends, then she was truly sorry for him. She picked the newspaper up and read it again.

An announcement concerning the Matrimonial Plans of a certain Sixth Marquess of R. is expected within the month. The Polite World is eager to learn the identity of the Mystery Lady who is to make the Marquess the happiest, or at least the most Fortun-ate, of Men. But the Writer will Keep his Counsel, saying only that she is not to be found in the Ranks of London Society at Present.

It implied, of course, that Hugo was planning to marry beneath him. But it didn't actually say so... An idea was forming in her mind, so fantastic in its audacity that her first impulse was to reject it. She hastily dropped the newspaper and walked away, then turned back to look at it where it lay. No one would ever know... Quickly she ran to pick the newspaper up, and read the paragraph once again. It was definitely possible. The identity of the lady was a complete mystery. Dared she do it? What harm would it do? None! And it could do a lot of good. She would do it! A husband was what her father wanted for her, and a husband—or at least the promise of one—was what her father was going to have! If it would give him peace of mind she would make a pact with the devil himself. Even Hugo Devenish was not as bad as that—not that he would ever know.

Refusing to let herself be daunted by the boldness of the step she was taking, she marched upstairs and entered her father's room. He was awake and looking stronger. She saw Nurse Tomkins out and returned to the bed, smiling down at the invalid. "How are you now, Father? Are you feeling more the thing? I believe you're looking a little better."

"Julia, you and I have never dealt in flummery. We both know I've been given my notice to quit. It's just a matter of time, child. And if I could be happier about your future I'd welcome the notion. It's not much of a life, tied up here surrounded by a lot of petticoats, but it's all I'd have to look forward to."

"Father, if you talk in this dismal vein I shan't tell you something that will please you very much. At least, I hope it will."

This bait was sufficiently intriguing to take her father's mind off his troubles. "Well, what is it? Out with it, Julia!"

"It is this, Father," said Julia, producing the *Gazette* with a dramatic flourish. "Whoever wrote this has forced our hand—you have to know immediately. I really cannot imagine how the vulgar Press got hold of it."

"I don't understand what you're saying, Julia. Stop maundering, girl, and tell me in plain words. What is it?"

"This, Father." Julia proceeded to read out the paragraph, expurgating the more malicious phrases. She added, "Hugo and I had decided to wait till you were stronger before he came to see you. Now the cat is out of the bag, and I would not for the world have you hear of it from anyone but ourselves."

"Wait, wait! What are you trying to say? What has that piece of impertinence to do with us?"

"Can't you guess the identity of the 'Mystery Lady,' Father?"

"Julia, are you trying to tell me that you have entered into a secret engagement? But why?"

Genuine tears glistened in Julia's eyes, giving her words more conviction. "You were so very ill, Father. Dr. Carfax said the least excitement would hurt you. I persuaded Hugo to wait a little—was that so wrong?"

"Who did you say? Hugo Devenish? Rostherne's boy?"

"Hugo's father is dead," Julia said gently. "Hugo is the present Marquess."

"This is a funny business," said the Earl querulously. "I can't say I like the way you've gone about it."

"It was for your sake, Father."

"I like what I know of young Devenish, mind. A bit of a Greek scholar. I've written to him several times. Usually got a very civil reply, too. Well, well. I suppose I shall have to agree. He's got a good head on his shoulders... He'll know how to keep you in order. Hugo Devenish, eh?"

He was smiling as he sank back against the pillows, and
Julia gave a sigh of relief. Her father obviously remembered Hugo's interest in classical architecture, but had forgotten, if indeed he had ever known, Hugo's part in Julia's
catastrophic Season. Her plan seemed to be working better
than she could have hoped.

Until Lady Thornton's departure the following morning,
Julia was on tenterhooks lest her father should say anything about her engagement. She kept their farewell interview short and made sure she was present. When the coach
finally swirled away down the drive she breathed again. Now
all she had to do was to keep the fiction of her engagement
to Hugo Devenish alive until... She paused. Until her father was strong enough to take the truth, she told herself
firmly. Meanwhile he would have the peace of mind essential for his recovery. But what about the lie? asked a small
voice inside. It had to be confessed one could not be happy
about that—but what harm could it do? Neither Hugo nor
anyone else would ever know. And it had made such a difference to her father's state of mind... Yes, she had done
the right thing.

She would have been less complacent had she known that
her aunt had sent Sophie to see her uncle the night before.
That Sophie, who did not scruple to eavesdrop whenever she
thought she might hear something of interest, had paused
outside the door of Lord Carteret's bedchamber and had
heard everything...

CHAPTER THREE

HUGO DEVENISH swore under his breath and swept the pile of papers on to the floor. He got up impatiently, went over to the window, and when his butler came in he was staring out on to the busy street unseeingly. Without turning round he said, "Whatever it is, Lydiate, the answer is no."

"Lady Daresby is here to see you, my lord."

"What the devil is she doing in London?"

"She did not say, my lord. Does your lordship wish to see her?"

"I'll have to, Lydiate. In fact, I'm surprised she's not already— Ah!" He broke off as an imposing figure sailed past Lydiate.

"Hugo, my dear boy!" The lady swept to a halt in front of her nephew and offered her cheek for his kiss.

"Aunt Honoria," said Hugo, making an effort to put warmth into his voice. This visit was as unwelcome as it was unexpected, but in spite of her formidable ways his aunt was one of the few people whose company he still enjoyed. "What brings you back to London so soon? Lydiate, see if you can find some refreshment for Lady Daresby."

"And never mind bringing me tea or ratafia, Lydiate. I'm too old to start maudling my insides with rubbish like that!" said Lady Daresby firmly, handing Lydiate a voluminous cape of the sort which had not been seen in London for the past thirty years.

"Burgundy, then," said Hugo, raising an eyebrow and smiling in spite of himself. Then as the door closed behind Lydiate he added, "You've shocked Lydiate, Aunt Honoria. He doesn't approve of ladies who drink burgundy in the middle of the day."

"Lord, Hugo. Lydiate's known me since before you was born. If he hasn't learned what I'm like in all those years then he should be put out to grass! Time he was, anyway. He shouldn't be rattling about London at his age."

The idea of Lydiate rattling about anywhere was enough to set Hugo's lips twitching again. "Lydiate refused to leave me," he replied. "He should be at Donyatt, of course, but since the house has been shut up I cannot persuade him to stay in Dorset. You will never get him to agree that I could manage with just one manservant here in London. He seems to think that my consequence would suffer if I did not have the services of a butler. And in fact, his duties are not onerous. You could count my visitors on the fingers of one hand."

Hearing the underlying note of bitterness in these last few words, Lady Daresby gave her nephew a penetrating glance.

"Well, you wouldn't have much space for them if they did come," she said unsympathetically. "What possessed you to hire a house with such a poky set of rooms?"

"All I could afford, dear Aunt, all I could afford!"

"Why d'you need a house in London at all? Ain't Donyatt enough for you?" she demanded. "There's plenty of space there. I thought you liked the place."

Hugo did not reply to this, but something in his face warned her not to pursue the subject. Lydiate's entry with the wine caused a brief diversion. By the time Lady Daresby was comfortably settled by the fire with her glass of burgundy and some biscuits, the awkward little moment had passed.

"I daresay y'know why I'm here, Hugo."

Hugo shook his head. "The burgundy?" he ventured.

"Don't talk such rubbish, boy! The burgundy's barely passable! Y'father would turn in his grave if he knew what you were giving to your guests. He made a good few mistakes in his time, but he had an infallible nose for a good wine—which this certainly isn't! And don't tell me it's all you can afford! But where was I? Oh, yes, it's this." She drew out of her capacious pocket a cutting from the *Gazette*. "I want to know the meaning of this!"

Hugo waited in patience while she took out her spectacles, polished them, cleared her throat and began to read. But after the first few words he stiffened and the expression on his face was once again forbidding. When Lady Daresby had finished she looked up at him challengingly. "That's why I've come, Hugo!"

"I would not have expected you to read such trash, Aunt Honoria," said Hugo stiffly. "Still less that you should pay any attention to it. However I still fail to see quite why you are here. If you have come to commiserate with me on the insult contained in the paragraph, then I assure you your concern is unnecessary. I have learned to put up with worse than that in the past eight years, believe me."

Lady Daresby's fierce expression softened briefly. "I know that, my boy. But no, that's not what I've come for. It's what it says about your marriage plans that worries me."

"I really cannot see why they should concern you, ma'am. Until my marriage plans are made public in the proper manner, they surely concern no one but myself and the lady in question."

"Y'mean there's some truth in it? Well, 'pon my word, Hugo, I'd never have believed it of you! And if you are planning to bring some damned underbred tradesman's daughter into the family, then it concerns us all!" said the old lady, her jaw working. "And it's no good lookin' down that beak of a nose at me! Your high and mighty airs sit ill on a man who's planning to marry out of his class—for money!"

Hugo's face was pale and he was obviously restraining his temper with difficulty. "Aunt Honoria, I admire and respect you, but—"

"I don't admire and respect you, and that's a fact! I know you've had your difficulties. I know the Devenish fortune is as good as gone—though God knows why your poor fool father got himself into the hands of the money-lenders. When m'father was alive we were one of the richest families in the south of England! Where did it all go, Hugo? Tell me that." She looked sharply at Hugo, who turned away and went to the window again. "Oh, I don't really expect you to tell me any more than y've told anyone else, so you needn't turn your back on me. But it's as plain as the nose on your face that John was at the root of it all. Useless from the day he was born, that young wastrel—going off to play politics in London... What sort of occupation was that for the heir to Donyatt?''

"John is dead, Aunt Honoria. Let him rest," said a quiet voice from the window.

"John may be dead, Hugo—and from what I've heard it's better he is!—but you and Donyatt are still paying for his sins. There are quite a few who believe that it was your affair with Thérèse which set him off down the road to perdition."

"I gave up denying the affair long ago," said Hugo, almost indifferently.

Lady Daresby got up and went over to him. "My boy, I didn't believe it at the time, and I still don't believe it. I think you went to Greece to escape from that... that harpy. But the story did you a lot of harm, Hugo. It was clear that John believed it to be true, the pool fool." Hugo nodded without turning round, and after a moment Lady Daresby went back to her seat. "Have you heard of Thérèse since?" she asked casually.

"No, nothing. I have not seen or heard of Thérèse de Lachasse since the day I left London for Greece. Why do you ask?"

"She had a child, you know."

Hugo turned round swiftly.

"Oh, you've no need to be anxious, Hugo. It can't have been of John's getting. She'd been back in France for long enough before it was born. But you'd be a fool to ignore her. Her future in France can't be looking as bright as it was when Armand Benezat was one of Bonaparte's closest friends."

"Armand who?"

"Lord, Hugo, don't you know anything? Armand Benezat—Boney's favourite. Thérèse is his wife, or his mistress—I'm not sure which. Just don't let her try any tricks on you—about Donyatt."

"Aunt Honoria—"

Lady Daresby swept on unheeding. "I tell you, Hugo, Donyatt is a damn sight better off with you in charge than f John and the harpy had inherited." The tone of her voice changed as her eye caught the cutting from the *Gazette* and she remembered her original mission. "But not if you're going to fill it with tradesmen's brats!"

Hugo took a deep breath and turned round. He was formidably angry. For a moment the two faced one another across the room, then Lady Daresby said gruffly, "I'm sorry, my boy. I should have remembered what a time of it you've had. Mind, I don't take back a word I've said, but I shouldn't have said it. I'm a foolish old woman and m'tongue runs away with me when I'm not watching it." Her voice took on an unaccustomed wheedling tone. "But why don't you give yourself time to consider before doing anything rash? Go back to where you belong—go to Donyatt!"

Hugo's eyes moved fleetingly to the papers on the floor. Then with careful courtesy he led his aunt back to her chair. He said, "Aunt Honoria, unless I find a substantial sum of money before next quarter-day, Donyatt will not be mine to return to. Along with the other remaining Devenish assets it will be sold to meet the demands of the creditors."

Lady Daresby was shocked into silence. When she finally did speak, her voice trembled. "But Donyatt has been in the family for generations! You're not serious, Hugo!"

"You may believe me, Aunt Honoria. Hockliffe has checked very carefully."

"You've worked so hard all these years. I quite thought you were succeeding!"

Hugo shrugged his broad shoulders. "Another year or two and we might have managed it. But the creditors have grown impatient and are demanding repayment by Lady Day. Hockliffe has been looking into the terms of my father's agreement with them. I'm afraid he has found no hope of reprieve."

Lady Daresby looked wordlessly at her nephew. She had known, of course, that Hugo's circumstances were bad, but not that they were as desperate as this. Hugo no longer confided in her as he had once done. She doubted he confided in anyone. It was not surprising. He had been forced to learn some bitter lessons in the years since his father's death. She sighed as she thought of Hugo as a boy—laughter always lurking in his eyes, and a smile never far from his lips. And he had grown into a charming rogue who had returned from Greece to take London society by storm with his engaging ways and ready wit. She frowned slightly. Even then there had been something wrong...something in his attitude to the young ladies who had all fallen over themselves to attract his attention—a touch of cynicism, perhaps? For that, she was sure, Thérèse was to blame. But the look of cynicism was now permanent, and the harsh lines in his face bore mute witness to the unhappy years since that time.

"How can I help you?" she asked suddenly. They both knew that her widow's jointure, though handsome for her needs, was a mere drop in the ocean compared with the sums required before Lady Day.

"You cannot," he said flatly. "A rich marriage is my only recourse."

"But why must you make such a *mésalliance*, Hugo? There's no shortage of young hopefuls in your own class— rich, some of them, too."

"My dear aunt, I have no time. And in any case, not one of the delicately brought up young heiresses about to make their debut this Season would think of marrying me! And even if they did, their mamas would disabuse them of the notion! No, society has shown its view of the Devenish family scandal very clearly—embezzlement and unexpected deaths in the family might eventually have been overlooked, but loss of wealth never! I must look for my rich bride elsewhere, and take consolation in keeping Donyatt. But you could help me afterward, if you would—by introducing my bride to the ton."

"I'll do that, Hugo—but only if I can give her a thorough grounding in the usages of society first!"

"Such as drinking burgundy in the middle of the day, perhaps? May I offer you some more?"

"No, I've had enough for today, and in more ways than one, Hugo, in more ways than one! I'll take my leave before I change my mind about your scheme. I can see your mind is set on it, but I cannot like it. Still, there it is. I don't suppose you've taken the decision lightly."

Lady Daresby departed as impressively as she had arrived, leaving Hugo alone with his thoughts. They were not happy. Lightly indeed! If Donyatt itself were not threatened, he would not for a minute entertain the notion of marrying for money. The bitter irony was that Donyatt would have been safe in one more year. If only the creditors had held off for just a little longer! He poured himself a glass of wine, sat down in the chair lately vacated by Lady Daresby, and gazed moodily at the untidy heap of papers on the floor. He was not the first of his line to marry to save his estates—Ralph de Venoix, the founder of their fortunes, had married a child less than half his age, a ward of the Conqueror himself. And the second Marquess's wife, a shrew of no mean order, had brought the fortunes of two previous husbands into the family coffers. From all accounts she and the Marquess had led a pretty cat-and-dog existence, but for all that they had produced a large family and survived to a ripe old age. He must resign himself.

HE WAS ROUSED by the entry of an elderly gentleman, who entered unannounced.

"I knew you were expecting me, my lord, so I came in without troubling Lydiate. How is your lordship? Dear me!" This last was occasioned by the sight of the mass of papers on the floor.

"As you can see, Hockliffe, I have given the papers you left with me my most earnest attention." Hugo paused and stared into the fire. There was a long silence during which Mr. Hockliffe wondered if he should say something. He had known Hugo all his life, but in recent years he had found it increasingly difficult to guess at his employer's thoughts. His lordship's father, the late Marquess, had been an aristocrat of the old stamp. He would have ranted and stormed, had indeed done so in the past, had even thrown the inkstand, a heavily ornate pewter affair, at Mr. Hockliffe on one memorable occasion. He shifted uncomfortably. The silence was oppressive. Even the throwing of an inkstand

might be more welcome. He began to gather up the papers
from the floor.

"You are perfectly right," said a toneless voice from the
fireside. "Unless we can find a substantial sum of money,
they will foreclose."

Mr. Hockliffe's training in law caused him to blink at this
unequivocal statement, but he was unable to refute it. He
expressed surprise at the unreasonable behaviour of Lord
Devenish's creditors and lamented even more the terms, including the extortionate rates of interest, under which the
late Marquess had borrowed such huge sums. At this
Hugo's face darkened and, rising swiftly from his chair, he
walked over to the window. "I have told you before, Hockliffe, these matters are not for discussion. Not here, nor
anywhere else. Do you understand me?"

Mr. Hockliffe replied somewhat stiffly, "I understand
very well, my lord. Your lordship does me an injustice in
imagining for one minute that I would discuss any aspect of
the late Marquess's affairs outside these four walls. But I
have conducted the business of the Devenish estates for
more years than I care to count, and it has caused me great
personal distress, I assure you, to see such a handsome pat-
rimony reduced, in spite of my most earnest representa-
tions, to its present miserable state in the course of the
three—no, two—short years preceding your father's death.
Your brother—"

"Enough!" Hugo cut him short. There was a brief silence. When Hugo spoke again his voice was calm. "Believe me, Hockliffe, I am grateful for all you have done these
past years. No one could have worked harder or with greater
devotion to the interests of the estates. We both know however that, though another year might have seen us through
the worst, time has run out on us and more drastic action is
needed."

"Your lordship is thinking no doubt of our discussions
with Mr. Prendergast?"

Hugo nodded brusquely. "You will hear from me very
soon, Hockliffe. I wish you good day."

Mr. Hockliffe took himself off, shaking his head sadly. It

came as no surprise to him that his employer had decided to seek a bride among the classes made rich in the new manufacturing industries. As a practical man of business, Mr. Hockliffe thoroughly approved of such a course. But Lord Hugo, as Mr. Hockliffe still thought of him, was most unlikely to find a congenial companion in the person of Miss Rosabel Prendergast, who was a vulgar, hoydenish creature with few pretensions to refinement or beauty. She was young. Perhaps she could be trained to fit the great position she was about to fill? He doubted it. He was really very doubtful. Mr. Hockliffe sighed as he walked up Cheapside, and arrived at his lodgings with a heavy heart.

AFTER HOCKLIFFE'S departure Hugo sat down at his writing table with the air of a man about to perform a hateful task, and wrote a short note. This he dispatched immediately. It was not in his nature to shirk unpleasant duties, and his reluctance to commit himself to the Prendergast family irritated him. Why the devil was he feeling such distaste for his projected marriage? He was no longer such a fool as to imagine that a love-match existed outside the playhouses or the covers of a romance. Nor did he wish for one! Love was a dangerously unpredictable madness. It had destroyed his brother John—and the family with him. He wanted no further part of it. It would, however, have been pleasant to choose a woman from his own world, one of sense and breeding, who would have shared some of his interests. Well, that course was closed to him, and far from feeling this reluctance to take the final step he should be blessing his good fortune in coming across the Prendergasts.

Hugo had known Josiah Prendergast, retired ironmaster, for just three weeks. Josiah had amassed a huge fortune from his foundries in the Midlands, and it was now his dearest wish to see his only child established as a member of the aristocracy. Hugo had been invited to dine at the Prendergast mansion, and after a long and overpoweringly grand meal he and Josiah had come to a tacit agreement. Miss Prendergast had signalled her willingness to be approached—indeed her large, slightly prominent pale blue eyes had stared at Hugo throughout the meal rather as a dog stared at a particularly luscious bone. So far Hugo had hesitated to take the final step, but there was now no other way to save Donyatt. If things went as planned he would soon become—how had that damned impertinent paragraph put it?—"the most fortune-ate, if not the happiest, of men", or something of that nature. Well, if such a marriage could be a success, he was determined to try to make it so.

FOUR DAYS LATER Hugo was standing in Mr. Prendergast's overfurnished library, consumed with a rage he was not troubling to hide. "Am I to infer that your daughter has changed her mind, sir? Or is this some misplaced jest? If so, you must forgive me if I fail to see the humour of it."

"No, it's no joke, your lordship. Before you come running after my Rosabel, I'd advise you to sort yourself out a bit better. I'm not giving my daughter, nor the 'andsome fortune that goes with her, to a man who's busy making a fool out of us all! Josiah Prendergast isn't the man to throw his wealth down the drain. You just look at that!" Mr. Prendergast, who was almost as angry as his lordship, thrust a paper under Hugo's aristocratic nose. "You read that!"

Hugo looked with contempt at the page before him and turned away. "It is not my practice to read the trash conjured up by the gossip-mongers."

"You should, then!" cried Mr. Prendergast. "You might learn a bit about yourself. I did! From what it says 'ere, Rosabel's not the one you've set your 'eart on at all! And I'm not 'aving Rosabel made un'appy by any loose aristocratic ways and that's flat! With all the money I've got, don't think I can't do better for 'er than a Marquess with nothing but 'is title to recommend 'im. There's better fish in the sea nor ever came out of it."

Hugo's lips tightened. Then he said with thinly veiled contempt, "Your daughter would have had no reason to complain of my behaviour if she had had the good fortune to become my Marchioness, Prendergast. However, I think you are right. Miss Prendergast and I should not suit. Pray convey my excuses to her. I will bid you good morning."

As he turned to go, Miss Prendergast herself burst into the room. "But Pa, you promised I should have him!" she

cried. "And a tiara. And a big house." She drew a deep
breath. "I shall scream, Pa. I shall scream if you let him
go!"

Hugo made his way out, reaching the front door almost
before the footman could open it. As he left the house, the
noises coming from the would-be Marchioness were filling
the air. Profoundly grateful as he was to escape, his rage at
being forced to undergo such humiliation was such that he
decided to dismiss the coachman and walk back to Dover
Street. However, the walk did little to improve his temper.

"My congratulations, Hugo!" shouted one young buck
as he passed in his curricle. And as he approached Berkeley
Square an elderly dowager who hadn't spoken to him for a
year said, "What a naughty man you are, leading us all on
like that!"

What the hell were they talking about? And why the hell
couldn't they mind their own business? In the light of what
had happened in Prendergast's library that morning, it was
damned annoying. Then he paused. It had been at least ten
days since the paragraph speculating on his marriage to the
ironmaster's daughter had appeared in the *Gazette*. Why
was everyone reacting now? There must be more to it. He
had been so enraged by Prendergast's impertinences that he
had paid little attention to what he had actually said. Hugo
was frowning more heavily than ever as he strode into his
house. Lydiate received him at the door, taking his hat and
cane. One glance at his master's face was enough to warn
the elderly butler to tread carefully.

"A lady is waiting to see you, my lord."

"I don't wish to see anyone. Tell her I am not at home to
visitors. And Lydiate—bring a bottle of brandy and yesterday's *Gazette* to my room straight away—after you've
shown the lady out."

"The lady was very pressing, my lord. She said the matter was extremely urgent—"

Hugo continued across the hall. "I cannot conceive of
anything in the world more urgent to me at this moment
than a large glass of brandy in my room. Are you going to
perform the duties I pay you for, Lydiate, or am I to serve

myself? I think our visitor has addled your wits. Who is she?''

Lydiate cleared his throat nervously. ''The lady refused to give me her name, my lord—''

Hugo stopped short at the foot of the stairs. ''You let her in? You showed her into my study without getting her name? What the devil has happened to you, Lydiate? I begin to think you really have gone mad. Get rid of her, before you lose your position as well as your wits. I'll be in my room.''

''If you are annoyed with anyone, Lord Rostherne, it should be with me! Your man did all he could, short of using physical force, but I refused to be put off. I must discuss a rather...difficult matter with you.''

The voice, clear and musical, with an attractively husky overtone, came from a figure in the shadow of the study door.

CHAPTER FOUR

HUGO SET HIS TEETH. "You must forgive me, ma'am, if I seem to be taking this invasion of my home and my privacy in bad part. However, I will be plain. I do not wish to speak to you at the moment. Do I make myself clear? If you will leave your name and direction with Lydiate I will endeavour to see you in the near future. Good day, ma'am. Lydiate?"

As the butler went towards the door and Hugo put his foot on the bottom stair the visitor came forward, removing her veil. "How very foolish of you, Lord Rostherne. You must know that no lady would ordinarily be so insistent unless the matter were truly important." Hugo was about to reply, but she forestalled him. "No doubt you are ready to observe that my behaviour would not immediately lead you to believe that I was a lady. Am I right? I assure you, however, that I am."

Hugo was intrigued in spite of himself. He took a closer look at his visitor, who put up her chin and bore his inspection with composure. He saw a tall, graceful woman in her middle twenties. She was quietly but very fashionably dressed in dark green velvet, and had the air of one used to command. Her face was pale and her features unremarkable except for a pair of large, widely-spaced grey eyes. She regarded him calmly while he struggled with a faint memory of a silver-eyed girl hiding among the plants in Lady Godfrey's winter garden. "Good God, you're Sophie Mersham's cousin—"

He would have said more, but the lady put a finger to her lips. "Pray do not mention my name. Not here." She glanced at Lydiate, who was standing stiffly by the door with an expression of disapproval on his long face.

"Lydiate's discretion is complete, I assure you. But though I know you are a Marchant, it is so long since we met that I cannot for the life of me recall your Christian name. Jane? Georgina? Something like that."

The lady's voice acquired an edge it had not possessed before. "It is Julia. Will you give me five minutes of your time? In private?"

Hugo looked at Lydiate, who now seemed puzzled, and dismissed him with a glance. "Very well, Lady Julia. However, I sincerely hope that what you have to say is as important as you think. If I remember correctly, your ill-judged pranks caused me some annoyance when we last knew each other. So far you appear to be running to form."

Julia suffered a pang of conscience at these words, and it was fortunate that she had her back to Hugo as he ushered her into the study, for he might otherwise have noticed her look of guilt. By the time they were facing each other again, she had recovered her composure.

Hugo offered her a chair, but she shook her head. "What I have to say, Lord Rostherne, is better said standing. I have a confession to make." She hesitated and he said impatiently,

"Well, what is it? I cannot conceive of anything which would occasion all this fuss. Please continue."

"I should first tell you that my father is gravely ill—so ill that he is not expected to live above a month."

When there was another pause, Hugo said stiffly, "You have my sympathy, Lady Julia. Lord Carteret is one of the few men in England whose scholarship on the antiquities of Greece I whole-heartedly admire. If there was anything I could do to help you I would. But our acquaintance is so slight..."

"That's just it! I'm afraid that in the eyes of the public at large it isn't."

"Lady Julia, I have had a long and harassing morning, and though I have sympathy for your present situation my patience is not inexhaustible. I cannot imagine what you are trying to say. Will you please explain before I send for Lydiate again?"

Julia thrust a copy of the *Gazette* into his hand. "I think perhaps you should read this first."

Hugo's frown grew heavy again as he read the marked paragraph. Prendergast's angry reaction was explained. Couched in tones as malicious as the first, the paper announced a mistake in its original surmise about the Marquess of R.'s marriage plans. The *Gazette* now had it on good authority that the lady who was about to bestow her affections—and her large fortune—on the happy Marquess was Lady Julia M., daughter of Earl C...!

Hugo uttered something which was fortunately inaudible as he flung the paper into a corner. Then, turning on his heel, he strode up and down like a caged tiger. Julia stood where she was, to all appearances unaffected, but in truth extremely apprehensive. Finally he stood still and said in tones which sent a shiver up Julia's spine, "By God, I'll have the paper ruined for this! Their first piece of scurrilous innuendo I ignored. It was at least based on a grain of truth. But this goes beyond what I will tolerate." He paused and, visibly restraining himself, said more gently, "My apologies to you, Lady Julia, for suggesting that what you had to say was unimportant. But...forgive me, was it wise to come here? Surely it will only give rise to yet more gossip?"

"Lord Rostherne—" began Julia. She was not allowed to continue.

"My hope is that the consequences of this announcement are not as serious for you as they have already been for me. But I cannot immediately see a way of protecting you without causing yet more scandal. Believe me, I will find out who has initiated this outrageous story about us both, and will make him sorrier than he has ever been in his life before." He grew angry again. "Be assured I will not rest until I have run him to earth!"

Julia took a deep breath. "It was me," she said in a small but steady voice.

"I beg your pardon?"

"I didn't send any information to the newspaper. But I started the rumour. That's why I am here. To confess."

There was an appreciable silence. Hugo stared at Julia for what seemed like an age, but was probably less than a minute. She had once stood on the slopes of Etna, and had experienced the same unbearable tension. Suddenly her knees gave way and she sat down on a chair nearby. When he eventually spoke his voice was dangerously calm.

"I find this...difficult to believe. You must forgive me if I appear to be dull-witted. Did you say *you* started the rumour, Lady Julia?"

She swallowed. "Yes, I did," she said, a little hoarsely.

"May one ask what possible motive you could have had for interfering in my private—my very private—concerns?" he asked, still in the same soft tone.

"I didn't intend any harm, Lord Rostherne—" began Julia, but she was startled into silence as he strode towards her and snarled,

"You didn't intend me any harm...! You have my permission to put me in Bedlam, ma'am, if I believe that for one second. I now remember the last occasion on which we met. You have never intended me anything else!"

She winced as he shouted these words in her ear, but replied bravely, "You do me an injustice, Lord Rostherne. It's true that I once in a fit of childish rage swore you enmity, but you surely do not mean to suggest that I would carry on such a ridiculous vendetta for—what is it?—nearly ten years? Especially as we have not even met in all that time."

"How am I to know what is in that twisted mind of yours? What other reason could there be for making up such a tale? Do you realise what damage you have done?" he demanded. "What a stupid question! Of course you do— you would not have done it else!" He turned away as if he could not bear the sight of her. She got up and followed him.

"Lord Rostherne, I'm truly sorry if I have inadvertently caused you embarrassment—"

"Embarrassment!" exploded Hugo. "By God, your gift for understatement is unsurpassed, ma'am!"

"But I swear I never intended what I said to go beyond the walls of my father's bedroom. And as soon as I learned that it was more widely known I came here to warn you and to apologise. Believe me." When he remained unresponsive she added, "If there is anything I can do to put it right—"

"Have no fear on that score. I already intend to publish categorical denial in tomorrow's *Gazette*. That is the very ast I shall do."

"Oh, but you can't!" cried Julia.

"Can't, ma'am? Can't? Who will stop me, pray? Surely ot you? Or are you prepared to be the laughingstock of ondon for a second time?"

"I beg you to let me explain the situation," pleaded Ju-a. Something of the desperation in her voice seemed to each Hugo, for he said,

"I shall give you three minutes, ma'am." He indicated a hair and they sat down.

"I told you that my father is...is dying," she began. "Dr. arfax says he must have rest and quiet, but this is impos-ble while his mind is tormented with the thought of my uture." She looked down at her hands. "You obviously emember my catastrophic London Season, Lord Rosth-rne. Of course, I was far too young—and too ignorant of e ways of society—to be launched. For this my father lames himself, and it is his belief that this disastrous ex-erience has destroyed my chances of making a suitable natch." She looked up defiantly. "He is wrong, of course. ut I cannot persuade him to believe otherwise." She aused, and looked at Hugo, who was sitting back in his hair with an air of sardonic patience.

"Pray continue this affecting tale, Lady Julia."

"When I saw the first paragraph in the *Gazette* I realised nat since it did not mention the name of the lady in ques-on—not even her initials—I could turn it to good use. In rder to set my father's mind at rest I told him..."

"Yes, Lady Julia?"

"I told him that you and I were secretly engaged," Julia inished.

"And your father no doubt swallowed this...this Ban-ury story, not even stopping to ask why we should think it ecessary to enter into a secret engagement, or why he hould have heard nothing from me? I suppose he was the ne who found this charmingly original way of announcing ur engagement to the world at large? What sort of a fool do you take me for? You'll have to do better than this, my girl, if I am not to deny your story."

"I cannot tell you who sent the information to the *Gazette*, for I do not know, Lord Rostherne," said Julia with dignity. "But my father is a sick man, and so less critical than he would normally be. He believed what I told him. And now, if you publish a denial, I shall have to tell him the truth, and his peace of mind will vanish. Surely you see that? It is such a little thing to ask. You may deny it all you wish after... afterwards."

"Tell me, Lady Julia, do you feel no pangs of conscience? Oh, I would not be so foolish as to expect that you might have some regard for my feelings, or worry about the effect your action might have on my plans—"

"I told you! I didn't think you or anyone else would ever know!"

Hugo ignored the interruption. "But had you no qualms at deceiving your father, who you say is not likely to live?"

"Of course I had!" cried Julia. "That lie will be on my conscience for the rest of my life. But my father's peace of mind means more to me than my own, Lord Rostherne. The paragraph in the *Gazette* was like an answer to a prayer, and I used it. I would do so again if the choice were before me a second time."

"You read the paragraph out to him, you say?" When she nodded he continued bitterly, "So your father, whom I have always admired, now regards me as a damned fortune hunter."

"I didn't read that bit out to him. It seemed to me that it was written in purest malice. But..." She hesitated, and then asked quietly, "It's no more than the truth, is it? I mean, you are marrying for money, aren't you?"

"I'll thank you to keep your confoundedly impertinent observations to yourself, miss!" he said, angrily glaring at her. "Little though you seem to think it, my private affairs are no concern of yours. Shall I repeat that, so that there can be no possibility of misunderstanding? Stay out of my affairs, Lady Julia, or by God it will be the worse for you!"

At this point the door of the study opened to admit the Mershams, followed by a flustered Lydiate. At the look of outrage on Hugo's face, the butler hastened to explain. "I'm sorry, my lord. When Lord and Lady Mersham called to see your lordship I explained that you were otherwise engaged, and showed them into the very small parlour. But on hearing Lady Julia's voice, Lady Mersham was so anxious to speak to her that she found she could not wait until you were free... my lord..." The old man's voice trailed away miserably, and when Hugo took pity on him and released him he tottered out gratefully.

"Your family appears to be determined to reduce Lydiate to a quivering wreck, Lady Julia," observed Hugo pleasantly. Lord Mersham hastened forward with apologies.

"Hugo, I'm dashed if I know what got into Sophie's head. Th'thing is, she's so impulsive, she can never bear to wait for anything. Y'll have to excuse her—y'know what she's like. Lady Julia, your servant, ma'am. But the truth is, when m'wife heard you were here she couldn't wait to see you."

Sophie had been standing by the door, gazing with greedy speculation first at Julia's flushed face and then at Hugo's all too evident anger. But now she stepped forward, saying, "You really have no need to make excuses for me, Peter. Of course I had to come! Living as Julia does in the heart of the country, she is probably unaware that it is shockingly indiscreet of her to be visiting Hugo unchaperoned, even if she is engaged to him. He will tell her so himself. Perhaps he already has? Was that the reason for the little disagreement I could hear as we came in?"

"Who told you we were engaged, Sophie?" asked Hugo stiffly.

Sophie opened her eyes wide. "Why, surely that is what the paragraph in the *Gazette* meant? I must admit I was never so surprised in my life. I wasn't aware you had even seen Julia since... since your little contretemps. And that was years ago. But now it's to end happily ever after. How fortune-ate for you, Hugo! At this particular time, I mean."

Hugo checked a sudden movement towards her. "Is this a social call, Peter? Or do you have something particular you wish to discuss with me? If so, I can see you in a very few minutes when Lady Julia and I have finished what we have to say. Perhaps you'd care to wait in the small parlour?"

"But Hugo," protested Sophie. "Surely now that we are here to chaperon her, Julia can join us. I cannot wait to know her wedding plans."

"My love," Lord Mersham said hastily, "you are presuming too much. Come, leave Hugo and Lady Julia to settle their affairs in peace. Come, I insist!" He took his wife firmly by the arm and led her to the door. But suddenly she stopped, turned round and said,

"You know, Peter, it's my belief they aren't engaged at all! I know that at Ju's age one doesn't exactly go into raptures when one is about to be married, but these two don't look as if they even like each other! It's all a hum! There isn't an engagement after all, is there, Hugo?"

Faced with this sudden challenge, Hugo unaccountably hesitated. Sophie clearly knew or suspected something. He looked at Julia. To all outer appearance she was perfectly calm, but he somehow knew that she was under an almost unbearable strain. He could not bring himself to betray her—not in front of Sophie's spiteful curiosity. He said, "Peter, you should restrain your wife's impatience. Matters are not always as easily or as quickly arranged as she thinks. Lord Carteret's illness naturally causes a number of problems, which will have to be discussed before any proper announcement can be made. Now, if you will permit Lydiate to show you to the small parlour...?"

As soon as Hugo had shut the door behind the Mershams, Julia sank into a chair and put her face in her hands. Hugo's expression softened as he looked at the downbent head. "Would you like me to get you something, Lady Julia? Or would you prefer to be alone?" At the sound of his voice she took a deep breath and stood up. They regarded one another in silence for a moment.

"Why didn't you tell them?" Julia asked at last. Hugo found himself at a loss. It had been an absurdly quixotic impulse, one that he could hardly afford.

"It wasn't the moment for a public denial," he said coldly. "Sophie Mersham would waste no time in creating scandal and gossip. I cannot afford that at present."

"I see."

He knew that she must be disappointed by his response, but there was no sign of it in her demeanour. Remembering the gawky, vulnerable child of seventeen, he was astonished at the grace and poise of the grown woman.

"Then I must not keep you from Sophie and her husband any longer, Lord Rostherne," she said in a cool voice. "I am sorry for any difficulties my impulsive action has caused you. If you could see your way to giving me some warning before issuing your denial, I should be grateful. I will take my leave of you."

Hugo once again experienced an absurd desire to reassure her, to tell her he would wait, but he restrained himself. He would have to see Hockliffe again before he could allow any delay in the plan to save his lands. The Prendergasts were lost to him, but there might be others. "I will engage to keep you informed, Lady Julia." He hesitated, then added, "I hope your father's state of health is not as desperate as you fear."

A shadow crossed her face fleetingly and then was gone. She gave a small inclination of her head. "Goodbye, Lord Rostherne."

She left without looking at him again, and Hugo joined his guests in the small parlour. He firmly resisted all Sophie's attempts to draw him on the question of his engagement, and kept the conversation on general topics. He and Peter Mersham had quite a lively discussion on the state of the English Turf and the prospects for that year's Derby, until Sophie pouted and said she was bored with all this sporting talk, and the Mershams, to Hugo's profound relief, left.

When he rose the next morning Hugo was conscious of a lightening of the spirit. At first he was unable to account for it, for the vexed question of what to do about Julia Marchant was now added to all his other problems. And with the loss of the Prendergast connection his financial difficulties were worse than ever. That was it! The fact that he no longer faced the prospect of living with Rosabel Prendergast was enough to give him a new optimism! He smiled at the absurdity of this. There was no reason to suppose he would fare better with any other wealthy industrialist's daughter. And why should he? A bargain was a bargain—his title and position in return for the bride's dowry. Personalities did not enter into it. He would be lucky to find anyone as suitable as Miss Prendergast. All the same he found himself whistling as he ran down the stairs to breakfast.

CHAPTER FIVE

MR. HOCKLIFFE was sitting in the study, anxious to hear the result of the previous day's visit to the Prendergasts. He was shocked to hear that Hugo had, so to speak, been refused, but when Hugo told him the reason his sense of propriety was outraged.

"I can hardly believe it, Lord Rostherne! Whatever is the world coming to? A young lady to put herself forward like that, to announce her non-existent engagement to you, more or less because she feels like it! What a very forward and underhanded way of behaving! And she allowed it to be published! The *Gazette* must issue a retraction immediately—it could do you irreparable harm. Indeed it has done so already! Dear me, dear me!"

Mr. Hockliffe's agitation increased as he considered the disastrous consequences of the second announcement in the *Gazette*. He asked to see it. Hugo sent for it, but warned the lawyer, "I'd like your opinion, Hockliffe, but the situation is not straightforward. The girl had her reasons. I will decide myself how best to deal with it."

"Your lordship may have no choice but to issue a complete denial immediately. If the estate is to be saved we must have no delay in finding a successor to Miss Prendergast." He took the *Gazette* and examined it. "Now, who is this dangerous female? Well, bless my soul! Lady Julia Marchant! But why should Lady Julia wish to embarrass you in this way?"

"To be fair, I must tell you that she had no intention of making it public," said Hugo. He proceeded to explain the circumstances in which Julia had made her original announcement.

"Then how did it get to the ears of the *Gazette*?"

"Lady Julia has no idea. I, however, have my own suspicions."

But Mr. Hockliffe was occupied with a fresh idea. "Lady Julia Marchant, eh? Your lordship is no doubt aware that the Marchant fortune is a very large one? A very fine one indeed! The estate itself is entailed, of course, but a considerable amount of capital and lands lie outside the entail. And, if I remember correctly, Lady Julia inherited handsomely through her mother, too."

Hugo's expression grew forbidding. "You will abandon that train of thought on the instant, Hockliffe. I will not involve Lady Julia in any mercenary schemes."

"It seems to me she has involved herself, Lord Rostherne, and to no good effect," said Mr. Hockliffe tartly.

Hugo got up and walked about the room. "I cannot help admiring her devotion to her father, Hockliffe. And I believe her when she says it was not her intention to cause me harm, though the consequences have been unfortunate."

"Unfortunate! They might well be disastrous! I will do my best to find another connection as suitable as the Prendergasts, but I fear it may be difficult. Fortunes such as theirs, attached to fathers who are eager to rise in the world and daughters who are willing, do not grow on trees, Lord Rostherne. And time will soon run out."

"How much time do we in fact have, Hockliffe?"

"Strictly speaking, the bills will be presented for payment on Lady Day. However, if your lordship were to announce his engagement to a person of known fortune before that date, I am sure we could contrive something." He coughed and added drily, "The announcement must be a formal one, phrased and presented in the proper manner, Lord Rostherne."

Hugo gave a short, humourless laugh. "I don't suppose Lady Julia will meddle any more in my affairs, Hockliffe. No, with good luck and your good offices, the *Gazette*'s next use of my name will be to publish my engagement as formally as you please." He threw himself into a chair. "Lord, what a distasteful business this is! I sometimes ask myself if even Donyatt is worth it all."

Mr. Hockliffe was shocked. "All great families go through periods of difficulty, my lord. But whatever the feelings of an individual member, it is his duty to do all he can to preserve as much as possible for future generations."

"I know, I know. Would to God this particular burden had never fallen on me! It should have been John's lot... But then the Devenishes would not be in these straits without his foolish, wicked weaknesses."

Mr. Hockliffe held his breath. Never before had Lord Hugo voluntarily mentioned his elder brother's name. But his lordship quickly recalled himself and said in a brisk voice, "What are you waiting for? Go out and seek a suitable heiress, Hockliffe!"

"It is not my usual line of business, as your lordship is aware. However, I will do my best. I should point out that it would make matters considerably easier if we inserted a denial in the *Gazette* of any involvement with Lady Julia."

"No," said Hugo slowly. "On reflection, Hockliffe, I have decided I will do nothing about that. We shall ignore it. But you may deny it as much as you please to any anxious fathers."

"Are you doing this to help Lady Julia, Lord Rostherne?"

"I cannot help her as she would wish. But I'll give her as long as I can before the rumour is publicly denied. From what she said of her father's state of health, it might be long enough."

"Lord Rostherne—" began Mr. Hockliffe.

"You must do your best without that, Hockliffe. Good day to you."

MR. HOCKLIFFE did his best to some purpose. Less than a week later he arrived at Dover Street with the welcome news that Sir Herbert Sockridge, a former East India merchant, who had failed to purchase his way into the peerage by any other means, was now prepared to give his well-endowed daughter to the Marquess of Rostherne.

"And Miss Sockridge?" asked Hugo. "What are her views? She's not another Rosabel, I hope?"

"No, no! She is a very quiet, ladylike girl," said Mr. Hockliffe. "She seemed complaisant enough, though I do not remember her expressing any firm opinion."

In the event Miss Sockridge proved never to have any opinions. Indeed it would have been difficult for her to do so, for Sir Herbert regarded the holding of opinions as strictly his domain. He was a large red-faced man, and both his wife and his daughter clearly went in dread of him. There ensued several interminable evenings when Sir Herbert's prowess in the hunting field, his acumen in the acquisition of wealth and his views on estate management were propounded with great satisfaction by the master of the house. Hugo gritted his teeth and consoled himself with the thought that, though Miss Sockridge never gave any indication that she liked him or was even interested in him, she must surely welcome an escape from this pompous, opinionated bore. Matters proceeded swiftly, and an announcement for insertion in the *Gazette* was in the process of being formulated when Hugo's plans received another sudden and devastating check.

JULIA WAS IN low spirits on her journey back to Downings. Her effort to make her father's last days happy seemed to have gone seriously wrong. Hugo Devenish had said he would let her know before he issued any denials, but she could see for herself that he could not afford a very long delay. His financial situation was obviously even more serious than she had thought, and if she had indeed jeopardised his plans to marry an heiress then she could well understand his anger. Indeed, she reflected, after his initial burst of rage he had been more sympathetic than she deserved. She sighed, and then called herself to order. Instead of repining she should be devising ways of telling her father the truth. But after wrestling with the problem for a while she gave up. There was no easy way. Her thoughts took another, no less unhappy direction. Her father had not questioned her on her sudden decision to go to London but had insisted that she stayed the night there with her aunt. She had given way—she liked the thought of travelling back in the dark even less than her father did. She now wished she

ad returned the night before. In her father's present state
f health so much could happen even in two short days.

In the event, she found him in better spirits than he had
een for some time. His eyes were brighter and he seemed
o have regained some of his strength. His speech was much
mproved. "I see I shall have to leave you more often, Fa-
her," she said, smiling affectionately down at him. "My
bsence seems to have done you good!"

"Don't talk such rubbish, girl! Sit down and tell me how
oung Devenish is. I suppose you saw him when you were
n London?"

"I had quite a... quite an interesting talk with him, Fa-
her, but we were interrupted when Sophie and Peter Mer-
ham arrived. She was very shocked that I was seeing Hugo
nchaperoned, and so I came away."

"Meddlesome cat! Did she think Devenish would seduce
ou in broad daylight under his own roof? Besides you're
ngaged, or as near as makes no difference. 'Quite an inter-
sting talk', eh? Not very loverlike! What did Devenish say
bout the *Gazette*?"

"Er... He was extremely angry. Indeed, I had a difficult
me with him, but I think we have sorted it out—for the
oment."

"Good! Well I've missed you, Julia, but I believe I've
ent the time usefully. You needn't think you're the only
ne to have 'interesting talks'."

Julia was surprised. On the whole her father was not on
ood terms with most of his neighbours. And the last time
e vicar had paid a visit, the Earl had sworn that the
mealy-mouthed gospel gabbler" would bore him to death
ven before the doctor's damned potions killed him. So she
miled at him again and said, "I thought Dr. Carfax said
ou were to rest. Who were these interesting people?"

"I didn't say the people were interesting, Julia. But what
ey had to say was. I've been hearing about Hugo Deven-
h. You didn't tell me he's as good as drowned in the River
ick."

Julia stared at her father in consternation. "Is he?" she
aid feebly.

"Dammit, you must know that, Julia. You're not a fool.
And don't look at me like that. I'm not going to forbid the
bans just because the Devenish estates need your money.
From what I've heard, it's not young Devenish who went
into debt. It was his father bailing out his worthless
brother."

Julia had always known that her father's views were un-
conventional, but it gave her a shock to hear this practical
approach to Hugo's problems. And it made it so much
harder to extricate herself from her false engagement. She
decided to try nevertheless. "Oh, Father!" she cried. "Do
you think he wants to marry me just for my fortune?"

Her father gave her a sharp look. "Good God, Julia,
you're not an eighteen-year-old with a head full of romantic rubbish! Of course your fortune will be useful! That isn't
to say it's the only reason he's marrying you. And you can
set your mind at rest about his supposed affair with his sister-in-law, too. He may well have had a tendre for her—she
was a damned attractive woman from all accounts. But he
behaved just as he ought—took himself off to Greece out of
temptation's way. It was his fool of a brother who set the
tabbies' tongues wagging about his wife and Hugo. No, no,
there's no reason for second thoughts there. Anyway, you've
accepted him and that must mean you think you'd be happy
with him. You're a sensible girl, Julia, and I trust your
judgement. I shan't object if you two wish to make a match
of it."

"Thank you, Father," said Julia hollowly. "I think it's
time for me to have a word with Mrs. Tomkins. I must
thank her for looking after you so well."

As she escaped from the room she thought she heard her
father laugh, but decided she must be mistaken.

THE FOLLOWING weeks passed slowly for Julia. Lord Carteret's health continued to improve, and for this she was
grateful. But since she feared that his recovery resulted to a
large extent from her "engagement," she was in hourly
dread of hearing from Hugo Devenish. Though she thought
of little else, she was no nearer to finding a satisfactory way
of making her confession to her father. A conversation with

Dr. Carfax did little to make her happier, for he warned her that Lord Carteret was still very seriously ill and could easily suffer a setback.

"I am sure it is unnecessary to tell you, Lady Julia, that your father would not survive a third attack."

After this she increased her efforts to make her father rest, but in spite of all her remonstrances he insisted on "putting his affairs in order" as he described it. "Let me alone, girl. I know what I have to do, and you don't. You can't inherit this house or the land that goes with it, you know that. Damned entail! But what's-his-name—Geoffrey Marchant—is plump enough in the pocket. The estate won't come to harm if everything else goes to you. Funny to think of it—young Geoffrey in my place. He'll do better by the land than I did. I was always too interested in travelling to bother much with it. Left it all to the agents to do."

"But Father you settled all this months ago when Cousin Geoffrey came to visit. Don't you remember? His wife came with him."

"Ha! Now there's a man who lives under the cat's paw! It's my belief he spends most of his time out of doors to escape from that Friday-faced dame."

But Julia was not to be put off. "So surely you need not see the lawyers so frequently? Mr. Farleigh has been here three times in as many days."

Her father stared at her then said, "Perhaps you're right. I'll send a message to Farleigh. He shan't come again."

Julia would have been seriously worried by this apparent meekness if she had not suspected that her father had finished whatever business he had been conducting.

A COMPARATIVELY peaceful time ensued. Julia read the *Gazette* to her father, played a gentle hand of picquet with him when he felt strong enough, and brought him books and documents from the library when he wished to study. Among these was a collection of drawings and notes on the Greek temple on Aegina. When she admired them her father mocked her for not recognising Hugo Devenish's work.

"They're excellent stuff. He should be doing more of this instead of contriving ways and means. That's no business

for a gentleman. Still, he'll be free of those worries whe
you're married. He'll be able to travel again then. Or are yo
going to keep him here at home?"

"I'd go with him, you know that. Or do you think h
would expect me to remain at home? I'm not sure I shoul
like that at all. Oh, Father, do you think I should marr
Hugo?" Poor Julia was still trying to find some way of ge
ting her father to change his mind about her "engage
ment". But all her attempts to present Hugo in poor ligh
failed. She had known of old that once Lord Carteret ha
an idea in his head it was impossible to persuade him t
change it. And he was now convinced that Hugo Devenish
was the right man, indeed the only man, for his daughter.

THE NEXT AFTERNOON Julia was in the library replacing th
folio of Aegina papers. Though the drawings were meticu
lously done, Hugo had obviously been in a great hurry whe
he had sent them, for the accompanying note had bee
hastily scrawled and the papers were untidily arranged. Ju
lia decided to put them in order. She spent some time ad
miring the drawings as she worked, and was intrigued whe
she came across a scrap of paper which was stuck to th
back of one of them. The paper was badly stained and th
writing was not Hugo's firm hand, for it wavered an
slanted as if the writer had been ill. She had succeeded i
deciphering one word—"prevert", or was it "prevent"?—
and was trying to work out the rest—"ru...de squat..
eons"—what could it be?—when Chard, the butler, cam
in to ask if she was at home to Lord Rostherne.

Her heart leapt into her mouth and the paper fluttere
unheeded to the floor. Then calling on all her reserves o
strength she said calmly, "Of course, Chard. Show Lor
Rostherne in."

It was as well she did so, for Hugo swept in almost befor
Chard could turn. He had obviously ridden from London
and was equally obviously in a rage.

"How wrong was I to change my mind about you!" he
said as soon as Chard had left the room.

"Good afternoon, Lord Rostherne. You have clearly
ridden hard. Shall I send for some refreshment?" said Ju

ia, in an attempt to reduce the charged atmosphere. It failed lamentably.

"Don't you try your polite airs on me, you Jezebel! I won't be taken in again by your damned play-acting!"

Julia became angry herself. "And I will not be spoken to in such an uncouth manner, Lord Rostherne," she said icily. "Unless you restrain your language I will leave this room on the instant. What has put you in such a rage that you forget all propriety?"

"Don't pretend you don't know, Lady Julia. Please spare me that!" Julia walked swiftly to the door and had just grasped the handle when he strode over and put his hand on hers. "If you leave this room now, your father will know of your machinations without delay." They stared angrily at each other for a moment. Then he went on, "I mean it, Lady Julia. You will not cozen or bluff me into silence again."

Slowly Julia let her hand fall, and turned back into the room. "I am in your hands, Lord Rostherne, you know that," she said bitterly. "Does it gratify you to torment me like this? Why else are you here if not to tell my father? But surely a letter to me would have been enough? At least I could then have attempted to soften the blow for him. I truly thought I could trust your word, fool that I was. Why did you not do as you promised?"

"Oh, you're very good," he jeered. "I suppose you will now claim ignorance of the notice in today's *Gazette*, look at me with those enormous eyes, and expect me to believe everything you say. Not any more, Lady Julia. Believe me, not any more."

"What notice?" she cried desperately. "I don't know of any notice! You were to put one in the *Gazette*, not I!"

"But not one like this, Lady Julia. Read it—if you insist on carrying out the farce to the bitter end."

He confronted her with a copy of the morning's *Gazette*, pointing aggressively at an announcement just under the Court Circular. Julia read out in incredulous disbelief. "'A marriage has been arranged between Hugo, Sixth Marquess of Rostherne of Donyatt Abbas, Dorset, and Julia, only daughter of Earl Carteret of Downings Castle, Surrey. The marriage will take place shortly at Downings Castle."'

She sank into a chair and put her hand to her brow. "I don't understand," she whispered. "I don't understand at all."

"I've already admired your histrionic skills, Lady Julia. Sarah Siddons herself could hardly do better. But now I wish you to tell me without further waste of time the reason for all this." He slapped the paper with his hand. "Is it simply that you wish to ruin me? If so, you have accomplished it beyond your wildest imaginings. There is now no hope that I can meet my creditors' demands. Donyatt is lost to me completely..." He turned away from her and seemed to be fighting for control of his voice. Then he continued, "But why should you bear me such malice? Surely not because of what happened years ago? You said yourself it was over." A thought occurred to him and he came right up to her, taking her chin in his hands and forcing her to look at him. "Or is it not over even yet, Lady Julia? Do you still cherish a secret admiration for me? Is this some ruse to force me into marrying you after all these years? That must be it, though I can hardly believe it."

Julia did not attempt to break away, but looked at him scornfully. "You are right to have doubts on the subject, Lord Rostherne. It is true—and I am ashamed to admit it— that when I was too young and too foolish to know better I believed you to be a gentleman worthy of my admiration. However, I came to my senses and quickly changed my mind. My recent acquaintance with you has given me no reason to suppose I was wrong to do so. I find you eminently resistible, believe me."

He let her go, and faint colour appeared in his cheeks. "Forgive me," he said stiffly. "I am certainly in no position to think highly of myself—nor to imagine that anyone else of quality would, either. You must put it down to the thought of losing Donyatt. It has been the Devenish home for nearly three hundred years...and I am attached to it. Deeply attached."

There was a short silence. Then he added suddenly, "But if you did not put this notice in the *Gazette*, who did?"

"Some enemy of yours? Someone who really does wish to see you ruined?"

Hugo did not immediately dismiss this as a piece of nonsense. He considered it carefully. "It's possible," he said briefly. "But not probable. And I'm still not convinced that it is totally unconnected with you, Lady Julia."

"Then I can see no purpose in continuing this conversation, Lord Rostherne. I am sorry to be so disobliging, but since I have not the slightest notion how the *Gazette* came to publish this announcement I cannot help you any further."

"Help me!" exclaimed Hugo, losing his temper again. "I would have no need of help if it were not for you, Lady Julia! Allow me to remind you that this whole damned mess arose from your feather-headed scheme to comfort your father!" Julia was about to make an equally heated response when Chard knocked and came into the room.

"Excuse me, my lady. Lord Carteret requests you to bring Lord Rostherne up to see him."

Julia gazed at Hugo in consternation, then said quickly, "I do not think my father is well enough to receive visitors, Chard. And...and Lord Rostherne is just leaving..." She looked pleadingly at Hugo, but he made no effort to help her. "Perhaps later, when my father is feeling stronger."

Chard said in neutral tones, "His lordship was most insistent, my lady. He has ordered refreshment to be served in his bedroom immediately." He went out. The two left behind in the library looked at each other in silence. Finally Julia said,

"You now have the opportunity to reveal my deceit to my father, Lord Rostherne." She paused, and her voice trembled in spite of her efforts to control it. "I...I beg you to tell him as gently as you can. He is really not very strong."

Hugo hardly seemed to hear her. He was looking as if a new and startling possibility had occurred to him. "I wonder," he said softly. "I begin to wonder... Come, Lady Julia. We have said some harsh things to one another. Perhaps some of them at least were undeserved. Be assured I would not willingly harm your father." They went up the stairs together.

CHAPTER SIX

HUGO AND JULIA were greeted by a vision of Lord Carteret sitting by the fire in the splendour of a wine-coloured brocade dressing-gown, a Turkish cap and embroidered slippers. His cheeks had more colour in them, and his eyes were sparkling in anticipation of the coming interview. "You've persuaded him to come up, I see, Julia. Good! Rostherne, I'm glad to welcome you. Forgive me if I don't get up. The truth is, I can't. Come here, my boy, and let me have a look at you." His face inscrutable, Hugo placed himself near Lord Carteret. "You've the air of your father. D'you have his hasty temper, too?" the Earl said at last. Worried though she was, Julia could not help a most unladylike snort and hastily turned it into a cough. Her father ignored her, his eyes never leaving Hugo's face. "I'll wager you're not the fool he was, though. So you want to marry Julia, eh?"

Julia held her breath. Now was the moment of truth. What would Hugo say? How would her father's frail strength cope with the shock? But Hugo's reply was a puzzle.

"Why did you do it?" he asked.

"Ha! I was right!" said the Earl in delight. "The boy has his wits about him!" He looked slyly up at his guest. "Do what, Rostherne?"

Unsmiling, Hugo replied, "It's my belief that today's... somewhat premature announcement of my engagement to Lady Julia was inserted in the *Gazette* at your bidding, Lord Carteret. May I ask why?"

"Don't put on your high and mighty air with me, boy! Why shouldn't I? It was high time someone did something to clear up your situation. And I may have been ill and confined to my room, but that don't mean to say I can't find out what's going on. That notice will keep your creditors at bay until you marry her."

Julia saw that Hugo was controlling himself with difficulty. She came swiftly forward. "Father, the truth is—"

"If you're about to tell me that your secret engagement was all a hum, Julia, then you can save your breath. I've known that since before you went to London." Julia gazed at her father speechlessly.

"If that is indeed the case, sir, I should like to know why you allowed your daughter to continue with her singularly ill-advised scheme," said Hugo coldly. "You could have saved me a great deal of trouble, and Lady Julia a great deal of distress."

"But that wasn't my aim, young man! Julia deserved to suffer after treating me as if I was in my dotage, unable to put two and two together or read a newspaper for myself. And as for you—what sort of a slow top are you not to see that the match is exactly what you need? Julia's every bit as rich as the tradesmen's daughters you've been making a bid for—and a damn sight more presentable. She doesn't want for intelligence when she's not mawkishly worried about me. She'd make a first-rate wife. You ought to thank me—"

Julia and Hugo interrupted at the same time.

"Father, how could you?"

"Lord Carteret, I am conscious of your age and the state of your health, otherwise, I assure you, I would call you to account for such unpardonable interference in my affairs."

"Rubbish! You'll thank me before you're through, see if you don't."

"Father, I cannot marry Lord Rostherne. We should not suit . . . if you only knew . . . Oh, this is all so humiliating! I have never been so ashamed in all my life. How could you, Father?" Julia was perilously close to tears. She walked quickly over to the window, struggling to regain her self-possession.

"Lady Julia—"

"Pray do not say another word, Lord Rostherne," she cried desperately. "This is all my father's doing. I cannot tell you how sorry I am that you have been subjected to this treatment."

"Bless me, I quite thought you had started it, Julia!"

"But I never intended it to go beyond these four walls, Father! How did it get to the ears of the *Gazette* in the first place? You didn't—?"

"No, I don't know who gave it to the *Gazette*, but I rather fancy Sophie took the word to London. We should all be grateful to her."

"Grateful! That I find myself in an impossible position with Hugo Devenish for a second time? Forgive me, but I think you must be mad, Father!"

"Time will tell, my dear, time will tell. Now you've had your say—and not to much purpose. What about you, Rostherne?"

"If you are asking me if I think you are mad, sir, then no, I do not. Devious, perhaps. High-handed, certainly. I should like you to tell me what you thought you would gain in publishing that notice in the *Gazette*, however. You have told us yourself that you already knew Lady Julia's original story to be false. So why are you trying to force us both into a match which is desired by neither?"

"Sit down, sit down, both of you. We can't have a reasonable conversation if the two of you tower over me like this. Come over here and sit down!" said the Earl. "And while I put my thoughts in order you might pour some wine for us all, Rostherne. It's too important an affair to be rushed. I must make you see what's best for you both."

With a small bow, Hugo handed Julia a glass of claret. He looked not unsympathetically at her distress, and rested a hand on her shoulder for a moment. Then after serving some wine to Lord Carteret he sat down and waited with a sceptical air.

When the Earl began to speak his voice and manner were very different from his usual trenchant tones. He might have been lecturing at a university, or talking to the Royal Society, for he chose his words carefully and spoke with deliberation.

"We've all three studied the Greeks," he began somewhat surprisingly. "And I have always tried to convey to you, Julia, my admiration for their gift of logic, of rational thought. I'd be surprised if you haven't felt the same admiration, Rostherne." He looked enquiringly at Hugo, who gave a brief nod without speaking.

"Well now, let me review our present situation in the light of reason. You, Rostherne, have not attempted to hide that you are urgently seeking a rich wife. You are a man of culture and feeling, yet, according to my informants, the brides you have so far sought have neither taste nor education, and are ill-equipped to share the great position you would offer them. In short, you have resigned yourself to a miserable existence in order to save your inheritance and, in particular, Donyatt, for future generations. Am I right?"

Hugo studied the deep red wine in his glass and said in a low voice, "Miss Prendergast was not what I would have chosen in a wife. But Miss Sockridge seemed to be a quiet, well-bred girl, and...amiable. I had a hope of happiness with her."

"So quiet and so amiable," mocked the Earl. "Do you know she has twice tried to run away with a young officer to whom she is devoted?"

Hugo looked up, startled. "No, I did not. But how do you know?"

"I have my own intelligence systems, my boy. You may trust my information."

Hugo looked angry, but said nothing more.

"Now we turn to the Marchants—*'père et fille'*. I blame myself severely for the fact that Julia has never married. In my arrogance I insisted that she should enter society when wiser voices said she was not ready for it. I was wrong, and Julia suffered a setback from which she has never recovered. Your share in the fiasco of her London Season is not unknown to me, Lord Rostherne." Julia gasped and Hugo started to speak, but the Earl held up his hand. "I do not blame you in the slightest degree, my boy. Indeed, the only person to blame is myself. I exposed my only daughter to a situation in which she was bound to fail. I have no need to tell you how I have felt since that time. But in spite of that, Julia and I have been happy together. She is a delightful companion, and for many years she has run this household for me very competently. I suppose that is why I have selfishly not made a greater effort to see her established." Here the Earl paused and took a sip of wine. Hugo glanced curiously at Julia, but she ignored him. She was still stunned at the extent of her father's knowledge.

Lord Carteret continued, "But now I have been told that my life hangs on a thread, and my chief—indeed my only—preoccupation is Julia's future. I believe you to be honourable, intelligent and capable of making my daughter content. You have a great deal in common with her—far more than with Miss Sockridge, for example. And the fortune she brings you—you see I make no bones about it—will not only save Donyatt, but will free you from further financial worry. Is it not worthy of consideration?"

"I would have preferred to consider it, Lord Carteret, without the pistol of a public announcement at my head."

"If I hadn't put that notice in the *Gazette,* would you be here today? Of course not. I haven't time for finesse and a waiting game, Rostherne. I'm not here for much longer, and I want to see Julia safely settled before I go."

Julia interrupted them. "But you can't force us to marry, Father! Cannot you see that we have no wish to do so? I can lead a very comfortable life of my own."

"A spinster? With your hired companion and your pug dogs? Unable to travel, restricted to female company? Don't be a fool, Julia! What do you say, Rostherne?"

Julia got up in exasperation and returned to the window as the two men faced one another. They seemed to think she would accept any decision they made without protest. Well, they would see!

"Your arguments are persuasive, Lord Carteret, and I am honoured by the confidence you appear to have in me. But, strange as it may seem in the light of my recent efforts, I feel some scruples in asking any lady of quality to marry me. It was different with Miss Prendergast and the others. I felt I was making a fair bargain with them—my title for their money. Lady Julia has no need to enhance her position in the world. Indeed, since it will take time for me to reestablish myself in society, in marrying me she would diminish her position. I have nothing to offer her."

"You have security, a home, children to offer her, sir!"

A stifled exclamation came from the window.

"Lady Julia!"

"A more soulless, inhuman bargaining I have yet to hear. Has neither of you any regard for my feelings, or respect for your own? I would rather die in loneliness than be a party to this . . . transaction!" said Julia, her voice trembling with rage.

"When I was a boy, my lady, you'd have been told to marry him and that would be the end of it!" said the Earl, losing his judicious tone as anger got the better of him. "And as for you, Rostherne, if you don't want my daughter, say so and have done. But don't try to put me off with your so-called scruples." He broke off short, his mouth working. "'Pon my life, I don't know what the world is coming to. What are you looking for, both of you? A love-match? Pshaw!" He threw himself back against his cushions. Julia looked at her father in concern. It was obvious that the Earl was growing too excited. His breathing had become uneven and his hands were trembling. She fetched some of his cordial, knelt beside his chair, and anxiously gave it to him.

"I wish I had never seen that wretched paragraph," she said unhappily. "Or that I had had the sense not to try to make use of it. Oh, Father, what can I do to put things right?"

He looked at the anguish in her face and shook his head. Then he leant back with a sigh and closed his eyes.

Hugo had observed this with a thoughtful look. Now he said slowly, "If you will excuse us, sir, I should like to talk to Lady Julia alone." He looked at Julia for her agreement, and then asked, "May I call your man?" The Earl nodded slightly, his valet was brought in, and Julia followed Hugo downstairs to the library. Here he saw her seated and, standing with his back to the fireplace, he said, "Lady Julia, apart from one delightful interlude at Lady Godfrey's ball, our relationship has not been a friendly one. It would not in the slightest surprise me if you found it difficult to consider a life together. I will be frank enough to confess that I would have preferred to find my own solution to this . . . this wretched crisis in my fortunes—one that did not involve you. But your father is right. I have no other means of saving Donyatt." He paused and then went on slowly, "I can also see that your father is so set on a match between us that he will have no ease of mind until it is accomplished. So I am asking you to reconsider."

"Reconsider what, Lord Rostherne?"

"Your very strong determination to die of loneliness rather than to enter into a business transaction."

"A business transaction?" echoed Julia.

"I believe that is how you described marriage to me."

Julia grew paler than ever. "You are asking me to marry you, Lord Rostherne?"

With a touch of impatience he replied, "My dear girl, pray pull yourself together! You are not usually so slow-witted. Yes, I am asking you to marry me. It seems to me to be the only course of action left for us."

"But I cannot marry you! We do not love each other!"

He looked at her derisively. "I agree that few would describe it as a love-match. But then, I have never looked for one. Have you?"

"Yes," she said quietly. "Once, when I was young and foolish, I did."

"You have made the point for me, Lady Julia! 'Young and foolish', indeed. But we are neither of us so young any longer, and we should not be so foolish, either."

She flushed angrily. "I am not yet at my last prayers, however! And to marry you at this juncture would be to abandon forever any hope of happiness with someone I could love and respect!"

"And what sort of love and respect do you think you deserve, Lady Julia? Tell me that! I cannot imagine that any man of principle would look with complaisance on your recent conduct." Julia was stunned. She had never considered the effect her escapade might have on her own future. Her thoughts had not gone beyond her father's illness. Without waiting for her reply Hugo went on, "By God, I find women beyond belief—and you more than most! You started this farce with no thought of the consequences either to yourself or, God help them, to anyone else involved. Oh, yes, I know you are going to protest that it was for your father's good, but not even you can honestly tell me that he is now in a happier frame of mind! And I surely do not need to tell you what your actions have done to my life! Yet you refuse even to consider the only way you can make amends. You sit there so damned demurely, talking of 'love' and 'respect'." He strode towards her and Julia shrank back in her chair as he bent over her. "If you were a man I could call you out for taking such liberties with my name and person!"

"If I were a man, Lord Rostherne, this situation would not have arisen," said Julia defiantly. They stared at one another, then Hugo turned away to stride about the room in frustrated fury. "And may I ask what hope of happiness you think we would have, when we can hardly be in a room together for two minutes without your raving like a lunatic at me? No, no, you need not think you can bully me into compliance."

Hugo stopped where he was and ran his hand through his hair in exasperation. Making a visible effort to speak calmly he said, "You may disbelieve me if you wish, Lady Julia, but I am not in general so ill-tempered, whatever your father may say. You will allow that I have suffered more than a little provocation of late." His voice grew more conciliatory. "I believe I could offer you a reasonably comfortable life. We should spend most of our time at Donyatt, and from what I observe you are happy in the country. I think we share more than a few interests—am I right? In time I think we could deal amicably together." Julia gazed at him doubtfully as he went on, "After all, you may not regard me with favour, but my desire to save Donyatt is surely not unworthy of your respect. The estate is not now as large as it once was, but it is all I have left, and in spite of many setbacks I have fought hard to keep it. There have been Devenishes in Dorset since the days of the Conqueror. Is it so wrong to wish to preserve seven hundred years of tradition?"

"Is there really no other way?" Julia asked, somewhat desperately.

"No."

"Could my father not lend you the money?"

"I would merely be substituting one set of creditors for another. No. Besides, that would not answer your father's fears for you."

It was Julia's turn to move restlessly about the room. Finally she asked, "What sort of marriage would it be? Purely a business transaction? Would you expect...expect more of me than the use of my fortune?"

"Eventually I would hope to have a son, Lady Julia, to inherit Donyatt."

Julia nodded and walked about the room again. Hugo watched her in silence.

"I will marry you," she said at last, "but there are conditions."

Hugo looked wary. "Which are...?"

"After we are married I would wish to stay with my father for as long as he needs me. I...I do not think that will be long."

Hugo nodded. "And?"

"After that I would like to have time to get used to you before...before I am asked to provide this son—or daughter. And if our relationship should prove impossible I would wish to be free to go on my own way."

It was Hugo's turn to spend time in thought. "During this time that you spend 'getting used to me'—is our relationship to remain totally platonic?" A glint appeared in his eyes. "And at what point do you decide you are sufficiently 'used to me'?"

"I don't... I don't know," she stammered. "But I couldn't possibly live with you as your wife at the moment."

"Shall we let the future take care of that, Athene?"

"No! I would want something more definite than that! And if you wish me to consider any kind of alliance between us, Lord Rostherne, you will not call me by that name!"

"Very well. You may have a year—one year in which I shall endeavour to persuade you that I am not such an ogre."

"And if you fail?"

"I refuse to consider such a possibility—but yes, if you insist, you may then go your own way. But it will not happen. Ath—Julia. You see—" he drew her towards him "—I shall take pains to keep you." She was grasped firmly in his arms and kissed. She wanted to protest, to say this was just the sort of thing she did not wish for, but to her delight and despair she was immediately transported into the past, into the alcove at Lady Godfrey's ball. The feeling of enchantment she had experienced nearly ten years before, and never since, returned. When Hugo would have released her she held on to him, confused and dizzy. He laughed, and whispered, "Athene? Julia? You'll marry me?"

Julia was on the brink of telling him that she would do anything in the world he wanted, but then she took a deep breath and pulled herself together. "Yes," she replied as coolly as she could. "Yes, Lord Rostherne, I will marry you." He would have kissed her again, but she held him off. "On the terms we have agreed," she said firmly.

WHEN THEY RETURNED to Lord Carteret's room he was in bed. The valet expressed himself anxious about his lordship and suggested that Dr. Carfax should be sent for. Julia nodded and hurried over to the bedside. He was propped up against his pillows, breathing with difficulty. His eyes were shut, but when he heard Julia approach they opened. There was a question in them.

"Lord Rostherne and I have agreed to marry, Father." She looked round and Hugo came up to the bedside.

"I will take good care of her, sir. I promise you that."

A faint smile appeared on the Earl's face. "Course you will, Rostherne. Made for one another. She'll be good for you, too. That's good. That's...very...good..."

The Earl's voice died away as he closed his eyes and appeared to fall asleep. Julia looked anxiously up into Hugo's face. "He's not...?"

"No, he's just very tired. He needs to sleep. Come, let me give you another glass of wine. We'll drink to our... What shall I call it, Julia?"

"Our bargain," said Julia calmly.

LORD CARTERET improved slightly after Dr. Carfax had visited him, but the little doctor's prognosis was gloomy. "He should never have exerted himself so much. He has very little strength left, Lady Julia. All these visitors he's been having... And then, to cap it all, he gets up! It should not have been allowed, not at all!"

Hugo, seeing that Julia was unable to reply, answered for her. "Dr. Carfax, when Lord Carteret's mind is set on doing something, have you ever known him to pay attention to anyone?"

The doctor had to acknowledge that he had not, and departed unhappily.

But Lord Carteret had not yet accomplished all he had set out to do. A few minutes later Hugo was summoned to his lordship's bedside where he was asked to marry Julia without delay. "There's no reason to wait, is there? And as far as I am concerned there's every reason to hurry. I might not be here next month. Can you do it, my boy?"

"Yes, of course," replied Hugo. "I would be delighted to marry Lady Julia as soon as possible. And afterwards," he added firmly, "Lady Julia will remain here with you—until I have finished my business in London."

"Ah, yes, you'll need time to deal with the lawyers. Farleigh has the details of the settlement for Julia and so on. You see to it, my boy."

"Don't worry, sir. Julia's future will be safe."

So they were married very quietly at Downings Castle ten days later. There were no guests, and little fuss was made. Julia simply wore her best dress—an elegant primrose silk—and after the ceremony the newly married couple spent the evening with Lord Carteret. The next day Hugo departed for London and Mr. Hockliffe. "I shall come whenever you need me, Julia," he said gently before leaving. They both fell silent. Lord Carteret was surviving by sheer force of will, and they both knew it would not be long before Julia would be sending for her husband to take her to Donyatt.

"Don't look like that, Julia. I shall do what I can to make Donyatt a pleasant place for you to live."

"I know, I know," said Julia, her eyes filling with tears. "It's just that Father and I have been so close. It will be strange without him. But don't worry. I promise to be a more cheerful companion at Donyatt.''

JULIA HAD NEARLY eight weeks with her father, then he died in his sleep. Though she was deeply unhappy at her own loss, she felt she must be glad for him. He had been increasingly frail and in constant pain towards the end. Their last conversation of any length had taken place the day before. After talking for a while of their travels together he said suddenly, "You'll be happy with Rostherne, Julia. He's a man you can put your trust in. He's had a bad time with one thing and another, but that's over now. You'll have a good life together.''

Conscious of the bargain she had made with Hugo, Julia did not know how to answer. Her father chuckled and added, "Oh, I know I've thrown you two into a marriage neither of you wants. You may even have some notion that it won't last. But it will. I knew what I was doing when I drove you into it. You're both headstrong, but you're made for each other. I wouldn't be surprised if it don't turn into a love-match...'' Still laughing at his joke, her father fell asleep, and that night he died.

Julia held on to her father's last words as she sadly started the business of packing up her personal belongings. The new Lady Carteret proved to be unexpectedly kind and helpful. Her taste was not for the exotic objects and furnishings which the late Lord Carteret had gathered on his extensive travels, so most of these were carefully packed and left for Julia to collect later. As she sorted and directed, Julia wondered about her new home. What would Donyatt be like? It would be hard to imagine a more difficult beginning to a marriage, but she and Hugo would have to come to terms. However harsh and cynical he appeared to have become, something of the old Hugo must still be there. There had been moments during the past weeks when he had shown kindness...

WRAPPED UP in her own concern for her father and the radical changes which were about to take place in her personal life, Julia took only a cursory interest in the fate of the nations battling it out in Europe. She knew, of course—who in England could remain ignorant?—that Napoleon Bonaparte had suffered disastrous reverses of fortune, and that during the previous October the French army, largely composed of young, inexperienced recruits, had been decimated at Leipzig. Now Napoleon, after years of dominating Europe, had been forced to abdicate, and the Bourbons in the person of Louis XVIII had been reestablished on the throne of France. But how could she have foreseen these events, so distant, so apparently unconnected with her personal life, would have a profound effect on her future? For with the restoration of the French monarchy, the position of Thérèse Benezat, born de Lachasse, formerly married to John Devenish, and later a star of Napoleon's court and wife to one of his chief advisers, became highly uncomfortable. Snubbed and rejected by the returning Royalists, who considered her a traitor to her class, she began to look for a future elsewhere—across the Channel, perhaps...

CHAPTER SEVEN

HUGO WAS IN London during the intervening weeks, spending most of his time with Mr. Hockliffe and the other lawyers. As the news of his marriage spread, followed just two months later by the death of his father-in-law, he was afflicted by a stream of callers wishing to congratulate him or condole with him with varying degrees of sincerity. Society had apparently now decided to forgive him. Lady Thornton was one of the first. In recent years she had found Hugo too intimidating to be completely at ease in his company. Nor was the memory of Julia's behaviour during that fateful Season a comfortable one. But although she was somewhat disturbed by the haste and secrecy of her niece's wedding, she was unaffectedly happy that Julia had married.

"For I must tell you, Lord Rostherne—oh, forgive me, I suppose I may call you Hugo now." She gave a nervous laugh. "I must tell you, Hugo, that you are a fortunate man. Julia will make a perfect wife." Encouraged by Hugo's smile, she went on, "Dear me, little did I think all those years ago that you two would finally make a match of it! But there, however badly she may have behaved, Julia was always rather taken with you, you know. I cannot say how happy I am for you both." She went away with tears of sentiment in her eyes.

A second well-wisher arrived in the person of Lady Daresby, who demanded to meet her new niece and was very put out not to find her with Hugo. When she heard of Lord Carteret's death, however, she instantly understood. "Poor girl! Of course she won't want to face society just yet! It wouldn't do, in any case—she'll be in black gloves for a good bit." She expressed her delight at the match. "I knew you wouldn't let the family down, Hugo! Tradesman's daughter indeed! The Marchants are almost as old a family as the Devenishes, but I dare say you know that. I may suppose you were having a joke at your aunt's expense, eh?" She poked him in the ribs with her stick. "Mind you, there are those who say that the joke is on you..." She cackled with laughter when she saw that Hugo was looking puzzled.

"The Maypole, Hugo, the Maypole! She waited ten years but she finally captured you after all! The girl's got stamina, as well as a handsome fortune! I wonder who put her up to it? It was a masterly scheme, you have to grant that. Well, your troubles are over, my boy, and I'm glad of it. Though you'll have to watch your step with that wife of yours, mind. She'll have you dancing to her tune if you don't watch out!"

She went away, still laughing, leaving Hugo once again uneasy about Julia's motives in marrying him. Had it all been a very clever plot? His doubts were not set at rest by a visit from the Mershams. In his kindly way Peter was eager to reassure Hugo that his hasty wedding was perfectly understandable in the circumstances.

"Only thing to do, old fellow! To marry before m'wife's uncle died. Would have had to wait a year otherwise—impossible situation. Very sensible, I call it. Doesn't matter what anyone else says—"

Sophie interrupted him. "We're very pleased for you, of course, Hugo. And I am not afraid to admit that I never imagined for a minute that Julia would succeed... I mean that you would agree to her scheme..."

"What scheme's that, my love?" asked her husband. "Hugo, have you been hatching schemes with Julia?"

"Pray do not say another word, Mersham!" exclaimed Sophie. "I can see that Hugo knew nothing about it. Well, what a clever puss Julia is after all! All her problems solved!"

"I say, Sophie," protested Lord Mersham. "The poor girl has just lost her father..."

"Sophie, I don't wish to hear any more," said Hugo. But Sophie had a score to settle with Julia and would not be stopped.

"Oh, but you're one of the family now, Hugo! And you surely don't believe for a minute that Julia's chief concern was her father, do you? Why, what a saint you must think her! No, no. As soon as she saw that paragraph in the *Gazette* she was on to it like a bird. I was there at Downings at the time. You remember, Mersham? It was just before you bought me that sweet little phaeton. And Julia talked to me about you then, Hugo. It was fortunate that I happened to be returning to London the next day... Oh, don't look at me like that, both of you! Perhaps it was naughty of me to see that the *Gazette* got the hints about you and Julia, but we girls must stick together." She tapped Hugo playfully on the arm. "Gentlemen can be so difficult to attract. And Julia was always nutty on you. Of course, my poor dear uncle would always do anything Julia wanted..."

Hugo knew Sophie of old and would normally have discounted most of what she said as malicious gossip. He had begun to like what he knew of Julia, to feel that this marriage might well turn out better than he had hoped. But on this occasion he was easily persuaded that his instinct had been wrong. For one thing, his experiences in the past had not encouraged him to believe that anyone's motives were to be trusted, least of all those of a woman. For another, the two aunts, who were both unquestionably fond of Julia and himself, had also implied that Julia had intended to marry him from the first.

So from that point on Hugo began to review the events of the past few weeks with a more jaundiced eye. He had been prepared for the gossips' sly remarks and insinuations about fortune-hunting, and could easily shrug them off—he had grown an extra skin since his father's death. But was he now to regard himself as a gullible fool, victim of a clever woman's machinations? That would be more difficult to bear. He spent some time going over the meetings with Julia since she had first come to see him in Dover Street. She had certainly been very convincing. In spite of his own difficulties he had felt an overpowering desire to comfort her in her distress—

as he had done ten years before. And look at the trouble that
had caused him! It seemed he had a blind spot where Julia
was concerned—he would not normally have been such an
easy target. Yet she had not appeared to employ any arts to
attract him . . . she had defied him, rather. There had even
been times when he had wanted nothing more than to beat
her! Or kiss her out of her mind. Now where had that
thought come from? It was curious. Perhaps it was as well
that Julia had asked for a year's grace. Perhaps he, too,
needed time to get to know his "partner"! And, after all, he
now had what he had most wanted—the means to save
Donyatt. He might have to wait a little before acquiring an
heir, but after that . . . If Julia were as devious as Sophie had
implied, she could go her own way as much as she damn well
pleased—and so would he!

IT WAS AS WELL that Julia knew nothing of the effect of Sophie's efforts, for it might have been the last straw. She was
exhausted, both physically and emotionally. Her life seemed
to have been in turmoil ever since her father's first attack.
The constant vigil at his bedside, her desperate stratagem to
comfort him, and its catastrophic results, were all taking
their toll. So when she set off with Hugo for Donyatt Abbas
in Dorset just ten days after Lord Carteret's funeral, she was
content to sit for hours gazing at the countryside or leaning
back with her eyes closed as they travelled westwards. Hugo
was at his most charming, pointing out the sights on the way
and constantly checking that she was comfortable, but there
was something about his manner which disappointed her.
She had felt closer to him when they had been quarrelling
before their marriage than she did now when she was his
wife and he appeared to be taking every care of her. Once or
twice he started to say something, but then shrugged his
shoulders and was silent. Finally Julia said, "What is it,
Hugo? What is wrong?"

"Nothing, my dear. What could there be?" He smiled
down at her and then asked casually, "Did Sophie Mersham stay at Downings when your father was ill?"

She was surprised, but answered, "She came down while
my aunt was with us, yes."

"Did you discuss the paragraph in the *Gazette* with her?"

Julia hesitated and flushed painfully as she remembered the discussion with Sophie. "I...I...think so. Why do you ask?"

She caught sight of a flash of anger in Hugo's eyes, before he smiled and said gently, "It's of no real consequence. I was simply curious to know how you arranged to get the item linking our two names into the *Gazette*?"

Julia looked at him blankly. "What do you mean? I've told you before, I don't know who arranged for that item to appear in the *Gazette*. Was it Sophie?"

"She said so, and implied that it was at your instigation."

"But it wasn't!" said Julia. "You must have misunderstood her."

"Perhaps I did. As I said, it's of no real consequence."

"But—"

"We shall forget what she said, Julia. After all, we both achieved what we most desired. Have you observed the spire in the distance? I think we must be approaching Salisbury."

He would not be drawn further on the subject of Sophie, but talked lightly and amusingly on a wide range of other topics, always with that cynical air. He was behaving as if they had only just met. Julia's apprehension grew as the journey continued. What had she done? Why had she committed herself to Hugo Devenish? Admittedly there had been one evening of enchantment ten years earlier, but that had been followed by weeks of humiliation and misery. Their recent brief and stormy acquaintance was hardly a basis for a successful marriage, and now she was faced with this stranger who seemed to be hiding his real thoughts behind a mask of polite indifference. She began to remember the stories about the Devenish family. People said Hugo had run off with his sister-in-law, though her father had said that wasn't so. Whatever had happened then had clearly left Hugo with a dislike of women. But what had happened to Thérèse? And what were the true facts behind the deaths of the old Marquess and his heir, and the loss of so much land and wealth? Most people agreed that John had stolen government money. But why had his father shot himself? And above all, why was Hugo so different now? During the period immediately before her father's death he had seemed genuinely sympathetic, had appeared to be making an effort to get to know her. But now that they were away from London and on their way to this remote part of England he was very different. Which was the real Hugo? Her fears affected her physically and she suddenly felt stifled in the coach. She fought the sensation for a while, but had to give in to it in the end. Fortunately they were on a reasonably good stretch of road with wide views over Salisbury Plain.

"Hugo, I should like to stop for a while. I need some fresh air."

"Here? Are you sure? This is a desolate spot, Julia. There isn't an inn for miles."

"I said I wanted to get out! Stop the coach at once!"

She was ashamed of her outburst when she saw the surprise on Hugo's face, but it had the desired effect. The coach was drawn to one side and stopped. Almost before it had come to a halt Julia had scrambled out and was walking swiftly away from it. When Hugo caught up with her and took her arm she pulled it away.

"What's wrong, Julia? What have I done to make you shy away from me like that? Are you mad?"

"I begin to believe I may have been. I don't know you, Hugo. I don't know you at all!"

He must have sensed her panic, for when he next spoke his voice was gentle. "I thought that was what your year was for—for us both to get to know each other."

"I'm not sure I wish to know you!" She turned away from him.

"My dear girl, your nerves are stretched to the limit. Perhaps I was selfish to bring you to Donyatt so soon?" He smiled ruefully and for a moment he almost sounded sympathetic. "I just wanted you to see it as soon as possible. It might have been better for us to stay in London for a while—"

"No!"

"Then what do you want?" There was a trace of impatience in his voice. "Don't you think you're being a touch foolish? Where else can you go? Not to Surrey. Your cousin is already installed there.''

He waited for her to speak, but she stood in silence. Finally he said with decision, ''Come back to the coach—with luck we'll be at the Red Lion before nightfall, and you'll be able to rest there. There'll be a good meal—Bainbridge is famous for them and he's expecting us. Come, Julia!'' He would have taken her arm again, but Julia thrust him away.

''Don't touch me!''

Hugo lost his temper. ''This is ridiculous!'' he said, sweeping her up into his arms. ''If you won't walk back to the coach then I'll carry you! I'm damned if I'll miss my dinner for anyone.''

Julia kicked wildly. ''Put me down! Put me down, I say! How dare you!''

''Oh, I dare anything when I'm hungry. And, Julia,'' he said as he set her down in the coach, ''you might remember that you're no longer a spoilt daughter, free to do as she wishes. You're my wife! I doubt you'll find anyone who will dispute a husband's right to his wife's company, when he likes and where he likes! So try for a little wifely obedience, my love!''

''So much for our bargain, then!''

''Oh, I'll keep the bargain—as long as you don't provoke me. And remember, it takes two to keep a bargain. For a moment there I thought you were in danger of forgetting your side of it.'' Julia's eyes were enormous in the shadows of the coach and Hugo's face softened. ''I'm really not an ogre, Julia. Don't look like that. Come, I'll promise to be more patient in the future if you'll only smile now.'' Astonishingly, in view of what had just happened, Julia was reassured. She smiled tremulously at him and watched his face become transformed as he smiled in response. He leaned forward and kissed her gently. ''Are you ready to continue? Where's your bonnet?''

''I think it must have fallen off when you—er—brought me back to the coach.''

''Ah, yes, there it is.'' He held it up. ''It's very fetching,'' he said gravely. ''But the trimmings are a trifle rustic, do you not agree?'' Julia smiled reluctantly as he held the bonnet up to reveal mud and grass clinging to the lower side. As she leaned forward to take it from him he held her chin for a moment and looked into her eyes. "Shall we go on?"

She nodded. He gave the order to the coachman and got in. After a while she found him studying her closely.

"Which is the real Julia, I wonder?"

This was such a close echo of her own earlier thoughts that she stared at him, amazed. It had never occurred to her that Hugo might be as uncertain of her motives as she was of his. She said slowly, "I suppose only time will tell, Hugo, for both of us."

He nodded thoughtfully and then proceeded to make undemanding conversation until she slept again. She woke when the coach was clattering into the yard of an inn, gave a little moan of protest, and shut her eyes again, for she felt comfortable and warm where she was. Then she sat up with a start and turned to see Hugo rubbing his arms and stretching. It was obvious that he had been holding her while she slept. In some confusion she allowed the landlord to hand her out of the coach and lead her into a private parlour. After mine host had gone out, assuring them that he had a positively succulent repast and two handsome bedchambers prepared for them, Julia said, avoiding Hugo's eye, "Forgive me. Are you very stiff?"

"A little, but it's no great matter. Are you feeling more the thing, Julia? Will you manage Bainbridge's 'succulent repast'?"

"You know him? Of course, you have travelled this road many times before."

"But never in such charming company, I assure you," he said.

She looked at him uncertainly and was then forced to smile as she looked at her crumpled dress and ruined bonnet, her dishevelled hair and dirty shoes. "I can see that your reputation as a man of taste will be in serious danger if I don't go to my room immediately for some urgent repairs to my person. But I shall be ready to join you for a meal . . . in half an hour?"

His eyes warmed in admiration as she went past him. He caught her hand and kissed it. "Spoken like a true Amazon, Julia."

She sighed as she went up the stairs. What sort of man had she married? And how was she to account for the violent swings in her feelings towards him—one minute having heaven knew what ugly suspicions about him, the next warming to his charm and feeling the full force of his attraction? As far as she could judge he seemed to be having the same problem about her, though she had no notion why. She must make it her business to find out. Hugo and she must learn to trust each other, otherwise there was not much of a future for their marriage.

HUGO STILL HAD his more approachable air when she rejoined him in their parlour, and over the meal Julia asked about Donyatt.

"The original building goes back to the Middle Ages. It was part of a Benedictine abbey, and one of my ancestors bought it after the Reformation."

"I thought you said that your family had been in Dorset for seven hundred years?"

"But not living in such grand style. The Reformation ancestor made his fortune under Henry—it's probably best not to ask how—and bought the abbey in order to live up to it."

"Wasn't it a slightly uncomfortable place to live?"

"Not at all. The abbot was no ascetic, I assure you! But in any case, there isn't much of the original building left now. The setting is still the same, but the second Marquess practically rebuilt the house at the beginning of the last century. I ... You'll have to learn to put up with my ravings about Donyatt, Julia. I'm afraid I think it is perfect. You'll see it tomorrow."

Julia felt a sudden pang when she heard the tone of Hugo's voice when he spoke about his home—a mixture of reverence, pride and love. Just so might a man speak of a woman he loved. And what woman would not be deeply touched?

EARLY THE NEXT evening, as they came over the top of a
rise, the coach stopped, and Hugo touched her arm and
pointed. Donyatt lay on a level piece of land halfway up the
hill on the other side of the valley. Julia's apprehensions and
doubts were forgotten when she first saw the house, and
Hugo's passion for it seemed all at once to be perfectly understandable. The serene harmony of its proportions and the
beauty of its golden limestone were breathtaking. Towards
the south, terraced lawns set with oaks and lime trees led
down to a large lake, which was sparkling in the May sunshine. The countryside of copses and meadows, with the
broad sweep of the Dorset hills beyond, was a perfect setting. Julia turned with wonder in her eyes. "It's beautiful,
Hugo. And there's such an air of peace about it."

"I was used to think so," Hugo replied sombrely. Then
he smiled down at her. "And there will be again. Drive on,
Tom."

The coach wound its way down to the valley and then up
again. But as they drew nearer Julia could see that a veil of
neglect, invisible from above, lay over the house. Its broad
drive was overgrown with weeds, and cracks where creep-
ing plants had been allowed to penetrate the stone marred
the fine flight of steps leading up to the portico. Discol-
oured streaks on the golden stone walls bore witness to un-
mended gutters, and the magnificent doors were cracked
and stained. The house had obviously been deprived of
money and care for many years. As they went up the steps
Hugo looked at her shocked expression and said bitterly,
"Yes, it's not so lovely when you're near enough to see, is
it? And do you know what the cause of Donyatt's decay
was? A weak man's desperate efforts to forget that he had
lost the woman he loved."

"You're talking of your brother?" asked Julia, once
again wondering what had happened to Thérèse Devenish.

"And his wife." Hugo seemed to have read her mind.
"And, do you know, Julia, she wasn't worth a single stone
of it." Julia was distressed at his words, and more by the
harsh tone in which they were uttered. Hugo seemed to have
withdrawn again behind his wall of cynicism. Whatever had
happened in the past seemed to have affected his view of the

world—and especially his view of women—very deeply.
Could she ever overcome this prejudice?

"Oh, don't look so worried, Julia. One woman nearly
destroyed Donyatt and the Devenishes, and now another—" he made a sweeping bow in her direction "—will
save us all. Is that not poetic justice?"

Julia said in a troubled voice, "You sound almost as if
you hate women?"

"What nonsense! I simply find it difficult to trust them,
that's all. Even you. For instance, some day I should like to
know your true motives in marrying me, Julia."

"You already know them. There's no secret about them."

"Really? We'll see. But until then I'm happy to settle for
your fortune for Donyatt."

Julia took a deep breath, but then decided not to try to
argue with Hugo in his present mood of bitterness. Instead
she said calmly, "Very true, if not very generously expressed. And now that I have seen Donyatt I cannot think
of any better use for my fortune." She walked into the hall,
a slender figure in black. Hugo looked at the gallant lift of
her head and felt a strange mixture of remorse, and pride in
her courage.

CHAPTER EIGHT

WAITING TO RECEIVE them was a rather untidy group of servants led by an elderly couple whom Hugo introduced as the Chiddocks. They seemed uncertain of what to do, and Julia guessed they had been recruited in a hurry to prepare the house for occupation. That they had only partially succeeded became obvious as Hugo led her into a small parlour off the hall. The room was beautifully proportioned, but devoid of all personality or comfort, and its general appearance was lack-lustre. Hugo sent the servants off to bring in the baggage and prepare some refreshment, and he and Julia were alone for a moment.

"I'm sorry," he said stiffly.

Tired though she was, Julia made an effort to find the right words. "It's still a beautiful house, Hugo. All it needs is time and, as you said, money."

But Hugo for once had not been thinking of Donyatt. "You misunderstand. I was apologising for my words on the steps."

"Oh." Julia was disconcerted. "I agree that they seemed unworthy of you. But you were distressed at seeing Donyatt in this state. Knowing how you feel about it, I understand some of your bitterness."

"I shouldn't have spoken so to you, all the same. It was a poor welcome."

Julia was prevented from responding by the entry of Chiddock bearing a large tray of rather crudely prepared food and a bottle of wine. There was silence when Chiddock busied himself with serving the food, and Julia sat in a daze, listening to the other servants taking the baggage upstairs, and longing desperately for her bed. Finally Hugo dismissed Chiddock and came over with a glass of wine for

er. "Try to eat something. The Chiddocks have done their
est, but they are not trained for this sort of thing. They
ave been caretakers here since my father died and the house
vas closed."

After the meal Hugo said, "Hockliffe will be here very
oon, and he will bring Lydiate with him. That will be a
tart. Lydiate is old, I know, but he's had years of experi-
nce at Donyatt." He went on to talk about other servants,
inishing up with, "And your maid is already here—she
ught to have unpacked your valises by now. Would you like
ne to see you to your room?" He smiled as he saw that his
vife was almost asleep in her chair. He picked her up and
tarted to carry her upstairs. Julia was suddenly wide awake.

"Hugo, you can't!"

He stopped and looked at her, devilment in his eyes.
"Can't I?"

"I'm too heavy!"

He laughed down at her. "Oh, is that all? I thought you
ad other grounds for objection! Don't worry, Julia. I'm
ot about to collapse under your weight. Hold tight and
hut your eyes, and we'll make it to the top."

When she lay in bed afterwards, having submitted to
Ruth's ministrations without really noticing them, one
roblem was plaguing Julia more than all the rest. Hugo had
leposited her in her room, called her maid, and then qui-
tly departed. Since that was clearly what one would have
xpected him to do in view of their bargain, why was it that
ter chief feeling had been one of disappointment?

THE ROOM WAS DARK when Julia awoke, and for a moment
he wondered where she was. She could hear sounds out-
ide, and concluded it must be morning. Sliding out of bed,
he groped her way to the window and pulled open the cur-
ains. Light flooded in, dazzling in its brightness. When her
yes had adjusted to it she could see that her room over-
ooked the lawns down to the lake. She opened the window
nd leaned out. The view was incredible, and the air went to
ter head like wine. She suddenly felt happier than she had
lone for some time. The unknown, which had seemed so
errifying the day before, now seemed to hold an exciting

challenge—there were things to do here! She could hea
Hugo's voice down below giving instructions to one of the
gardeners, and leaned out a little further to see him. He
looked up and smiled, and Julia felt her heart give a strange
little leap. Ignoring it, she hastily retreated from the win
dow and rang for Ruth. In a creditably short time she wa
on her way downstairs, where she found Hugo waiting fo
her in the hall.

"I'll show you the way to the breakfast parlour. I don'
have to ask you if you slept well—you look a differen
woman."

After breakfast he took her on a tour of the house. Now
it was even easier to see evidence of neglect and the fami
ly's straitened circumstances. The lack of pictures on the
walls, the absence of any distinguished furniture, the dirty
grey brocade on the walls of what had once been the blue
drawing-room—all told the same story. Julia could not bear
to look at Hugo's face as the sorry state of Donyatt un-
folded. But, as she examined the splendid proportions of the
rooms and the simple elegance of its architectural details, a
picture of Donyatt as it should be—as it would be—was
growing in her mind's eye. When they returned to the
breakfast parlour Hugo, who was once again looking grim,
said, "Well, Julia? Does your heart quail at the thought of
this decay? Even I can see that there isn't a room fit for you
to live in. When I remember what it was like in my grandmother's day..."

"I don't intend for one moment to live in rooms like
this."

Hugo's mouth tightened as he said, "I thought we had
settled this on the journey down. There is no question of
your return to Surrey. Your place is here with me—for a year
at least."

"Much as I dislike your autocratic tone, Hugo, I agree
with you. You misunderstood me. I cannot deny that Donyatt is in a poor way, but I can do much to restore it in quite
a short time—if you agree, that is...?" she added meekly.

He gave her a sharp glance, as if he suspected she was
making fun of him, but evidently decided not to follow it
up.

"I would be delighted," he said somewhat formally. "But would like to make Donyatt self-supporting as soon as possible. I will have to use a large sum to pay off the debts, but I will not drain your resources more than I have to."

"But apart from the money and property settled on me when we married, Hugo, it is all yours!"

"I will not feel it is mine until you live with me as a wife—completely." He smiled wryly as she looked startled. "I have more scruples than you apparently credit me with, Julia. Donyatt must stand on its own feet as soon as I can arrange it, and that means working to restore the lands. We cannot afford to do that and undertake costly refurbishments inside the house at the same time."

"Mmm... But we'll have to do something, won't we? Let me do it! Hugo, please...I promise to be careful!"

Hugo looked at the animated face before him. Gone was the poised creature of their meeting in Dover Street, gone the pale ghost of their journey. Julia had regained her colour, and her grey eyes were sparkling—she was irresistible. He felt a sudden urge to give her anything she wanted, but then hesitated as his aunt's voice echoed in his mind. "You'll have to watch your step with that wife of yours—she'll have you dancing to her tune if you don't look out!" He said brusquely,

"I'll see what can be done. I'll discuss it with Hockliffe. You'll have to excuse me now—there are some people I must see about the estate," and he went out of the room.

Julia looked after him thoughtfully. Hugo might well have people to see, but his departure had had more than a faint touch of a retreat. Why? She sighed. It was not going to be easy to get to know this husband of hers. Her fears of the day before seemed ridiculous now—Hugo was no monster. His attitude to her fortune was that of a man of honour—almost quixotically so. But his temper was uncertain—particularly on topics associated with his family. He was still under a great strain; that was obvious. She must try to see how best to help him, and meanwhile be as patient as she could. Hugo was right. It *was* important that the estate was brought to a point where it could be self-sufficient again. But that did not mean that she would allow him to treat her

as a cypher. Oh, no! The house could fairly be described as
her domain, and it too was going to be restored, whatever
Hugo said. She went to the window, looked out at him as he
strode down the lawn to the lake, and said firmly to his re-
treating back, "Not *'I'll see'*, Hugo, but *we'll* see. *We'll* see
what can be done, and *we'll* discuss it with Hockliffe!"

JULIA SPENT SOME TIME considering how to present her
point of view to Hugo. It was far from easy. She wanted to
avoid any suggestion that her claim to be consulted was
based on the source of the money. Indeed, it would have
been easier for her to refurbish Donyatt out of her own very
generous settlements without saying a word to anyone, but
she wanted him to recognise from the outset that their marriage was to be a partnership, based on honesty with each
other. She believed that she would best achieve her goal by
using reason and logic rather than confrontation. But on the
evening before Mr. Hockliffe's arrival she ended up losing
her temper with him all the same.

She had taken care with her appearance that evening, en-
livening the dark colour of her dress with a white fichu. She
had exerted herself to talk entertainingly during their meal,
and had then invited Hugo to sit with her in the small parlour to discuss something important to her. He had responded well to her conversation at dinner, they had
laughed together, and towards the end of the meal he had
raised his glass to her with a look in his eyes which was almost a caress. As they rose from the table it seemed quite
natural that he should offer her his arm to lead her into the
other room. Once there he seemed reluctant to let her go.
She looked up at him, puzzled, and he turned her to him. He
cupped her face in his hands and kissed her slowly. She
wondered why such a gentle kiss should make her feel as if
she hadn't a bone in her body, and clutched his arms for
support. "Julia," he murmured, smiling at her, and then he
gathered her close to him, kissing her again and again—a
shower of kisses on her lips, her cheeks, her eyes. For a
moment Julia was lost in a whirlwind of feeling such as she
had never before experienced. It frightened her, and she
pulled away from him.

Hugo laughed when he saw her confusion. "Don't look like that, my innocent Amazon! It's all very natural, you know. It's called love..." He would have pulled her back, but she resisted.

"I don't think so, Hugo. Not yet. A strong attraction perhaps, but not...not love."

"Is there a difference? Does it matter what you call it?"

"Yes. To me it does."

Hugo considered her for a moment. Then he said slowly, "Are you now trying to change the terms of our bargain, Julia? I sincerely hope not, for you will be sadly disappointed if you are." He paused for a moment's thought. "I suppose it's natural that you should be reluctant to embark on a closer relationship before we really know each other, though it is by no means unusual for comparative strangers to marry, you know. But I trust you are not trying to tell me that you will not sleep with me until I am 'in love' with you for, if you are, then I must disillusion you. I may, when I was young and foolish—your phrase, Julia—have imagined that I was in love. That deceptive and degrading experience is not one that I should ever allow myself to repeat."

Julia knew she ought to let the matter rest. Hugo was right; their marriage was not one in which passionate love—a total commitment of heart, soul and body—would play a part. And at the moment, it would clearly be unwise to argue the point with him. She ought instead to concentrate on her own immediate interests, her intention to have a share in the decisions about Donyatt. But in some obscure way she felt that she was fighting for something important. So, almost against her better judgement, she persisted. "You sound very determined. It is quite unnecessary, Hugo. I know the terms of our bargain and do not plan to change them. However, do you not think your view of love is somewhat jaundiced? Not all love is 'deceptive and degrading'."

He said swiftly, "In my experience it is, Julia. But come, I believe you to be too intelligent to obscure the issue of our relationship with talk of romantic 'love'. We can find a great deal of satisfaction in each other's company without such nonsense. Indeed, when you look as you do tonight I find it hard to resist you." He would have taken her in his arms again, but she pulled away. He smiled and shrugged his shoulders. "There's time enough, I suppose. Very well." Then he led her to her chair and asked calmly, "You said after dinner that you wished to talk to me?"

Shaking off a vague feeling of depression, Julia broached the subject of Donyatt's redecoration, and her desire to take part in any discussion on the matter.

There was a long silence. He turned abruptly away from her and walked swiftly to the window.

"What is it, Hugo? What have I said? It is surely not so unreasonable—" She was shocked at his next words.

"Was this the purpose of all the affection and high-minded talk a few minutes ago?" he asked harshly. "To cozen me into giving you your way?"

"Hugo!"

"Don't 'Hugo' me, ma'am! Believe me, I am far too experienced in the wiles and guiles of women not to recognise a campaign when I see one! Tempting smiles, delightful conversation, beguiling looks, spurious sincerity... Faugh! To think I had begun to believe they were wrong about you, that you at least were different! But I see now that your earlier success has gone to your head. Let me inform you, Julia, that you may have tricked me once. You will not do so again!"

"Tricked you? In what way? You are insulting, sir!"

"Am I indeed? Then tell me why half of London believes you manipulated me into marriage, ma'am!"

Julia's face was as white as her fichu as she stood up to say, "They are mistaken. It is the other half which knows the truth—that you married me for my fortune!"

"But not willingly, by God! Not willingly!"

Julia drew a sharp breath. Rage was consuming her; she wanted to hurt Hugo; she wanted to hit him, rail at him, force him to admit he was wrong. Then, as suddenly as it had come, her anger evaporated as she realised that Hugo's bitter suspicion must have its roots in the past. She was the victim, not the cause of his angry distrust. Clasping her hands to stop their trembling, she said in a voice as calm as she could make it, "This must stop!" She could see he was surprised at her moderate tone, and went on, "I truly thought we had made a bargain in a situation which was impossible for both of us—a bargain in which you gained Donyatt, and I gained peace of mind for my father. I cannot imagine how you came to the conclusion that I tricked you into marriage. I assure you it was not so. If you have been influenced by anything Sophie Mersham said, then you cannot know her as I do. As for London society, we both know—you even better than I, perhaps—that the scandalmongers will distort and invent to suit their own purposes. They have no time for the real truth. They would not begin to understand my love for my father, nor yours for Donyatt."

Her words seemed to impress Hugo, though he was not yet fully convinced. "You're right about society," he said, "And about Sophie. I would not normally give her stories any credence at all. But Lady Thornton and my aunt both said something to the same effect—based on your behaviour ten years ago, I must admit—"

"Does the world never forget the follies of our youth?" interrupted Julia with a sob.

Hugo had not moved from the window, but there was a touch of sympathy in his voice as he said sombrely, "Not in my experience, Julia." He paused and went on, "Perhaps I was wrong to judge you so harshly. And in my case, we are now married—for better or for worse. Forgive me."

Julia looked at him uncertainly, but he was serious. She replied, "I should not have said what I did, either. I was angry because you had accused me of dishonesty. I had employed no wiles to encourage you to listen more favourably to my ideas."

Hugo gave a twisted smile. "You may not have been aware of them, my dear."

"I beg your pardon?"

"Nothing, nothing. What were they, these ideas?"

Haltingly at first, then more confidently as Hugo appeared to listen to what she was saying, Julia put forward her reasons for wishing to be more closely involved in Donyatt affairs. At the end she paused and looked anxious, ready to argue a point or two.

"I agree," he said.

"To what?"

"To it all. You are right. I ought to have thought of it myself. My excuse is that I have had to work on my own for so long that I am not yet used to the idea of a partner. When Hockliffe arrives we shall set about the work together."

Hugo had once again taken her breath away, thought Julia. When would she know him well enough to predict what he would say or do next?

MR. HOCKLIFFE ARRIVED the next day, and the serious work of sorting out Donyatt's financial affairs began. Much to his surprise, and initial disapproval, the new Marchioness was included in all their discussions. As time went on, however, Mr. Hockliffe became increasingly impressed with Lady Rostherne's grasp of essentials. Hugo looked on in resigned amusement as Julia slowly won first the respect of his man of business and finally his admiration—indeed, he ended up quite often quoting her.

One night Hugo congratulated her on her conquest, ending by saying, "But I am sure that even now poor Hockliffe has no idea how very clever you are, Julia."

"What do you mean?" She looked at him doubtfully. His voice gave no clue to his own thoughts on the subject, but she wondered whether Hugo disapproved of clever women. "What do you mean, Hugo?"

"You were very persuasive in your support of my road scheme. You even persuaded Hockliffe that the plan was a good one, when five minutes before he was convinced it was far too unorthodox."

"What nonsense, Hugo! I merely reminded him of some of the advantages. But the decisions were yours and Mr. Hockliffe's, not mine."

"Oh, no! You cannot pull the wool over my eyes so easily, ma'am. If I didn't watch you like a hawk you'd soon have everything your own way! But tell me, why did you allow him a free rein on the question of its ways and means?"

"You are talking nonsense again, Hugo! I am quite certain I could never deceive you, nor would I wish to try. As for Mr. Hockliffe—it is not for me to 'allow' him anything.

However—" she looked at him demurely "—I think he will embrace the scheme with more enthusiasm if he feels he has decided something about it for himself. Do you not agree?"

"You are a little minx, Julia," said Hugo, laughing in spite of himself. "What can a mere man do against you?"

He was amused to see Julia blush like a débutante at his compliment.

In truth, Hugo was himself impressed with Julia's intelligence and capacity for work. Far from languishing in her room as he had half imagined most women would, Julia was already busy with plans for the house. She had heard that her cousin had introduced some of his own staff into Downings Castle, and had immediately sent off to Surrey to see if her old housekeeper would come to join her at Donyatt.

"Not that I mean to import many outsiders," she said to Hugo. "Donyatt should be a source of work for our own people here. However, I shall need someone to train them, and Mrs. Staple is just the person. Moreover, I believe she has a nephew living in Dorchester, so a move to Dorset is not an inconvenient one."

He looked at her quizzically. " 'Our own people', Julia? You are more attached than I thought—to the people of the estate, at least, if not to their master."

She coloured in embarrassment. "I was forgetting. They are your people, of course," and she stared at him in annoyance as he laughed at her confusion, caught her to him, and kissed her soundly. He went off, still smiling.

Julia was left once again to wonder what he really thought. She had now been living at Donyatt for some weeks, but he remained something of an enigma. She had seen for herself that he was a good master and had all the attributes of a good landlord. In his dealings with the people on the estate—especially the older ones—she saw flashes of a younger Hugo, one totally devoid of the cynicism which still occasionally chilled her soul. On most evenings their discussions ranged over a wide field of topics, and she had found him to be an amusing, stimulating companion. On the surface, at least, she and Hugo were achieving a harmonious relationship. Indeed there were times when they laughed together or touched each other when she felt a kinship that she had found with no one else. But there was still a long way to go before she could claim to know the real Hugo. There were areas in his life which remained uncharted territory—and her uncertainty about these, she felt, prevented her from achieving true progress in their relationship.

CHAPTER NINE

IT WAS VERY PLEASANT in the rolling green and gold countryside of Dorset as high summer drew nearer. The neighbouring families began to pay calls which were returned, and the Donyatt estate, which had been asleep for ten long years, slowly began to come to life again. The work on its fabric continued, and each day Julia fell more in love with the place. In other circumstances—in what could be termed an "ordinary" marriage for example—she could have been jealous of Hugo's devotion to his home. But she had known from the beginning how important it was to him; indeed, it had been the primary reason for their marriage. So whenever she found herself wondering somewhat wistfully what it would be like to be first in his affections, she firmly told herself to be content with what she had—a lovely home, pleasant companionship and many shared interests. She might perhaps in time win something more—her husband's confidence, for example. Hugo made no further reference to their discussion on the nature of love and its relevance—or lack of it—to their marriage bargain, but seemed content to wait for Julia to come round to his way of thinking. And though he constantly made it clear that he found her a delightful companion, teasing her, laughing at her, even hugging her and kissing her briefly, he made no attempt to confide in her, or to reveal any of his deeper feelings. Julia was of the opinion that he had been alone for so long that he had forgotten the art, but it did not enable her to feel that she really knew him.

In spite of Hugo's preoccupation with the Donyatt estate he did not forget Julia's interests. They made several visits to her properties in other counties, where he acquainted himself with her people there. But when he had satisfied himself that they were capable and honest he was content to leave them to it, merely introducing them to Hockliffe and making sure that they knew how to reach him in cases of doubt.

Hugo and Julia were returning from one such visit when they were overtaken by a series of mishaps which seriously delayed them, and they found themselves unable to reach Donyatt that night as they had originally intended. The latter part of the journey was unpleasant, and the state of the roads after a sudden summer storm had caused Julia's maid, normally a hardy traveller, to be coachsick. Julia was herself feeling slightly queasy, so that when they came across the Golden Galleon they decided to put up for the night. However, unlike its name, the inn was modest, obviously unused to wayfarers of such quality, and also undergoing some much needed repair work. After many apologies and some delay, the landlady showed them into a large, low-ceilinged bedchamber, scrupulously clean and pleasantly scented with lavender. Julia was prepared to swear it was the landlady's own. The grooms were to sleep in the stables, and Julia's long-suffering maid would be accommodated in a makeshift room on the other side of the stableyard. Beaming with goodwill, the landlady promised Julia that she would provide them with the best-cooked meal in Dorset. She arranged to serve it in an hour and made to leave.

"Wait!" said Julia. "My husband's room? Where will he sleep?"

The good woman looked at her benignly. "Why here, yer ladyship! Roit where 'e belongs. Where else?" Then her rosy face clouded over. "Oh, Oi forgot! His lordship would possibly loike another room. But what's to do? We 'aven't one, yer ladyship. Not one as 'd suit. The inn's being re-roofed and we'me be terrible short."

Hugo came in at that moment and asked what the trouble was. The landlady curtsied and explained, whereupon Hugo said calmly, "Then my wife and I will share." He shepherded the landlady out, shut the door, and faced an irate Julia. "What would you have me do? Sleep in the stables with the grooms? A fine story that would make for the servants' hall at Donyatt! And she's right—there's nowhere else, I've looked. If it were not so late the landlord would probably choose to let us go on to the next hostelry. However, that is impossible. Oh, don't look so worried, Julia! I'll remember our bargain and keep my distance!" His tone of slightly impatient scorn reassured Julia, who agreed with a fair degree of composure that sharing the room seemed to be the only solution. In any case she was too weary to argue. But when Hugo wasn't looking she eyed the bed warily. It seemed to dominate the room, but then perhaps it was as well it was large. She completed a hasty toilet and was ready to go downstairs when the hour was up.

The landlady's boast was not a vain one. They ate a handsomely prepared dinner accompanied by some wine which was so good that Hugo was prepared to swear it had never found its way to that modest little inn by legitimate means.

"The coast isn't far away. I suspect it's a bottle held back from a consignment for the local squire. Enjoy it, Julia. Wines of this quality are rare and should be savoured. And if you should hear bumps in the night, close your eyes and go to sleep again. It's more than likely some harmless free-trader."

"Is there much free-trading in these parts, Hugo?"

"Lord, yes. It's practically a local industry. The Excise men have a hard time of it—the coast here is almost impossible to guard."

"Then it's lucky that the war is over, before the French found that out!"

"Ah, now that's a different matter. Our friends here work in small bands with local look-outs to help them. A whole army is more difficult to conceal!"

"But there was probably traffic on a smaller scale—I dare say quite a few spies came and went, for example." Julia's comment had been idly made, and she was astonished to see Hugo's face close up. For a moment he looked—frightening. What had she said? He relaxed with a visible effort as their landlady came to acknowledge their compliments on her cooking and to bid them goodnight. They took her hint and retired to their room. In the dim candlelight Hugo's shadow loomed over the bed. Julia jumped as he turned to her.

"My dear girl, pull yourself together. I was only going to say that I would take a turn outside while you prepare yourself for bed. Can you manage without your maid—or do you wish me to help?" he added with an ironic smile.

With dignity Julia thanked him and refused. "It's all very well for you, Hugo. I dare swear you have shared a room with any number of the opposite sex, but I never have!"

"I'll ignore the slur on my morals and point out that if ours had been a real marriage from the start, Julia, as I'm beginning to believe it should have been, you would now be well used to seeing me in your bedchamber—and more besides."

Julia blushed scarlet. "Hugo, please," she begged.

"Be sure you're safely tucked up before I get back. I'll sleep on top of the sheets," was all he said before he disappeared.

In spite of her lack of a maid, Julia had never undressed so quickly. In no time she was in a nightgown which covered her from her neck down. With its long sleeves and elaborate tucking, she was more modestly dressed than in an evening gown. Thankful that the June night was surprisingly cool after the storm, for otherwise she would have died of a heat-stroke, she snuggled under the bedclothes and wrapped them firmly round her. For a while she started at every sound, but gradually the wine and her exhausted state had their effect. Hugo returned to find her swaddled like a mummy in the bedcovers and fast asleep. He shrugged his shoulders, removed his cravat and jacket, took off his boots, and lay down beside her.

Julia awoke in the night to the sound of voices outside. She was unbearably hot. She slipped out of bed and cautiously pulled back one of the shutters. Moonlight flooded in, filling the room with a gentle silver light. She opened a window. There was a sudden scrabble of boots on cobbles, and then silence. Hugo's smugglers, no doubt. If so, they would not take it kindly if she spied on them. She returned to the bed. Hugo was lying sprawled on his back, his breathing deep and slow. In repose he looked much younger—the Hugo of Lady Godfrey's ball again. She examined his face in the soft moonlight—the broad brow, the arrogant nose and thin cheeks, the mouth...a beautiful mouth, now that the harsh lines of cynicism and self-discipline were relaxed in sleep. Almost without volition she slowly bent forward and gave it the lightest of kisses. In an instant she was seized and held fast.

"No, Julia. Oh, no! That really isn't playing the game."

"You cheated," she panted. "I thought you were asleep!"

"I enjoy kissing better when I'm awake," he growled, and proceeded to show how much.

"Hugo, no!" gasped Julia. "Let me go! Please..." Her voice died into a long sigh as Hugo kissed the heart out of her. Her arms, which had been attempting to push him away, crept round his neck and she pulled his head closer. After a moment of surprise Hugo gave a delighted laugh and turned to hold her more tightly than ever. He kissed her eyes, her cheeks, her lips. He undid the ribbons of her nightgown and kissed her throat and shoulders, the hollow between her breast. Julia was lost in a whirl of passion. Nothing existed but their two entwined bodies.

Hugo gave a triumphant laugh. "I dared not hope it would come to this, Julia. I saw you at the window and it was all I could do not to come over and carry you back to bed. That's why I pretended to be asleep—it was the only way I could remain still. And then, when you kissed me..." He clasped her face between his hands and kissed her hard. "Now try to tell me that you want to wait the rest of the year! Try to deny that you feel the same as I do! Isn't this excitement, this delight the only thing that matters between a man and a woman? Isn't this enough?" He kissed her again, more deeply this time, his hand moving down to caress her breast. But for Julia his words had destroyed the magic. The moonlight was a cold, alien invader, lighting up the tumbled bedclothes and her own disarray, and hiding Hugo's face in shadows.

"No!" she cried, pulling away from him and scrambling off the bed. "No! No, it isn't enough. I want more, much more than this!"

Hugo's eyes narrowed and he said softly, "I don't like teases, Julia."

Julia's face was white in the moonlight, her eyes enormous. "Believe me, Hugo, please believe me, I don't wish to tease you. I was wrong to kiss you. I don't know why I did. And for a while, I...I..."

"Forgot yourself? Forgot your stupidly romantic notions? Come, Julia—admit it! You were as wild for me as I was for you. Look, this isn't some poet's dream, it's reality! Don't be ashamed of what you felt—it's the most natural thing in the world. Come here, Julia."

"No!" she said desperately. "It's not what I want. Leave me alone, Hugo! You promised me! We made a bargain!"

"I haven't forgotten the damned bargain! Would you call this keeping your share of it?"

"I need time!" Julia cried. "I don't know you, Hugo! I don't know you at all! Being your wife isn't easy."

"Just as long as you remember that you are a wife, Julia, with all that that entails. Marriage is more than living in the same house and having friendly conversations, my little spinster."

Julia flushed angrily. "I know that! But it's more than mating like animals, too, Hugo. You laugh at my 'romantic notions', as you call them. Perhaps you are right, and I am stupid even to think of them. But...but I have to feel that we at least trust each other, even that we like each other— and I don't feel that at the moment. I... I'm sorry if I gave you the wrong impression."

"Ha, that's rich! 'The wrong impression' indeed! Why, you little wanton, there was no mistaking the impression you were trying to convey, however much you regret it now! I ought to teach you not to play with fire..."

Julia shrank back as Hugo advanced towards her. "Hugo, I'm sorry, I'm sorry! Please don't..." and she burst into tears.

"Oh, God, save me—a woman's last resort," he said contemptuously. He watched her for a minute, then gave a sigh of exasperation and said, "You can stop crying, Julia. I'm going out for a walk. You might pray that I don't meet with any smugglers, for I feel a remarkably strong desire to engage in a fight." He went out of the room, and a moment later she heard him striding swiftly over the cobbles.

After a while Julia's sobs calmed, and she lay in the huge bed, watching the stars pass the open shutter. Was she being a fool? Was it stupid to feel that she and Hugo must share more than their bodies? But Hugo was still such a stranger to her—and, she thought sadly, tonight's events might well have set them even further apart. What should she do? Gradually the sky grew light and the new day dawned. By the time Hugo turned up in time to shave and make himself respectable for breakfast, Julia had decided that she must do her utmost to repair some of the damage done to the delicate fabric of their relationship.

Hugo seemed to have reached the same conclusion. They were alone in the carriage for the rest of the journey—because of her sickness the previous day, Ruth asked if she might travel on the box with the coachman—and he talked with understanding of Julia's fears of the night before. "You went to my head last night, Julia. It isn't easy to exercise restraint—not for a man. But we made a bargain and I must stick to it, I know that. I'm sorry if I upset you. Of course you must take whatever time you need to feel you know me. I'm not a monster. You're so easy to talk to most of the time that I forget what a sheltered life you have in fact led. Am I forgiven—yet again?"

"There is nothing to forgive. I'm sorry that I'm so foolish. I suppose that even at the best of times adjusting to a marriage must be difficult, and ours began in more unpromising circumstances than most!" She looked shyly at him. "I truly intend to keep our bargain, Hugo."

He smiled, caught her hand, and kissed it. "Then I shall possess my soul in patience. I am sure it will be worth every second of the wait!" The rest of the journey passed swiftly in very pleasant conversation. Never had Julia felt more at ease with him.

CONSCIOUS OF HUGO'S NEED for economy, Julia employed few outside specialists in her transformation of the house. She concentrated instead on her band of servants from the villages round about, who had proved themselves eager to learn and ready to work hard. For this she had to thank not only the awe with which they regarded Mrs. Staple and Lydiate, but also their own local pride. Donyatt had been in eclipse for many years, and now all worked with a will to make the "Great House" once again the jewel in Dorset's crown. All day they scrubbed and washed, polished and cleaned. Nothing escaped Mrs. Staple's eagle eye. Silver, china, hangings, carpets—all acquired new life. Experts were brought in to restore the painted cartouches over the stairs and to re-gild the ceiling in the state dining-room. Otherwise, to universal approval, Julia used local crafts-men and labour. The big house was alive with cheerful ac-tivity.

Then one day Mrs. Staple came to see her with an air of exasperation. "I don't understand it, Lady Rostherne. The women are simply refusing to work in the library. They've never given me a moment's difficulty before, but now they just purse their lips and shake their silly heads."

"Have you spoken to Lydiate?"

"Yes, but he just shook his head too and walked away! It's my belief he knows why, but won't say."

Julia thought for a moment, and then suggested that Mrs. Staple should try giving the women something to do else-where. The housekeeper returned a few minutes later to tell her they were working as willingly as ever in the east bed-room.

"I thought as much," murmured Julia, and dismissed the housekeeper with a reassuring smile. "I'll try to find out what the trouble is. But meanwhile, leave the library till later."

THAT EVENING after dinner she tackled Hugo about it. She was totally unprepared for the strength of his reaction. "The stupid fools! I'd hoped we were done with all that rub-bish." He turned to look at Julia, and her heart sank at his expression. The harsh lines which had begun to disappear from his face had returned in full force, and he was glaring at her as if she were an unwelcome stranger. But Julia was beginning to know something of Hugo's character. She was prepared to swear that behind that mask of anger Hugo was hiding something else, something too painful to reveal. If Hugo and she were ever to get closer to each other, then she must try to persuade him to share it with her.

"What is it about the library, Hugo?" she asked quietly.

"The library, Julia, is where I found the bodies of my father and my brother. As the world knows, they had been shot. Do you wish me to continue? I've no doubt that Sophie Mersham and her friends lost no time in telling you all they knew of my father's death, but there are perhaps one or two details which they have overlooked. How can I best satisfy your morbid curiosity?"

"That's not fair of you, Hugo! I don't think I deserve that! Sophie did say something, it is true, but I would not listen to her. And I certainly don't wish to—"

"My dear wife, don't pretend you're different from your sisters. I've never yet known a woman who could resist a juicy scandal. Come!"

He took her hand, and pulled her with him out of the room and across the hall to the doors of the library, where he stopped.

"Hugo, please—"

"Oh, don't be afraid, my love. There's nothing left to show that two men died here—no blood to offend your delicate sensibilities, no evidence of the violence and despair that this room has witnessed."

"Hugo!" cried Julia. "Hugo, stop this! I've been in this room before now. I know there's nothing frightening in it."

"Ah, but you're wrong, Julia." He opened the doors and pushed her in before him. Then he walked alone into the centre of the room. "The ghosts are all around us."

There was such conviction in his voice that, in spite of herself, Julia looked half fearfully over her shoulder. The room occupied the south-western corner of the house. Five large windows were set into the wall to the west, the middle one of which extended down to the ground, forming a door to the terrace outside. The windows were hung with heavy tapestry curtains which obscured half the light and must— even on the brightest day—make it difficult to read. As it was, the setting sun cast a lurid glow over the huge mantelpiece on the eastern wall, and was reflected in the mirror above it, so that the rest of the room was bathed in red. The day had been cool, and the flickering remnants of a fire were still in the hearth. "Hugo?"

"Don't worry, Julia. The ghosts only exist in my own mind—and in the superstitions of those ignorant women."

"Real or not, they haunt you, Hugo. Tell me about them."

He seemed not to have heard her at first. Then he went and stood by the centre window, blotting out the sun. "He was here," he said. "John was lying here. We couldn't open the window at first because his body was blocking the doorway. He'd been shot in the head. My father..." He paused and then continued in a voice from which all emotion had been banished, "My father had been shot while sitting at his desk." The voice was controlled, but Julia felt an almost overwhelming desire to comfort him. But she restrained herself. The anguish she sensed in him was too deep for facile expressions of sympathy. Wrapped up in the past as he was, he was hardly aware of her existence. He continued, "No pistol was found, and the coroner's jury concluded that an intruder had murdered them both."

It was now dark in the room, except for the firelight. Julia got up and went over to him. "You had removed it—the pistol."

"Why should I have done that, Julia? Or do you think I shot my brother? It would, God knows, have been a kindness to both of them."

"I don't believe for a moment you did."

"Why not? I was next in line—there are those who say I would have done more than that to inherit Donyatt."

"But we need not pay any heed to them—and nor should anyone else." She met his gaze with calm assurance, as she continued, "But I do believe you might have removed the pistol—as a last service to your father. If, for example, you thought that he had shot himself after...after shooting your brother."

He gave a short, humourless laugh. "You don't wrap things up, do you, Julia? Not a soul in London dared to say that to my face, though all would agree with your conclusion. However, I advise you not to speculate on the matter

ere. You would quickly lose your popularity if the local
people thought you were trying to rattle that particular
skeleton in the Devenish cupboard. They all know it's there,
you see.''

"Dear God, I don't want to rattle any skeletons! Nor am
I concerned with what anyone in London says, or at this
moment, with the question of my popularity with your
people! I'm trying to help you!''

"What makes you think I want your damned help?'' he
demanded savagely. "But I'll confirm your suspicions, if
that's what you want. Yes, I did remove the pistol. I even
opened a window to give credibility to the story of an intruder. And yes, I believe my father shot my brother and
then attempted to kill himself. He almost failed. It took him
two days to die. Are you satisfied? And now, if you'll excuse me, Julia, or even if you won't, I've had enough—I'm
going for a walk. Goodnight.''

He opened the doors on to the terrace and went out. Julia watched helplessly as he strode away and disappeared
into the night. Whether Hugo wanted her to or not, she was
beginning to understand him better. The causes of the profound change in Hugo's nature over the last ten years were
becoming clearer. It wasn't the lack of money, or even the
loss of his "friends" in London—the old Hugo would have
laughed those off. The fear of losing Donyatt might have
accounted for some of the bitterness. But what must it be
like for him to live with the knowledge that his father had
killed his brother? That was something of which he would
never be free. Her money might settle his debts and make
Donyatt safe. In time, if he wished, he could reinstate himself in society. But nothing, nothing in this world could
eradicate the pain of that deadly knowledge. She sat in
thought for a long time. The noises of the house died away
as the servants went to their own quarters. Hugo had still
not returned when she finally went up to her own room.

CHAPTER TEN

THE NEXT MORNING Hugo appeared as usual at the breakfast table. From his pallor and the way in which he winced
when Lydiate dropped a spoon, Julia surmised that he had
sought oblivion in brandy the night before. She forbore to
comment. He had needed something to help him forget.
However, during her own sleepless night an idea had formed
in her mind. She could not remedy the tragic past, but she
could reduce its legacy a little.

"Hugo, may I talk to you about the library?" His frown
grew even heavier. "About its decoration."

"Why must you talk to me about that? I thought we had
agreed it to be your domain."

"But this is slightly different. I wish to alter its use." She
hurried on before he could object. "The blue drawing-room
would make a much better library—its lighting is brighter
and more even. And the expense of moving the bookshelves into it could be set against the very costly business
of renewing the brocade on the walls of the drawing-room."

Hugo put his hand to his head and said carefully, "I suspect you are at your machinations again, Julia, and that
when I have time to think it through it will not be so evident a saving as you would have it appear."

"'Time,' Hugo?" said Julia delicately.

"A clearer head, then," he snapped. "I knew you would
not be able to refrain from some comment on my indul-
gence last night."

Julia kept calm in the face of this manifestly unfair attack. "You are right," she said, "I should not have bothered you this morning. Do you wish to consider it further,
or may I proceed?"

"Dammit, do what you like! You'll probably do so anyway. And take that damned complacent smile off your face before I change my mind!" he roared, and then groaned as his head got the better of him.

After asking a dubious Lydiate to offer a headache powder to his suffering master, Julia sent for Mrs. Staple and the estate carpenter. The sooner she set her plans in motion, the better.

LATER THAT DAY Hugo sought her out in the little parlour which Julia had taken over for her own use. She was engaged in writing to her cousin at Downings, requesting him to send the various objects and furnishings from the East which had been waiting in their packing cases since she had left. She now had a use for them. When Hugo came in with a purposeful air she was at first anxious lest he should have changed his mind about such a radical rearrangement of the rooms in the house, so she was relieved as well as disappointed when he announced that he found it necessary to spend some time in London.

"When are you thinking of going?"

"Tomorrow. We shall not stay away longer than we have to—"

"We?"

"I am taking Hockliffe with me. I need him for some negotiations with the creditors and some other business. You look disappointed." His tone of voice, which had been guarded, grew warmer, and he came to sit by her. "I assumed that you would prefer to stay here, but if you wish to spend some time in London it could be arranged."

"No, no. I have a great deal to do here, and, as you know, I am not particularly fond of London—especially in the summer. No, I was merely wondering whether you really had business in London. You might have been running away."

"I beg your pardon?"

"Hugo, you have said many times that you trust no one, least of all any woman. Last night you appeared to have forgotten that. I thought you were now regretting it and escaping from temptation by going to London."

"You flatter yourself. I did not reveal anything last night that was not already common knowledge," he said stiffly.

"I saw something of your feelings, Hugo. I would like to think that showed you have some trust in me. You do not in general confide those to many people, I believe?"

He paused to reflect. "I was angry," he said dismissively.

Julia put her hand on his. "Come, Hugo—I saw more than anger."

He stared at her hand, apparently debating some difficult question in his mind. Then he took hold of it and grasped it hard. "There's more to the story than anyone else knows."

"I thought there must be," she said gently. "Your father's behaviour is difficult to comprehend otherwise."

"Why do you say that?"

She chose her words carefully. "While I was in London, seeing you in Dover Street after... after..."

"After you had announced to your father that we were engaged, is that right?"

Julia nodded. "He had enquiries made about you. By the time I returned he knew a great deal about you and your family."

Hugo got up and went to the window. With his back to her he said, "I am surprised he allowed the engagement to stand—still more that he actively promoted it."

"He said that, though your brother had behaved badly, he had found nothing dishonourable in your conduct."

Hugo turned round swiftly. "He said that?"

"Yes. It was very like him. He always refused to pay heed to rumours and gossip. He said very little of your father's death. But he did say that your brother... your brother..."

"He told you of John's gambling debts. Yes, it would be difficult for anyone not to know of those."

"He also said he had found some foundation for the rumours that John had stolen some money, and that your father had been forced to replace it in order to save him from prison," she finished in a rush.

"Nothing more?"

"No. But it isn't the whole story, is it, Hugo?"

"Why do you say that?"

"Because it makes no sense! Your father wouldn't save John from arrest, merely in order to bring him home here and then shoot him! There must be something else!"

"John's debts ruined the family. My father had already paid out vast sums before he replaced the money John had 'borrowed'—his word—from the Navy Office."

Julia shook her head. "It still isn't enough," she said obstinately.

"You're right, of course. Come over here—please, Julia." Puzzled, she walked slowly over to join him at the window. He took her face in his hands and examined it. "You have beautiful eyes, do you know that, Julia? A most unusually clear silver-grey, wide-spaced and with an expression in them which is almost irresistible—frank without any hint of boldness, shy but honest. There's intelligence there, and something more. Integrity? I am tempted to trust them, those eyes. Am I being a fool, I wonder?"

Julia held her breath. If Hugo could once bring himself to confide in her, then she might have the key to their whole future. Suddenly he seemed to reach a decision. "Come for a walk, Julia," he said. "I don't want any of the servants to interrupt—or overhear. Do you need a bonnet?"

SOON THEY WERE sitting in a little summer-house high on the hill overlooking Donyatt. Hugo did not immediately say anything. He stared down at Donyatt with the now familiar expression in his gaze—that mixture of tenderness, pride and love. It caused Julia a sudden pang of . . . what? Surely it wasn't jealousy? How could one be jealous of a house? She was relieved when he began, somewhat abruptly, to speak.

"John never gave a fig for Donyatt. I always found that difficult to understand, and so did my father. But from the day he was old enough John wanted to live in London and play a part in government. Donyatt merely provided a background for his political ambitions. My father did his best for him, but the Devenishes have never had much influence in government circles. Our interest was always in the land. So it was essential that John make a politically advantageous marriage, and he was all set to do so when he met Thérèse de Lachasse and fell desperately in love with her.''

Hugo fell silent. Julia was so anxious not to distract him that she hardly breathed. But what had all this to do with what had happened in the library?

"She destroyed my brother and damn near destroyed us all."

Julia was shocked into protest. "Hugo!"

"I mean what I say. A little while ago you protested when I described love as degrading. That is exactly the effect your precious 'love' had on my family. John was its worst victim. It drove him to betray everything—family, honour, friendship, loyalty... It destroyed him and it almost destroyed me. I assure you, Julia, rather than fall prey to that kind of madness, I would cut my throat."

"But not all love is like that, Hugo!" It seemed important to Julia that she should persuade Hugo that he was wrong. She cast about in her mind for a suitable analogy. "What do you call the feeling you have for Donyatt, for example? Wouldn't you say that was love?"

"'Love'? No, I would prefer to say that Donyatt is part of me, Julia. I can't explain. I want to protect it, cherish it, would sacrifice anything to keep it safe... And I feel that in return Donyatt will never betray my trust, never be unworthy... Oh, as I said, it is impossible to explain!"

"Isn't that the best kind of love, Hugo? Can't it exist between men and women, too?"

Hugo laughed sardonically. "Not the sort I've experienced, my dear. And I would not compare that with what I feel for Donyatt."

"Then you have not experienced the kind of love I mean."

"I've told you, Julia—there's no such thing! Or have you found this love?"

"I... No, I haven't. I agree it's rare. But it exists, Hugo, it exists."

"In a romance, perhaps. But not in real life, Julia. You have only to look around you."

Julia sighed and gave up for the moment, returning instead to Hugo's story. "What did Thérèse do?"

"She married John. My father hadn't wanted the match, but he did his best for them. He gave them their own London establishment, he made them a more than handsome allowance, he even let Thérèse refurbish Donyatt throughout, though her taste was far from his. But she was never satisfied and eventually she left him. And John...John went slowly to the devil." He moved restlessly, and Julia wondered if he was remembering the part he might have played in the drama. But he went on, "You have heard the stories of my brother's career after that. I assure you, they are all true. When I first returned from Greece I couldn't believe it. Though John was not a strong character, there had never been any vice in him. But after Thérèse deserted him it was as if he had gone mad. He became a vindictive, dangerous man. Only in the last few hours of his life did he come to his senses and try to repair some of the damage he had done."

"He came to beg your father's forgiveness?"

Hugo hesitated. He looked at Julia, who steadily returned his gaze, then he turned his head away. "For more than theft, Julia. John was a traitor. He had sold secrets to the French."

After a shocked pause Julia said, "I don't believe it!"

"His guilt is beyond question. I was there when he confessed. Oh, he was full of remorse, swore he had never meant it to go so far. He said it had started with unimportant details." Hugo gave a humourless laugh. "However it had started, it certainly ended disastrously enough. The day before John set out for Donyatt he had heard that a Navy frigate had been intercepted and sunk by the French. They knew where to find it because they had been informed of its rendezvous position with the rest of the fleet. All hands were lost. For the first time John was faced with the full significance of his treachery."

"What did your father say to him?"

"I don't know. My father ordered me out of the room. He wanted to talk to John alone about what he must do. So I went out to the stables. I should have known what would happen! My father was always too impatient to handle John properly. He was totally uncompromising in his standards of conduct, and expected others to be the same. It's my belief that John was reluctant to take the honourable way out, and my father took the matter into his own hands—shot him, and then shot himself afterwards.''

THEY SAT IN SILENCE for some minutes. Donyatt lay before them, bathed in sunlight, surrounded by serene English countryside. The dark events of the past seemed to belong to another world.

Hugo aroused himself and said wearily, ''I always swore that my brother's crimes should die with him, that I would tell no one the real truth behind what happened that night. I am not sure even now why I have burdened you with it.''

Julia moved round swiftly to kneel in front of him. She looked up into his face. ''I cannot tell you how glad I am that you have, Hugo. It was time for you to share the pain. Indeed it was essential that you should. Now you can begin to feel free—to look forward, not back.''

''It was wrong of me all the same to marry you without first telling you of it. You should not be involved with this. You could be forgiven if you wished to go your own way immediately, without waiting a year.''

Julia said steadily, ''My involvement, whatever it is, is with you, Hugo, not with your brother or anyone else in your family. I have yet to learn that you have done anything dishonourable.''

For the first time that morning Hugo's smile lightened his face. He took her hands in his. ''Like father, like daughter. I believe you mean it. I should have recognised your quality ten years ago, Julia. What a fool I was!'' He smiled again at her confusion as she blushed and stammered. She finally managed to say,

''I had a lot to learn, Hugo. I would not have suited you at all at that time! Besides, you had your heart set on someone else—someone who was everything I was not. Beautiful, accomplished and, above all, familiar with the ways of society.''

''Ah, yes,'' he murmured. ''Mary Strangway—the Honourable Mary. A very lovely girl! You're right, Julia. She was a jewel. And so well versed in the ways of society that it took her very little time to decide we should not suit, after all—once the Devenish fortune went."

"Then she was not worth a great deal!" said Julia, unable to help herself.

With a return to his old cynicism, Hugo replied, "Ah, but then she had thought that I would be worth a great deal to her!" He laughed when he saw Julia's face. "Oh, don't worry! You were wrong to suggest earlier that I was in love with her. I had simply decided that she was beautiful, well-bred and well-behaved. And unlikely ever to lead me the sort of dance that Thérèse had led John. I assure you 'love' did not enter our relationship."

"All the same, Hugo, though you had rejected the idea of 'love'—" Julia managed a fair imitation of the scorn in Hugo's voice "—had you also abandoned the idea of loyalty?"

"It would not occur to me to ask it of a woman."

"You are not very kind to my sex. What qualities do you look for in a woman, then?"

Hugo turned with the familiar glint of devilment and slid his arm round her waist. It was some time since he had touched her like this, and again she felt that little leap of her heart, but she resisted it and met his eyes steadily. His smile faded and he drew a deep breath. He started to say something, stopped, and looked puzzled. He said uncertainly, "Julia?" Slowly he pulled her to her feet and held her close. They kissed, a long, deeply passionate kiss, a kiss that left them both breathless, and afterwards Hugo buried his head in Julia's hair as if he was seeking her comfort and support. Then he held her away from him and stared at her as if seeing her for the first time. He gave a short, incredulous laugh and shook his head as if to clear it. "What was it you asked? The qualities I look for in a woman? Up till a moment ago I was in no doubt. Now..." He paused, then said slowly, "I am no longer sure, Julia. I'm no longer sure!"

CHAPTER ELEVEN

THE NEXT MORNING Hugo and Mr. Hockliffe set off for London before the rest of the household was fully astir. Julia watched from her bedroom window as the coach bowled down the drive. She had not slept well, for the episode on the hill with Hugo had left her restless and confused. He had avoided her the rest of the day, pleading last-minute business on the estate, and in the evening he had seemed *distrait*. More than once she had caught his eyes on her, with a strange look, almost of bewilderment, in them, but each time he had looked away again as if he wished to keep his thoughts from her. At the end of the evening he had spoken to her about the management of the estate and had then taken his leave of her courteously, but with evident relief. What was wrong with him? On the hill he had seemed so close—if he had asked her immediately after that kiss to forget about waiting the year she might even have agreed and she would now be his wife in more than name. But something had stopped him, and afterwards he had distanced himself from her. Surely she could not have imagined the completeness of their rapport. Could it be that their very closeness had taken Hugo by surprise and that, suspicious as he was of deeper feelings, he was afraid? Or was she deceiving herself? Was there another explanation, less agreeable to her self-esteem? She was so inexperienced in these matters that she might well have misinterpreted their encounter. She sighed and decided that she would have to wait for his return to get an answer.

In the meantime, Julia concentrated on her self-appointed task of ridding Hugo of the presence of the ghosts in the library. In less time than she would have thought possible, the dirty brocade in the blue drawing-room had been stripped

and the library bookshelves had been transferred to their
new home. The former library was soon empty, its heavy
tapestry curtains and worn druggets consigned to the attics.
And by the time the carpenters and painters had finished
their work the carrier's drays had arrived with Julia's possessions from Downings. Local upholsterers and seam-
stresses were called in, and new curtains and wall-hangings
put in place. There was no end to the activity. Furniture
which had been relegated to the attics by Thérèse Devenish,
some of it in the Chinese style of some sixty years before,
and all of it beautiful, was brought down, restored, and arranged in the new rooms. The former library was renamed
the Chinese drawing-room, and the household agreed that
it was many years since a handsomer apartment had been
seen in Donyatt—though the more conservative among
them expressed doubt about the foreign birds and trees
which rioted over the walls in Julia's wall-hangings. Julia
herself was delighted with the results of their labours. There
was now no trace of the dark library, heavy with remembered tragedy, in this airy, elegant drawing-room.

But July passed into August and August was very nearly
over before Hugo returned to Donyatt, and when he came
Julia was shocked at his appearance. He was pale, he
seemed thinner than ever, and his temper was, to say the
least, uncertain. He refused to answer her very natural
questions about his stay in London, and after a while she
thought it wiser to ask no more. She was relieved when he
decided to go to bed, and was not in the slightest surprised
when she was told the next morning that Hugo was flushed
and hot, and that he had spent the night tossing restlessly in
his bed and murmuring incoherently. She sent one of the
grooms for the doctor and went to see her husband. As she
came up the stairs she could hear Hugo ordering his valet to
bring his damned clothes. She went swiftly to Adcombe's
rescue, dismissing him as she came in through the door.

"I have told Adcombe you are not to get up until Dr.
Trent has seen you," she announced, growing a little pink
as she realised that Hugo was stark naked under his dressing-gown.

"Did you indeed? Well as you can see, Julia, I am perfectly fit and well able to get out of my bed. I intend to dress, starting now. I have no desire to offend your sensibilities, so I advise you to leave the room."

"Don't be so pigheaded, Hugo! Dr. Trent will be here shortly and I am positive his advice will be that you should be confined to your bed for some days. You look quite dreadful."

"Thank you," he growled. "I'll get up just the same."

"You cannot," she said baldly. "I've sent Adcombe to fetch some barley water from the kitchen. He isn't here to dress you."

"In that case I'll dress myself," he began, standing up. He sat down again. "Confound it, I'm as weak as a kitten."

In spite of her embarrassment, for Hugo was a splendid sight in his half-open dressing-gown, Julia hurried to the bed. She helped him to get under the covers, and when Adcombe returned she insisted, in spite of a lively argument, that Hugo should sip some of the barley water. She was encouraged by his ill-temper. A very sick man would not resist her attempts to make him comfortable so strenuously. When Dr. Trent arrived he confirmed what Julia had already suspected. Hugo had a slight fever, probably picked up in London. A few days' bed rest was essential, but then the patient would rapidly recover. After the good doctor had departed, promising as he went to send round one of his own concoctions, Julia set about organising the sick-room. Hugo's fever-bright eyes followed her round the room.

"Aren't you afraid you'll catch it?"

"Of course not! You forget. I have been living a quiet life here in the country, not knocking myself up in town. What on earth have you been up to, Hugo?"

His face took on a closed expression. "Nothing," he said. "Business with Hockliffe and the others. I'm tired, Julia. I'd like to sleep for a little. Adcombe will see to me."

She stood still for a moment. "Of course," she said woodenly. "Sleep well, Hugo."

His voice stopped her at the door. "Julia!" She turned. "I'm glad to be back."

Her eyes filled with tears. "Donyatt is glad to see you again, Hugo," she said, as calmly as she could. Then she made her escape.

The fever ran its course and for three days Julia, Adcombe and the doctor managed to keep Hugo in his bed. On the fourth day after his return he became so angry when they tried to persuade him to remain there any longer that Dr. Trent gave in.

"To tell you the truth, Lady Rostherne, your husband would not benefit from further bed rest. This agitation of his spirits is more harmful than a little judicious exercise."

"'Agitation of his spirits'!" said Julia crossly. "Your tact does you credit, Dr. Trent. I would call it plain bad temper!"

"Invalids—especially an invalid of Lord Rostherne's energetic mode of life—are notoriously difficult. You will need a great deal of patience, my lady."

"Hmm! You are sure he is fit enough to come downstairs?"

"Oh, yes. The fever was not a serious one. I think if Lord Rostherne had been in an easier frame of mind he could have thrown it off quite easily. The mind, Lady Rostherne, plays curious tricks on us. Do what you can to set his mind at rest, and you will see your husband fully recovered very shortly."

The doctor departed, and Julia went to seek out Mr. Hockliffe. It was no more than she had suspected. Something had happened to Hugo in London in spite of his denials, and she must do her best to establish what it was. Perhaps it was something to do with the estate?

"Lady Rostherne, I wish I knew!" was his disappointing response to her question. "We worked long hours on the final details of the loan repayments, and it all went very well. Very well indeed! The estate is now clear of all encumbrances. There are no problems there which cannot easily be solved with time and good management. Lord Rostherne seemed very satisfied and, I thought, eager to return. But then, just as we were about to come back, he suddenly decided he had to stay in London another week, and in fact it turned out to be ten days. I used the time to complete other

less urgent tasks in the City, but his lordship was otherwise
engaged. He did not see fit to tell me the reason for the delay.''

Julia was left to her own thoughts. So Donyatt was once
again completely Hugo's. Was...was he now regretting the
price he had been forced to pay? She heard his steps on the
stair and quickly pulled herself together. Regrets were useless. Hugo's way to recovery was before him, not behind.
She hurried into the hall and greeted him gaily.

"Hugo! You are looking much more the thing. Let me
help you.''

"Thank you, Julia. I am perfectly capable of negotiat-
ing a few stairs by myself. I would be obliged if you could
manage to convey that to my totally unnecessary atten-
dants,'' he said, glaring at Adcombe and one of the footmen who had been helping him downstairs. Julia nodded to
them and they disappeared.

"Come, I have much to show you," she said, leading the
way towards what had been the old library.

"Julia!" She turned to find Hugo standing in the middle
of the hall, looking paler. She ran over to him and grasped
his arm.

"What is it? Do you feel ill again?"

"No, I am well enough. But I cannot face that room today."

"Nor will you ever again. Look!" She led him firmly to
the doors, threw them open, and ushered him in. The sun
was just beginning to move round to the long windows, but
the room hardly needed the extra light. Gone were the heavy
bookcases, the dark tapestries, the dingy walls. In their place
were light-hearted panels of exotic birds and shrubs, pale
straw-coloured silk curtains, and walls in the same delicate
colour. The rugs on the gleaming floor, the china cabinet
against the wall, and two large vases on stands echoed the
theme of the room. "May I present you, Lord Rostherne,
to the Chinese drawing-room?" said Julia, sweeping him a
lavish curtsy.

Hugo walked slowly into the room and gazed all around
him. His silence began to unnerve Julia, who was waiting
apprehensively at the door, "There's my grandmother's

writing table!'' he suddenly exclaimed. "And the chairs, and stands—'' He whirled back to her. "Where did you get all this?"

"Most of the furniture came from your own attics, Hugo. The furnishings were mine. My father brought them back from China."

"It's so different..." He walked round the room, brushing his fingers over the writing-table, examining an ornament, standing in front of a picture. Julia remained where she was, stiff with tension. Hugo returned to the door, put his arm round her shoulders, and drew her into the centre of the room. "Athene the wise, dispelling the ghosts in her own way. Thank you." He raised her hand to his lips and kissed it. Julia suddenly found it difficult to get her breath.

"I... I enjoyed doing it," she stammered, feeling every bit as gauche as the shy seventeen-year-old at Lady Godfrey's ball. Hugo obviously remembered her too. He smiled as if at a delightful memory, his eyes danced, and then he slowly bent his head and kissed her. The sweetness of the kiss took Julia's breath away. This was the old Hugo, the Hugo she had fallen in love with all those years ago! She stared at him in delight and then gasped as Hugo suddenly grew serious and pulled her closer, kissing her hard, kissing her desperately again and again. Passion flared between them as Hugo groaned her name, and Julia flung her arms around his neck, returning kiss for kiss. She felt gloriously, magnificently alive. How could she have doubted him? This was where she belonged, had always belonged! She wanted to be one with Hugo, one body, one flesh, one life. The intoxication of the moment lasted a short while longer, and then she felt Hugo's hands gently putting her away from him. They faced one another in confusion.

"I... I'm sorry, Julia."

Julia was incapable of any sensible response, or even of meeting Hugo's eyes. She felt he was looking at her averted face, and struggled to say something. After all, the loss of control had by no means been his alone! Then he repeated, "I'm sorry. I didn't mean that to happen."

The passionate regret in his voice penetrated Julia's whirling thoughts. What did he mean? She forced herself to

look at him. Hugo was trembling almost as much as she
was, his eyes dark in a paper-white face. He looked worse
than ever. With an enormous effort she pulled herself to
gether and said softly, "Come, you must sit down. I'll ring
for Lydiate and order some tea—or would you prefer
something else?"

"Julia, I...I..." His voice was so unhappy that her heart
misgave her. She rallied and said with a small smile,

"I'm sure what you have to say is important, Hugo, but
you must leave it for the moment. Rest for a while."

"Damn it, how can I rest? There are things I must tell
you, though God knows how... It's all such a mess, Julia!
Why in heaven's name did I ever marry you?"

It was Julia's turn to grow white. She stopped short on her
way to the bell, paused and then, still with her back to him,
she said in a voice devoid of all expression, "To save Donyatt, I believe."

"I should never have done it. I should have stayed with
my first plan and married one of those girls Hockliffe found
for me."

"Except that, as you've so often said before, I made it
impossible," said Julia harshly, finishing the thought for
him.

"Julia—"

"You must excuse me, Hugo. I...I don't feel very well.
I have a headache." She forced a small laugh. "Pray heaven
I have not, in spite of my brave words, taken your fever af-
ter all."

"Julia!" Ignoring his call, she ran to the doors and disappeared, and Hugo was left swearing quietly in the centre
of the beautiful room Julia had created in an attempt to
bring him peace of mind.

JULIA AVOIDED HUGO for the rest of the day. She stayed in
her room for the most part, pleading a headache and refusing to come down for dinner. A tray appeared later for her,
and she forced herself to eat a little. She must not become
ill; she must retain her strength. She had had such bright
hopes while Hugo had been away in London. She had believed that she could eventually break down the barriers

which he had erected against all who would get close to him, had believed that he was slowly beginning to trust her. She had not really considered what might lie beyond that—a friendly, contented existence together at Donyatt? Or might there have been something more, something she had caught a glimpse of during those moments in Hugo's arms? Whatever it was, it was now clear that Hugo had not felt the same. She cringed as she wondered if he had seen how powerfully he had affected her and was now trying to indicate that her loss of self-control was distasteful. Those girls he had mentioned, they would have taken his title and his position in return for their money, and would not have dreamed of asking for his . . . his what? His love? This was ridiculous! She was no longer a green seventeen-year-old, and she was surely past the age of looking for wild romance! She would most certainly not find it with Hugo Devenish, for he had expressly rejected the idea of "love" with devastating scorn. No, if she did stay with Hugo the most she could hope for would be a life of friendship and shared interests, looking after Donyatt and her children, perhaps travelling a little and occasionally visiting London. Most of the women of her class would not dream of expecting more. Indeed, she ought to count herself fortunate that she had so much! By the end of a long and wakeful night Julia had persuaded herself that her behaviour that afternoon had been a momentary aberration, and when Hugo sought her out the next day to request her to accompany him on a walk up the hill, she was able to face him with reasonable equanimity.

"I was a clumsy fool yesterday," he began. They were sitting in the little summer-house overlooking Donyatt, resting after the steep climb.

"Please, do not say any more. It was foolish of me to react so badly."

"But I must!" he insisted. "I hurt you quite unintentionally. I only meant—"

"I know what you meant, Hugo, and if there was any way I could undo the past I would. But I can't, and we must learn to live with it. Now please, unless you wish me to become agitated again you will drop this subject."

He ran his hand through his hair. "What a mess it all is! Very well, I will leave the matter until you are calmer, Julia, but, I warn you, it cannot be postponed forever."

Julia ignored the latter half of this, and said brightly, "Thank you. I was reading in the *Gazette* recently that many of the French émigré families have returned to France, now that the monarchy has been reestablished there. They added such a distinct flavour to society. I'm sure they will be sadly missed." Hugo frowned slightly and she went on hastily, "Of course, London is always thin of people at this season. Where is the Prince Regent spending the summer, do you know?" Julia babbled on in a manner which was totally alien to her, and Hugo listened patiently enough at first. But he finally found her unnatural, artificial tone so unwelcome that he could bear it no longer.

"Julia, if you hoped to fend me off with this inane chatter—I will not grace it with the name of conversation—then you have failed. You must listen to what I have to say. It is vitally important to us both."

Julia shrugged her shoulders in a tiny gesture of defeat. "Very well. If you must."

"I went to London to clear up the remaining details of the loan repayments. The business went well. All I wanted to do was to get back to Donyatt to start a new life." He took her hand. "The past will always be with us, Julia, but I truly thought that we could make something of the future. My financial worries over, I was looking forward to a contented life here with you—children, perhaps, and above all peace to enjoy Donyatt as it was always meant to be enjoyed. But then, just as I was about to return, something happened." He paused. His mouth was set in a firm line, but Julia could sense the turmoil inside him. She regarded him calmly and asked,

"What was it?"

But Hugo was swearing quietly under his breath, and when she followed his gaze she could see why. Mr. Hockliffe was toiling up the hill towards them and was nearly within earshot.

"Confound it, is there never to be a moment when we can be alone? What does he want now?"

Julia interrupted this speech before the lawyer heard it.

"This is a hot day to be hurrying like that, Mr. Hockliffe," she smiled. "Sit down and rest a minute."

"Lady Rostherne, you are too kind, too kind. Thank you. I have brought some good tidings."

Hugo muttered something inaudible. In view of the expression on his face, Julia was glad it was. She said hastily,

"How intriguing! What is it, Mr. Hockliffe?"

"I have here the missing receipts for his lordship. I am sure you will be delighted to know that that completes every last detail of our negotiations, Lord Rostherne," said the little man, smiling in genuine relief. "And . . . I have a note for her ladyship."

"For me? How pleasant! What can it be?" But a minute later Julia gave an exclamation of astonished dismay.

"What is it?" asked Hugo anxiously.

"Sophie Mersham is on her way to visit her mother-in-law in Bath and is proposing to call on us."

The silence that followed was broken by Mr. Hockliffe, who began to remark how agreeable it was to receive one's friends in the country. He received a glare from Hugo and stopped short.

"I take it Peter is with her. When do they plan to arrive?" Hugo asked.

Julia was rapidly scanning the page. "No! I can't believe it!" she wailed. "They're arriving tomorrow evening! Oh, this is too bad! How dare they give us such little notice?"

"Let me see," said Hugo, taking the note from her. "There must have been some delay in the mail, Julia. This note was dispatched over a week ago."

"What are we to do?"

"I'm afraid there's no help for it—we'll have to receive them. If they are on their way to Bath they won't stay long— a day or two at the most. Can you do it?"

Julia was already getting to her feet. "I must find Mrs. Staple. Mr. Hockliffe, please come with me. There's so much to be done. You can perhaps advise me on where to find . . ." Her voice faded as she and Mr. Hockliffe went down the hill.

"Damn!" said Hugo. "Damn, damn, damn!"

CHAPTER TWELVE

JULIA UNASHAMEDLY used the excuse of this unexpected visit to avoid Hugo. She knew that she was behaving foolishly, but after his behaviour in the Chinese drawing-room she dreaded what he might say. She would postpone it as long as she could.

Instead she concentrated on her preparations for the Mershams' visit. She had good cause to bless her original inspiration in sending for Mrs. Staple, for that good woman rallied to the rescue with all her considerable force. Without saying a word out of place she had managed to convey to the servants that Donyatt was on trial. The result was that no one grumbled as they laboured to transform the reopened bedrooms into comfortable apartments for the visitors and to finish off the work in the new library. The Mershams were lodged at the opposite corner of the house from Julia's own apartment. It was true that Hugo's bedchamber adjoined hers, but the communicating doors were always locked, and the last thing Julia wanted was for Sophie's prying eyes to observe the sleeping arrangements she and Hugo had adopted. She knew her cousin well enough to imagine the capital Sophie would make of that!

By the time the Mershams arrived, Donyatt was as ready as it could be. It would have been impossible to wipe out more than ten years of neglect in a few months, but the reception rooms and the Mershams' chambers were as elegant as they had ever been, and the main façade of the house was once again gracefully beautiful.

"Lord!" grumbled Sophie as they came up the steps. "What an out of the way place to live, Ju! I declare my poor bones feel quite shattered. Those appalling roads! It took us an age to get here. How can you bear it?"

"I love Donyatt," smiled Julia.

"Yes, you always were a country mouse," said Sophie with distaste. However, she brightened up considerably as they reached the portico where Hugo was standing. "Hugo, how charming of you to have us here! You must forgive us for intruding in this shabby manner on your idyll, but I had to see how Julia was—I miss her dreadfully, you know!"

It was not immediately obvious that Sophie had missed Julia, for when they were all together most of her conversation and all of her smiles were directed at Hugo. Only after dinner, while the gentlemen stayed in the dining-room for a while, were Sophie and Julia alone in Julia's Chinese drawing-room. The gay charm of the wall hangings, the calm beauty of the furnishings were lost on Sophie, who fidgeted and yawned while Julia enquired after her aunt and persuaded Sophie to talk about her children.

"I had thought that Peter's mother would be glad to see them?"

"I wouldn't dream of taking them to Bath! They're much better off in London where they have their tutors and nurses to look after them. I couldn't bring everybody! And if you're going to suggest that it's too hot for them in London, Ju, you can save yourself the bother. My mother is taking them with her to Worthing." Sophie paused for breath, obviously recalling an argument on the same subject with Lady Thornton. She went on fretfully, "Old Lady Mersham is always so critical of them—and of me! Besides, children are such a nuisance on a journey. They get sick, they are constantly demanding attention—my nerves couldn't stand it. No, Peter's mother is quite enough to cope with. But tell me, how is Hugo now that his fears for Donyatt are at rest? I have to confess I never imagined for one minute that your engagement was a real one."

"Then why did you tell the *Gazette* it was imminent, Sophie?" asked Julia.

Sophie looked as if she were about to deny this, then she visibly recalled that she had said as much to Hugo. She opened her large china-blue eyes wide and said in an injured tone, "I thought I would help you. After all, there was poor, dear Hugo desperately searching for a rich wife, and

there were you—nearly thirty and desperate for a husband.
I think I was rather clever, so you needn't look at me in that
accusing way, Ju. You did very well out of it. But why did
you have such a hasty wedding?''

With some constraint Julia reminded Sophie of her father's illness, and explained that the Earl had wanted to see
his daughter married.

''Well, it's understandable that he wanted to be sure Hugo
came up to scratch, I suppose. However, I do hope you
haven't made a mistake, Ju, pushing ahead like that. I know
my mother was most concerned. People do talk so, don't
they?''

By the eve of the Mershams' departure, Julia was heartily sick of her cousin's visit. Sophie's eyes were everywhere,
and though she rhapsodised on the beauties of Donyatt and
its surrounding lands in Hugo's presence, she never ceased
to convey her scorn of the many deficiencies in Donyatt's
condition when she was alone with Julia. Julia resented this
with a ferocity which surprised her. Good manners alone
kept her civil. But there was worse to come. Afterwards Julia was to ask herself whether this had been the chief reason
for Sophie's willingness to make a large detour along indifferent roads in order to visit them.

After dinner that evening Sophie suddenly said, ''Come,
Ju, we'll take a turn in the garden. There's still plenty of
light—you dine so bucolically early here.'' Then when they
were well away from the house Sophie said casually, ''I
thought Hugo had given up the town house, Ju?''

Julia knew that tone of old. Sophie was up to some mischief. What lay behind this seemingly innocent enquiry?
''The lease still has some time to run,'' she said calmly.

''Oh, so that's why...'' Sophie stole a glance at Julia.

''I expect you saw Hugo there when he was in London
recently. He and Mr. Hockliffe were finishing off some estate business. It was useful that the house was still avail-
able. But we'll find something better when we eventually
spend a Season in London. The Dover Street house is
somewhat small.'' That ought to silence Sophie, Julia
thought, if her delightful cousin was trying to suggest that
Hugo couldn't wait to get away from his new bride.

"You know, Ju, I really admire you," Sophie continued, undismayed. Julia braced herself. It was worse than she had thought. Sophie sounded like a cat with a whole dairy of cream.

"Thank you, Sophie. Shall we go in now? The men will be wondering where we are."

"I think you are so brave—and so sensible!" said Sophie, undeterred. "But who is she?"

Julia could not think of a thing to say. To ask Sophie what she was talking about would be to court disaster. She remained silent.

"I mean the little lady who was staying in Dover Street with Hugo. Who is she? She looked very striking, though I only saw her at a distance. Hugo didn't seem to want to introduce us. What part does she play in the estate business, Julia?"

Only because she had prepared herself for a shock was Julia able to keep her self-possession. She forced herself to smile. "You must ask Hugo that, Sophie," she said gently. "You're surely not asking me to betray his confidence, are you? And now, if you are to be ready to leave early tomorrow morning, then I really think it is time we went in. I have hardly spoken to Peter since he arrived."

By exerting every ounce of her self-control Julia managed to remain a gracious hostess until Sophie's departure the next day. She had the satisfaction of knowing that her cousin went to Bath still uncertain of how much Julia had already known of Hugo's mystery visitor.

It was the only satisfaction. Julia might have saved her face, but she was unable to save her heart. It was fortunate that Hugo had gone out for the day on an urgent visit to one of the outlying farms, otherwise she might so far have forgotten herself as to challenge him. As it was, she had a whole day to come to terms with the unpalatable truth that Hugo had made no mention of faithfulness in their initial bargain. She had assumed it, that was all. It was by no means unusual for a man to have a mistress. And if she considered it rationally it would be very likely that Hugo, denied his wife's bed, would seek consolation elsewhere. But to her dismayed astonishment she found that she couldn't even begin to consider it rationally! She was a raging mass of jealousy and despair. So this was what Hugo had been attempting to confess to her! This was why he was regretting their marriage! Had he planned to endure a tame, unexciting existence at Donyatt with her, Julia, and to add spice to his life with a mistress in London? And was his conscience now urging him to confess? Or was this woman more precious to him than he had imagined? Had Hugo been picturing her when he had held Julia in his arms so passionately? Had he seen her face when he had looked so tenderly at Julia's? Did he imagine that she, his wife, would sit there listening tamely to his confession of love for another woman? It was not to be borne! Julia strode restlessly about the house and garden in a vain effort to regain her self-possession. Finally she ordered her horse to be saddled and, refusing the services of her groom, took off for the open country.

During a long, hard ride she took herself to task. This was no time to permit herself to believe she was in love with Hugo Devenish! It would be the height of idiocy even to contemplate it. She doubted he was capable of the sort of love to satisfy her—one that demanded and gave total commitment—but even if he were, it would not be for her. She came a very poor third in his priorities. Donyatt was his consuming passion. For that he would do almost anything; he had said so. And now there was this woman. Had she been part of his life even before Hugo had been forced to seek a rich bride? Very probably. Damn her! Damn them! Julia rode on and on, tormenting herself with these and similar thoughts, until at last a kind of drear exhaustion brought common sense. It would be better for her, she decided, if she could learn to keep her rioting emotions under control. Having reached this eminently sensible conclusion, she admired the rolling hills around her for fully two minutes, but then angry resentment mounted within her again. How dared Hugo conduct himself so in public, exposing her, Julia, to the gossip of cats like Sophie Mersham? She spurred her horse to another gallop in a vain attempt to return to equanimity, but after a short time she came to a halt again in despair. It was useless! She had to confess that she would be totally indifferent to anything a hundred cats like Sophie Mersham might say if only Hugo loved her! However hard she rode, she would never escape from the melancholy truth. Her love for Hugo Devenish had never really died; it had merely been dormant for all those years. And now it had resurfaced as strong as ever, and far, far more dangerous. Well, she had suppressed it before and she would do so again, if it killed her! With this firm resolve she turned for home—and realised that she had no idea where she was. Indeed, she was hopelessly lost!

Julia spent the next hour going round in circles, or so it seemed. She was growing anxious—this part of the county was not densely populated, and her horse was showing signs of fatigue. So it was with relief that she eventually found a herdsman who was able to direct her to the "Big House." But after leading her horse down to the valley and walking a mile along a rough lane, she found to her dismay that one herdsman's "Big House" was not the same as another's. This was not Donyatt. The drive was overgrown, and ivy covered the windows of an ancient, rambling manor house. She braced herself. Without help she could not go much further, so she must seek it even in this unlikely spot.

The massive door was opened by a neatly dressed housekeeper—a most reassuring sight for poor Julia, who was by this time distinctly nervous. Clearing her throat, she said with commendable calm, "Good evening. Is your mistress at home?"

The housekeeper looked at her somewhat suspiciously, but decided that the visitor deserved an answer in spite of her dishevelled appearance. "Well, the master's back, ma'am. Do you wish to see him?"

"Er—yes. Please convey Lady Rostherne of Donyatt's compliments to him, and ask him if he might spare her a few minutes. She finds herself in a slight quandary."

The housekeeper curtsied and with a wide-eyed, "Yes, y'r ladyship. If y'r ladyship would care to wait here." She showed Julia into a low-ceilinged hall with tall chairs ranged about the walls, and scuttled away. Even on this bright summer day the room was full of shadows. Julia sat with a sigh of relief and in a few minutes heard footsteps in the passage opposite. A door was flung open and a man's voice said, "Thérèse? I can't believe it! You've got what you wanted, after all! But what on earth are you doing here; isn't it rather dangerous?" Julia stepped forward into a patch of light and he exclaimed, "Good God! Who the devil are you?"

Drawing herself up, Julia said coldly, "I am Julia Devenish, Hugo Devenish's wife. I think you have confused me with my husband's sister-in-law, sir."

Her host stood stock-still for a moment, then came forward, his face showing deep concern. "Lady Rostherne ... ma'am ... what can I say? Pray forgive me—you were in shadow, you see. For a moment I thought ... It was stupid of me. It must be ten years at least since John and Thérèse visited me here. And...and now I remember, John died years ago without ever inheriting the title. You must be Lord Hugo's wife. I have only just returned after being away for some time ... Age is addling my wits, Lady Rostherne. I have spent so much time in remote regions of the East that I have quite forgotten how to behave in civilised society. Will you forgive me?"

At that moment Julia would have forgiven him a great deal, so relieved was she at finding herself with a friend of the family, so to speak. Besides, though he looked contrite, there was an engaging twinkle in his eye which seemed to be inviting her to share the joke of his gaffe. She smiled back, almost in spite of herself. "You should rather forgive me, sir, for breaking in on you in this cavalier fashion. The fact is I am lost! I don't even know where I am now—or whose hospitality I am enjoying... ?"

"Oh, excuse me, my name is Greenfield, Lucian Greenfield. And this is Arbury Manor. You have not strayed a great distance, Lady Rostherne. Donyatt is some six miles away."

"Six miles! It seemed much further. But I think I must have wandered from the direct route."

Mr. Greenfield was more polished than he had at first appeared, for he allowed himself to show no surprise at a gentlewoman roaming the countryside without even a groom for company. He said merely, "How can I best help you, Lady Rostherne? What about your horse?"

"She's outside. I cannot think of riding her back. She is quite exhausted." Julia's eyes were full of remorse. "I am ashamed of myself, Mr. Greenfield. I'm afraid I gave little thought to poor Starlight in my abstraction." Julia's cheeks were flushed and her silver-grey eyes were luminous.

Mr. Greenfield looked at her admiringly for a moment, then said, "Pray do not distress yourself any longer, Lady Rostherne. Your horse will be well looked after in my own stables overnight and I shall see she is safely delivered to you tomorrow. Perhaps you would like to rest and refresh yourself while I see to it? Then I shall take you back to Donyatt in my carriage."

"May I meet your wife?"

"I have no wife, Lady Rostherne." He twinkled at her as she grew confused again. "You will probably now say that my ill behaviour is easily accounted for—and you would be right! Elderly bachelors are notoriously curmudgeonly creatures, graceless in company, and quite incapable of treating beautiful visitors as they ought. However, I assure you that I shall be on my best behaviour from now on. I'll fetch Mrs. Needham—she'll see to your needs."

With that he went away and came back shortly after with the housekeeper. Then he disappeared again and Julia was taken upstairs. She was shown into a handsome guest-chamber where she could tidy herself up, and refresh herself with lemonade and some delicious little cakes and biscuits. By the time she was down again Mr. Greenfield was back, with his carriage harnessed and waiting outside. He refused to allow her to express any thanks, saying only that he regarded it as a privilege to help any member of the Devenish family, especially the pretty ones. Julia laughed and disclaimed. His manner was so avuncular that she was not at all embarrassed at his compliments, but his admiration soothed her bruised heart a little.

On the journey she quizzed him as discreetly as possible about his friendship with those other Devenishes, but though he appeared to answer her questions frankly she later realised that he had not in fact told her very much. Thérèse was very pretty, John had been very much in love with her; it was a tragedy that they had not managed to stay happy together. But Julia could not waste this opportunity to find out more about Thérèse.

"Is my sister-in-law in England, then?"

"What makes you think that, Lady Rostherne?"

"You thought she might be at your house this afternoon. Am I . . . do I resemble her?"

Mr. Greenfield's laughter rang out. "Not exactly! Thérèse is...a little dab of a thing. Not at all my style, I assure you. And, of course, she must be well into her thirties by now, whereas—if I may say so without offence, Lady Rostherne—you are still in the bloom of youth!" Julia's cheeks acquired a faintly rosy touch as Mr. Greenfield looked at her with discreet admiration. However, she composed herself enough to ask,

"And my husband—did he visit you with John and his wife?"

His manner grew more reserved. "Lord Hugo was only about eighteen or nineteen at the time. I saw very little of him—but he was an extremely engaging young man. You may well say that that was the trouble, I suppose. But it's all past history now."

He would say no more, turning aside her questions with a laugh and adding that he was not yet so old nor so dull-witted that he would talk to her of another man—and that man her own husband! He told her of his travels, and Julia could almost forget her own problems for a while in the fascinating accounts of his journeys in the East. Time passed very swiftly.

CHAPTER THIRTEEN

IT WAS LATE afternoon before Hugo returned to Donyatt, though he had pressed hard to finish his business at Three Mile Farm. With the departure of the Mershams he would at least be able to have his long-delayed talk with Julia. He wanted to be free of his burden, wanted Julia to know the truth behind his delay in London and his doubts about their marriage. She had been hurt the other day, and that worried him. Julia deserved better than that. He was keenly disappointed, therefore, to find that Julia was not there. As he waited for his wife in her Chinese drawing-room he considered the Mershams' visit. Peter was an old and loyal friend and, God knew, he had few enough of those. But he was glad to see the back of the couple all the same. He had grown impatient with Sophie's trivial chatter, her constant scandalmongering and her sly digs at Julia. It had been stupid to let Sophie's malice influence his attitude at the beginning of his marriage. Now that he knew Julia better he was sure that his first instinct to believe in her had been sound—she had not manipulated him. It would surprise Sophie, he thought grimly, how easily he had seen through her façade of girlish charm, and how angry he had grown at her constant attempts to belittle Julia. Julia was worth ten of her—no, a thousand...

He got up impatiently, went on to the terrace, and gazed down the drive. It was time Julia was home, surely? He stood for a minute or two, but the drive remained empty. Where was she? He wanted to see her, he needed her here... He realised with some surprise that he thought more highly of Julia than of any other woman, more than of any other person, in fact, of his acquaintance. His wife had a quality that was all her own, compounded of so many contradictions—cool, silver-grey eyes, hair with the warmth of new chestnuts, a queenly grace of movement, yet an unexpected compliment could cause her to blush in confusion like an inexperienced girl. She was intelligent and clear-sighted, yet capable of unquestioning loyalty, and his pulses quickened as he remembered how her air of modest dignity could melt into passion... Yes, Julia was unique...

But where was she? He wanted to know how she would react to what he had to tell her. Surely she would not leave him? He could manage without her, of course! No woman was that important to him. But there had been times during these last months with Julia when life at Donyatt had proved very pleasant. Very pleasant. Surprisingly pleasant! But where the devil was she? He went in search of Lydiate.

"When did you say Lady Rostherne went for her ride?"

"Not long after your lordship left this morning."

"Did she give any indication of where she was going, or when she would return?"

"No, my lord. She seemed anxious to be gone. She didn't even wait for her groom."

Hugo looked at his butler in disbelief. "Let me understand you properly, Lydiate. Am I to infer that Lady Rostherne has been out all day, without her groom, and no one has seen fit to tell me?"

Lydiate quailed at the look on his master's face, but answered with dignity, "We did inform your lordship. As soon as your lordship returned!"

"Not that Lady Rostherne was alone, you fool! Send for the groom. No, I'll go myself."

Hugo strode to the stables, brushing aside an anxious Mrs. Staple with a curt, "I know, I know!" Here he found Julia's groom, and in five minutes had convinced that worthy that it would have been better if he had never been born. But at the end of it Hugo was no wiser. Julia had left Donyatt that morning and had not been heard of since. Had she known he was at Three Mile Farm for the day? Had she tried to join him there? Refusing to give in to the dread that was taking hold of him, he dispatched numbers of men to the outlying farms.

He had just reached the house again, and was about to change back into his riding clothes to go in search of Julia himself, when he saw a carriage coming up the drive. By the time he had reached the steps to meet it a stranger had just emerged. Full of foreboding, he hurried forward, but stopped short at the sight of Julia laughing down into the stranger's face as he handed her out. His sense of profound relief rapidly gave way to anger, and he stood in silence as Julia approached.

"Hugo! Such an adventure as I have had!" She spoke in the same unnatural, artificial tone she had used a day or two before when she had refused to let him tell her about London. Julia was up to something.

"An adventure, Julia?" said Hugo woodenly.

She gave a little laugh and went on, "Oh, you mustn't misunderstand. That would never do! I completely lost my way, and—"

"Your groom would have advised you, Julia, had he been with you."

Julia flushed, looked at the stranger, and said in a cool voice, "You are right, of course. But Mr. Greenfield cannot be interested in this discussion. Indeed, he deserves your thanks, for he has been most kind. I believe you already know him?"

Annoyed that his feelings had led him to forget his manners, Hugo stared at the stranger and then said with a touch of hauteur, "I do not think so."

Julia said sharply, "He was a friend of your brother's, Hugo."

Hugo frowned and Mr. Greenfield said hastily, "My acquaintance with your husband was of the slightest, Lady Rostherne. I am not at all surprised that he does not remember me. I believe he was seldom at Donyatt when his brother and sister-in-law lived here." He looked at Hugo with a sly twinkle in his eye. "I heard a great deal about you, of course, Lord Rostherne."

Hugo was about to ask him what the devil he meant when Julia intervened. "Mr. Greenfield was so good as to bring me home when I had completely lost myself. He has even arranged for Starlight to be brought back tomorrow."

"I am obliged to you, sir," said Hugo stiffly. "Will you come in?"

"You are too kind, Lord Rostherne, but I believe it is rather late," replied Mr. Greenfield, with a slight smile at the lack of enthusiasm in Hugo's voice.

"Oh, but you must!" cried Julia. "We cannot send you away without some kind of refreshment! Hugo, if you will escort Mr. Greenfield into the breakfast parlour, I shall see Mrs. Staple."

She hurried away and the two gentlemen slowly ascended the steps. Donyatt was looking its loveliest, the rays of the setting sun turning its stones to warm gold.

"You have a beautiful home, Lord Rostherne."

"Yes," replied Hugo. He caught sight of his guest looking at him in amusement and asked abruptly, "Do you live near, Greenfield?"

"Some six miles away—at Arbury."

"Arbury? Arbury Manor?" He stopped and gave Greenfield a hard stare. "Perhaps I do remember something . . ." His tone implied that, whatever it was, it was not to Mr. Greenfield's credit, but they had by this time reached the small parlour, so his visitor merely smiled again. Julia came forward.

"Now I can welcome you to my home and hope you will feel as kindly received as I was, Mr. Greenfield. I consider it most fortunate that I was directed to Arbury, however mistaken your herdsman was! Pray help yourself to some of Mrs. Chaffcombe's famous biscuits, and James has some wine for you here."

Hugo could not stop himself. He asked, "Julia, how was it that you were so far afield?"

Up to this moment Julia's manner had been cheerful, almost gay. But she now flushed slightly and her tone was restricted, "I felt I needed some fresh air, Hugo," she said after a perceptible hesitation. Mr. Greenfield's eyes were on his glass, but Hugo was sure that he was missing none of the nuances of the conversation. Damn the man! He would wait till they got rid of their visitor before he made any further attempt to find out what Julia had been up to. Conversation languished after a while. Hugo contributed little, and apart from the most trivial of generalities every other topic was hedged about with difficulties. John and Thérèse Devenish were in all their minds, and mentioned by none of them.

When Mr. Greenfield finally got up to go, Hugo made no effort to detain him, and the three of them made their way to the front doors. Julia thanked their visitor charmingly, and looked at Hugo in a slightly puzzled manner. "Yes, yes!" said Hugo heartily. "We're most grateful, Greenfield, most grateful. Let me see you to your carriage. No need for you to come, Julia." He went down the steps and said, as his unwelcome visitor left, "By the way, I'll send a groom over for Lady Rostherne's horse. No, I insist. We mustn't put you to any more trouble. Goodnight!"

As Hugo strode back to the house a small voice inside him told him that he was behaving like a fool, but he ignored it. How dared Julia go off into the blue like that, without even her groom to protect her? How dared she return in such a carefree manner when he had been more than a little worried about her? How dared she return in the company of such a man, even insisting on inviting him in! Well, that was one matter which was easily remedied—he would put an end to any idea she might have of making a friend of Greenfield!

He found Julia in the little parlour, sitting at the window. Her whole posture was so expressive of weary unhappiness that he paused for a moment, overwhelmed by a desire to comfort her, to hold her close and beg her to tell him what was wrong.

"Julia..." he began.

But when she heard his voice she stiffened and faced him in an attitude of unfriendly defiance. His heart hardened and he continued coldly, "I wish to hear an explanation of your conduct today."

"Really?" she drawled. "But perhaps I do not wish to give you one, Hugo. Indeed, I doubt there is much to explain. I went for a ride and got lost. That is all. And I am now going to my room." She rose and made for the door.

"Before you go, however, I must warn you that your friendship with Greenfield will not do. I do not wish you to see him again."

"Wish! You are full of 'wishes' today, Hugo! And what if I 'wish' to continue an acquaintance which I have found to be a welcome relief from the strains of my life here? I will see Mr. Greenfield when and how often I choose!"

Hugo grew pale. "Just what is this man to you, Julia?" he asked softly. "Is it possible that today was not the first occasion on which you 'lost your way'?"

"Hugo! How dare you?"

"You may 'Hugo!' me as much as you wish, ma'am. Greenfield is no friend of mine, nor was he made welcome here when my father was alive. I may not have known his name, but Thérèse's visits to Arbury Manor were a constant source of dissension and gossip. Be assured I will not permit history to repeat itself."

Julia's smile was as sweet as it was false. "I think you may have confidence in my discretion, Hugo. At the moment I hardly know the gentleman in question, but if I do choose to... develop my acquaintance with him, there will be no gossip. Not about me, at least."

"You will neither visit nor receive Greenfield, even if I have to watch you every minute of the day, my dear!"

"I am not—and never was—your dear, Hugo. Let us not forget that. Nor have I forgotten, any more than you have, that our 'bargain' made no mention of faithfulness. We are both of us free to have as many lovers as we wish."

Hugo looked stunned. "I didn't realise..." he began. "Is that how you view our marriage, Julia?"

She evaded a direct answer and got up to go. "Hugo, I'm very tired. This inquisition is really very silly. Can't we postpone it?"

He was slumped in a chair and did not reply as she bade him goodnight and left the room.

HOWEVER, THE DAY was not quite finished. After Ruth had come, tended her mistress, and gone away again, Julia found that, in spite of the exhausting events of the past days, she was not yet ready for sleep. It was almost dark and very warm—even sultry. She had discarded her Chinese silk wrapper in favour of a thin lawn shift and was standing by the window, grateful for the cooler air. She could see occasional flashes of lightning and hear the distant rumble of thunder. Perhaps it would rain before morning. She hoped so—Donyatt needed it. Such concern for Donyatt, she thought with a bitter little smile. It seemed at once an age, and no time at all, since she had sat on the hill with Hugo and had felt so close to him, had imagined a life of happiness together here at Donyatt. She had been deceiving herself, of course. But what was she to do now? The thought of remaining to share Hugo's life with another woman was unbearable. She would rather return to her spinster state.

There was a knock on her door, and without waiting for a reply Hugo came in. The light was so dim that she could not see his face, but his voice came out of the darkness. "I have to talk to you, Julia."

The room was lit by a brilliant flash of lightning. "I will talk to you in the morning, Hugo." Julia forced herself to walk calmly to her bed and put on her wrapper. "Not tonight."

A faint thread of amusement and something more disturbing could be heard in Hugo's voice as he said, "Too late!"

"I beg your pardon?"

Again, although Hugo's voice was mocking, it had the same disturbing undercurrent as he replied, "Short though that flash of lightning was, it revealed every line of your delectable body. The wrapper cannot deprive me of memory."

Julia felt a surge of anger, and her precarious self-control almost slipped. How dared he? How dared he force his way in here and say such things? He could keep his compliments for his mistress—she might appreciate them! She took hold of herself and said scornfully, "Is that what you came to tell me, Hugo?"

"No, but for a moment it removed any other thought from my mind." His voice changed and acquired an unusual note of uncertainty. "I came to say that I behaved like an autocratic fool, Julia. To explain." As he spoke he came

slowly forward, a dark shape in her dark room. Julia's
nerves were stretched to their limit. Only her pride kept her
from screaming at him to keep away from her. There was
another brilliant flash of lightning, followed immediately by
a deafening clap of thunder. She gave a frightened cry and
turned to face the window. Hugo's arms were around her;
he was turning her back to hold her face against him.

"It's all right, Julia—"

"It's not 'all right, Julia'!" she cried, and struggled to set
herself free. A demon seemed to have taken possession of
him, for the more she struggled the more firmly he held her.
"Let me go!" she shouted.

"Hush, Julia! I mean you no harm. Just be quiet, my
love— "

One of her arms was free. She swung it with all her might
and there was a loud crack as her hand met its target.

Hugo was almost startled into letting her go, but then as
the pain hit him he gave a furious roar and caught her cruelly to him, holding her arms behind her back. In another
flash of lightning Julia could see his eyes burning with anger. She was sobbing with rage herself as she twisted and
turned in a vain attempt to release herself. Finally she threw
her head back and faced him defiantly. They stared at each
other while the lightning flickered in the distance. Though
he still held her, his fury slowly died.

"Oh, God, Julia!" he groaned. "I want you! How I want
you!" He bent his head and she braced herself to repel his
kiss. When it came it was not the savage onslaught she had
feared, but a slow, endlessly seductive caress. Only the
thought of his mistress in London kept her from responding mindlessly. She stood stiffly within the circle of his arms,
and when he eventually released her she wrenched herself
away and escaped to the other side of the bed.

"No, Hugo!" There was a silence, then out of the darkness came an infinitely weary voice,

"You're right. It is not the moment. Though I could wish
you had not reminded me. We'll talk."

"To what purpose?" Then before he could ask her what
she meant she said, "Please leave my room now. If you wish

to talk, we'll talk tomorrow. Now go!'' Julia's voice was
unsteady and held a pleading note.

"Very well. But I have already waited too long to tell you
of my visit to London. It will not be put off any more. I'll
see you tomorrow morning. Goodnight, Julia.'' He went,
leaving Julia to her own miserable thoughts. Eventually she
decided that Hugo was right—the situation between them
clearly could not continue as it was. She had put off her talk
with him as long as she could. Now it looked as if the next
day would decide her fate, and whatever the outcome she
must be glad to have it settled.

IMMEDIATELY AFTER breakfast the next morning Hugo took
Julia's arm and said firmly, "A short turn in the park, don't
you think?'' He ushered her out through the window, down
the steps at the end of the terrace, and on to the lawns. Here
he stopped and said abruptly, "Things reached a crisis point
last night. I'm sorry if I upset or frightened you. It was
never my intention.'' He gave a short laugh. "Another
apology! I think you have had more from me than all the
rest of my acquaintance put together! It's this ridiculous
bargain of ours. I should never have agreed to it. But in the
circumstances perhaps it's as well. Will you forgive me—
again?''

Julia nodded. "We seem to have a strange effect on each
other, Hugo. I have never before so far forgotten myself as
to hit anyone.''

"So you're suffering under the bargain, too?''

"I . . . I am ashamed of my behaviour last night.''

He grinned and fingered his jaw. "Er—some time you
must tell me where you picked up your boxing skills. They
are considerable.'' He became serious again. "But that's not
what I really have to say to you now. I wish to tell you about
London.'' He paused and they walked towards the lake in
silence. Julia glanced up at Hugo—he seemed to be finding
difficulty in beginning. Finally he said, "I met Thérèse
there.''

This was worse than Julia had feared. "Thérèse? It was
Thérèse?''

Hugo stopped again. "You knew about it?''

"Sophie told me she had seen you with someone in London. She didn't know who it was." She added desperately, "You have no need to tell me any more, Hugo."

He looked at her averted face and said, "On the contrary, if Sophie has been talking to you, there is every need! I have no doubt that she made the most of it!" Julia's silence was confirmation enough. "Did you believe what she undoubtedly implied?"

Julia nodded and then added almost involuntarily, "I was very angry."

"Was that why you went tearing off yesterday to visit Greenfield? To punish me?"

No! She wanted to say. No, I spent the day trying to reconcile myself to the fact that you loved someone else. And I failed! But instead, she resumed their walk, finally replying, "I went out because I wanted time to reflect, to come to terms with the new situation—new to me, at least. And I foolishly failed to take note of where I was going. I simply lost my way, and came to Arbury Manor by chance."

"I see." He glanced down at her. "And what conclusion did you come to during the ride?"

Julia turned her head away and said in a stifled voice, "That whatever I felt . . . that I was wrong to be angry. Our bargain gave me no claim on your fidelity. Especially as I had demanded that you should wait, perhaps as long as a year."

"I see... So you thought I had been unfaithful—and your comment last night didn't refer to your own conduct, but to mine!"

By this time they had reached the edge of the lake. Hugo regarded the water-fowl quarrelling and splashing in the reeds as he added apparently indifferently, "Do you feel free to take a lover, Julia?"

Julia felt a sudden impatience with his questions. "What does it matter what I feel, Hugo?" she asked bitterly. "Surely what you feel for your brother's widow is more important?"

Hugo put his hands on her shoulders and spun her round to face him. His air of indifference was belied as he said fiercely, "Whatever anyone may have said, and in spite of all Greenfield's insinuations, I have never had an affair with Thérèse! If it is of any interest to you, Julia, you are the first person to whom I have ever bothered to deny it—apart from my brother, on whom the effort was wasted. But it is none the less a fact. Thérèse is not, and never was, my mistress."

"Not even now that your brother is dead?"

"Not even now."

"Then why was she staying in Dover Street?"

"She intends to be in London for a while and has taken the rest of the lease over from me. Julia, I do not intend to defend myself further. Either you believe me or you do not." His words were arrogant, but his eyes and his grip on her shoulders betrayed anxiety. Julia studied his face for a moment and then gravely nodded. The feeling of a great weight behind lifted from her heart was almost physical.

"Why does she wish to live in London, Hugo?"

"Thérèse's fortunes in Paris have declined since the restoration of the French crown. The returning Royalists treat her as an outcast, and she now thinks she will do better in England."

Something in Hugo's voice roused Julia's curiosity. "What does she want of you? And why were you so disturbed when you returned from London?"

"It's a long story. But the end of it is that she is attempting to blackmail me. She threatens to tell the world of John's treachery!"

CHAPTER FOURTEEN

"THAT'S WHAT I'VE BEEN trying to tell you for so long, Julia—and why I said in my clumsy fashion that I regretted marrying you. I had to discuss Thérèse's threat with you, had to give you the freedom to disassociate yourself from the Devenishes. If Thérèse carries out her threat, then we're in for another time of social ostracism. I couldn't inflict that on you without giving you the choice."

Hugo spoke seriously, but Julia could have laughed with joy. Hugo did not have a mistress, and his reservations about their marriage arose out of concern for her! She smiled brilliantly at him. "But there isn't a choice, Hugo! I am married to you, whatever happens. And it would be a poor sort of wife who would run away when life became difficult. That's just the time when you need me!"

Hugo regarded her in silence. It was impossible for Julia to guess what he was thinking, for his face was a mask. He said in neutral tones, "I don't think you understand what it means, Julia. How could you? You have not experienced it as I have. It will be bad. The tale will lose nothing in Thérèse's telling of it, for she has a love of the dramatic and few scruples. It will be bad."

"Hugo, I for one am very happy here at Donyatt. If Thérèse is so unscrupulous as to expose her dead husband to the censure of society, and society so unjust as to punish you for it, then I can very well do without both!"

He looked as if he was having difficulty in believing what she said. Then he gave a crack of laughter, caught her in his arms, and swung her round. "Spoken like a true Amazon! You never cease to surprise me, Julia—but I should have known, I should have known! Thank you, my love!"

"Hugo! Put me down!" Julia frowned as she spoke, but her glowing cheeks and sparkling eyes betrayed her. Hugo set her on her feet again, but kept his hands at her waist.

"Have you any idea what a rare delight you are, Julia? Not one woman of my acquaintance—and not many men, either—would have spoken as you just have. I begin to believe the Devenish luck is turning at last." He bent to kiss her, but she evaded him. She was still vulnerable after the emotions of the night before and wanted no repetition of them for the moment. She started walking back to the house, but when Hugo caught up with her and took hold of her hand she could not help smiling at him. To the annoyance of the woman observing them from the terrace, they gave every appearance of being a devoted couple.

THEY WERE MET at the edge of the lawn by a flustered Lydiate.

"My lord, I am afraid there is a visitor in the drawing-room. When I could not find your lordship, I thought that the place to ask her to wait—"

"Who is it, Lydiate?" asked Hugo.

"Lady John, my lord. Er...Madame Benz... Your lordship's sister-in-law." Lydiate was floundering in his attempts to make the identity of the visitor clear. To Julia it was obvious. Their unwelcome visitor was Thérèse.

"Hugo!" she said urgently. Hugo dismissed Lydiate with a nod.

"What is it?"

"What does Thérèse want in return for silence? Money?" Hugo shook his head. "What, then? I must know!"

Hugo hesitated, then said, "To stay at Donyatt. To live with us here." Then he started walking towards the steps of the terrace. Julia ran after him and caught his sleeve.

"Is that all? You cannot be serious, Hugo! You're prepared to risk such a terrible scandal just for this?"

"Yes, Julia." He started off again.

"But you mustn't! You can't!"

Hugo stopped and looked down at her, a cynical twist to his mouth. "Changing your mind, Julia?"

"No, of course not! But why? It's such a small favour to grant her—and she is a Devenish, after all—"

"You are wrong. It's a very big favour—too big. Don't meddle."

"But Hugo..." It was too late. Hugo was halfway up the steps to the terrace where Thérèse was waiting.

Julia's first reaction when she saw Thérèse Devenish was one of surprise. Whatever she had imagined, it was not this. Mr. Greenfield's description fitted her perfectly—"a little dab of a thing, well into her thirties." It was hard to believe that this tired, sallow-skinned woman was the siren who had brought ruin to the Devenish family, and now threatened more. By the time Julia reached the top of the steps Hugo was already speaking.

"I told you not to come here, Thérèse. You have had my answer to your...suggestion."

"But you were always so impetuous, Hugo," the lady said in a attractively accented voice. "I could not believe you really meant what you said, *chéri*. Come, do not quarrel with me, I couldn't bear it, *je t'assure*. Tell me instead who this charming lady is, hmm?"

"As you very well know, this is my wife. Julia, may I present my brother's widow, Thérèse, to you?"

Dark eyes met Julia's, the huge shadows under them inviting her sympathy. "He can hardly bear it, Julia, that we should meet. You hear how he speaks of me? As if he wished I, too, were dead?"

"I am sure Hugo cannot wish anything so dramatic. You must forgive us if we find it difficult to welcome you here, Madame Benezat," Julia said in a cool voice. "You cannot fail to understand why. Shall we go inside?" She led the way into the drawing-room. But before Thérèse would agree to sit down she clasped her hands together and said with a slight break in her voice,

"You misjudge me, both of you. I beg you to forget the things I said, Hugo." When Hugo continued to regard her unresponsively she turned to Julia. "Always, Hugo and I, we quarrel, and I get confused and angry. Of course I do not wish to bring shame and scandal to the Devenish name— after all, it was once mine also! But I felt so alone in Lon-

don, and...and I had been ill, and Hugo was so...so cold
and unfeeling. I wanted to frighten him, *c'est tout*! Please
say you forgive me, Julie!''

Julia looked doubtfully at Hugo, who was standing at the
window with his back to the room. She invited Thérèse to sit
down. ''I cannot answer for Hugo, Thérèse, but you succeeded in frightening me. Why is it so important to you to
stay here?''

''Is that what he said?'' Thérèse exclaimed sharply.
''Simply that I wanted to stay here?'' Hugo swung round
and there was a curious pause. Then Thérèse said plaintively, passing her hand across her forehead, ''But where else
could I stay when I am in England? I am, after all, a member of the family.''

Since this echoed her own sentiment, Julia found it difficult to reply. A voice came from the window,

''A former member, Thérèse. You gave up the privilege
of belonging when you deserted John. And you surely cannot have forgotten that you have since married Armand
Benezat?''

Thérèse gave a melancholy smile. ''*Hélas*, Armand is
dead! He never returned from Russia—like so many others. It is cruel to taunt me with this, Hugo—you have grown
very hard, I think. As for John—it was so many years ago!
And you know why I had to leave him.''

''I am aware of the reason you gave John. But it was not
altogether the truth, was it?''

''No. But the wish was there, Hugo. You cannot deny
that!''

''For a short while. It was soon over, Thérèse.''

Julia felt like a spectator at some fencing match, possessing a little knowledge of the game, but not nearly enough.
She intervened firmly, ''And now we have to consider the
present. Hugo, if you agree, I will have a room prepared for
Thérèse—at least for tonight.''

Hugo made a gesture of protest, but before he could say
anything Thérèse thanked Julia, adding with a glance in his
direction, ''I am very naughty, I know, to arrive without any
warning. But even you must agree, Hugo, that it is impossible that I should start back to London today. And *à vrai*

dire, I cannot think you would wish your friends to hear that I was forced to lodge in the village!''

"This passion for respectability sits ill on one who once scandalised the whole neighbourhood without a second thought," said Hugo grimly.

But Julia had had enough. "Of course you may stay, Thérèse. Pray wait here and I will see Mrs. Staple. Excuse me." Julia left the room, trying not to make it obvious how glad she was to escape. She was puzzled by Hugo's behaviour. Why was it so important to him that Thérèse should not stay at Donyatt—apparently not even for a night? What was he afraid of? But she had found no answers by the time she returned to the drawing-room. Ignoring the charged atmosphere, she suggested that Thérèse might like to see her room, and gave her into Mrs. Staple's charge. As soon as they were alone Hugo said, "I hope you will not regret this, Julia. Thérèse intends to stay for as long as she needs—or can."

"I don't understand why you are so set against it. What can she do to us here? I must confess I find your animosity towards her excessive, Hugo. Thérèse seems to me to be a tired, sick woman—she even seems to have changed her mind about her threats. Perhaps she is genuinely sorry for what she has done and is anxious to make amends? If that is the case, you were not very kind to her just now. I think we ought to give her a chance."

In the end Hugo said irritably, "Very well, very well. She may stay for a short while—a very short while—until her health has improved. But that is all! And you would do well not to trust Thérèse de Lachasse, Julia, in spite of her penitent air."

HUGO WAS RIGHT in one thing. Thérèse gave every indication of remaining at Donyatt as long as she could. For the first few days she spent a good deal of her time in her room, and when she was downstairs she presented a picture of a frail, saddened woman. Hugo's attitude to her remained guarded and cold, and Julia often found herself sympathising with her guest and in private taking Hugo to task for

his manner. But then a different Thérèse began to emerge—
so gradually to begin with that Julia hardly noticed.

This Thérèse had more colour in her cheeks, her hair was
arranged in saucily flattering curls, and her drab style of
dress had been replaced with elegant silks and modish bonnets. At first Julia welcomed these signs of Thérèse's improved health and spirits—they led her to believe that she
and Hugo might soon be rid of their guest. But she discovered that the change in Thérèse's appearance was accompanied by increased confidence—more than that, arrogance—in her manner. She behaved almost like the mistress of the house, and never for one moment showed any
sign of wishing to depart. Julia eventually came to the conclusion that her original assessment of Thérèse had been
completely false. She had been deceived by a sort of extra
skin, adopted as a disguise, and now that it had served its
purpose it was being sloughed, thus revealing the true nature of Thérèse de Lachasse. She admitted her mistake to
Hugo, but then added, "I still think it is a lesser evil than
having the Devenish name dragged through the mud once
again."

They were walking in the park, something they had taken
to doing in order to escape from their guest's all-pervasive
presence, and had almost reached the summer-house on the
hill. Hugo did not immediately reply, then he said, "I blame
myself. I know Thérèse and should not have allowed her to
outmanoeuvre me."

Julia sat down and drew a deep breath. She had to get
Hugo to confide further in her. Her instinct told her that this
might be the last, and most painful secret. She said, "Hugo,
I think it is time you told me more."

"Of what?" he said, his manner guarded.

"Of everything! I am tired of hints and insinuations! You
have said that Thérèse was never your mistress, and I believe you. But why was John so difficult to convince? There
must have been something."

"I . . . can't tell you, Julia."

"I thought you were beginning to trust me."

"Not with this. I . . . I am ashamed."

"Tell me all the same, Hugo," said Julia softly, drawing him down beside her. He hesitated, looked away down into the valley, then back at Julia, as if he couldn't decide how to begin. Finally he said, "Yes, there was indeed 'something.' For a while I persuaded myself I was quite desperately in love with her. Your kind of love, Julia—the all-consuming passion. If I hadn't gone to Greece when I did I might well have betrayed my family as badly as John did later. I loved her almost to distraction," he said. Julia was not deceived by his indifferent tone. With the heightened awareness that her own love for him gave her she could feel the pain behind his words. So now she knew. Rumour had always maintained that Hugo had been attracted to his sister-in-law, but this was evidence of a Hugo she had never known—neither the light-hearted, cynical rogue of Lady Godfrey's ball, nor yet the sceptical, touchy master of Donyatt, but a vulnerable human being at the mercy of an emotion almost too strong for him to bear. What a fool she had been to hope that she could ever arouse this man's devotion, persuade him that "love" existed! The love, the devotion, the commitment she had hoped for had been commandeered long, long before she had ever met him.

Hugo seemed to read her silence as disapproval. He took his hand away. "Yes, it was contemptible, wasn't it? I didn't realise, you see, I didn't realise I was falling in love until it was too late, and then however much I despised myself for it I couldn't stop. Thérèse was like a...an addiction, like an infection in the blood." He turned to Julia. "You don't know her, Julia. I think in past times she would have been burned as a witch."

"'The woman tempted me'—is that what you're saying, Hugo?" Julia's voice must have revealed some of her bitterness, for Hugo's cheeks flushed a dark red.

"I'm not trying to defend myself. At nineteen I knew the difference between right and wrong. At first I hardly noticed her. She was a few years older than me, and my brother's wife. But then she seemed to become so unhappy...she was so helpless, so lonely in England... She said she enjoyed my company." He gave a short laugh. "You've seen how tiny she is—she arouses a man's protective instinct without even trying!" Julia winced, but Hugo didn't notice, absorbed as he was in his story.

"Everything went well and, I assure you, I felt a very great fellow. But then things began to change. I didn't know what was happening to me." He smiled wryly. "You probably find that hard to believe. I would myself now. But in fact I had led a very uncomplicated life, Julia, divided between studies at Oxford and my life at Donyatt. I'd had affairs, of course, but I was totally unprepared for the sort of attraction I started to feel for Thérèse. She could look at a man with those huge dark eyes and he was lost...damned... I left London in an attempt to escape, but she and John came down to Donyatt when I was there. One day he took her to task about her visits to Arbury, and when I intervened he turned on me... John and I were never reconciled from that day on. Then there was a scene in London... In the end I went to Greece in order to escape before the family was destroyed. I didn't know Thérèse would leave John more or less at the same time, nor that John would believe that we had gone away together. But then I didn't know she had told him that we were in fact lovers—not until much later, and by that time it was already too late. You know the rest."

"What about now?" When Hugo looked at her, his attitude guarded again, Julia said impatiently, "It's now obvious to me that Thérèse is the last woman to play the part of a poor relation, living here quietly with us. I'm not a fool, Hugo. I want to know what she really wants!"

Hugo shrugged his shoulders and said reluctantly, "It was a shock to her to find that I was married. She refuses to accept that it is impossible for us to be divorced. She wishes to replace you as my wife."

"Why didn't you tell me this before?" Julia cried.

"Because it will not happen. You are my wife, Julia, and I have a duty and an obligation to you. Even if it were possible, I should not wish for a divorce. So it really wasn't necessary for you to know anything about it, and if you are now distressed it is your own fault. I warned you not to meddle." Hugo's voice was so totally devoid of warmth that

Julia felt as if a great chasm had opened up at her feet. In spite of her fear she took a step towards it.

"And...and what are your feelings toward Thérèse now?" she asked, bracing herself.

With a sudden movement Hugo got up and faced her, his face a mask. "You've had enough self-confession from me, Julia! I've told you what I want—a peaceful, prosperous life with you at Donyatt! I want no more of...of passion and torment. Now let it rest—for your own sake as well as mine!"

Without waiting for her, he strode off down the hill, presumably to the stables, for the next time Julia saw him he was galloping up the valley as if chased by all the fiends of Hell. With a heavy heart she walked down to the house.

THÉRÈSE WAS SITTING in the Chinese drawing-room. After the revelations on the hill Julia saw her with new eyes. Yes, Thérèse was transformed. Now she looked small— "tiny" had been Hugo's word, she remembered, wincing again—slender and elegant. Her striped silk dress was elaborately frilled and tucked, and artfully placed curls framed a heart-shaped face, dominated by her eyes... When Julia met the lambent gaze of those dark eyes she suddenly felt taller and clumsier than ever before. She almost stumbled, such was their power. Thérèse gave a little satisfied smile, and then looked around her with disapproval. "Why have you changed everything, Julie? This was the library. Why is it now a drawing-room?" She rolled the "r" with impressive scorn. "It cannot be a question of—how do you put it?—a new brush sweeping clean. Most of this—" she gestured contemptuously at the furniture "—was in the house before I threw it out. Where did you find these antiquated relics?"

"In the attic. I believe Hugo's father ordered the servants to put them up there. He didn't want to lose them altogether." Julia glanced at the exquisite little writing-table which had belonged to Hugo's grandmother. How pleased Hugo had been to see it again! He had kissed her...oh, Hugo! She pulled herself together, for Thérèse was looking at her again and this was no time to weaken.

"You are unhappy, Julie?"

"Yes, I am. I'm afraid I shall have to ask you to leave Donyatt, Thérèse. I think you are now recovered from your illness—indeed, you are quite your old self again. No doubt you have other friends you would wish to visit."

"I see that Hugo has told you what I really want!" said Thérèse. "And you wish to be rid of me. That is natural."

"It is also Hugo's wish."

"*Zut*! He is obstinate, that one!" After the exclamation the dark eyes were almost opaque, as if Thérèse wished to hide what she was thinking. Then she said slowly, "There must be more to you than I thought. You know that I promised Hugo I would tell London of John's...misdeeds?"

"Yes," said Julia with resolute calm. "I cannot say I admire your methods, Thérèse. They are hardly even sensible, for you surely could not have expected Hugo to give in to coercion? But then, when one is desperate one is seldom wise. Amuse London society, if you wish, with tales of your dead husband. I will stand by mine."

For a moment Thérèse's exquisitely made-up face grew old and ugly as anger consumed her. Then just as suddenly she was smiling. "Such devotion!" she mocked. "One is surprised—" again the "r" rolled in contempt "—that the door between the bedchambers is kept permanently locked. Whose idea is that, I ask?" She got up, and Julia felt a shiver run up her spine as Thérèse gazed at her. But she, too, stood up, and returned the gaze steadily.

"How soon can you leave, Thérèse?"

"Since you are so unkind—and so foolish—as to refuse me the hospitality of Donyatt, I shall have to find somewhere else to stay. It will take me some time, perhaps a month or more. Then I shall go." Thérèse walked towards the door. "You have a little time for reflection, Julie. I should consider very carefully if I were you. Scandal is not the only disaster that can befall Hugo—not even the worst."

When Thérèse had left the room Julia sank back onto her chair. She was trembling. What had happened to her? It had taken all her will to oppose Thérèse in that last encounter, particularly when her sister-in-law had looked at her with

her black, witch's eyes. She could now more easily understand the young Hugo's infatuation with the woman. Well,
at least Thérèse would shortly leave them—Julia felt it could
not be too soon.

In fact, she saw little of their unwelcome guest in the en-
suing weeks. Thérèse joined them for meals, when she teased
Hugo about his sober face and talked of friends they had
known in London—even sometimes of John, for whom she
adopted a tolerant, slightly contemptuous tone. Aside from
that Thérèse avoided the rest of the house and seemed to
spend a great deal of time either walking in the park or req-
uisitioning one of the carriages for lengthy excursions. Julia began to wonder whether Thérèse was meeting someone,
for she often returned looking sleekly satisfied, like a well-
fed cat. In reply to a casual remark, she said that she had
been to Arbury Manor, adding with an injured air, "I have
to visit old friends in the short time I am here, Julie! You
cannot object to that, surely! You grudge me the coachman, perhaps?" She glanced shyly at Julia. "And then I
sometimes meet Hugo, and we talk of old times. Time
passes very quickly then. Oh, what a sour face, Julie! It an-
noys you that I meet him? I must confess it is not always
accidentally." Disgusted at these insinuations, Julia got up
and went towards the door, but Thérèse swiftly rose and intercepted her. "I thought this marriage of Hugo's was a
business arrangement?" she said, with wide-open eyes. "It
certainly doesn't look like one of the…heart? Those locked
bedroom doors…"

"I doubt very much that Hugo would discuss our marriage with you, Thérèse. Nor will I."

"But one must be reasonable about these things! Hugo is
a man of strong feelings, of passion—who would know that
better than I? How can a bargain like yours satisfy such a
one? But I think you would be very silly to become angry
about it, Julie!" She smiled sweetly. "I assure you, however much Hugo may feel for someone else, he will never
leave you—he feels he owes you too much! And, of course,
he would be sorry for you."

Julia's patience gave way. "Thérèse, I will listen to no
more of your mischief. Hugo will behave as he wishes, and

we both know that Donyatt is paramount with him. Now please forgive me, I have things to do elsewhere.''

Thérèse's voice floated after her. ''But have you asked yourself if Hugo is happy, Julie?''

IN SPITE OF JULIA'S determination to ignore Thérèse's mischief-making, it was difficult to keep her worries at bay. There had been a time when Hugo had loved, really loved Thérèse. Did one ever quite forget such feelings? She sincerely doubted that Hugo would arrange clandestine meetings with Thérèse, but was certain that Thérèse would have no scruples about waylaying him when he was out. And it was obvious that Hugo's mood recently had been sombre and difficult.

Julia was out on the terrace a few days later when her suspicions were aroused at the sight of Thérèse making purposefully for the summer-house. A surge of fury swept through her as she wondered if Thérèse had arranged to meet Hugo there. Without stopping to think, she followed at a discreet distance, taking the side path in order to gain shelter from the shrubs and trees on the way. But when she reached her goal the summer-house was empty. She listened for a moment and gradually became aware of Thérèse's voice coming from somewhere behind, speaking in rapid, angry French. Though Julia could barely make out what she was saying, she got the impression that Thérèse wanted her listener to do something, and was being refused. The man's voice was much less clear. Perhaps he had his back to the summer-house? Then Thérèse said, so slowly and distinctly that Julia understood every word, ''You will help me in this, Prevert, for, if you do not, I shall tell the world what really happened here when John and the old man died!'' Julia could hardly breathe. What was Thérèse saying? Who was this man? She pulled herself back into a dark recess as Thérèse passed swiftly by the summer-house and made for the house. There was a rustling sound as the man made his way through the trees behind, but Julia dared not peer out. By the time she emerged, all was quiet.

CHAPTER FIFTEEN

JULIA SAT in the summer-house for a while, not only to wait until Thérèse was away but also to ponder on what she had heard. It was obvious that her sister-in-law knew more about John's death than she ought, considering she had gone to France four years before it had taken place and had only recently returned. And who was Prevert? Prevert...Prevert... The name had an elusive familiarity. Where had she heard it before? Still deep in thought, she walked slowly down the side path to the house. Thérèse was nowhere to be seen, but Hugo was in the library. She stood at the door, looking at his dark head bent over his papers. A wave of love swept her. Why was life so complicated? Hugo had had enough of storms and tribulations. He deserved peace; peace to pursue his interests and enjoy life at Donyatt. But she was forgetting—was that what he really wanted, deep in his heart? Or was he still in love with Thérèse even after all these years? Julia knew all too well how an almost forgotten love could flare up again. What would she do if the same had happened to Hugo? Her involuntary movement of pain at the thought caught Hugo's attention. He looked up and smiled at her with such warmth and tenderness that her heart missed a beat.

"Julia! Don't stand there, come in!" He got up and came over to her to lead her to the huge desk in the middle of the room. On it lay the notes, drawings and sketches he had made in Greece.

"Look! Do you think these are good enough to publish?" His arm was round her shoulders, in a gesture of unconscious affection. Tears came to her eyes, blurring the pages in front of her, and she turned and buried her face against him. His arm went round her and he drew her close.

"What is it, Julia? What's wrong? Come, this is no behaviour for my Amazon! Spitting defiance is more her style." Though she despised herself for it, Julia could not reply, for the tears were now rolling down her cheeks. "The drawings are surely not so bad, are they?" he said with mock anxiety. She shook her head. "Well, then, look at me and tell me what this is about." He put a gentle finger under her chin and forced her to look up. "Oh, God, Julia," he said in a gruff voice, kissing her wet cheeks. "Don't cry any more. You cannot imagine what it does to me! Tell me what is wrong, please!" He took her over to the sofa, took out his handkerchief, and wiped her face with it. "Now? Is it . . . is it that you're not happy at Donyatt?"

"No! I mean, yes, of course I am. I . . . I'm a little tired. My nerves are a little strained, that's all. Goodness, I sound like Sophie! Please forgive me for making such an exhibition of myself, Hugo. I'm quite recovered now."

"It's Thérèse, isn't it? She's the unsettling influence," said Hugo, his voice sombre.

Julia shied away from asking him in what way. She said abruptly, "Hugo, I was up in the summer-house just now. Thérèse is meeting someone in secret up there."

"For God's sake, can't we forget about Thérèse just for a short while?" he burst out. "She's a troublemaker, Julia. She always has been!"

"Yes, but she was talking about your father's death—to someone who clearly knew something about it."

"Tell me what she said."

Julia repeated as much as she could remember of the conversation up by the summer-house. Hugo listened carefully, but his expression was unencouraging. He said finally, "I agree it's odd but there's not much substance to it. I suppose we now know who told Thérèse about John's activities, but the fact that a French accomplice witnessed what happened on the night my father died, and then escaped, doesn't change anything. No, Julia, the events of that night are best forgotten now."

"But Hugo—"

"Please, Julia!"

It was clear that Hugo was determined not to discuss the matter any further. Julia sighed and gave in. "Let me see your work, Hugo."

They spent a pleasant half-hour looking through Hugo's folios. The drawings were exquisitely done, with a great deal of detail, and a sheet of notes in his neat, firm handwriting was attached to each. Julia remembered how impressed her father had been with them, though she herself had almost preferred the little sketches of life in modern Greece decorating the notes—a goatherd sitting with his flock on Mount Ida, a woman in Turkish dress posed by a village fountain, wild flowers on Aegina . . . Aegina! She put out her hand to stop Hugo from closing the folio. "Wait! Let me look at that!" She turned the papers over carefully. Yes! There it was! A torn, stained scrap of paper, covered in writing that was wavering and faint. "Prevert...ru...de squat...eons." The rest was impossible to read. "What is this, Hugo?"

He took it, frowned at it and said finally, "Rubbish. I don't know." He made as if to throw it away, but Julia stopped him.

"It's intriguing. I'll keep it, if I may." She tried to sound casual as she asked, "Hugo, did your father ever look at this work?"

Hugo's tone was affectionate as he smiled and said, "Not often. His interests were all outdoor ones. He seldom expressed an interest in any other pursuits. He looked at these drawings just to please me, I think. In fact..." He sighed. "In fact it was almost the last thing he did. He had been looking at them just before John arrived that last day."

Julia felt a sudden surge of excitement as another little piece of the puzzle fell into place, but kept it to herself. Hugo had made his position clear and, anyway, her suspicions were so fantastic that she was reluctant to voice them. As they left the library Hugo looked down at her.

"It won't be long, Julia. Thérèse will be gone shortly, and then we shall start to build a peaceful new life here. Be patient." He went away to an appointment with one of the tenants, and Julia went to the privacy of her room.

Here she examined the scrap of paper once again. "Prevert . . . ru . . . de squat . . . eons"—the rest was stained.

She shivered. Had Hugo's father written this in his dying moments? If her suspicions were correct then this bit of paper had lain on the desk on the fatal night, and the stains on it were bloodstains. In the confusion and haste after the discovery of the bodies, the small scrap of paper had been caught up in the notes and drawings scattered on the desk. But what had the late Marquess been trying to convey?

Julia's first impulse was to consult Hugo, but then she paused. Hugo had been very reluctant to take the question of Prevert seriously. Her theory was, to say the least, somewhat wild. The connections—the paper to Hugo's father, John to Prevert, Prevert to Thérèse—were all so tenuous. She had no real proof. Hugo might well refuse to discuss his father's death once again. Or, worse still, he might ask Thérèse about Prevert, perhaps during one of those "long conversations" that Thérèse had mentioned, and she would be sure to deny all knowledge of him. Yes, those conversations... With sadness Julia admitted that at the heart of her reluctance lay an uneasy feeling that Hugo's undoubted friendship, affection even, for his wife might be severely strained by a confrontation with Thérèse. She did not wish to put them to the test.

Her doubts were reinforced by the sight of Hugo and Thérèse driving up to the house, talking animatedly. Hugo looked serious, but the sound of Thérèse's laughter floated in through the window, and Julia clapped her hands to her ears and turned away. Was this the "tenant" Hugo had been to see? She instantly rejected the thought as unworthy, but its poison spread in her mind all the same.

At dinner that night Thérèse was in brilliant form. Her red silk dress was a perfect foil for her dramatic colouring, and the diamonds in her ears sparkled no more brightly than her eyes. If the ensemble was a trifle overdone for a simple evening in the country, Thérèse showed no sign of worrying over it. She proved to be wickedly witty, setting herself out to entertain and charm her dinner companions. With Hugo she failed for, apart from normal courtesies, he was silent. Julia in her half-mourning dress of grey muslin and feeling like a rather large sparrow in the presence of a hum-

ming-bird, was still enticed into occasional laughter, in spite
of what she knew of her guest. Eventually Thérèse said,

"*Oh, mon Dieu*! Hugo! You are impossible! I thought
you would be happy that I am departing the day after tomorrow, and instead you are so gloomy!" With a sly look
at Julia she said, "Look at him, Julie! Perhaps in spite of
what he says he does not really wish to see me go, *hein*?"
Then she added with a trill of laughter, "But you do, Julie!
Oh, you do! I am a nuisance, am I not? Always in the way?
Always visiting your friend Greenfield! No, do not answer!
I am very naughty to tease you."

"You say you're leaving, Thérèse? On Wednesday?"
asked Julia in astonishment.

"Yes, *hélas*! I must be in London by the beginning of next
week."

Hugo broke his silence. "There is one matter which still
puzzles me, Thérèse. Before you leave I should like you to
tell me how you knew of John's misdemeanours?" Julia
looked sharply at her husband. Was he testing Thérèse?

"Why should I not? He was my husband."

"But from what he said, John did not actually begin
selling information until long after you had left him and
were back in France. How did you learn of it?"

There was an appreciable pause. Then Thérèse said gaily,
"I cannot really remember when or how I learned of it,
Hugo. I am not as exact as you! It may have been when
John came to visit me in France."

"That must have been difficult," said Hugo in tones of
extreme scepticism. "Until recently our two countries were
at war for nearly twenty years."

"Must I give you a lesson in history, *mon vieux*? There
was a short peace, and that is when John came," Thérèse
said with exaggerated patience. "Look, I returned to France
early in 1802, as soon as the peace of Amiens made it safe
to do so. The war did not recommence until the middle of
the next year. John came looking for me just before
that...in April, I think." Again a note of contempt coloured Thérèse's voice when she spoke of John. Julia felt a
pang of pity for the poor wretch—Thérèse must have been
merciless with him. "He was seeking a reconciliation. You

are surely not about to dispute it, are you, Hugo? You, if you remember, were in Greece—and in any case, John was very discreet about it.''

"Then I cannot dispute it, can I?"

"But you need not fear that anyone else knows of it," said Thérèse reassuringly. Before she could stop herself Julia said,

"Except Prevert."

"Prevert!" Thérèse exclaimed. Her eyes glittered into Julia's, then they grew opaque, and she said, as Julia had known she would, "Who is this Prevert?"

Before Julia could reply, Hugo answered for her. "It was a name Julia heard. What made you think of that, Julia?"

"I just wondered if Thérèse was familiar with the name, that's all."

Thérèse made some pretence of thinking, then shrugged her shoulders with a masterly show of indifference. "I do not know this name. But I have something more important to tell you. I think I will not, for the moment anyway, make public John's perfidy." She waited for Julia's reaction. When there was none she asked, "Why do you remain silent? Are you not pleased, Julia?"

"It is more Hugo's affair than mine. It is for him to say."

"But Hugo knows already. I told him this afternoon."

"If he is happy then I am too." There was an undercurrent of malice in Thérèse's tone which made Julia unwilling to say more. Whatever had caused Thérèse to change her mind, it was not good will towards her; of that she was sure!

HAD JULIA HEARD the whole of Thérèse's last interview with Hugo before leaving, she would have seen how right she was not to trust Thérèse's motives.

"Hugo, I have come to bid you *au revoir*." The knowing look in Thérèse's eyes belied her pathetic demeanour as she faced Hugo in the library.

"Then I wish you a safe journey."

"You are so cold now, Hugo," mourned Thérèse. "You have been forced to hide your true feelings for so long that you have forgotten how to show them, I think. It was not always so."

"I hope I am wiser now than I was at nineteen, Thérèse. I certainly have more sense."

"Wisdom! Sense! What have they to do with love?"

"Nothing—which is why I have rejected it in their favour."

"Your wife would not be happy to hear you say so."

"Julia and I have a relationship which you could not possibly understand. No, I do not love her in your sense, but I have deep affection for her—"

"Affection! That's a lukewarm emotion to take to bed with you, Hugo! But then, you do not, do you?"

"What do you mean?"

"Merely that this great affection is apparently not enough to tempt her into sharing her bed with you! Or am I wrong? Perhaps she unlocks the door into her bedchamber each night, and locks it again in the morning?" Hugo's lips tightened at Thérèse's mockery, and he said curtly,

"I will not ask you where you acquired your information, Thérèse. I do not propose to discuss the matter with you at all. Are you now ready for your journey?"

"But, Hugo," protested Thérèse, opening her eyes wide, "I merely wished to make you aware of the danger of your situation. You may think you can make do with this dull—and celibate—'affection' you speak of, but are you so sure that Julia can? What if she is looking for a more exciting experience—or has indeed already found it? You were angry with me when I warned you of Lucian Greenfield's interest in her, but his conversation is tediously full of 'Julie,' *je t'assure*! Perhaps your wife's reluctance to open her bedroom door to you has a more sinister cause than you think?"

Hugo's face darkened. He strode over to Thérèse and grasped her arm. "You poisonous bitch! Leave now, do you hear?"

"Why don't you forget this stupid bargain with her, Hugo?" she murmured, swaying closer still. "She could never love you as I do. And remember how desperate we were all those years ago... Such a strong passion could not have disappeared entirely. You will never love this Julie while I remain in your heart. You have said as much. Love me again, Hugo, and be happy!''

Julia had come in search of Thérèse to tell her goodbye. She stopped short outside the library door as she heard Thérèse's words. There was a moment's silence, then Hugo's voice, deep, calm and determined said, "It is not in you to understand what I feel for Julia, Thérèse. No, I do not love her, but I have great affection and respect for her. And, since she is my wife, I also have a duty and obligation to be loyal to her. Now go."

"Very well. But I shall not give up, Hugo! I know that you will not be satisfied for long with 'affection.' You and I will meet again and then...ah, then...! But—I will give you time to think it over."

Julia walked swiftly away, and when Thérèse emerged from the library she was waiting in the hall in the shadow of the front doors. Thérèse looked angry. She stood where she was for a moment, putting on her gloves with great concentration. Then she nodded, as if she had come to a decision, and walked to the doors. Her eyes widened when she saw Julia. She looked speculatively at her and then said peremptorily, "I have something to say to you, Julie. Come with me to the carriage."

"I do not wish to hear anything you might say, Thérèse. I have heard enough," said Julia stiffly. "The horses have been standing some minutes—it is time you went."

Thérèse looked at the servants in the background. She drew close to Julia and said softly, "But if you will not listen to what I now tell you, then Hugo will lose Donyatt."

This was so far from what Julia had been expecting that she was startled into exclaiming, "What rubbish are you talking now, Thérèse? You have no power over Donyatt!"

"*Ma chère Julie,* I have a great deal of power. Come with me to the carriage and I will tell you why."

Julia walked reluctantly down the steps. What was the woman up to? Thérèse ordered the coachman to take the carriage to the gates at the bottom of the drive. "Lady Rostherne and I will walk—we still have things to say."

"Thérèse, if you have anything to say about Donyatt, you should say it to Hugo, not to me."

"Be silent and listen! You will soon learn why I am talking to you." Thérèse waited until the coach was on its way. Then she said, "You know, I suppose, that John was older than Hugo?"

Puzzled, Julia nodded.

"So you will agree that John's child would inherit Donyatt?"

"But he had none!"

"You are wrong. I have a son."

Julia looked disbelievingly at Thérèse. "He isn't John's!"

"No? You know this? You could prove it perhaps?"

"But you couldn't, you wouldn't take Donyatt from Hugo! It means everything to him!"

"I am glad you realise this, Julie. It will make things easier. Come, you are not walking."

Julia forced herself to speak calmly. "The English courts would never accept your claim."

"They would have to if the proof was there! After all, I was still married to John when the child was born."

Something in Thérèse's voice caused Julia to stop. "The child isn't John's, however, is he? You wouldn't have let John touch you after you left him."

Thérèse narrowed her eyes. "How very perceptive of you, Julie! As I think I have said before, there is more to you than I thought. But John was in France at the relevant time, I assure you. Or near enough. Since we are two together with no one near enough to hear, I will admit to you that the child could not possibly—no, not in a million years—be John's. But Hugo would find that very difficult to prove."

"Believe me, Thérèse, he would find a way."

"*Vraiment*? That might take a very long time. And lawsuits are notoriously expensive, are they not? What would happen to the estate of which he is so proud while the ownership was in dispute? It might well go to ruin, I think."

There was a silence. Then Julia said, "Why are you telling me this, Thérèse? Surely it's Hugo's affair, not mine?" There was another short pause. "What do you want? Money?"

Thérèse raised her hands in a gesture of repudiation. "You know, Julie, much as I like the English, I find they have little or no *délicatesse*. You are so blunt! But surely you are not suggesting that I would take money to deprive my child of his birthright? Fie, fie!''

"Your resources cannot be infinite. If Hugo disputes what appears to me to be a very shaky claim to the title, you might find that you are ruined, too."

"My claim is not a shaky one. Prevert will see to it that it is incontestable! You see, I now admit to you that I do know Monsieur Prevert, though I should like to know where you heard the name! No? You will not tell me? No matter. He is an old ally of mine, and knew John very well. But to return to more important matters—you can keep your money, Julie. That is not what I want."

"Then what?"

Thérèse stopped and looked up into Julia's eyes. Her own were gleaming like a cat's at night, the pupils large and dark. "There have only ever been two men of importance in my life, Julie, and one of them is dead."

"Not John," Julia stated with certainty.

Thérèse laughed contemptuously. "John? John was never anything to me. I married him because my parents told me to. He was rich, well-connected, and mad for me. They were happy to see me so well established in England. But the marriage was a disaster from the beginning. No, the first man in my life was Armand Benezat. When he was alive I needed no one else. But now he is dead."

"So we come to the other. Hugo?"

"The other is Hugo. And I want him, Julie."

"He is not mine to give you."

"No, *au fond* he is already mine."

"Then take him. Threaten him with the loss of Donyatt."

"Don't be a fool!" said Thérèse sharply. "Do you suppose Hugo would abandon you, and all his 'duties and obligations' as he calls them, for his own pleasure? And what would he think of me? No, he would sacrifice himself and me—and we would, all three of us, be condemned to an unhappy future. You must make it easy for him. Leave him. Make him believe you are bored here at Donyatt."

"It isn't possible, Thérèse. This isn't Revolutionary France. A divorce would be out of the question."

Thérèse gave a little smile. "I am no bourgeoise, Julie. We will forget the question of divorce for the moment. I will be content to stay here with Hugo with or without marriage."

"And if I don't agree to go? If I decide that I wish to hold Hugo to his bargain with me?" asked Julia defiantly.

Thérèse smiled pityingly at Julia and began to walk again. "I will tell you why you will not do that, Julie. You love him. Am I not right?" She took Julia's silence for agreement, and continued, "And since you love him, you could not bear to see him forced to part with the only thing that really matters to him. He, on the other hand, does not love you. He married you in order to save Donyatt. And you will leave him so that he can keep it."

Julia walked in silence, then she said, "I don't believe that Hugo would be happy with you, Thérèse, with or without Donyatt. He despises himself for feeling as he does about you!"

"Leave Hugo's feelings to me. He may not like me—but what do I care about that? I am in his blood, as he is in mine. I am part of him—as Donyatt is." They had reached the end of the drive. "What is it to be, Julie?"

"I need time to think. I will let you know."

"My dear Julie, there is really no choice. Hugo does not love you—he has said so. What would remain without Donyatt?"

"All the same, I will not throw everything away without thinking very carefully first. You will have my answer soon."

They bade each other farewell coldly, and Thérèse was driven off.

CHAPTER SIXTEEN

JULIA RETURNED slowly up the drive to the house, but when she got to the steps she turned away towards the hill. A chill wind had got up, though the sun was bright on the fields around. Unlike some parts of England, Donyatt had had a good harvest, and the young men returning from the wars had found much needed work here. Now the green and gold of summer had given way to the russet tones of autumn, and a few of the trees had already lost their leaves. But down in the valley the scene was still one of tranquil peace. Donyatt was incredibly lovely.

As Julia wandered on she noted all this through a kind of daze, as if her eyes belonged to someone quite different. Eventually, however, the numbness which had enabled her to talk so calmly to Thérèse wore off, and she was then filled with such desolation that the pain was almost physical. Thérèse was right. There was no choice. Hugo's heart had been captured when he was too young to see his sister-in-law for what she was, and despite his disillusion it had remained hers ever since. His passion was for Thérèse, his love, his pride and his reverence were for Donyatt. There was nothing left for her, nothing but a sense of obligation and perhaps a little affection. No—her mouth twisted wryly at the thought—there was certainly a lot of affection. But how long would the affection last in exile from Donyatt? It was not a thing she could ask Hugo—the decision had to be hers. But the answer lay in everything he had ever done or said about his home. There was no choice. With a heavy heart she returned to the house and went to her room.

ONCE SHE HAD ARRIVED at her decision Julia wasted no time in setting her plans in motion. She wrote to her lawyers telling them that she wished to arrange a confidential interview with them in the near future. She wrote a curt note to Thérèse to say she would see her soon, and then she set about preparing Hugo's mind for a visit to London.

"It's high time I saw my aunt, Hugo—she will think I have forgotten her. And it's also time I refurbished my wardrobe and paid some attention to my appearance. My hair has been sadly neglected. I am getting painfully provincial—a real country bumpkin. What Sophie would say if she saw me now, I cannot imagine."

"On the contrary, you know very well what Sophie would say—or very nearly. Since when have you been concerned?"

"I suppose you are right. But I should still like, for my own sake, to pay a little attention to my appearance. And though I cannot yet play a full role in society I should like to renew some acquaintances."

"I rather hoped we should spend Christmas at Donyatt, Julia."

"We..." Her voice faltered and then became firm again. "We may well do so. But that is still quite a few weeks away! We could surely fit in a short visit, could we not?" She recalled the wheedling tone that Sophie used when she wanted something badly. "Please, Hugo?"

He smiled down at her. "I don't see how I can refuse you. I can't have my wife looking like a dowd, can I?" The teasing note in his voice was nearly her undoing. She looked down quickly to hide her feelings.

"Then I shall write to my aunt straight away."

Hugo stretched out his hand and caught hers. "Don't change too much, Julia."

"What do you mean?"

"I like you as you are."

"That is just because you have grown used to me—rather like a familiar coat or a favourite pair of slippers."

"On the contrary. I find your intelligence a challenge, your ability to run Donyatt impressive, and your beauty constantly refreshing."

The compliment threw Julia into confusion. Avoiding Hugo's eye, she said as calmly as she could. "I have often been thought too clever by half, Hugo. I was brought up from an early age to run a large household, so there is no virtue in that. But beautiful I am not. I never have been, and I don't suppose I ever shall be."

"Modest, too," murmured Hugo.

Julia said sharply, trying not to smile, "I warn you, Hugo, we shall fall out if you persist in these ridiculous compliments!"

Hugo looked at her with a grin. "Well, that puts me into a bit of a dilemma. For however lovely I find you, I shall never dare say so again. I remember another of your accomplishments, you see." Julia looked at him enquiringly and he fingered his jaw. "As true and straight an aim as I have come across. I've no desire to risk that again, my love." He smiled in relief as Julia burst into laughter. "That's good. I thought I was never going to hear you laugh again, Julia." She was instantly serious.

"What nonsense! Besides, you have not been very cheerful yourself."

"Things will be different now. You may be assured of that. I think I can say that our problems are over." He got up to go. "Except for the tower of the parish church. I have to see the vicar about it at four. Excuse me." At the door he paused. "You know, Julia, you may not think yourself beautiful. And now, of course, I dare not argue with you. But by God you're desirable. The waiting time is becoming very tedious." With that he vanished, leaving Julia staring after him in amazement. It had almost sounded as if Hugo had meant it!

LADY THORNTON expressed herself delighted to receive them for as long as they wished, and promised Julia a list of the latest modistes. Within a few days Hugo and Julia were on their way. But as they lurched and jolted along the mud-covered road, Hugo was puzzled. This was one of the worst times of year for travelling—and for such a frivolous purpose, too! Julia must be missing her aunt more than he thought. But then, now he came to think of it, Julia had not seen Lady Thornton since April, and had only left Donyatt once or twice on dull business journeys to view her own properties. He was being selfish in wishing they could have remained in Dorset—Julia needed a change. He looked at her now. She had fallen asleep in spite of the uncomfortable conditions, and he marvelled at her beauty in repose. How could he ever have thought this woman "unremarkable"? His finger traced her cheekbone and the delicate line of her jaw. Her skin was clear, a faint flush colouring her normally pale cheeks. With a frown he took note of the dark blue shadows under her eyes—had she been sleeping badly at night? One lock of her hair had fallen over her shoulder, a swathe of dark bronze silk against the grey velvet pelisse. He leant forward and gently kissed her. She sighed contentedly and her eyes opened. She smiled at him sleepily and his heart turned over in his breast. "Julia!" he said.

In an instant she was fully awake. "Oh, goodness, what a sight I must look! Forgive me, I think I must have dozed off. Where are we?"

She held him at bay with questions of his journeys abroad, falling into silence again as he described the trips they would make together in the future. Now that the Monster of Europe was safely confined on Elba, France, with all its sights, was open once again to the English visitor. Occasionally he caught a wistful look in her eye, but she turned his questions with a laugh and some further enquiry.

They arrived in London on a murky November afternoon. Lady Thornton welcomed them warmly, and they were soon comfortably established in a suite of rooms on the first floor of her house. Here Julia cast her bonnet aside and sank on to a day bed by the fire, while a maid unpacked her valises.

"It seems to me that you hardly need another dress," was Hugo's comment. "Where will you find room for your new ones? Perhaps we should engage another coach? Julia?"

Her failure to respond to his teasing disappointed him, but he smiled when she looked up with a start and said, "What? Oh, forgive me, my mind was full of modistes and plans for my stay. I shall give my old dresses away, of course!"

For the next few days they saw little of one another. Julia was out most afternoons, though where she went her aunt could not have said, for Julia kept her own counsel. Even Sophie Mersham was unable to find out.

"I'll swear Julia has a secret lover, Mersham," she remarked to her husband.

"Nonsense, my dear. Julia and a lover? Hugo would never allow it. Didn't she say she was visiting her dressmaker?"

"But Madame Rosa hadn't seen her yesterday. I asked. I'd give more than a guinea to know where Julia goes. Four so-called visits to the modiste in as many days is too many!"

SOPHIE WOULD HAVE BEEN disappointed, for Julia's forays were not at all scandalous. Apart from Madame Rosa, she visited her father's lawyers several times, where the various confidential tasks they were asked to perform caused more than one raised eyebrow, and finally paid a call at a very respectable address in Dover Street.

"Milady is at 'ome, *madame*," said the little maid in a strong French accent. "Oo shall I say is 'ere?"

Julia gritted her teeth and said calmly, "Lady Rostherne." The maid looked doubtful, but announced her.

Thérèse waved a scented handkerchief at Julia and said, "Ah, Julie! I am enchanted to see you. Pray forgive me for not getting up. Jeanne, take Lady Rostherne's pelisse and bring in some tea. You see how English I become, Julie? Do sit down—it is very fatiguing to look up such a long way." Thérèse looked at Julia, a cruel little smile on her lips. "So what have you decided, Julie? *Oh, alors!* Why do I ask? There is nothing to decide! Not for you."

"Before I agree to anything, Thérèse, I should like some guarantees," replied Julia. "For instance, what assurance can you give me that you will not press the claims of your son at a later stage? What if Hugo rejects you even after I have left him? He's a man of principle—and from what I have observed you are devoid of anything of the kind. What if he finds it impossible to live with you?"

Thérèse laughed merrily. "*Oh, là là, là là!* There speaks the old maid! My dear Julie, try not to talk of things you don't understand—men don't take principles to bed! They soon forget that sort of thing when they're between the sheets! Dear Hugo will be kept happy, I assure you."

"But what guarantee can you give me?" insisted Julia.

Thérèse shrugged her shoulders. "None. I find it impertinent that you should demand it. You are in no position to bargain or beg for guarantees, Julie."

"Nevertheless, I will not agree to your scheme without one." Though Julia sounded determined, she was bluffing. She knew she had very little room for manoeuvre, but there would be even less afterwards. She must fight for what she could now.

"*Mais c'est ridicule*! What would you have me do? You cannot imagine I would be idiot enough to write anything down...? Unless..." Thérèse sat in thought for a moment, then she laughed and clapped her hands. "Yes, why not? Listen, I will give you a kind of guarantee—but I do not know whether you are gambler enough to like it! It is very good of me, I think, for I have no need to grant you anything, you know."

"What is it?"

Thérèse's eyes were sparkling. "We will have a ... a contest of wits. I will give you a clue as to where Prevert can be found. He knows the truth about my son's birth, and, if I know him, he will have evidence of it. You might be able to persuade him to tell you. The game is this—I'll wager I can convince Hugo that his true place is with me before you can find Prevert and persuade him. Is that not generous?"

Julia might have rejected the challenge immediately, except for one thing. Unknown to Thérèse she already had some information about Prevert. Perhaps if the two were put together she would find him sooner than Thérèse imagined. And if Prevert had indeed been a Napoleonic spy, then the present French authorities would be only too willing to help her. She looked up. Thérèse was siting back on the *chaise-longue* looking elegantly relaxed, but the knuckles of the hand holding her handkerchief were white. This was important to her. Why? Was it part of some scheme against Prevert? If that were the case it could be dangerous... But what did that matter? What had she to lose? She would have to find something to do with her life after... after she left Hugo. Removing Thérèse's source of power over him might not be a bad thing to do. She decided to take the risk. "I accept your challenge, Thérèse. What is the clue?" A flash of triumph in Thérèse's eyes, though quickly concealed, confirmed Julia's suspicions. But Thérèse merely said,

"Not yet. You must leave Hugo first. How soon can that be arranged."

"I need two days."

"You must make your departure convincing, Julie. No
heroics. Hugo must have good reason to believe that you no
longer wish to live with him." When Julia did not reply,
Thérèse said more sharply, "You understand?" It would be
better for Hugo if he could dismiss her with an easy conscience, thought Julia.

"Yes," she said. "I'll make sure."

"Then I will give you the clue in two days' time. *Au revoir*, Julie. I felicitate you on your good sense. Jeanne!"

Julia rose to go. As she went out of the room she heard a
call of "Good luck!", followed by mocking laughter, floating after her.

JULIA DID NOT immediately return to her aunt's house. She
first went to a small house in Islington, which had been
leased on her behalf by her lawyers. Here she visited an elderly Frenchwoman whose services she had engaged some
days previously. Unlike many of the other French émi-
grées, Madame de Luthigny had nothing left to return to in
France. Her husband had died some years before, leaving
her with very little to live on, and she now supplemented her
income by acting as a companion or chaperon to those who
needed her. In her earlier years she had been an enthusias-
tic member of the salons in Paris and had also travelled all
over Europe with her husband. Julia was hoping to find a
congenial spirit in this lively lady, and, once matters between Hugo and herself were sorted out, she planned to
spend some time travelling in Madame de Luthigny's company. Until that time Julia intended to live quietly here in
Islington, safe from society's unexpected piece of good fortune that she had chosen a Frenchwoman to be her companion, and indeed *madame* was delighted when she heard
of Julia's intention to visit France. She was undeterred by
Julia's warning that there might be some danger in the en-
terprise, and only asked with a smile and a slightly coy look,
"An affair of the heart, perhaps?"

Julia started to deny it, paused, and then nodded sadly.
It could be so described, though not in the way Madame de
Luthigny undoubtedly suspected, and it might even serve the
useful purpose of satisfying Madame de Luthigny's obvious curiosity about the sudden change of plan.

Having done all she could for the moment, Julia returned to her aunt's house, where she pleaded a bad head and retired to her room. Fortunately Hugo was out till late and Lady Thornton was preoccupied with preparations for a soirée which she was holding the following evening. "I will leave you to rest today, Julia, and tomorrow, too. You have been doing too much; you do not look at all the thing, child. I cannot have my guest of honour looking so worn out! Send for me if you need me."

The headache was a painful reality, but Julia did not use the time for rest. First she spent a short time deciding what to leave with her aunt and what to take with her to Islington, and then she sat down to consider what to say in her letter to Hugo. Finally, with dogged determination, she wrote what she had to—that she had decided that they did not suit after all, that the quiet life at Donyatt that Hugo evidently wished for would not satisfy her once her year of mourning was over, and that it was within the terms of their agreement that she could choose to live apart from him.

I am aware that the year we agreed on is not yet up, but I really cannot bear another moment of our situation. This letter is in the nature of a farewell. However, knowing how important Donyatt is to your happiness, I have done all I can to ensure that it will be safe. The financial arrangements made by my father at the time of our marriage will still stand. There will, no doubt, be some inconvenience attached to my departure, but, since you have always maintained that our relationship did not involve any feelings other than those of friendship and respect, I know I am not causing you any lasting pain. Please understand, and forgive me.

She signed and sealed it, and put it safely away for later use.

THE NEXT EVENING was a glittering occasion. The Mershams were there, of course, together with other influential members of the ton, who all complimented Hugo on his bride. Madame Rosa had surpassed herself in her creation of a robe of white crêpe, worn over a sarsnet slip. The dress was beautifully cut, its simple lines suiting Julia's tall, slender figure to perfection. It was cut low, but Julia's only ornament was a black, jet-trimmed ribbon round her throat. Her hair had been brushed until it shone like dark copper, then wound into a Grecian knot on the top of her head. She looked stunning.

Hugo could not keep his eyes off her. He had grown accustomed to seeing Julia in her modest, sober gowns, suitable for their quiet life at Donyatt. This was a different creature altogether. This was a queen of society.

As the evening wore on, Julia's success seemed to go to her head like wine. She sparkled and laughed, enchanting all around with her wit and charm. Sophie was furious.

"Hugo! Cannot you stop your wife making such a spectacle of herself? She has been flirting with Lord Northbury for the past half-hour, and now even Mersham is making sheep's eyes at her. Stop her, Hugo!"

"Julia is enjoying a little harmless fun, Sophie. I wouldn't dream of stopping her! She leads a quiet enough life at Donyatt."

"That's the trouble, Hugo. That's why a little social success has gone to her head so quickly—and it's only because she's such a novelty. Poor Julia would soon discover how fickle her admirers are if she spent any length of time in London. It would be a kindness to give her a word of warning, Hugo."

Hugo excused himself. Sophie was really more than he could tolerate.

He found Julia sitting in an alcove while Lord Northbury fetched her something to drink. She smiled brilliantly as Hugo approached.

"Is this not a splendid occasion, Hugo? I confess I had forgotten how pleasant company can be!"

Hugo frowned fleetingly, then turned as Lord Northbury came up carrying a glass of champagne. "Northbury! Just the man I was seeking," he said, firmly removing the glass. "Lady Thornton was asking for you. I believe she has someone she wishes you to meet."

As a reluctant Lord Northbury made his way to see his hostess, Julia said in a puzzled voice, "But my aunt has just gone upstairs to repair the hem of her dress, Hugo."

"Exactly so!" said Hugo with satisfaction. "It will take that old fool quite a time to track her down. What the devil do you mean by flirting with him, Julia? You'll turn his head."

"Was I doing that? I didn't know. What fun!"

"It's more fun to flirt with me. Do you remember the first time we sat in an alcove together? I kissed you...like this."

Julia closed her eyes... Then she pulled herself away with a laugh. "I can't remember the alcove, Hugo. Where was that? Oh, there's Peter Mersham—you know, he's really quite charming once he's away from Sophie. I want to talk to him. You must tell me about the alcove another time..."

She was gone. A small frown creased Hugo's brow as he gazed after her. Julia was very different here in London. He had thought he knew her, but this will-o'-the-wisp was a stranger. Was he seeing the real Julia? Surely not! Perhaps Sophie was right—Julia's success had gone to her head a little.

By the end of the evening Julia was near breaking-point. She had laughed, flirted, avoided Hugo and encouraged others till her head was aching almost as badly as her heart. When Hugo would have sat down with her after the last guest had departed she said pettishly, "Oh, Hugo, not now! You are always so serious, and I am in a frivolous frame of mind. Do let me go to bed. I vow I am asleep on my feet." She moved away, apparently preoccupied with practising a little dance step. "I can hardly wait till my year of mourning is up! Think of all the ton parties I shall go to! I never realised how very agreeable they could be! Goodnight, Hugo!"

CHAPTER SEVENTEEN

DURING THE LONG NIGHT that followed, Julia was so often tempted to give up her plans that she had to remind herself over and over that Hugo would never have loved her as she wanted. Without Thérèse's ultimatum she might eventually have settled for second, or even third best and stayed with Hugo as his wife. She tried to comfort herself with the thought that she might later have been even more unhappy than she was now. If that were possible. Finally she got up shortly before dawn and assembled the personal possessions she had sorted out the day before. Then she wrote to Mrs. Staple to say that she would be away for some time, and asking her to keep Donyatt running smoothly until other arrangements were made. She gave the housekeeper Mr. Farleigh's address in London, and asked her to write to the lawyer in case of difficulty. She did not broach the question of her possessions at Donyatt. Thérèse would probably wish them to be removed but there would be time for that. The thought of her Chinese drawing-room caused some more pangs, but she determinedly pulled herself together before she melted into tears. By this time the light was stronger, and she could hear movement about the house. In a few moments she would go to her aunt.

Lady Thornton, roused from sleep, was decidedly unsympathetic to Julia's news. She was essentially conventional, and deeply shocked that Julia was planning to leave her husband. Nor could she understand the reasons Julia gave her.

"But Julia, I'm sure Hugo will indulge you in your wish to mix in society again. He seems to be a very reasonable man. Why do you have to leave him merely because you are bored with Donyatt? I thought better of you, I really did. What if you *have* found your marriage was a mistake? People are often disappointed—especially when, as you did, they achieve their heart's desire after waiting so many years. That's it, isn't it? You've had an ideal picture of Hugo ever since you were a girl, and now that you are living with the reality you find it's not what you wanted after all.''

"I... Yes, Aunt Alicia. That's it. I should never have married Hugo. I was too set in my ways.''

After more discussion, which tried Julia's patience to the uttermost, Lady Thornton, who had always been very fond of her niece, grudgingly agreed to help. With tears in her eyes Julia kissed her aunt, saying, "Try not to think too badly of me, Aunt Alicia. Believe me, I would not do this if there were any other way.''

As she came out of Lady Thornton's bedchamber she met Hugo, who had come in search of her. He took her into the drawing-room. "Julia, is there something wrong? You seem so different. What is it?''

Mindful of her role, Julia turned petulantly away from him and said, "If you must know, Hugo, since I came to London I have grown to like it here. My unfortunate Season when I was a girl gave me a jaundiced view of society, but now I find it very pleasant to be courted and flattered. Oh, I know you will say it doesn't mean anything, but it is so agreeable!'' She turned round defiantly. "And you must admit, life at Donyatt has not been very amusing of late, has it?''

"Why didn't you say something before this? I didn't realise...'' He shook his head. "I've been very selfish. I thought you liked living at Donyatt. I'll see Hockliffe about leasing a house in London next season.''

"Oh, you'd only be miserable away from your precious Donyatt! Confess!''

"It's true I prefer country life to that of the town, yes. But I can be reasonable, Julia. If you wish for more town life we can compromise.''

This evidence of Hugo's innate fairness almost undid Julia. There was genuine desperation in her voice as she said, "For heaven's sake, Hugo, don't be so self-sacrificing!''

Hugo stiffened. "You seem to be spoiling for a fight. Well, I have no intention of indulging you. Perhaps when I come back you'll be in a more reasonable frame of mind.'' He made to go.

"Hugo!"

He stopped at the door. "What is it?"

Julia came over and looked up at him. "I am right, aren't I? Donyatt is the most important thing in your life?"

He was still offended. "Yes, of course," he said shortly. "Why do you ask?"

She stretched up and kissed him slowly. "Forgive me, Hugo."

"What is it that's wrong, Julia? Look, I'll cancel my appointment with Hockliffe, and talk this over—"

"No, no!" she cried in a panic, then she forced herself to laugh. "That really isn't necessary. Don't keep Mr. Hockliffe waiting." When he still hesitated she said, "Besides, I have an appointment myself. Do please go, Hugo!"

He went out. She ran to the window and watched his broad-shouldered figure striding away.

HALF AN HOUR LATER Thérèse was handing Julia an envelope. "The clue, Julie. You are quite sure you have left Hugo?"

"Quite sure. My aunt will give him my letter when he returns."

"No affecting speeches or heroic sacrifices?"

"No, he will believe that I have left him because I no longer wish to live with him. But I warn you, if you make Hugo unhappy, I will tell him everything."

Thérèse gave her trill of laughter. "Hugo will not be unhappy! I will be so careful. But, in any case, what makes you think he will ever again listen to anything you have to say? Are you going to open your clue?"

Slowly Julia opened the envelope. She read, "'Prevert is to be found among the birds in Paris.' Paris is a large city, Thérèse."

Thérèse had her head cocked on one side, her eyes sparkling with malice. "I did not say it would be easy, *ma chère*. Give it up! It is in any case wasted effort."

"I will not give up."

"In that case, I will bid you adieu, Julie."

"And I shall say *au revoir*. Remember what I have said about Hugo's happiness."

Julia went straight from Dover Street to Islington. She must allow herself no time for thought, for it would be all too easy to fall into a melancholy. She might never see Hugo again, but, in concentrating on saving Donyatt yet again for him, she might forget some of her misery. This puzzle set by Thérèse might well be her salvation.

Madame de Luthigny proved to be an incorrigible romantic. The mystery of Julia's "affair of the heart" intrigued her and, though she at first expressed doubts about two women setting off for France without an escort, she then, almost in the same breath, found the solution. Her nephew, who was at present in England, would very shortly be returning to France and would be delighted to travel with them. More than that, he offered them accommodation in Paris at his family home near the Tuileries. Julia accepted gratefully and, in the bustle of preparation that followed, sometimes felt she was escaping from her heartache. She overlooked the fact that this problem, which concerned Hugo and Donyatt so closely, did nothing to release her from the bonds which held her. She never for one moment considered what she would do after her return from France. The immediate future was all that occupied her.

Before setting off for France, Julia visited her aunt, having first ascertained that Hugo had left London.

"Julia, why did you not tell me where you would be staying in London? No, don't tell me where it is now, for Hugo will very likely murder me if he finds out that I have known your direction without informing him. My dear child, how could you do this to him? He was in a fearsome rage. I really thought he would go mad. Oh, you're safe at the moment. He has just gone storming off to Banbury, don't ask me why. I think he is making a systematic search through every property you own! Why did you do it, Julia? The poor man is distraught."

"My dear aunt, you exaggerate. He will recover," said Julia, with more confidence than she felt. "I will in any case not be in England after tomorrow. I am leaving for France."

"France! Julia, what are you thinking of? Why are you going to France? Whatever will you do next? I think you are both mad, you and Hugo!"

"Aunt Alicia, I...I've written two letters, one for you and one for Hugo. They are to remain sealed unless something should happen to me." Lady Thornton gave a scream and clutched her throat. "I assure you I am in no danger," added Julia hastily. "Pray do not worry on my account. But in the very unlikely event that I meet with some accident—very unlikely, Aunt Alicia—I should like you to send one to Hugo and open the other one yourself. Here they are. But meanwhile Hugo must remain in ignorance about my whereabouts. Now, what would you like from Paris?"

Julia eventually coaxed her aunt into viewing the excursion to France more calmly. They parted affectionately, and the following day, two weeks after Julia had left Hugo, Julia, Madame de Luthigny and her nephew were on the Dover road.

HUGO HAD SPENT the intervening weeks searching everywhere he could think for Julia. He had visited all her estates and properties, had subjected himself to the surprised questions of her cousin, the present Lord Carteret, in Surrey, and had demanded to see her lawyers in London, who after some acrimonious discussion had finally given him the Islington address. But though Hugo went there straight away Julia had already gone—where, no one knew. He went back to Lady Thornton's, heavy of heart, without any clear idea of what he would do next. Initially he had set off to find Julia in a fury. How dared she leave him? She was his wife, she belonged to him, and her place was at his side! He had sworn that once he found her there would be no more nonsense of bargains and the like! Julia was his, and the sooner she was his in fact as well as in name the better it would be for both of them! But then, as time went on and Julia was still not to be found, his anger died and a great fear took its place. Did she not know he would have done anything—anything at all—to keep her? Had she no idea how much she meant to him? Perhaps she hadn't—he hadn't realised that himself till now. Why, Julia was everything to him! He must find her!

When a note was brought round asking him to call at Dover Street, he thought for one wild moment that Julia might be there. His disappointment, therefore, was intense when Thérèse proved to be alone. He hardly listened to her expressions of delight that he had come so promptly, and

when she would have gone on he cut her short with an im
patient, "Do you know where Julia is, Thérèse?"

"Does it matter?"

"Of course it damn well matters! I have to talk to her!"

"Hugo, why can't you forget this stupid Julie? Surely i
is enough that she has gone, and that you are now free o
any obligation towards her? We are both free, Hugo. Come
we shall sit down here and talk, you and I."

He thrust her roughly away from him, and she sat dow
with a jerk on the sofa. "I haven't time to talk to you
Thérèse. You were my last hope here in London. If you can'
help me, then I shall go back to Donyatt and start lookin
from there. I must find her, I must!"

Thérèse jumped up and caught him by the arm. "Don'
be such a fool, Hugo! Julie has left you. She won't come
back." Her voice became soft and pleading. "Take me to
Donyatt with you—we could be so happy. I swear you wil
soon forget her!" She gazed up at him, her large dark eye
magically luminous. He looked at her coldly for a moment
and then his own eyes narrowed.

"You know something. By God, I believe you know
something! Tell me what it is, Thérèse!"

Thérèse drew back from him. "You've changed," she
said slowly. "I think you don't love me any longer
Hugo—"

"Love you! I never loved you, Thérèse! What I felt fo
you was a madness, a sickness—and whatever it was, it wa
over long, long ago. I may not have realised it at the time
but I know it now. Abandon any thought of living with me
at Donyatt or anywhere else. It is out of the question."

The black eyes now burned with anger. "You will regre
this, Hugo. More than you know—"

"Tell me where Julia is, or I shall force it out of you
Thérèse..." Hugo's voice was full of menace.

They stared at each other in silence. Then Thérèse smiled
maliciously. "I do not think you will be happy to know this
Hugo."

"Tell me!"

"Before I do, I ask you to remember that I did warn you
Julie is a comparatively young woman. You neglected her
shamefully in your passion for Donyatt, and your..

memories of the past. Is it so surprising that she sought companionship elsewhere, that she was not alone when she left for Paris?"

"Paris! Why Paris? And who was her companion? Tell me, damn you!"

Thérèse shrugged her shoulders. "I really cannot say for certain. I only know that she was accompanied when she left London. But perhaps their ultimate destination is not Paris? Perhaps a certain gentleman of our acquaintance wishes to show her the delights of the East? I told you that she was interested, did I not?"

"You've always been a lying bitch, Thérèse, but this time you've overreached yourself. Julia wouldn't do such a thing. She may have left me, but not for this. I would stake my life on it. But I am obliged for the information." He made to go.

"Wait!" cried Thérèse. "I wish to say something about Donyatt—"

"Donyatt can wait!" Hugo was almost out of the door. "I must first find Julia."

CHAPTER EIGHTEEN

ONCE IN PARIS, Julia wasted no time. She called immediately at the Embassy and obtained the names and directions of various officials at the French Court who might be able to help her. She debated whether to take Madame de Luthigny fully into her confidence, for her help in communicating with these people would be invaluable, but decided against it. The fewer people who knew the truth about Prevert the better. So, leaving her companion at home with her family, Julia visited every official on the Embassy's list. But though they all showed a lively interest in a Napoleonic spy in Paris, they could offer no help in finding him.

"Milady, it is impossible," said one, shrugging his shoulders. "The King has been back such a short time, and all is confusion! No one will admit to knowing anything about Bonaparte's regime," he added cynically, "except when they are whispering about former friends! It is difficult—no, it is impossible—to get any real information from anyone." She showed him her scrap of paper, which he dismissed as rubbish, then let him see the clue which Thérèse had given her. He was polite, but harassed by the huge amount of work he was burdened with, and had little time for puzzles. "'Birds'? 'Among the birds'?" He gave her directions to aviaries, to gardens with peacocks, to parks with lakes for water-fowl—all in vain. Day after day she went back to the house by the Tuileries tired and dispirited.

Madame de Luthigny had observed all this without making any comment. But one day she drew Julia aside. "Lady Rostherne, I have till now respected your obvious desire to keep your affairs to yourself, but I think you have been looking for someone—so far without success. Is there no way I can help you? I do not like to see you so unhappy." As

Julia hesitated, *madame* added with a sentimental smile, "He is obviously someone important to you."

Julia's first impulse was to tell Madame de Luthigny that the matter was not really an affair of the heart, that it would not end, as *madame* clearly imagined it would, in a lovers' reunion. But she stopped herself. It would be safer if her companion remained under the impression that the story behind Julia's search for Prevert was a touching romance—rather than an ugly tale of treachery and betrayal which could bring disaster to the Devenishes. So she contented herself with nodding. *Madame* continued, "Even now, after all these years, I still have friends at Court. One in particular knows Paris very well indeed, and you may be assured of his discretion. Shall I ask him to visit us here?"

When Monsieur de Litry arrived, Julia gave him a carefully edited version of the truth. She was looking for a certain Monsieur Prevert, who lived in Paris. She had reason to believe that he had worked as an agent for the French government, and he had certainly been in England on at least two occasions, one quite recently.

"You have been to the British Embassy here in Paris? What did they say of this?"

A faint colour rose in Julia's cheeks. "I have not told them. It is . . . awkward."

He smiled sympathetically. "Ah, yes, I understand perfectly. You would not wish word to go back to England, is that it? But Milady, there is very little to work with here. Is there really nothing more?" Julia silently handed him Thérèse's "clue." "Who gave you this, *madame*?"

She hesitated, then told him, "Thérèse Benezat, my...my husband's former sister-in-law."

His eyes widened. "Armand Benezat's wife, eh? Now that is really interesting. 'Among the birds.' May I assume that you have already looked in all the obvious places?" Julia told him of her searches. "No, it would not be as simple as that. Have you nothing more to help us?"

Julia had been reluctant to show her two helpers the torn scrap of paper, but now she held it out to him. They examined it carefully. Monsieur de Litry gave Julia a sharp look.

"This looks as if it has a dramatic history, *madame*?"

Julia merely replied, "Its history is well in the past, *monsieur*. It is some years old. I wondered..." she hesitated, but after an encouraging nod from Monsieur de Litry she went on. "Could it be an address?"

He looked again at the paper. "'Among the birds,'" he mused. "'...eons.' Pigeons?"

Madame de Luthigny gave a little screech of excitement. "Of course it is! And I know where! It's the Rue des Quatre Pigeons! It's quite near where I used to live as a child." She turned joyfully to Julia. "We have found him for you, Lady Rostherne! You will see him very soon. Oh, *l'amour, l'amour*—how romantic it is!"

"One moment, *madame*, if you please." Monsieur de Litry spoke in a serious tone. "If you will permit me, Lady Rostherne, I should prefer to investigate a little further first. For one thing, it might not be the right street—"

"Of course it is!" said Madame de Luthigny.

"And if it is," continued Monsieur de Litry firmly, "we still do now know which is Monsieur Prevert's house. I could perhaps ascertain both of these." His tone grew even more serious. "And lastly, though I do not wish to offend your sensibilities, *madame*, I must warn you. If this man has been a...a spy—for that is what you meant, is it not?—then, however fond he may be of you, he will possibly be very angry that he has been traced. The matter could be dangerous."

"What nonsense, Jean-Pierre! He will be overjoyed to see Lady Rostherne!"

"All the same, I think I should call first."

"No!" said Julia. "No, you must not call on him. If you could make discreet enquiries—I mean with total discretion, *monsieur*—then I should be in your debt. I agree it could be difficult if I called on a...a stranger. But Prevert must not know that I am in Paris. That is important."

Monsieur de Litry looked faintly puzzled, but agreed to do as she asked. Two days later he was back with the information they had sought. Monsieur Prevert lived at number thirty-two Rue des Quatre Pigeons. He lived quietly, and was apparently away a lot.

Julia was slightly surprised at a change in Monsieur de Litry's manner. On his previous visit he had been business-like and brisk, but the atmosphere had been cordial. Now his manner was reserved, even cold. It was as if she had offended him in some way. Madame de Luthigny noticed it, too.

"What is it, Jean-Pierre? Something has happened—tell us."

"It is nothing," he said curtly.

"Jean-Pierre, I know you too well to be fobbed off. Lady Rostherne might be going into danger—you said so yourself. Now tell us what has made you so cold."

"Very well. Lady Rostherne may not be aware of the fact that Monsieur Prevert has a wife and children. They live there with him. It might be better if she arranged a—" his lip curled slightly "—an assignation with him elsewhere."

Julia grew scarlet at his tone. "*Monsieur*!"

"Forgive me, Lady Rostherne. I am as broad-minded as the next man, I believe, but in this case my sympathies are with Madame Prevert. From what I have heard, the poor woman has had more than enough to bear already. She was deeply distressed at the loss of her only son when he was just sixteen, and has since received little comfort or support from her husband, who is nearly always absent. There seems to be grave concern about her state of mind. A visit from you might well precipitate a crisis."

Julia saw now that her little deceit was threatening to hamper her mission. But what could she do? Her two aides would hardly believe a new story now, nor did she wish to tell them the truth. "I assure you that, whatever I do, I will bear this in mind, *monsieur*. I have no desire to cause unnecessary pain," she said at last. "I am obliged to you for your help and consideration, but I must now act as I see fit."

Monsieur de Litry gave her a stiff little bow, and made for the door. Here he paused. "I should be failing in my duty, Lady Rostherne, if I did not warn you again. You are playing a dangerous game." Then, bidding them both farewell, he left.

Julia was in a fever to go to the Prevert house. Ignoring Madame de Luthigny's expostulations, she changed into walking dress, and was waiting impatiently in the hall for a carriage to be brought round, when her companion appeared, also dressed for an excursion. She followed Julia outside. "I am coming with you!" she said firmly.

"No!" exclaimed Julia. "I must go alone, *madame*, I must! The matter is too important and too delicate for anyone but myself."

Madame de Luthigny looked affronted. "I am not inexperienced in matters of delicacy, Lady Rostherne! You may rely on me."

"I will not have you with me!" said Julia, too nervous to be tactful. "Pray go back into the house, *madame*. I refuse to discuss the matter any further."

Madame de Luthigny pressed her lips together disapprovingly, then said as she went in, "As you wish, Lady Rostherne. It is not at all *comme il faut*, however. I hope you may not regret it."

Number thirty-two Rue des Quatre Pigeons was in one of those faceless, apparently impenetrable terraces of large houses found everywhere in the cities of France. Julia asked the coachman to wait, and knocked at the door.

"I would like to speak to Monsieur Prevert, if you please," she said to the maid. She decided not to give her name. "Tell him that I am an acquaintance of Thérèse Benezat."

The maid returned with a request for Julia to enter. So far so good, thought Julia, her heart beating faster. Thérèse's name had had an effect. It was an effect she had not bargained for, however. A woman stood regarding her with burning eyes as she came into the ornate salon. She was heavily built, but very pale, with dark circles under her eyes. She neither invited Julia to sit, nor gave her any greeting, but began abruptly, "You may give a message to your friend, Madame Benezat, *madame*. You may tell her that she is welcome to my husband—I have had enough—"

"Madame Prevert, pray forgive me for interrupting you, but I am no friend of Thérèse Benezat's, nor in any position to deliver confidential messages to her. I am sorry if you have that impression. I have come to seek information from your husband. Is he here?"

Madame Prevert drew a shuddering breath, sank on to the sofa, and covered her face with her hands. Her shoulders shook and a sob broke from her. It was quickly followed by others.

"*Madame*, please. You will make yourself ill. Let me fetch your maid."

Madame Prevert shook her head and said through her sobs, "She went out after letting you in... She has to help with the children... They've been staying with my sister while... while I've been ill."

"Then let me fetch you something to restore you." Julia brought the distraught woman a glass of brandy, sat down beside her on the sofa, and saw that she sipped a little of the spirit. "How can I help you? Shall I stay with you until your husband returns?" In her concern for Madame Prevert, Julia had quite forgotten her mission. But this suggestion brought forth renewed sobs from *madame*.

"Why isn't he here now? He's never here when I need him!" She looked piteously at Julia. "*Madame*, can you imagine what it is like to hear of the death of an only son? And to have no one to comfort you? No one to share your sorrow? He's the boy's father! Why wasn't he here?"

"How long is it since you lost your son, *madame*?"

"It's more than a year now—he was killed at the battle of Leipzig. Thousands of them were, most of them not much older than he was." She burst out, "And the only comfort his father could give me was that he had died gloriously for France! Gloriously! Boys, herded like cattle to certain death. Oh, Marcel, Marcel!"

Julia said nothing, but gently chafed the cold hand clutching hers. After a while Madame Prevert whispered, "You are very kind, *madame*... very kind. I am sorry I spoke to you as I did." She made an effort to pull herself together. "My husband is out. He went out about half an hour ago. I don't know when he'll be back. May I know who you are?"

"My name is Devenish, Julia D—"

The woman on the sofa widened her eyes. "Devenish? From England, then? But you know my husband, Lady Rostherne!"

Julia shook her head, and was about to ask how Madame Prevert had known her title, when the door to her salon opened.

Madame Prevert drew a quick breath. "Here he is now," she said.

Julia turned round to face the newcomer, and for a moment shock kept her silent. Then she said in a strangled voice, "Of course! Why didn't I see it before? Prevert.

'Pré'—field, 'vert'—green. Greenfield. How ingenious!''
Her voice grew stronger and she said contemptuously, "I
never for one moment suspected that you were a common
spy, Mr. Greenfield!''

Lucian Greenfield stood quite still for a minute. Then he
shut the door carefully behind him and walked slowly forward. He smiled and said softly, "If I were as closely associated with the Devenish family as you are, my dear, I
should be more circumspect in my use of the word 'spy'!
Really, I am very hurt you should think that I am one. In
fact, much as I admire you, I could take serious exception
to your effrontery in searching me out and insulting me in
my own home in front of my wife—who, as you can see, is
not in good health. How did you find me, by the way?''

"Thérèse Benezat told me where to find you. And the
evidence for your being a spy may be circumstantial, but it
is enough to convince me—and, I believe, the authorities."

"Are you by any chance threatening me, Lady Rostherne? Now that would be most unwise, I assure you."

"I am not interested in exposing you, Greenfield." With
an effort, Julia disguised her scorn. "I would like you to
give me some information—about Thérèse Benezat's son. I
am prepared to... show my gratitude."

"You almost tempt me, Lady Rostherne—especially if the
payment were in kind." Greenfield swept her a gallant bow.
"But tell me first what you wish to know about Joseph Benezat."

Julia had flushed angrily at Greenfield's insinuation, but
said as calmly as she could, "I wish to know about his birth.
Thérèse said you knew the truth."

"Ah! Now I'm beginning to see! So Thérèse has claimed
Donyatt and the title for him already, has she? She said she
would. Does your husband know you have come here?"

"That need not concern you. Will you tell me what I wish
to know?"

"Lady Rostherne, I did not ask you to come here. You
sought me out. Unless you tell me what persuaded you to
make this arduous journey without your husband—I assume that is so?—I will tell you nothing." His face was cold,
his tone now quite different. Julia saw that she would have
to do as he asked if she was to learn anything at all. As

coolly as possible she told him of Thérèse's threat to oust Hugo from Donyatt, and her own actions to save him.

"But that is monstrous!" The exclamation came from Madame Prevert, who was sitting in the corner of the sofa, forgotten by them both. "Thérèse Benezat knows she has no claim! She was never properly married to the Englishman."

"Be quiet, Annette!" Greenfield said sharply. He looked at Julia. "My wife gets confused. Thérèse's career has been somewhat chaotic."

Madame Prevert cried angrily, "She married Benezat before she ever went to England, Lucien. You know she did. And she was still his wife when she 'married' John Devenish! Her career has been shameful, not chaotic. Where Thérèse Benezat is concerned, I am not confused." Greenfield walked towards his wife, who shrank back into the cushions.

"Leave her!" Greenfield stopped in astonishment at Julia's command. "Don't bother trying to stop her—the damage has been done and I know the truth. It doesn't matter whose child Joseph Benezat is, or when he was born. He could never inherit Donyatt, for the English marriage was never legal. Hugo's claim to Donyatt cannot be contested. Thank you, *madame*."

He turned round, shrugging his shoulders. "You have no proof."

"Now that I know what to tell my friends to look for, I am sure the proof will be found. Thérèse has lost."

"What makes you think so, Lady Rostherne?" asked Greenfield with a peculiar smile. When Julia looked surprised at the question he went on, "For an intelligent and sophisticated woman, you have been remarkably naive in this case. Did it ever occur to you to question Thérèse's motives in telling you where I could be found?"

"But she didn't! She challenged me to find you, not aware that I had other information to help me. She never thought I would find you so easily, Greenfield. In any case, I think she was possibly settling an old score with you."

"What a great pity! Such a waste of youth and beauty, and all because you have underestimated Thérèse Benezat—like many before you. What a woman that is!"

"I don't understand."

"You fool! Can't you see that Thérèse always planned to get rid of you so that she could marry your husband? And she intends me to do the work for her—as I now must."

"What do you mean?"

"I should have thought that was obvious. It means, Lady Rostherne, that in order to save my own skin I have to eliminate you. I cannot afford to let you leave this house alive!"

"But... but I had no intention of betraying you to the authorities—not if you stayed in France, that is."

"I have not survived for over ten years as an agent in England by dealing in 'intentions' and promises. The only certain way is to make betrayal impossible."

"As you did with John Devenish—and his father!" This was a bow drawn at a venture, but it met its target. Greenfield's lips drew back in a snarl.

"Did Thérèse tell you that, too? I can see that I shall have to deal with her when the time is ripe! Yes, I killed them both. John was getting squeamish, and being the coward he was he ran off to confess all to his father. Your husband will never know how fortunate he was to be sent away to the stables. If he had been present when John gave the old man my name, my address and the names of the rest of the spy ring, he would have died along with the other two. As it was, I had cause to be grateful to him. Thanks to your husband's efforts that night, there wasn't a soul in England who didn't secretly think that the old Marquess shot his elder son and then himself. One has to admire the irony." Without taking his eyes off Julia, he walked over to a small bureau and took out a pistol. "Now there's Thérèse and you, of course. But I hardly count you—much as I regret it, my dear Lady Rostherne, you will not live to tell anyone. And I can manage Thérèse."

"You will find it difficult to explain my death away, Greenfield. Here."

"I shall think of something—a lovers' quarrel perhaps?" He glanced at his wife. "Jealousy?"

Madame Prevert said in a low, intense voice, "I will not let you do this, Lucien. I am sick of death and destruction."

"You will not say or do anything to stop me, Annette—not if you wish to save our children from disgrace, that is.

Now, Lady Rostherne, you will walk out of this window here into the garden, if you please.''

Julia smiled contemptuously. "I do not please, Greenfield. If you are determined to shoot me, then you will do it here in your own salon. I will not move.''

Greenfield lost his temper. "Move, you stupid English aristo, or I will shoot! I mean what I say!'' He cocked the pistol. "Ten . . . nine . . . eight—''

"Lucien!''

"Be silent, Annette! Seven . . . six . . . five—''

"I will not be silent! This woman must not die! Marcel was enough. I cannot bear any more. Let her go, I beg of you!''

"Her death is not your burden. Five . . . four . . . three—''

Madame Prevert leapt from her sofa, crying, "It is, it is! I will not let you!'' She threw herself at her husband. He cursed and tried to push her back, but she clung to his arm, turning the pistol away from Julia. There was a loud report. Greenfield staggered, his eyes wide open in astonishment. Then he fell to the floor and lay there, his eyes still staring. Madame Prevert looked in horror at her husband's body, then she ran to the door, struggled to open it, and fled screaming into the street. Julia did not move. She could not. Her eyes were fixed on Prevert's face, but they were blank, like those of a doll. The stress of those last moments during which she had faced Prevert while he counted out her life, followed by the shock of his death, had put her in a trance, deaf both to Madame Prevert's screams and to all other noises from the street.

CHAPTER NINETEEN

HUGO HAD ARRIVED in Paris that same morning. His journey had been a tedious one, delayed by storms and dogged by difficulties of transport. His enquiries at Dover had confirmed that a party consisting of a tall young woman, an elderly lady and a gentleman had travelled to Calais and thence to Paris just over a week before. He was curious about Julia's companions, but had exercised caution in his questions about them. Although his faith in Julia's integrity was unshaken, he felt it was important to avoid any suspicion of scandal. As a result he had learned very little. What the devil had Julia been up to?

He visited the British Embassy as soon as he arrived. The ambassador was in London, but Hugo was welcomed by Sir Adrian Portway, an old acquaintance from his days in Greece.

"Come to join y' wife, eh, Rostherne? Don't blame you, man—though I don't suppose she's any different from all the ladies, eh? Here to buy Parisian fashions? They're all the same, bless their hearts."

Hugo was now faced with an unexpected difficulty. How was he to find out from Sir Adrian where Julia was staying, without revealing that he didn't already know? It took a great deal of ingenuity and involved long reminiscences of their time in Greece, but he managed it eventually. After this he got up to take his leave as soon as politeness permitted, but Sir Adrian seemed reluctant to let him go.

"Er—are you planning to travel a bit on the Continent, my boy?"

"I don't know, Sir Adrian. Why do you ask?"

"Well, if you'll take the advice of an old hand you won't plan to stay too long out of England."

Hugo stopped short. "Why?" he asked bluntly. "What's wrong?"

"Nothing, nothing! But..." Sir Adrian took Hugo by the arm, and said to him in a low voice, "You'll keep this to y'self, I know. The fact is—I wouldn't wager a great deal on the continued survival of the Bourbon regime, Rostherne. Some of the French are not too happy with their new masters—Louis makes himself agreeable enough, but he hasn't yet adapted to the new ideas, and Bonaparte still has his supporters among the people."

"It was the French who forced Napoleon to abdicate, surely?"

"Yes, yes. Let's hope I'm wrong. And anyway, you would probably negotiate your way out of any danger—I remember the way you bargained with Selim Pasha in Rhodes. Now he was a villain, if ever there was one!" Sir Adrian seemed prepared to launch once again on reviving old memories, but Hugo interrupted him.

"You must excuse me, Sir Adrian. If we are going to have to cut short our visit to France, then I must give Julia the bad news as soon as possible. When are you next in England?"

Within a few moments Hugo was on his way to the house near the Tuileries. At the de Luthignys' he thought it better not to give his own name, but merely asked to see Lady Rostherne on a private matter. He was shown into a small salon where he was received by an elderly lady in a state of some agitation.

"Lady Rostherne is not at present here, sir," she said. "May I ask what your business with Lady Rostherne is? And perhaps your name?"

"Forgive me, ma'am. I should like to first know who you are, and what *your* business with Lady Rostherne is."

The lady bridled a little, but replied stiffly, "My name is de Luthigny, sir. I am Lady Rostherne's companion, and fully in her confidence. Now your name, if you please."

"It is Hugo Devenish, Madame de Luthigny, and I am here to see my wife!"

Madame de Luthigny gave a little scream and sank back into a chair, fanning herself with her handkerchief. "*Oh, mon Dieu!*" she exclaimed. "We are lost!"

"What do you mean, *madame*? Where is Julia?" Hugo came swiftly over to her.

"Milord, you must restrain yourself. In France we are very civilised about such things, I assure you—" stammered Madame de Luthigny.

"Where is Julia?"

"I beg you, milord, do not spoil her happiness—"

"Where is Julia, Madame de Luthigny?" Hugo's voice was soft, but full of menace.

"Milord, pray do not look at me like that, you are frightening me!" whispered *madame*, shrinking back into her chair. "I am not to blame if Lady Rostherne has gone to see her lover—"

"Her *what*?"

"Her . . . her lover, milord."

"Julia has no lover!" he said fiercely.

"Of course she has! She told me so. Indeed, that is why we came to Paris." She glanced nervously at Hugo. "Did you not suspect something when she left you?"

"Her lover," said Hugo. His face lost its colour and he stood quite still.

"Let me get something for you, milord. It has been a shock, I think."

"So all the time . . ." He paused, then said in disgust, "What a fool I've been! Thérèse was right, after all." He got up, went to the window and stared out. After a while he swung round to Madame de Luthigny, who was hovering anxiously nearby. "Where are they? In Paris?"

She quailed at the look in his eyes and told him, not daring to prevaricate. He turned on his heel and strode out without a word, and Madame de Luthigny, sinking thankfully on to a sofa, called for her maid.

NO ONE DARED to object when Hugo commandeered a carriage from the de Luthigny stables and ordered the coachman to drive to the Rue des Quatre Pigeons with all speed. Here he leapt out of the coach, threw an order to the man to wait for him, and strode towards the house. He could hear loud screams coming from inside, and as he reached the door a woman came running out, still screaming. Hugo caught her, but failed to make any sense of what she was

saying. He thrust her into the arms of a neighbour who had
come to see what the noise was, and ran into the house.
When he reached the salon his heart stopped. Julia was
standing facing him, and at her feet lay a pistol. Near by was
the body of a man. It was Greenfield, and he was dead.
Hugo did not stop to think. He took Julia by the arm and
shook her. "You fool, Julia! You stupid fool! Why did you
do it? Come, you must get away from here before they come
for you. Come with me!" She turned her eyes to his face.
Her lips moved, but no sound came. Then her eyelids flut-
tered, and if he hadn't been holding her she would have
fallen to the floor in a dead faint. With a muffled exclamation he swept her up into his arms and carried her out to the
carriage. The screaming woman had disappeared, but an
excited crowd had gathered outside. Without waiting to hear
what they were saying, he placed Julia carefully in the carriage, then got in himself and ordered the coachman to drive
off immediately. When they were well clear of the Rue des
Quatre Pigeons he stopped the coach. Julia was now conscious, but very dazed.

"Can you talk, Julia?" The terrified grey eyes looked up
into his. He tried to give her a reassuring smile, which
seemed to work, for she nodded slowly. "Does anyone there
know who you are? Apart from...apart from your lover?"

She nodded. "*Madame...*" she whispered. "But he
wasn't my lov—"

Fury blazed in Hugo's eyes. "Don't even try to deny it,
Julia! Madame de Luthigny has told me everything." He bit
off anything more, and instead said with a visible effort at
control, "But that can wait. The important thing for the
moment is to get you away. This *'madame'*. Is she the
woman who came out?" She nodded again. "I doubt she
will be capable of saying anything to anyone for some time.
But we cannot depend on it. Right, coachman, back to the
de Luthigny house."

Here Hugo took charge completely. Julia was installed on
a sofa while a terrified Madame de Luthigny saw that Julia's clothes were packed immediately, and Hugo went in
search of a post-chaise. *Madame* needed little persuading
that it was in her family's best interests to cover up what she
could of Julia's part in the affair, and quickly agreed to stay
behind and see to it. Less than two hours after their depar-

ture from the house in the Rue des Quatre Pigeons, Hugo and Julia were on their way to Calais.

Julia was still in a trance-like state. She was completely passive, sitting like a doll in the coach, her eyes full of horror. Hugo was torn between a desire to take her in his arms and hold her close till that look disappeared, and an equally strong desire to shake her out of her lethargy and make her face the ugly truth. He did neither, but sat in silence, angry with himself for being so worried about her. They stayed at modest inns and, where there was no maid to tend Julia, Hugo tended her himself. She accepted his ministrations as passively as she took everything else. Though he was anxious about her state of mind, he pressed on as fast as he dared, eager to reach England and safety. At first Julia had refused to eat, but as they drew nearer to Calais she began to revive, and even started to do a few things for herself. After they were safely over the Channel and in England they were able to drive at a more leisurely pace, staying in comfort on the way. Hugo saw much less of his wife. She withdrew to her bedchamber as soon as they stopped for the night, and was attended by one of the maids, who brought her food and whatever else she needed. During the day she sat silently in a corner of the carriage, wrapped in her own thoughts, while he rode alongside, his face pale and stern.

THEY REACHED Lady Thornton's house in London ten days after leaving Paris. It was one week before Christmas. Julia's aunt was delighted to see them, and even happier to see them return together. She said so, and started making plans for their stay.

"Forgive me, Lady Thornton, but I'm afraid I have obligations in Dorset which mean that I must leave London immediately. Julia will, of course, stay here."

"Hugo—" said Julia piteously.

He looked coldly at her. "You must stay here, my dear. You are not . . . fit to come to Donyatt."

Lady Thornton decided to intervene. "Of course she isn't. She isn't even well enough to remain downstairs. Come, we'll see Julia safely installed in a comfortable bed, and then you and I, Hugo, will have a talk. No, I will not hear of any objection—it is, in any case, too late to set off for Dorset tonight. I will have a bedchamber prepared for you, too. Ring for Parsons, Hugo. He will bring you something to refresh you after your journey. Come, Julia."

Julia got up to follow her aunt, but stopped suddenly at the door. "No, I must talk to him... He has to understand... He must! Hugo!" She turned round and started towards him, but the effort was too much. Hugo caught her as she fell.

"Where is her room?" he asked grimly. "I'll take her there."

Hugo laid Julia on her bed, and was about to go when she opened her eyes, clutched his sleeve, and whispered feverishly, "Go and see Thérèse, Hugo. She sent me to Paris. It was for Donyatt. She said she could take it away from you. For God's sake don't look at me like that! I'm telling you the truth. Don't look at me like that!" She broke into a storm of weeping. Lady Thornton who had been hovering by the door, hurried over and, with a look of burning reproach, told Hugo to go down to the small parlour where she would see him in a few minutes. Then she took her niece in her arms and comforted her like a child.

When Lady Thornton eventually rejoined him, Hugo was sitting with a bottle of brandy at his side and a glass in his hand. She regarded him with some trepidation, for he seemed to be surrounded by a wall of ice. But her concern for her niece gave her courage, and she drew a deep breath and sat down facing him.

"Now, Hugo," she said. "What has happened? I was delighted that you had persuaded Julia to come back to you. I never for one moment believed her story, anyway, for I am convinced you are made for one another. But why did she leave you? And why are you now treating her so unkindly when it is obvious that she is ill? Indeed, I am astonished at your lack of consideration towards her—she should never have travelled from France in the state she is in! And why is she in such a dreadful state? Is it because of you?" Hugo finished the brandy in his glass and poured himself another, without replying. Lady Thornton said sharply, "Hugo!"

Hugo eyed the brandy in the glass, drank it and said, "Believe me, Lady Thornton, you would be happier not to know."

"But I insist! My brother trusted you to look after her, and now that he is dead I am the only person to see that you do. What is wrong, Hugo? What happened in France?"

Hugo looked moodily at the fire. "Julia had to leave France before they found out," he said.

"Found out what? Really, Hugo, I shall lose my patience with you! Put the brandy down, and tell me plainly what this is all about!"

"My dear Lady Thornton, I bow to your command," he said with a cynical smile. "But you will undoubtedly regret it. Julia was forced to leave France with all speed because she had killed her lover. There you have it—the plain truth."

"Her *lover*!"

"My reaction precisely. Julia deceived us both, it seems."

"Hugo, have you gone mad? Julia would never betray anyone in such a way—least of all you!"

"So I was beginning to believe. I suppose I should be thankful that I found out the truth before I made a complete fool of myself." His mouth twisted. "It's ironic, isn't it? Just when I was convinced I had, after all this time, found a woman to respect and admire—no, God damn it!— a woman I *loved,* a woman I thought I could not live without, it turns out she's a fraud. Just like the rest." He drank again.

"Have you talked to Julia?"

"No, she was too ill. Tonight was the first time she has attempted to say anything about it. But it wasn't necessary. It's over. The marriage was a mistake from the beginning. Oh, you needn't worry about a scandal. I've no intention of divorcing Julia. I just don't want to live with her again—in fact, I'd just as soon not see her again."

"You must! You must give her a chance to explain—"

He leapt up with a curse and faced her angrily. "There is no explanation possible!"

"Julia was trying to tell you something tonight, Hugo. You must see her again before you go away—to hear her side of the story. It is her right," said Lady Thornton gravely. "And in the meantime, why don't you go to see Madame Benezat?"

AT FIRST Thérèse received him warily. "Hugo! Back so soon? I still have not seen Julie, you know. Have you found her yet?"

"She was, as you said, in Paris," he said curtly. "With Greenfield."

Thérèse grew pale. "Oh, *mon Dieu*! You found them together? And ... And what happened?"

"I brought her back. Thérèse, Julia denies that Greenfield was her lover. She says you sent her to Paris. Something about a claim on Donyatt."

Thérèse was gradually regaining her confidence. She even appeared to be amused. "I sent her to Paris? *Mais c'est ridicule*! If she supposed that story would do, she must have been desperate! As if Julie would do anything at my bidding! Now *I* would have thought of something much more convincing. *A vrai dire*, Hugo, the English should leave intrigue to other nations—on the whole they lack the necessary imagination and finesse. But then I suppose you believe her?" He found the touch of pity in her voice galling.

"I don't find it easy to believe anyone, Thérèse. Certainly not any woman. Do you think you have a claim on Donyatt?"

She looked at him sadly, forgivingly. "You have told me that I have not, Hugo. I had hoped to live there with you, but that is not to be. I have no other claim. If John and I had had a son...ah, then it would have been another story! But in that case I would hardly have waited so long before claiming it for him, would I? Really, Hugo, there are so many flaws in Julia's tale that even you, fond as you are of her, would have to be blind not to see them."

"And what about Greenfield? What was he doing in Paris?"

"You know what he was doing, Hugo! He was—er—seducing your wife, I think, no?" She laughed as Hugo swore. "Did you fight a duel with him? Is he injured?"

"He's dead," Hugo said tersely. Thérèse clutched the arm of a chair and sat down.

"You killed him?"

Hugo avoided answering the question, though he would have refused to admit that he was still protecting Julia. Instead he eyed Thérèse closely. "Perhaps Greenfield was more important to you than I realised, Thérèse."

"He was an old friend, no more." It was clear that
Thérèse was thinking rapidly. "Hugo, I am desolate to ask
you to leave, but if you have no more questions...? I cannot pretend to be sorry that Julia is not the paragon you
thought her—I did warn you about her interest in Greenfield, did I not?"

"Who is Prevert, Thérèse?" Hugo shot the question at
her.

"Prevert... Prevert... You asked me that once before, I
think... I'm sorry, Hugo. I do not know. Now you must go.
Adieu, mon chèr! Do forgive Julie—if you can! Tell her to
polish her story a little!"

CHAPTER TWENTY

As HE LEFT the house in Dover Street, Hugo's frame of mind was not an agreeable one. He knew Thérèse to be a liar, but, as she had pointed out with such malicious satisfaction, Julia's story was so unlikely as to be incredible, and he was angry that he had been exposed to ridicule for nothing. He encountered the doctor at the door of Lady Thornton's house, and learned that Julia wanted to see him.

"But not for long, Lord Rostherne. Go carefully, sir, very carefully. Lady Rostherne has sustained a severe shock to the nervous system, and it will take time and careful nursing to restore her. Good day to you."

Hugo thought ironically that any woman caught by her husband seconds after she had killed her lover might be said to have sustained a severe shock to her nervous system. With a grim face he entered Julia's bedchamber to find her sitting in a chair by the window, her face pale but determined.

"Julia?" he said in a voice from which all expression had been removed.

"I had to see you," she began nervously. "I had to thank you for rescuing me from..." Her voice faltered. "From that house."

"I could do nothing else, ma'am. The Devenish name is hardly untarnished, but to have the latest Marchioness of Rostherne brought to trial for the murder of her lover would surpass anything that has gone before, I imagine."

"I did not kill him, and he was not my lov—"

"Whether you in fact killed him or not is immaterial, though I should have thought the evidence was plain enough."

"He was not my lover, Hugo. Thérèse sent me to find him." The sheen of moisture on Julia's forehead and her trembling hands betrayed her stress. But Hugo hardened his heart and said coldly,

"Since when have you taken Thérèse's orders, ma'am? What sort of tale is this?"

"You must believe me, Hugo!" Julia's voice rose hysterically. With a visible effort she forced herself to speak more calmly. "She said he would have information for me...about Donyatt..."

"About Donyatt."

"Yes, she was threatening to take it from you."

"How could Thérèse possibly take Donyatt from me? And why should she send you to France accompanied by Greenfield in order for him to tell you something about Donyatt? I make every allowance for your weakened state, but you could surely find a better story than this farrago! Pray waste no more of my time!"

"But I didn't know it was Greenfield. She told me it would be Prevert! And I didn't travel with him. That was *madame*'s nephew. And though she said there was a son, there isn't... Donyatt is safe, Hugo. I know now that no one can take it from you."

"That is perhaps the one undeniable truth in this whole unsavoury affair, ma'am."

"Must you keep calling me 'ma'am' in that odious way, Hugo? Can you not still think of me as Julia?"

"I shall try not to think of you at all!" He turned to go.

"Wait!" she cried. "You mustn't go like this! I...I..." She passed a hand over her forehead. "There's something else, I know, but I cannot at the moment recall it..." Her voice faded, then rallied as she said, "It concerned your father—"

He rounded on her savagely. "I do not wish to hear my father's name on your lips, madam! In fact, I do not wish to continue this conversation at all! For God's sake, let me leave you in peace to mourn the loss of your lover—"

She cried desperately, "Hugo, I swear he was not my lover. I beg you to believe me. You must see Thérèse. She will tell you the truth."

"If she were ever to do that, it would be the first time. But I should inform you, perhaps, that I have already seen Thérèse."

Julia leaned forward anxiously. "And?"

"Why did you lie to me, Julia? You must have known I should find out. Or did you hope Thérèse would support your story out of a desire for revenge on me?"

"I did not lie to you, Hugo. Thérèse sent me. Why won't you believe me? What have I ever done to make you dislike me so?" Julia's voice was rising.

"You must keep calm, Julia. The doctor has said you must rest. I do not dislike you. But I cannot trust you."

"Why not? When have I ever lied to you?"

"Apart from now, you mean? You have lied at least twice. You lied to your father, when you told him we were engaged. And you lied to me when you said you were leaving me because you were bored with life at Donyatt and wanted to stay in London. Within the month you were in Paris."

"But Hugo, I lied out of love because I loved my father, and I lied to you because I loved you!"

His air of calm deserted him, and Julia saw how very angry he really was. "What sort of fool do you take me for?" he asked furiously. "Loved me, indeed! Oh, I believe you when you say you lied out of love, Julia. That at least may well be true. But it was Greenfield I found you with in Paris! No, I will listen to no more of your tales. I am leaving for Donyatt within the hour."

"And what is to happen to us, Hugo?"

"At the moment I do not know." She hid her face in her hands in a gesture of despair. He looked at her sombrely. At last he said, "There are still three months left of the year we promised ourselves. We shall leave any final decision till then." He waited a moment, but when she did not lift her head he went quietly out.

LADY THORNTON did not allow Hugo to depart as he would have liked, however. She insisted on speaking to him in the privacy of her own little sitting-room, where she demanded to know what his aims were.

"You will forgive me, Lady Thornton, but that is not a matter I am prepared to discuss with you."

"All the same, I must remind you, Hugo, of your declared intention to avoid scandal. Have you now changed your mind?"

"No," he said, his voice stiff with anger.

But Lady Thornton was herself so angry that she was not to be put off. "Then you are a bigger fool than I thought! Oh, I have no intention of enquiring into what must be a private concern between you and your wife. But you must allow me to tell you, Hugo, that in abandoning Julia in London while you return to Dorset—especially when she is so ill—you are showing the same stupid blindness to what is socially acceptable as my brother did years ago when he refused to take my advice about Julia. Perhaps if he had been wiser then we should not now be in our present difficulties! As it is, you cannot have considered what the scandalmongers will say when they hear of your departure. In no time London will be alive with gossip and speculation about the Devenish marriage. I beg you to reconsider."

Hugo said somewhat desperately, "I cannot stay here in this house at the moment, Lady Thornton. I need time to reflect. And it would surely foster even more speculation if I went to stay elsewhere in London. No, you may make what excuses you wish to your acquaintance, but I must go to Donyatt for the moment."

"Then you must return before too long, to see how your wife does. I can hold the tabbies at bay for a short time."

Though Hugo refused to commit himself, Lady Thornton was reasonably certain that he had taken her point. She contented herself with wishing him a safe journey, in spite of the season, and a speedy return.

CHRISTMAS CAME and went unnoticed by either of the Devenishes, and for a while Julia remained in her room, seeing no one other than her aunt. As Lady Thornton slowly pieced together the story of her niece's involvement with Prevert and Thérèse, her indignation grew. "But you must explain all this to Hugo, Julia!" she cried.

"I have already done so, Aunt Alicia. He does not believe me."

"You must make him see that you are telling the truth—"

"Pray do not say anything more! It is useless. Please let us talk of something else!"

Lady Thornton took pity on Julia's distress, and talked trivialities from then on. But she was seriously worried about her niece, who seemed to be making little progress towards recovery. Julia always received her aunt with determined cheerfulness, but after a while her conversation would dry up and she would sit silently looking out of the window for minutes at a time. Finally Lady Thornton decided to take her to task.

"Julia, I would not be doing my duty if I did not ask you to bestir yourself. You told me you were in terror for your life in that house in Paris. What sort of life did that poor woman save, if you sit back and do nothing with it? You say that a reconciliation with Hugo is hopeless, though we both know you to be innocent. Does his lack of faith in you mean that you are never to be seen in public again? Where is your pride? What would your father say if he could see you now? Come, my dear—pull yourself together and take up your life again. As yet, society is unaware of any estrangement, so you need not fear curious eyes or impertinent questions. Hugo may have rejected you in private, but in the eyes of the world you are still Lady Rostherne."

These words had their effect and, though the memory of the terrible events in Paris and afterwards still haunted her, Julia began to make the effort her aunt was demanding. Lady Thornton also encouraged her to set about restoring her looks.

"For if you do not wish the gossips to conclude you are breeding, Julia, you will do your best to look less washed-out!"

"Why on earth should they leap to that conclusion?"

"Very easily. Newly married, not in your first youth—what could be more natural than you should wish for a family as soon as may be? You are not, I hope? That might prove very awkward!"

Julia assured her aunt on this score, but not without a hidden pang.

LONDON SOCIETY accepted without comment that Lady Rostherne was in London for treatment while her husband was forced to stay in Dorset. Julia paid and received calls, went driving in the park, visited the theatre and exhibitions and was fitted for new creations by Madame Rosa. She avoided the balls and larger gatherings, having the very good excuse that her year of mourning was not quite up. She hid her heartache behind a show of vivacity, and was generally regarded with favour by the ton. Her aunt was impressed with her courage, and decided to give a dinner party for her niece.

MEANWHILE, at Donyatt, Hugo had been trying in vain to resign himself to living alone there. A corrosive bitterness, worse than any he had experienced before, held him in thrall, and he could settle to nothing. At last he faced the truth. Without Julia, Donyatt was a wasteland. He doubted he could ever be happy there again. He half wondered whether to go back to Greece—it would be better than doing nothing, better than feeling this perpetual ache as he went through the rooms which had formerly been made bright for him with Julia's presence. Better than this useless rage at her perfidy, and the bitter thought that he had been so grossly deceived by her. How had he allowed her to become so important to him when he knew, had always known that nothing but unhappiness could come of giving your heart to a woman? Then the memory of Julia as he had last seen her, white and distressed, would return to haunt him. Had he treated her too harshly? Was she still as distressed? Perhaps she was ill? Perhaps he should return to London as Lady Thornton wished? If there was to be no scandal he must, and soon.

While he was still debating this he had a visitor, a friend on his way from London to Exeter, who sought two nights' respite from his gruelling journey. Hugo welcomed the distraction, and they had a pleasant enough time together. On the second morning his friend bade him a cheerful farewell.

"Thanks for the lodging, Hugo! A piece of luck for me that you're not in London with Lady Rostherne, though I don't suppose you're too pleased about it. She's a delightful woman—a hit with everyone, I assure you. You'd better make haste with your business down here if you want to keep her, old stick!" With a laugh at his joke he departed, leaving Hugo incandescent with fury. So much for a pale

and suffering Julia! By God, if he had her here now he
would wring her faithless neck! He spent the rest of the day
in a rage of activity, and set off the next morning for London, riding at a dangerous pace on the icy roads.

By the time he eventually arrived at Grosvenor Square,
Lady Thornton's dinner party had just started. A quick
word with the butler, a hasty visit to his room to change, and
Hugo was ready to face his wife.

WHEN HUGO ENTERED the dining-room the dinner party
was in full swing. A judicious use of rouge had improved
Julia's looks considerably, and she glittered with vivacity.
She had been fencing all evening with those who wished to
know more about Hugo's prolonged absence, and the dangerous game she was playing added sparkle to her eyes. She
failed to notice when the butler had a discreet word with
Lady Thornton, nor did she see her aunt get up with a quiet
apology and leave the room. But the startled hush that fell
on the assembly a few minutes later drew her attention to the
door. Her rouge suddenly stood out on her cheeks as she
grew deathly pale.

Hugo moved lazily towards her. She was reminded of a
panther stalking its prey.

"You see, my love, I couldn't stay away any longer," he
said lightly, but there was an undercurrent, perhaps only
noticeable to Julia, in his voice. He came round, took her
hand in a cruel grip, and kissed it. "How is my beautiful
wife?" he asked.

Julia looked desperately at her aunt, who frowned at her
and said, "Come, Hugo, I've had a place set for you here,
by me. You've made Julia speechless with delight. Don't
expect anything sensible from her for a little while, at least.
You can talk to her later."

Lady Thornton's guests resumed their conversations and
their meal, not without some curious looks at the newcomer and his wife. Her expression was hardly one of un-
alloyed pleasure. But as time passed Julia regained control
of herself, and soon her wit and liveliness were more marked
even than before. Hugo, too, was at his most fascinating.
For the first time in many years he displayed something of
the devilish charm of the old Hugo. Only Julia seemed to

notice the barbs in his remarks, the cynicism in his eyes. She resolutely suppressed the feeling of panic rising within her. What could Hugo do to her in her aunt's house?

After dinner they all went into the large drawing-room, which had been partially cleared for dancing. Though Julia would normally have refused to dance at all, this time she accepted the first request for her hand that came. But she was foiled in her attempt to avoid Hugo. In a voice that was full of lazy amusement, but which yet held menace, Hugo insisted that he had the prior claim. Julia's partners faded away like snow in sunshine. As his arm went round her waist, Julia closed her eyes. He had held her like this ten years before. She had fallen in love with him that night, and had loved him ever since, it seemed. Would she love him for the rest of her life? There was no reason to suppose she wouldn't.

"Look at me, damn you!" he whispered. His eyes were glittering with something approaching hatred. Oh, God, she was going to faint! She must not! She would not!

"Why are you here, Hugo?" she asked. "I thought I would never see you again."

"You mean you hoped you wouldn't," he said, cruel fingers crushing her hard. "Don't forget to smile, Julia. You're supposed to be delighted to see me, remember?"

"I . . . I can't!"

"Why not? You can pretend most other things." Then, as she stumbled, he held her in a travesty of a loving embrace, his eyes all the while burning with rage. "You were right, Julia, all those years ago. You do stumble a lot! I'm afraid you've stumbled right off the pedestal I put you on, poor fool that I was!"

Julia's pride came to her rescue. "A pedestal is a very boring place to be, Hugo. Especially at Donyatt."

"If you are wise you will not mention Donyatt tonight, Julia. I will not have the name on your lying lips."

She was in a nightmare. Only she could hear the words. The world saw the tender smile with which Hugo was regarding her, the apparently solicitous hold which was digging into her flesh.

"Hugo, I beg you . . ." His face suddenly whirled into a void and vanished.

When she came to she was lying on her bed. Hugo was standing by the fireplace. "What happened?"

"You fainted," he said coldly. "At least you appeared to. The others found it most intriguing. They are now speculating whether you are in what I believe is called 'an interesting condition.' Are you?"

Julia got wearily off the bed. Then she straightened herself and walked over to face him. "You know I am not," she said. "Why did you come, Hugo? Just to taunt me? It is unworthy of you."

"I came to see for myself. And I have seen," he said bitterly. "You're a success at last in London, Julia. I wish you joy of your gallants and cicisbeos, and I wish them joy of you. They can have you. As many times as they wish."

Before she could stop herself Julia smacked Hugo's face hard. His face was transformed with a look of murderous rage. He caught her wrists and, pulling her towards him, he kissed her savagely, cruelly. Then his arms went round her, holding her so tightly that she could hardly breathe. A shudder went through him as he groaned her name again and again. The bitter unhappiness, the despair in his voice, brought tears to her eyes and she tried to lift her hand to comfort him, but when he felt the movement he thrust her away. He turned round to face the fire, bringing his hand hard down on the mantelpiece. After a moment he said, "You will remain my wife as long as you are circumspect. But if you bring more shame to the Devenish name I swear I will divorce you, whatever the cost."

"And...and if I wish to come to Donyatt? To live with you there?"

"No! That is something I will not allow. I will not live with a faithless wife. Goodbye, Julia."

As he left the room he heard Julia say sadly and clearly, "It is you who are faithless, Hugo."

THAT NIGHT, as Hugo walked the streets of London, nightwatchmen and footpads alike left him severely alone, for he had the air of a man driven by demons. Julia's last words to him would not leave his mind, and Julia's face floated before him in a hundred different guises—vivacious, composed, asleep, awake, puzzled, alert, tender, angry...oh,

God, was he to be haunted forever by her? But she was false, as all women were false! He must remember that, for the temptation to return to Grosvenor Square, to beg her to forgive him for treating her so harshly, to plead with her to come back with him to Donyatt, was almost overwhelming. She had lied to him, he knew that. Unbidden, her words echoed in his mind. "I lied out of love, Hugo, because I loved my father, and I lied to you because I loved you!" How could anyone believe that? Her story had been a poor fabrication from start to finish. And yet... Julia was intelligent, no one could deny it. So why had she invented such a ridiculous story? He stood still as he wondered for the first time if he had been wrong. Of course he hadn't! There was all the other evidence—Thérèse's warnings, Madame de Luthigny, Greenfield himself, Julia's strange behaviour when they had left Donyatt that last time... How beautiful, how innocent she had looked in the carriage on the way to London! He cursed aloud as he found himself fondly smiling at the memory, and strode on more swiftly than before.

But her words would not let him escape. "It is you who are faithless, Hugo." How dared she accuse him? Why had she gone to Paris if not to be with Greenfield? But why had she shot him? He had never asked himself that. Why had Julia shot Greenfield? There had been another woman there. Was it out of jealousy? He found that difficult to believe of Julia. Then why, why, why? "It is you who are faithless, Hugo..." He was going mad! What was he to do? Towards morning the answer came, and when it did it was really quite obvious. He would go to Paris to find out the truth. He would have to take care to avoid involving Julia's name in any official enquiries, but the woman who had been screaming might have something to tell him. He would see about some letters of introduction—and Adrian Portway might help him in Paris. Hugo's tortured mind found some peace at last as he laid his plans.

JULIA, TOO, had been making plans. Hugo's catastrophic visit had made one thing very clear. He had never loved her, but he now no longer even liked her, and she must learn to live without him. In spite of her recent efforts, London life, she knew, was not for her. She would do as she had tried to suggest to her father. She would choose a companion—an intelligent woman who would share her interests—and live quietly on one of her properties in the country, and, in time, she would travel.

She hadn't expected to hear from Hugo again, and was surprised when a note was brought round the next day. He was going abroad—the note didn't say where—but he expected to be back before the anniversary of their marriage.

> By then I trust we shall have a clearer idea on our future mode of life. I apologise for my behaviour last night. Whatever the provocation, it was inexcusable. Please convey my excuses to your aunt also. Yours etcetera.

Julia read and reread the note. In spite of herself, a tiny seed of hope was sown in her unhappy heart. Hugo was still prepared to discuss their future life—together? But when she read the note again its formal tone gave her little encouragement. She decided to continue with her plans to settle in Esher, and leave the rest to fate.

CHAPTER TWENTY-ONE

"MAMA, WHY DO WE NEVER see Julia now? She was so taken with town life when she was here last November that I am surprised she has neglected us for so long." Sophie Mersham and her mother were sitting in Lady Thornton's drawing-room on a sunny day at the beginning of May. The Mershams had recently returned from yet another visit to Bath, and Sophie had brought the children round to see their grandmother. "I understand she had quite a success after Christmas, too," Sophie continued, "though we were in Bath, visiting old Lady Mersham, so I didn't see her then. I'm sure I don't know why we have to spend so much time in Bath. The old dragon never seems to get any better—nor any worse," she added gloomily. Her mind returned to Julia. "Of course, if she is increasing, as everyone seems to think she is, I suppose that would account for it. Is she? I suppose it is to be expected, but you have never mentioned it."

Lady Thornton appeared not to have heard Sophie, being absorbed in her youngest grandchild. Sophie continued, "But if that is the case, why is Hugo not with her—at least, I suppose he is not?" She looked again at Lady Thornton. When there was still no response she went on, "No, he would hardly take her abroad with him. The Continent is hardly a place for any woman at the moment, with Bonaparte on the rampage again. It is certainly no place for someone in a delicate condition. Though Julia was always so indelicately robust... Mama, did you hear my question?"

Lady Thornton looked up. "I beg your pardon, my love. What question was that?"

"Why do we never see Julia?"

"I thought you knew. Julia isn't in London."

"Well, where is she? Donyatt has been shut up for months. And she clearly isn't with you. Where is Julia?"

Lady Thornton was in a dilemma. She adored her only daughter, but she was not blind to her faults, and Sophie's love of gossip was not one of which she approved. Julia would not want the whole of London to know that she was living alone, except for a hired companion, in Esher. She decided that Sophie's first question was a safer one to answer. "She will visit us when she is feeling better. She has been . . . ill, you know."

"So she *is* having a child! And Hugo has gone off abroad, leaving the poor thing behind. I'm not surprised. Men are so selfish. They don't have any patience with the sufferings their wives go through for the sake of having their wretched children."

Lady Thornton thought of Peter Mersham's devoted care of his wife during each of her pregnancies, but held her tongue. Sophie was apt to get upset if she was contradicted. Instead she said, "Little Charlotte seems almost ready to walk. Was Peter's mother pleased with the children's progress?"

This was enough to divert Sophie's mind from Julia, and her complaints about the Dowager Lady Mersham's total want of sympathy with her daughter-in-law occupied the rest of the visit.

However, after she had gone Lady Thornton sat down with a most unaccustomed frown on her face. Where was Hugo? No one had heard a thing from him since the note to Julia immediately before his departure. Of course, things were very confused in Europe at the moment. Bonaparte's escape from Elba and his lightning march north to Paris had taken everyone by surprise. King Louis and most of the Allied embassies had been forced to make a most undignified exit from the capital, more or less leaving as Boney moved in. But there had been no fighting. Hugo was safe somewhere, but where? She got up with a sigh. She would visit Julia tomorrow to see how she was.

Julia received her aunt with genuine pleasure, showed her the improvements she was making to the small estate which surrounded the house, and gave every impression of contented activity. She and her companion, Mrs. Frensham, appeared to have a friendly, relaxed relationship with a good

many interests in common. They were busy planning a tour
of Italy to be undertaken when the present difficult situation had been resolved. But, though she dismissed her aunt's
anxious enquiries about her health with an impatient laugh,
Julia was painfully thin. And, if Mrs. Frensham was to be
believed, she spent much of the night pacing about her
room.

"At first she seemed quite happy here, Lady Thornton,"
said Mrs. Frensham. "Then five or six weeks ago she started
to show these distressing symptoms. And though I believe I
have her trust, I cannot get her to tell me what is wrong.
Perhaps you might . . . ?"

Lady Thornton was shaking her head. "I think I know
what it is. I'll try to persuade my niece to talk to me, but it
won't be easy. Leave me alone with her when she returns,
and I shall see what can be done."

However, Julia was quite prepared to talk to her aunt. "I
prefer to keep Mrs. Frensham in ignorance of the story of
my marriage," she said, "It will make life easier later. Yes,
it's Hugo. I foolishly allowed myself to hope he might be
prepared to discuss our situation again. He said he would.
He promised to see me on the anniversary of our wedding." There was a pause. "But he didn't come."

"Hugo has faults, but I have found him in general to be
a man of his word, Julia. Perhaps he has been delayed
somewhere?"

"With no word to me? For seven weeks? No, Aunt Alicia,
I must not deceive myself. Hugo was a deeply unhappy man
when I last saw him. It is not surprising that on reflection he
finds he has had enough of conflict and disappointment and
wishes to forget it all. He is probably in Greece."

"I am sure he will communicate with you before long."

"And I will not let myself hope any longer!" exclaimed
Julia fiercely. She swallowed and said, "You intend to be
kind, I am sure, but I would prefer not to talk of Hugo. It
is finished. As soon as I have the courage I shall go down to
Donyatt to fetch the rest of my possessions. It is unfortunate that they are so inextricably mixed with Donyatt's furnishings that only I can sort them out, otherwise I would
leave it to others. I plan to go at the end of next month."

"Do you wish me to come with you?"

"You are very kind but I think not. I prefer to go alone."
She gave a small smile. "A kind of pilgrimage, you might
say. I shall be perfectly safe. The servants are completely
trustworthy."

Lady Thornton left Esher with a heavy heart. What was
Hugo thinking of? Even Julia's strength of character must
falter under the twin burdens of suspense and injustice.

HUGO WAS IN FACT kicking his heels in an antechamber in
Berlin, chafing at the protocol and formalities which were
preventing him from delivering the message he had been sent
to deliver and returning forthwith to England. He hoped to
God that Julia had received his hastily written letter. Portway had promised it would be sent by the next courier, and
that had been before he had left Paris, over seven weeks before... Damn these bull-headed Prussians with their de-
lays, damn their stiff-necked officials! And damn Adrian
Portway for insisting he came here! If only he hadn't gone
back to the Embassy—he should have made straight for
England and for Julia...

Up to that point things had gone well for him in Paris—
if finding out that you had been a blind fool, who might well
have lost a treasure beyond price through his own intoler-
able, idiotic prejudice could be so described. He had gone
straight to the house in the Rue des Quatre Pigeons, but had
found it closed. After careful enquiry he had tracked down
Madame Prevert in her country retreat, and she had told
him everything. He now knew that Prevert and Greenfield
were one and the same man; he knew why Julia had come
to Paris and what she had discovered there. He knew her to
be innocent of all his accusations. What he did not know
and was desperate to find out was whether she could ever
forgive him.

His last piece of investigation, conducted in haste while
Bonaparte advanced on Paris, had led him to the house
owned in former times by the Benezats. Here he had received a surprise, for someone was in residence. As he entered the hall Thérèse had come running down the stairs,
looking radiant. But when she saw Hugo she stopped short.
"*Oh, mon Dieu*, what are you doing here, Hugo? You must
not stay—he'll be here any moment—"

"Who, Thérèse?"

"Why, Benezat, of course! Oh, Hugo, I am so happy! He is not dead. He has been working for the Emperor all this time. And now he is here in Paris—but you must go before he comes, quickly!"

"I'll go soon, Thérèse, but before I do I must know two things."

She dragged him into a small salon. "What are they? Quickly, Hugo!"

"First I wish to know about your marriage to Benezat, and your claims to Donyatt."

Thérèse looked at him feverishly. "You know, don't you? You've seen Prevert's wife. I heard. Yes, it's true. I was never legally married to John. Your stupid Donyatt is perfectly safe. What is the other?"

Hugo was prevented from speaking by the sound of activity in the hall. A short dark, thickset man came into the room, stopping when he caught sight of Hugo. His face, which had been full of good humour, darkened.

"Who is this?" he asked. Thérèse ran to throw her arms about him.

"Armand! Oh, Armand, it's you. I thought you were dead."

"Evidently. Is this my replacement?"

"This?" asked Thérèse, glancing nervously at Hugo. "Of course not. How could I ever replace you? This is Hugo Devenish, John's brother. He's here on business—something to do with the estate. Is the Emperor so close, then, Armand?"

"He'll be in Paris tomorrow," he said briefly. A fleeting look of contempt had passed over his face as she mentioned John's name. Now he bowed to Hugo and said, "Milord? You do not have the look of your brother."

"Really?" drawled Hugo. Thérèse interrupted before he could say any more.

"*Chéri,*" she said in her familiar wheedling tone, "have you seen Joseph yet? He will be over the moon to see you. I have nearly finished my business here, and then I will join you upstairs. Hugo is going very soon—he will have to leave Paris today if Napoleon is as close as you say."

Reassured by what he saw in Hugo's face, Benezat bowed and left them.

"What is the other question, Hugo?" Thérèse was very tense.

"It's Julia. I want to know why she left me."

Thérèse opened her eyes wide. "How should I know?"

"I think you do. But if you cannot tell me, I shall have a little chat with Monsieur Benezat. He is sure to be interested in your matrimonial plans in England..."

"He will kill me if he finds out about them!"

"I think that might be quite likely," Hugo agreed.

"But I think you too might kill me if I tell you about Julie..."

"Try all the same," said Hugo, smiling.

Thérèse shivered, and almost whispered the next words. "I blackmailed her."

"With what?"

Thérèse went to the door of the salon and, having made certain that no one was in earshot, she shut the door and said rapidly, "I said I would take Donyatt from you if she stayed. I told her I could make the courts believe that Joseph was John's son."

"Ah," Hugo said. "Now I understand your anxiety not to let Benezat know what you were planning to do with his son. And... and I understand Julia's motives at last." Thérèse looked sourly at his face, which was filled with a tenderness which she could never have aroused. Then he said briskly, "Goodbye, Thérèse. I'm sure you'll understand if I say that I hope never to see you again."

"Nor I you, Hugo!" she spat. Then she laughed and said archly, "But I could have made you very happy, I think!"

HE HAD HURRIED BACK to the Embassy to thank Sir Adrian for his help, before making all speed for England. And there he had been trapped. There had been no way out of this journey to Berlin. Portway had put it in such a manner that it was impossible to turn him down.

"It's vital that we not only warn the Prussians of Bonaparte's intentions, but we've got to convince them that they are needed, that it is in their own interest that they come out and fight. Blücher's all right. It's the ones at home in Berlin who need to be persuaded. I must get a message to von Kellenberg—you remember him from Greece, no doubt.

And you're the one to do it. You know von Kellenberg and you speak German. And, what's more, you could talk your way through a brick wall—I watched you do it in Greece. Prussian court officials are almost as thick!''

"It's no good, Sir Adrian. I must get back to England with all speed. It's just as vital as your message."

"Not quite the national interest, though, is it? This is. I'm disappointed in you, Hugo. I thought you might be glad of the chance to make a few amends.''

"Amends? What for?"

Sir Adrian had given him a cool, assessing look. "We know about your brother's treachery, Hugo. And his death didn't wipe it out—it merely prevented us from taking any action. This is a chance for your family to atone for the lives your brother lost for us. You don't want it?''

How could he have refused?

WHAT HAD BEEN Julia's reaction to his letter? Could she forgive him for his cruel lack of trust? What the devil were these Prussians up to? Why the delay? He should be in London trying to convince Julia of his overwhelming love for her, his desperate desire to make it all up to her.

Hugo was brought back to the present by the sound of his name. "Milord von Rostherne? Hofrat von Kellenberg will see you now. Please to follow." Two hours later he emerged from the oppressive grandeur of the palace to seek transport for England, his mission accomplished.

But it took nearly four weeks for Hugo to reach London, four weeks of a nightmare journey across a Europe preparing for battle. And when he arrived he found that Julia was not there.

HE HAD A COOL RECEPTION from Lady Thornton. Conventional courtesies were forgotten as she expressed her surprise and disapproval. "You can hardly suppose that Julia would wait all these months without a word from you and do nothing to establish a new life for herself, Hugo. The girl has much more spirit than that, I assure you." Stretching the truth a little, she added, "She is doing very well, too."

"I am sure she is the toast of London, Lady Thornton, but I must see her. Where is she? And what do you mean—without a word from me? I wrote to her over two months ago."

"A note—to say you were going away. Promising to be back for the anniversary of your marriage? Really, Hugo—"

"No, no! A letter begging her to forgive me..." Lady Thornton's expression was enough. He said in despair, "It didn't get here. Oh, God! What am I to do?" He walked to the window and gazed out blindly on to the Square.

"Where have you been, Hugo?" said Lady Thornton gently.

"What? Oh, in Paris—I went to find out the truth...and did."

"But what happened? Why did you not tell her what you were doing?"

"I was sent to Berlin. I thought I had told her—the letter must have gone astray. Damn Portway!"

"Hugo!"

"Forgive me, Lady Thornton. I... I hardly know what to say—or do. Where is Julia?"

Lady Thornton took pity on him and told him. "But you will not find her at Esher at the moment, Hugo. It is most unfortunate, but she and her companion are away—they did not tell me where. I can tell you, however, that Julia intends to visit Donyatt some time this month."

"Donyatt? Why?"

Lady Thornton avoided his gaze as she told him, "To collect her...to collect her possessions." There was a silence. "She thought you had gone forever, Hugo! What else could she think?"

"I know, I know." He came to a decision. "Then I shall go to Donyatt and wait for her there."

"Hugo!" Lady Thornton's voice stopped him at the door. "What are you going to say to Julia? I will not let you upset her again."

"I am going to beg her forgiveness—"

"Yes?"

"I am going to ask her to stay with me—"

"At Donyatt?"

"Anywhere in the world if she will have me."

"And?"

"The rest is for Julia's ears alone, Lady Thornton. But
shall try to keep her at Donyatt until she listens to me."

"I don't think that will take very long, Hugo. And I wis
you joy," said Julia's aunt, smiling at him.

WHEN JULIA and her companion returned to Esher, Julia
who was suddenly impatient to be done with all associatio
with Hugo, merely made a brief stop there before setting ou
for Donyatt—alone, except for her servants. All the wa
down, through Stockbridge and Salisbury, Shaftesbury an
Sherborne, bells were ringing and bonfires were lit. New
had filtered through of a great battle fought in Belgium, an
England was rejoicing, for Napoleon Bonaparte had bee
decisively beaten and Europe was safe. Waterloo was th
name on everyone's lips, and the Duke of Wellington wa
the hero of the hour. It was impossible not to be affected b
the general euphoria, and for some of the journey Julia wa
carried along by the mood of celebration at large in th
country. But as she drew nearer to Donyatt her feeling o
dread returned. How could she bear it? It would be wron
to say she had ever been completely, unreservedly happ
there, but she had experienced so many moments full o
bright promise. Compared with them, the future seeme
very grey. What would Donyatt be like? she wondered. Th
house had been closed for several months, and Mrs. Stapl
was living with her nephew in Dorchester. Julia warne
herself not to fall into melancholy just because a hous
showed evidence of neglect. But this was a very specia
house, a sad little voice inside her said. This house had take
her time, her energy and her heart. This house had been a
the same time her love and her keenest rival. And now nei
ther of them had won. Hugo was far away from then
both...

Julia paused at the top of the last hill and looked down a
Donyatt. "It's beautiful, Hugo," she heard a voice fron
another lifetime say. "And there's such an air of peac
about it..." She ordered the coachman to continue dow
into the valley. She had purposely arranged to arrive in th
middle of the day, hoping to find someone who would le
her in for a preliminary inspection. If not, she would see

ut Benson, the gardener cum caretaker, or one of the oth-
rs. They would not be far away. At the end of the drive she
topped the carriage and sent it on with the rest into the vil-
age. She would walk alone up to the house.

It stood, serene and golden, in the summer sunshine. She
ould not have had a lovelier rival. If nothing else had come
f her marriage, the restoration of Donyatt was surely worth
omething? She heard the voice again. "Now that I have
een Donyatt I cannot think of any better use for my for-
une." As in a dream she walked up the steps. The doors
vere open. That was surely careless? Perhaps Lydiate or
3enson was making the rounds of the house. Upstairs all
vas silent. She had taken most of her dresses and personal
possessions with her to London, and her room looked
mpty. But it, too, had its echoes. A sultry night and a
ummer storm... "Too late! Short though that flash of
ightning was, it revealed every line of your delectable
oody..." And then he had kissed her and said he wanted
ter... Julia fled downstairs.

Where was Benson? The house was empty. She toured the
round floor, the little parlour, the library, the east par-
our... Everywhere the voices were whispering, laughing,
lemanding without pause. Finally she came to her Chinese
lrawing-room and stopped. No, no, she couldn't go in. Not
tere. She'd get Benson or Lydiate—anyone else—to do what
vas necessary. But Julia found herself going in just the
ame, as if her legs had a will of their own...

The room had not changed. The birds and flowers rioted
over the walls, the Chinese vases were on their stands, the
hina cabinet still stood against the wall. And now the voices
vere clamouring to be heard, deafening her.

"Hugo! I've been in this room before now. I know there's
tothing frightening in it."

"Oh, but you're wrong, Julia. The ghosts are all around
ts."

They had worked so hard, she and the women, to get rid
f those poor ghosts for him. And now they had finally been
aid to rest. Her eyes wandered over the room. "There's my
randmother's writing table!" he had said. She had been so
tervous lest she had done the wrong thing, but he had put
tis arm around her... "Athene the wise," he'd called her,

and kissed her again and again... She closed her eyes to kee
out the sight, but she could not dismiss the voices.

"You know, Julia, you may not think yourself beautifu
but by God you're desirable...desirable..."

Julia was filled with sudden pain. Hugo might have d
sired her, but it hadn't been enough. "No, I do not lov
her... I have great affection and respect for her... I have
duty and obligation to her...duty and obligation..."

The voices were driving her mad; she couldn't bear it. Sh
had thought she could be strong, but she couldn't. "Hugo!"
she cried out. "Oh, God, Hugo! Why couldn't you hav
loved me?" She fell sobbing to the floor by the sofa, clasp
ing the cushions in a desperate search for comfort, curlin
herself up in a useless attempt to ease the pain.

CHAPTER TWENTY-TWO

HUGO HAD BEEN in the five-acre field, up on the other side of Donyatt, where the village was celebrating the great victory with a bonfire and feasting. He stayed as long as he could, but after a while the merriment grated on him and he was impatient to be back at the house, just in case... At the gate he looked eagerly up the drive, but there was no sign of a carriage. No Julia yet, then. But at the top of the steps he paused. The doors were wide open. He must have a word with Benson; today's celebrations had clearly gone to his head. He'd been told often enough to keep everything locked. Hugo walked cautiously into the hall. He paused again, every sense suddenly alert. There was a faint breath of perfume... something in his bones was warning him... Julia was here! She must be! Nothing else would give him this feeling of incredulous elation. He began to move towards the door of her drawing-room, his heart racing. Then he stopped short as Julia's despairing cry resounded through the house.

A few strides, and Julia was in his arms, his only thought to comfort her, to absorb her pain into his own body, to give her consolation.

"Don't, Julia, don't! I can't bear to hear you cry like this. Oh, my darling, my precious, precious girl, what have I done to you? Can you ever forgive me?" He took her face in his hands, kissing the tears away, then held her to him as if she were a treasure beyond price.

The grey eyes opened and looked into his. Then they widened and she pushed him from her. Holding him at arm's length, she said, "I thought you were in Greece. I thought you had left me forever, Hugo." Her lip trembled again and she looked away.

"Julia..." Hugo was unable to continue as he looked a the hollows in her cheeks, the shadows under her eyes. H said, "I've been a blind, idiotic fool. You called me faith less, and indeed I was." He would have taken her in his arm again, but she backed nervously away.

"It took a long time for you to find that out," she said.

"I've been in Paris. I saw Madame Prevert."

"Oh." Julia nodded. "Is she safe?"

Hugo was puzzled by Julia's manner. It now seemed un naturally calm. But he answered her question. "She wa when I last saw her. The authorities decided that Prevert' death was an accident, and she is now living in the countr with her children. She told me everything, Julia."

"So you have established my innocence to your own sat isfaction—with the aid of others."

"Julia, I went to Paris because I desperately needed t believe in you—"

"You said you would be back when our year was up."

"I was sent to Berlin. I wrote to you, but your aunt tell me you never received my letter."

"No, I never had it." She paused. "What did it say?"

"That I had seen Madame Prevert... and Thérèse. Tha I knew you had been telling me the truth. That I wanted t see you, to ask you to forgive me."

"Oh, I forgive you, Hugo. The evidence was strong, an what was there to put in the balance against it? Only m word."

"I should have trusted you, all the same. Your wor should have been enough. I knew you."

The calm broke. "You have never known me, Hugo!" Julia walked swiftly away from him and stood by the lon window, the window where his brother had once lain s many years before.

"Madame Prevert said you had established the trut about my father's death."

"Oh, yes. I trapped Prevert into confessing that he ha done it. I tried...I tried to tell you about it. But yo wouldn't listen—not to anything! And I couldn't explain. was ill..."

"Julia, please—"

"Please what? Forgive you? I've told you, I have! Believe me, I do understand, Hugo. You were very unhappy—and Thérèse was important, too."

"Thérèse was nothing! What I once felt for her was nothing compared with my feelings for you!"

Julia was standing with her back to the window, her face in shadow as she said harshly, "Affection and respect, duty and obligation, your friendship...? It was enough for me once, Hugo, but not now. I have rebuilt my life without you. It may not have the heights I once thought were possible, but it hasn't the depths, either. Pray do not ask me to share your life here on the old terms. I don't think I could."

Hugo grew pale and strode over to her. "To hell with affection and friendship and all the rest! I love you, Julia! I love you as I never imagined I could ever love anyone. Not even Donyatt could replace you, and when I think of the risks you took just to preserve it for me I could... I could shake you—or kiss you till you begged for mercy." He took her in his arms. "For God's sake, say you'll stay with me." He kissed her desperately, passionately, taking her breath away, until she gave a little cry. She was set free immediately. "Julia?" He took her hands. "I'll do anything you wish. Live wherever you say, in London, or in Greece, or on the moon if you insist! I'll leave you in peace if that is what you want, but please stay with me—we could share so much... laughter, ideas, interests—"

"And?"

"And love. So much love."

She looked at him searchingly, and what she saw in his face seemed to satisfy her, for she gave a little nod. But when she would have spoken he stopped her with a hand on her mouth.

"Julia, I have asked you this once before, but this time it is very different. I love you—forever. Will you do me the honour—the very great honour—of being my wife?"

Julia suddenly came to life again. She laughed and blushed and threw her arms around his neck.

"I will, I will! Oh, my darling, kiss me again!"

Hugo gave a great shout of joy and swung her round in his arms. There followed an interval when time stood still for them, when kisses were interspersed with snatches of explanation, with vows and endearments and more kisses. Eventually the sound of heavy footsteps coming through the hall brought them to their senses.

"Who's there? Doan't 'ee run away! I'm comin' in!"

When Benson's large form appeared in the doorway Hugo was retrieving Julia's hat from the floor and Julia was tidying her hair in front of the mirror.

"Yes, Benson?"

"Oh, I'm sorry, my lord, I thought it wur intruders— why, Lady Rostherne, ma'am! I dedn't see yer ledyship at first!"

"How are you, Benson?"

Benson's face grew red with pleasure. "Oh, tes good to see yer ledyship! Well, thank you kindly." He looked from one to the other, and something in the air seemed to reach him. "Er—the carriage? I dedn't see it in the drive?"

"It's in the village, Benson. I... I wasn't quite sure whether his lordship would be here—"

"But now we both are—and to stay," said Hugo, holding Julia's eye.

A broad grin spread over Benson's face and he said, "Well, if that ain't the best bit o' news I've heard—better even that Boney bein' beat! If yer lordship will excuse me I'll just go back to five-acre field—"

"Oh, no, you don't, Benson! Lady Rostherne and I will see the people of Donyatt for ourselves! You go and fetch her ladyship's carriage!"

LATER THAT AFTERNOON, after Julia had been given the kind of overwhelming welcome that Donyatt felt she deserved and Hugo's health had been drunk more often than was good for one or two of the weaker brethren, Hugo caught Julia's eye and whispered, "Shall we go?" They started to slip away, but were surrounded by a laughing, protesting crowd. Finally Hugo held up his hand.

"Lady Rostherne would like me to thank you all for the welcome you have given her today. She tells me she feels, as I do—and I hope you do, too—that Donyatt is the best place to be in the whole of England!" There was a boisterous cheer. "Now I am taking Lady Rostherne back to the house, for she has come a long way and needs to rest. Till tomorrow! And don't let Jack Benson drink all the ale."

The crowd accompanied them to the edge of the field, and then let them go. They walked slowly back till they came to the end of the drive, where they paused and looked at Donyatt. The house seemed to be smiling in the late afternoon sunshine.

"I cannot think why you said I needed a rest, Hugo. I have never felt more alive in my life."

"It was the only way I could get you to myself," said Hugo, taking both her hands in his. "But I'm glad you don't need a rest. To tell you the truth, I wasn't actually thinking of giving you one . . ."

Julia turned to him, an enquiring look in her eyes, then she blushed and said nervously, "It's just like the first time we arrived, is it not? Donyatt deserted, no servants, nothing prepared . . ."

"There is one major difference," said Hugo firmly. "This time when I carry my wife up to bed she will share it with me. The time for bargains is over, and from now on our marriage is going to be very real." He took her chin in his hands and forced her to look at him. "Isn't it, Julia?"

She nodded shyly. "As real, as true and as long as I can make it. I've come a long way—you said so this afternoon. But the most important thing is that it has all ended here at Donyatt.'

"Ended!" exclaimed Hugo. "My darling girl, it has only just begun!"

EPILOGUE

"MAMA, WHY DO WE still never see Julia?" said Sophie discontentedly. Once again Sophie and her mother were sitting in Lady Thornton's drawing-room on a sunny afternoon in May. "I imagined she would at least spend these last six months here in London, where she can have the best possible medical advice. After all, she's no longer young, is she? Perhaps she's afraid of letting Hugo loose on the town while she cannot go everywhere with him? But then, from what Mersham tells me, they are not planning to come to London even after Julia's confinement. I do hope they are not going to turn into one of those boringly rustic couples. Hugo deserves better than that."

"It is my opinion that Hugo and Julia are so much in love that they really don't mind where they are," said Lady Thornton gently. "And if Julia feels happier at present down at Donyatt, I am sure Hugo will not take her away from there. Besides, it is natural he would wish his son to be born there."

Sophie's face expressed her distaste for her mother's sentimentality, but she was prevented from comment by the entry of Mrs. Frensham, who was now her mother's companion. She entered in her usual calm manner, but those who knew her well would have noticed an air of suppressed excitement.

"Lady Thornton, I have here a letter for you. It has just arrived."

"From Hugo!" exclaimed Lady Thornton. "My dear Mrs. Frensham, pray do not go! You must stay to hear the news. Let me see . . . Oh! Oh, mercy me!"

Both Sophie and Mrs. Frensham ran to Lady Thornton's aid as she sank back into her chair. Sophie picked up Hugo's letter.

"Lady Mersham, I do hope it is not bad news?" asked poor Mrs. Frensham as Sophie frowned.

"No, no!" cried Lady Thornton. "It is wonderful, wonderful news—the best! Julia is well and she and Hugo have a son—Richard Hugh—"

"So Lord Rostherne has his son!"

But Lady Thornton had not finished. "And a daughter—"

"Mama!" Sophie sounded outraged. "It is bad enough, heaven knows, to have twins. But who on earth, except Julia, would call her daughter Athene?"